D0720460

Orphans and Angels

LINDA FINLAY

PENGUIN BOOKS

PENGUIN BOOKS

UK | USA | Canada | Ireland | Australia
India | New Zealand | South Africa

Penguin Books is part of the Penguin Random House group of companies
whose addresses can be found at global.penguinrandomhouse.com.

First published in Penguin Books 2017
001

Text copyright © Linda Finlay, 2017

The moral right of the author has been asserted

Set in 12.5/14.75 pt Garamond MT Std
Typeset by Jouve (UK), Milton Keynes
Printed in Great Britain by Clays Ltd, St Ives plc

A CIP catalogue record for this book is available from the British Library

ISBN: 978-1-405-93785-6

www.greenpenguin.co.uk

Penguin Random House is committed to a
sustainable future for our business, our readers
and our planet. This book is made from Forest
Stewardship Council® certified paper.

For my own Tuesday boy, Leon. My son, my friend.

I

Torquay, 1901

'Two deaths and it isn't even the end of January.' Mrs Daws shivered, in spite of the warmth coming from the range. 'I hope that old portent isn't coming true, Miss Sullivan.'

'And which one would that be?' Sarah asked, looking up from the early morning cup of tea she'd been enjoying. This was normally her favourite time of morning when the house was quiet.

Although it was nearly three months since her god-father had died, entrusting his beloved Red Cliffs into her care, she still had much to learn about the running of the place and time to herself was a rare commodity. So many people were relying on her to keep the school open and she was determined not to let them down. Luckily Mrs Daws, the indomitable housekeeper, was happy to give Sarah the benefit of her experience, and also her opinions.

Fond as she was of the woman, Sarah wished she would hurry up and answer, for once the children rose it would be all systems go until bedtime, especially now that Amelia, their temporary schoolmistress, had left, and she had lessons to plan as well.

'The portent that decrees everything happens in threes,'

Mrs Daws replied in her own time. 'Should have guessed when I saw all them crows on the lawn.'

'Really, Mrs Daws,' Sarah said, shaking her head at the woman's superstitions.

'You might well mock,' the housekeeper replied, kneading the dough vigorously on the scrubbed table. 'But nature's never wrong. You can't deny that both our dear Queen and Mrs Knight have been taken, and on the same day, too. Who's next, that's what I'd like to know.'

'Mrs Daws, Queen Victoria was eighty-one years old and had been ailing for some time, while Mrs Knight . . . well, I don't know her exact age, but she was elderly and had been confined to a Bath chair for many years.' Sarah bit down the lump in her throat. She had known Mrs Knight only a short time, but the old lady had helped her when she most needed it by arranging a sewing bee to make smocks and shirts for the children, and, as well as feeling grateful, Sarah had really valued her friendship.

'All I'm saying is . . .' Mrs Daws tutted as the door opened, letting in a blast of cold air. 'Do be quick, Master Higgins,' she chided the young schoolmaster as he stamped his boots on the doorstep.

'Won't be a minute, Mrs Daws,' he replied amiably. Sarah hid a smile, knowing that despite his assurances, the master would do things in his own time. He might look easy-going with his velvety hazel eyes and generous mouth, but he was a man who knew his own mind.

'You're letting out all the heat,' the housekeeper grumbled. 'Heat which is needed if the bread is to . . . oh . . .' Her voice trailed away as she noticed the young boy standing beside Harry Higgins. He was blackened with grime from his straggly hair to his bare toes and gripping a ragged bundle as if his life depended upon it. As he stood glaring at them with eyes darker than coal, the master gently pushed him into the room.

'This is Solomon and he has come to stay with us for a while, haven't you, old chap?' he asked, smiling down at the boy, who scowled back.

'Hello, Solomon,' Sarah said softly, her heart going out to the boy, who looked as though he'd slept in his clothes. 'Welcome to Red Cliffs.'

The boy raised his chin defiantly and clutched the bundle tighter to his chest.

'Don't amember saying you could use me name,' he muttered.

Recalling her godfather saying that children were often defensive when frightened, Sarah smiled and tried again.

'Fair enough, but we need to call you something. As today is Tuesday how about we call you that?' she suggested.

The boy gave a snort of derision.

'Now, young Solomon, I expect you're hungry,' Mrs Daws said matter-of-factly. He didn't answer, just stood there eyeing the closed door like an animal trapped in a cage. She put the dough aside to rise, then bustled over and crouched down beside him. 'Got some nice porridge cooking, if you're interested? Might even find a drop of creamy milk to go on top,' she added casually. This caught his attention and he turned and eyed the housekeeper solemnly. 'Trouble is, only clean children are permitted to sit up to the table so we'll have to get you spruced up a bit.'

The boy frowned down at his blackened hands, then shrugged.

'You go with Mrs Daws, Solomon,' Harry Higgins urged. 'She'll take care of you.'

'I already told you, I can take care of meself,' he snorted.

'So, you don't want any breakfast then?' the master replied.

'Does smell good,' the boy admitted, glancing over the pot on the range and sniffing the air appreciatively.

'I'll stay for a meal, then me father should be mended,' the child conceded grudgingly, but Sarah saw the tears glistening in his eyes before he blinked them away.

'Come along, young man,' Mrs Daws said in that encouraging voice she used on such occasions. 'We'll get you cleaned up and then you can have something to eat. Everything will look better once you've got a nice hot meal inside you.' She grabbed a towel from the pulley and ushered him outside.

As the door closed behind them, Sarah looked askance at the master. Despite the early hour, he appeared shattered and, unusually for him, a little dirty.

'Nasty accident at the foundry,' he explained. 'Mr Smith, Solomon's father, has been taken to the infirmary, badly burned and not conscious. I was on my way here when Sergeant Watts collared me and asked if we could take the boy in. Little blighter had other ideas, though, and put up quite a fight, insisting he could look after himself. Bit me so hard, he drew blood.' He held up his hand so that Sarah could see patches of dark red mixed with grime.

'I'd best bathe it,' she said, hurrying over to the sink and wringing out a cloth.

'You'd make a good nurse, Miss Sullivan,' he teased, then winced as she gently dabbed it with iodine.

'Hold still, you baby,' she chided. 'I suppose such a job would have its benefits,' she chuckled, enjoying her advantage over the handsome schoolmaster. 'There, no dressing needed. What about Solomon's mother?'

'According to Watts, she upped and left years since, saying she'd had enough of living in dirt and squalor.'

'That must have been hard on the boy. How long do you anticipate him staying?'

'To be honest they're not expecting the man to survive,' Harry sighed.

Mrs Daws, who'd come back into the room, shot Sarah one of her knowing looks. 'Happen the crows were right then,' she muttered. Sarah shook her head, amazed that such a sensible woman should believe in the old sayings. 'I left April helping Mrs Laver clean up the urchin. Thank the Lord, she had to come back today to finish off the laundry. Like a wild animal he was when he saw the copper full of hot water. Took both of them to prise those filthy rags off him. Said he didn't want no females pawing at him. Wasn't about to be parted from his precious bundle either, insisting they weren't to touch it.' She went over to the range and stirred the pot furiously. 'Poor little blighter.'

'Indeed, Mrs Daws,' Sarah agreed then, hearing footsteps thundering overhead, grimaced. 'Sounds like the children are up and about so I'll leave Solomon in your capable hands. As I'm taking the girls' classes until a new travelling mistress is appointed, I'd better go and make a start on the office paperwork. It means I won't have as much time to help you, though, I'm afraid.'

'Always managed before,' the housekeeper said philosophically.

'I have an invoice here from Bert for the work he did converting the front bedroom into another dormitory for the girls,' Harry Higgins said, looking at her ruefully. 'He's held it back for as long as possible but . . .' He shrugged and followed her through to her office.

'I know, and it isn't fair to keep him waiting for his money any longer,' Sarah agreed, remembering the handyman lived from hand to mouth. 'It's just that the budget we set for the first quarter has already gone to the wall and now there's another child to accommodate. Although we did say we wouldn't take in any more children, I don't like the thought of not being able to help Solomon, but . . .' She shrugged helplessly. 'I don't suppose the orphanage could have him?'

'I'm afraid not. With the deaconess still indisposed and her school closed, they are full to capacity. Besides, it was you who suggested we shouldn't take in any more children.'

'Only because we're trying to juggle the finances for those already here,' Sarah replied quickly. As Harry's hazel eyes searched hers she felt a pang of guilt. How could she be worrying about money when poor Solomon was likely to be orphaned within the day? After all, wasn't that why her godfather had opened his home, to help those children who desperately needed care? If only that invitation to meet with the school's benefactress would arrive. Although they were desperately trying to raise funds themselves, she couldn't deny that some financial assistance in the interim would help.

6

'You're right, of course. We'll do our best for Solomon, the same as we do the others,' she said, unable to tear her gaze away from his face.

'Don't worry, Sarah, we'll manage,' he said, patting her hand. At his touch, the familiar tingle travelled up her arm and she smiled. 'It's not only the budget that has gone to the wall, is it?' he asked softly. 'Things have been so hectic recently, we've yet to share that fish supper we promised ourselves. It's high time we remedied that, so, Miss Sullivan, will you do me the honour of escorting me into town on Saturday night?'

At his formal tone, a giggle bubbled up in her throat but, not wishing to upset his manly pride, she forced it down.

'I thought you'd never ask, Master Higgins,' she replied coyly.

'Good. Now that's arranged, I really must go and see how Mrs Daws is coping with our Tuesday child, as you've called him. I fear Solomon's not going to be an easy pupil and will probably need caging in class. Only joking,' he added when he saw Sarah's look of alarm. 'Talking of classes, I can be flexible with my timetable until the new mistress is appointed, so which afternoons will best suit you to take the girls?'

'Thank you, Harry,' she said, touched by his thoughtfulness. 'As you know, I intend working on boosting their self-esteem so that when they leave here they will have a chance of securing decent employment. Amelia has done a wonderful job of teaching them their stitches and I want to capitalize on that by showing them how to adapt the donated clothing to fit. Apart from their school smocks,

7

most of them have never had their own outfits and they are excited at the thought. If it's all right with you, I would like to increase their sewing lessons to three afternoons each week, starting this afternoon.'

Harry chuckled. 'Those girls have really grown on you, haven't they?'

'I can't deny I've become fond of them,' she admitted. 'It's a tough world out there, especially for females. One way or another, they've had a hard start in life and I want to ensure we do as well as we can for them whilst they are here. Sewing could be the best chance for some of them to gain financial independence when they leave.'

'Very commendable, Miss Sullivan. I'll see the boys receive comparable tuition, though not in needlework, of course, otherwise they'll be complaining the girls are getting preferential treatment and that would never do. You'd better use the classroom rather than the workshop, though. The boys are in the middle of making coops for the chickens and there's wood and sawdust everywhere. I hope this extra work won't make you too tired to walk out with me on Saturday night?' He grinned so that she knew he was teasing.

'I shall think of it as extracurricular homework,' she assured him, her heart leaping at the thought.

'Well, I guess that's better than detention,' he chuckled.

'And there's to be none of your threatened disciplinary methods,' she warned, shaking a finger at him.

'I'll try to remember,' he promised, his eyes twinkling mischievously. 'See you at breakfast.'

Hearing his laughter echoing down the corridor, Sarah

smiled. She knew the persona of stern schoolmaster he portrayed would be absent away from Red Cliffs and she looked forward to resuming their easy-going banter.

Catching sight of the leather-bound volume on her desk she pulled herself back to the present. The book was entitled *Principles for Trading and Profit* and had belonged to Mrs Knight, Amelia's grandmother. Flicking through the pages, Sarah saw they were covered in copperplate writing, as neat as her stitching had been, and contained masses of information the woman had collected during her years as proprietor of her draper's store. Amelia had thought Sarah might find it useful, insisting the old lady would have wanted her to have it. Knowing she'd been a shrewd and successful businessperson, Sarah hoped she might glean some wisdom on how to save Red Cliffs. Turning back to the first page, she began reading.

> *The only way to succeed in business is for income to exceed expenditure. It is essential therefore the proprietor be aware of the total running costs of the establishment.*
>
> *First Principle (a): Set a Budget for Expenditure and Endeavour to Keep Within It*

Well, she'd failed in that already, for although she and Harry had sat down and worked one out at the beginning of the year, the bills were flooding in faster than funding became available. Finding money to keep going was an ever-present headache. Now they had another pupil to care for and she daren't even think of the roof that needed repairing. With a sinking heart she read on.

First Principle (b): If outgoings should exceed income, find a way(s) to address the shortfall sooner rather than later either by increasing income or reducing costs. Only by doing this can you keep your business a viable proposition.

Outgoings were definitely exceeding income at the moment so what options did she have? There was the offer from the developers, of course, but she was adamant the magnificent house that had been her godfather's home, and which he'd generously opened up as a school for ragged children, shouldn't be turned into a hotel for the idle rich. Quite apart from that, selling would mean finding new premises and relocating the school. She stared around the shabby yet comfortable room and shook her head. Out of the question.

There was still some funding due from the Local Authority but the forms had only recently been submitted and money from that source would take time to materialize. The garden produce that had been carefully stored, whilst abundant, was only sufficient to feed the school and Sunday soup kitchen, although Harry had got the pupils digging up the lawn at the other side of the house to increase the size of the vegetable plot – an action that had been met with disapproval from some of their neighbours. Although the houses were set well apart, they deemed this to be an up-and-coming area and weren't backward in voicing opinion that the school lowered the tone.

Mrs Daws had suggested turning the extra produce into chutneys, jams and pickles, which they could sell at the Church Fayre, but that wouldn't be until much later in the year and besides, the woman had enough to do already.

There was still her forthcoming meeting with Lady Chorlton, whom she had recently been informed was the school's mystery benefactress, but Sarah was still awaiting her invitation to visit. Her solicitor, Mr Fothergill, had promised to let her know as soon as he received word from the lady but, under the circumstances, Sarah wondered if she dared prevail upon him to instigate an early consultation.

Hearing the gong sounding, she snapped the book shut. Breakfast was always a busy time and with the new arrival to be settled in the housekeeper would need her help. Mrs Knight's pearls of wisdom would have to wait until later.

2

Opening the door to the kitchen, Sarah saw the girls standing on tiptoe, their noses pressed to the glass as they peered outside. Then she heard the commotion coming from the yard.

'What on earth is going on?' she asked.

'It's poor Bunter, miss, he's getting hurt,' Monday explained, her periwinkle eyes grave as she turned to face Sarah. At six years old, she was a sensitive child who hated any sign of aggression.

'That new boy's duffing him up,' Kitty added. Being a few years older and much tougher, there was nothing she liked more than a bit of action to liven up the day. 'Coo, he can't half land a punch.'

'Now the master's trying to separate them. Blimey, he's just caught a blow to his chest,' Edith gasped.

'Right, girls, that's quite enough. Go through to the dining room and stand behind your chairs,' Sarah instructed.

'Knew that one'd be trouble,' Mrs Daws sniffed, as she lifted the pot from the range and set it on the trivet on the scrubbed table. Sarah was about to go to investigate when the door opened and the master came in, holding each boy by an ear.

'This is not the kind of behaviour I expect from my pupils,' he growled. 'Apologize at once or there'll be no breakfast for either of you.'

'I only 'ad a wash so's I got fed,' Solomon protested. Sarah saw his head was already shaved and his dark eyes appeared large and luminous as they contrasted against the white of his scrubbed skin. In comparison, Bunter was red in the face and panting heavily. 'And it were his fault,' he cried, glaring at Bunter. 'He tried to snatch me things and I told him, me name's Smith not Sniff.' He clutched his bundle to his chest defensively.

'Apologize to Master Smith,' Harry ordered, staring at Bunter.

'But he were sniffin' and he wiped his nose on his sleeve. You said that was a dis . . . er, disgusting 'abit,' Bunter informed the master self-righteously.

'I ain't stayin' 'ere to be called disgustin',' Solomon said, breaking free from the master's grip. 'Like I said, I can take care of meself,' he shouted, clutching his bundle tighter. He made a sudden dash towards the door, then stopped at the sound of a sharp rap on the knocker. As the helmeted face of Sergeant Watts appeared through the glass, Solomon blanched and stood there looking scared.

'Right, boys, into the dining room,' Sarah said briskly. 'We don't want that porridge getting cold. Ah, April,' she added as a red-headed girl emerged from the pantry. An ex-pupil whose facial scar had left her too shy to seek employment in the outside world, April took her position as maid seriously and Sarah knew she could rely upon her to keep the curious girls under control. 'Please go and supervise the breakfast.'

'And ask Pip to sit these two miscreants either side of him. Any more fighting and there'll be trouble,' Harry added, pushing the boys firmly on their way.

'Do come in, Sergeant,' Mrs Daws said, opening the door.

'I'm afraid I bring bad news,' the man said, carefully removing his helmet before stepping into the room. 'I regret to tell you that Mr Smith has been pronounced dead.'

'"Twere them crows,' Mrs Daws murmured.

'Don't think so, Mrs Daws,' Sergeant Watts frowned. 'There'll be an autopsy to establish the exact cause, though. The man never regained consciousness, which was probably a blessing as his body was burned almost beyond recognition.'

'Right, girls, this afternoon I'm going to show you how to fashion a new garment from this,' Sarah told them, holding up a green sprigged cotton dress. After the traumatic morning, they were all on edge and she was eager to restore calm and normality.

'Are we really going to have our own dresses?' Edith asked, her eyes bright with excitement.

'Yes, Edith, using the clothes from the donations box, you are each going to make yourself an outfit to wear. However, before you can begin sewing you need to learn how to carefully unpick the existing garment without cutting into the material, then study its pattern. I've chosen this pretty dress to demonstrate how it is done,' she added, spreading it out on the table.

'May I join in, miss?' April asked, bustling into the room. 'I've finished my household chores and Mrs Daws said she could spare me for this lesson.' She stood staring at Sarah hopefully.

'Of course, April,' Sarah smiled. 'Come in and take a seat. Goodness, whatever is that noise?' she asked, at the commotion coming from outside.

'It's the new boy, Solomon. He's been kicking up worse than ever since he heard his father died. Mrs Daws reckons it's best to let him get it out of his system so Master Higgins' given him an old cushion to bash the living daylights out of instead of the apple tree,' April told her. 'He says we must all be extra kind to him while he adjusts.'

'Yeah, I tried being friendly already,' Edith nodded. Sarah smiled encouragingly, knowing that the girl's brash exterior hid a caring nature. 'I told him it must be awful hearing his father's been burned to a cinder like that. But he just glared at me and cuddled his bundle like a blinkin' doll.'

'Well, I guess his clothes are all he has left . . .' Sarah began.

'More likely 'e's got his tools in there,' Kitty remarked. 'I mean, a workman 'as to look after them or 'e can't do his job,' she said, focusing her knowing grey eyes on Sarah.

Of course! Why hadn't she thought of that, Sarah wondered, marvelling again at the worldly wisdom of this young girl.

'Like I takes this everywhere,' Monday piped up, caressing the little globe her father had given her. It lived in the pocket of her smock and she refused to be parted from it. 'I love 'olding it and would feel 'orrible if it was taken away from me.'

Sarah smiled at the little group. 'Well, it's a terrible thing to have happened and we must all do what we can to help young Solomon settle in. Now let's concentrate on taking this dress apart and whilst we do, perhaps we can remember the "h" at the beginning of our words.'

'Oh yeah, I keeps forgetting about that,' Kitty replied.

Thoughts of the new boy were put to the backs of their minds as the girls watched Sarah take up the little implement that enabled the unpicking of seams without cutting into the material. When she'd finished, she spread the fabric out over the table.

'There ain't enough there to fit you, miss,' Edith commented, assessing Sarah with her calculating eye.

'Well done, Edith. You're absolutely right and that's why we are going to remodel this dress to fit April.'

'Me?' April squeaked, her eyes wide.

'Yes, you, April,' Sarah replied, smiling at the maid's look of astonishment. 'You're the oldest girl here so it's only fair you should have the first outfit.'

'She's a woman, not a girl,' little Monday piped up, gazing at April so adoringly Sarah felt a pang. Reminding herself she shouldn't get too attached to any one child, she pulled herself together. Gazing around the little group, she recalled Harry's words earlier and realized what he'd said was true. She had become extremely fond of them all.

'Of course she is, silly me,' Sarah laughed, pulling herself together. 'Now pass me that tape and we'll get measuring.'

The girls gathered around again and by the end of the afternoon, the dress had been reshaped and pinned to fit April's slender form.

'Now, April, as you've seen how to unpick and remodel, you can spend the next lesson sewing while the rest of us work on another garment.'

'As long as Mrs Daws lets me have the time off.'

'We'll be sewing on Saturday afternoons, too, don't forget,' Sarah assured her. 'I know you have free time then.'

'Oh, yes,' April replied, then sighed. 'I just hopes I don't mess this up with me wonky stitching, miss,' she murmured, gently stroking the cotton material.

'I can help if you like,' Edith offered eagerly.

'Phew, that'd be a relief. Your stitches all go the right way. I still can't believe I'm goin' to have me own dress,' April replied.

'Who's next, miss?' Ellen asked excitedly.

'To make it fair, we will work in order of age,' Sarah replied.

'That's me then, miss,' Maggie shrieked, jumping up and down.

'Me'll be an old lady afore it's me turn,' June lisped.

'I will be an old lady before it's my turn,' Sarah corrected automatically.

'Yeah, me an' all,' the little girl sighed.

'As I'm fortunate enough to have my own dresses, I'm happy to wait until last, Miss Sullivan, or even forgo a new one if there's not enough material,' Sally offered. Sarah smiled at the earnest ten-year-old. Even though she'd been uprooted from the more salubrious surroundings of the deaconess's school, and was used to better things, she never complained.

'That's kind of you, Sally. However, I'd like you all to learn how to adapt clothing as it will be a useful skill to have. It might even help some of you gain employment. And don't worry, June, nobody will wear their new outfit until you all have one,' she assured her.

'We should have a party then so we can wear them, shouldn't we, miss?' Kitty cried.

'I'm sure we can do something nice to celebrate,' Sarah smiled, delighted at their enthusiasm. 'And I'm certain Mrs Daws will show you how to make a special cake. Talking of which, let's tidy everything away and then we'll go and see what she has prepared for our supper.' With the promise of food to come, the girls busied themselves, then left the school room. Outside the air was cold with a stiff breeze blowing in from the sea.

Sarah glanced into the workroom where Harry was helping the boys with their woodwork. It was satisfying to see them all engrossed in their work and she noticed the coops were already taking shape. Five-year-old Luke, Kitty's younger brother, was contentedly sawing away and Sarah was happy to think he'd settled in so well. Harry glanced her way and the warmth of his smile made her heart jump. But then he looked beyond her, his expression changing to a frown. Turning, she saw Solomon slumped on the grass, his bundle clasped to his chest, a brooding look on his face. Walking over, she crouched down beside him.

'Want some company?' Sarah asked softly. He shook his head and turned away but not before she'd seen his red-rimmed eyes. 'It's hard losing your father, isn't it?' When he didn't respond, Sarah reached out to pat his shoulder but he shrugged her away. The wind was freshening, bringing with it the tang of salt, and Solomon shivered. 'It's time we went inside,' she told him, getting to her feet. 'It's nearly supper time and Mrs Daws will have a nice fire going in the dining room.'

'Call those few lumps of coke a fire?' he snorted. 'We 'ad a real one at the foundry. Red flames with sparks shooting right up to the roof.' Goodness, Sarah thought, no wonder the place had burned down. 'It were so 'ot you could fry yer mutton on yer shovel.'

'Really?' Sarah gasped. 'Have you brought your tools with you?' she asked, gesturing towards his bundle. Immediately, his guard went up and he lapsed into silence once more. 'Well, I don't know what Mrs Daws has cooked for us but it's bound to be something tasty,' she said brightly. 'Come on.' She held out her hand but he ignored it. Gently does it, Sarah, she told herself. Slowly she began to walk towards the house and was gratified when, after a few moments, she heard the crunch of gravel behind her. Then the sound was replaced by squeals of delight as the boys were let out of the work-room.

'Hey, miss, we've made the bestest coops ever,' Black cried.

'Yeah, you should see them,' Brown added as they hared past her, jostling each other in their eagerness to be first into the dining room.

'How about you, Luke? Are you enjoying making them?' she asked the boy.

He nodded vigorously. 'Master 'Iggins said I 'ad a good feel for woodwork,' he told her proudly. 'Them coops will soon be ready for the chooks.'

'Well done, Luke,' she replied. 'I'm sure all that work has made you hungry so off you go and get something to eat.'

Glancing over her shoulder, she saw Harry chatting

amiably to Solomon as he steered him towards the house. The boy looked so sad and lost, Sarah felt a pang of conscience. How could she have even thought of sending him to the orphanage? Not only would he stay, but she'd never even think of turning a child away again. Funding the school might be a constant worry but she was determined to run Red Cliffs as her godfather had. She would make it a viable proposition so the school inspectors could find no cause for complaint when they revisited in May.

Supper passed in its usual manner, the children falling quiet as they devoured their food. Sarah noticed Pip nodding reassuringly at Solomon and marvelled again at the boy's caring manner. Then as the children busied themselves clearing away and carrying out their chores around the house, Sarah and Harry could at last relax over their cups of tea. It was a time they both enjoyed as they caught up on the events of the day.

'Judging from the excitement ensuing from the girls' table, I gather the sewing lesson was a success,' Harry commented.

'It was indeed. You should have seen April's face when she learned the material we were working on was going to be turned into a dress for her. They are planning a party for when their new outfits are ready to wear. From what I saw through the window of the workshop the boys have been busy, too. Even Black and Brown, who as you well know, are not renowned for being industrious, were excited at how well those coops are coming along.'

'They are almost finished and will soon be ready for their new occupants,' Harry told her. Hearing the pride in his voice, she smiled. There really was nothing more satisfying than encouraging the children's creativity. 'Luke has an amazing aptitude for woodwork and the others are keen not to be outdone,' he continued. 'Couldn't get Solomon to join in but that's understandable. It's been a traumatic day for him, poor lad.'

Sarah nodded. 'Solomon wanted to go to the infirmary and see his father but Mrs Daws managed to persuade him he would want him to remember him as he was.'

'It was certainly a nasty business. I understand the fire had taken such a hold on the foundry, they had to leave it to burn itself out. Poor Solomon has no home to return to even if he wanted to.' Harry stared around the room. 'This place might be shabby but at least he'll have a roof over his head. Even one that leaks,' he grinned ruefully. 'I must confess to being curious as to what's in that bundle the boy's been carrying around since he arrived.'

'I thought it might have been clothes but Kitty reckons it's more likely to be his tools.'

'Of course,' Harry cried, slapping his hand to the side of his head. 'Why didn't I think of that? Perhaps I can encourage him to use them to help us finish off the coops tomorrow. Goodness knows, we could do with some decent tools. The ones Farmer Jim loaned us are rusted to ruination, bless him. I've tried cleaning them up but . . .' He shrugged.

'How is he?' Sarah asked.

'You know Jim: pretends he's on the mend but we all realize his crushed leg will never heal. I'm taking the boys to help tidy up the farm on Saturday afternoon but he really needs to take on a full-time helper. Bess keeps telling him it's time he retired but he reckons that'd be the death of him. Between you and me, it's his beloved cows that keep him going.'

'Talking of keeping things going, we need to work out another budget,' Sarah said, getting to her feet.

'You're some slave driver, Sarah Sullivan,' Harry said. 'Give me one good reason why I should spend another of my precious evenings working?'

'You mean the prospect of a couple of hours alone in my office with me doesn't appeal, Master Higgins?' she teased.

He grinned and jumped to his feet quickly, making her laugh.

'Your eagerness is gratifying,' she told him. 'Not at all, Miss Sullivan. I just can't abide to see a woman looking down at me. Besides, by your own admission, my grasp of mathematics is so much better than yours. I'll just check the boys are all right, then I'm all yours,' he teased.

'Goodness, there's no need to go overboard, Master Higgins,' she replied, gathering up their tea cups. 'It's only your brain I'm after.' She looked up then frowned as Pip came hobbling into the room with a grim expression. 'Is something wrong, Pip?'

'I was checking the front gates were locked when I heard this awful banging coming from the workroom. Went to investigate, but by the time I got there whoever it was had scarpered, leaving them chicken coops all bashed up,' he cried.

'What?' Harry growled just as Mrs Daws hurried into the room.

'Is young Solomon in here?' the housekeeper asked, peering around as if the boy might be hiding behind one of the chairs.

'No, Mrs Daws, he isn't. I'm sure he left the room with the others after supper,' Sarah replied, exchanging a look with Harry.

'Well, he must have run off then. I've just done a head count before bed and there's no sign of him or that bundle of his.'

'Thank you, Mrs Daws. You go back to the kitchen and I'll take a look around outside,' Harry replied, grabbing his muffler from the back of the chair.

'I'll come with you,' Sarah offered, but he shook his head.

'If the children have got wind of this they'll be bursting with curiosity and Mrs Daws will need a hand supervising them before bed. It's best we keep them to their routine and should anyone ask about Solomon just say he's feeling his father's death and needs time to himself.'

Fighting down her irritation at the way he assumed charge, Sarah managed a curt nod, but he was already striding from the room with Pip hobbling after him.

3

A glance at the mess in the workroom was enough for Harry to see Pip hadn't been exaggerating. There were smashed wood and splinters everywhere. All that work and wood wasted, he thought as he headed towards the gates that the lad was already unlocking.

'Shall I come with you, Master Higgins?' he asked.

Harry glanced down at Pip's leg and, seeing the cold weather had made his limp more pronounced than usual, shook his head. 'No, stay here. If Solomon returns take him to the kitchen and keep him there until I get back.'

'Yes, sir. I'd only hold you up anyway,' Pip replied, correctly interpreting the master's thoughts. He didn't often lament the infliction he'd been left with after suffering typhus as a young boy but sometimes, like now, he wished he could be of more use. 'Guess you'll be making for the foundry, or what's left of it? Poor blighter, it's a rum do, isn't it?'

'It is,' Harry replied, shivering as a sudden gust of wind caught him unawares. He pulled his muffler tighter around him. 'It's cold out here, Pip, so on second thoughts, leave the gates unlocked and go inside. Keep watch from the window in case Solomon returns. I'll make sure everything's secure later.'

Hurrying down the road, he stared around, grateful no one appeared to be peering out of their windows. The neighbours always seemed to sense when something was amiss and the last thing the school needed were more complaints about disturbance. He broke into a run, his breath snaking in wisps before him in the cold. Was that snow he could smell on the air?

Even before he reached the burned-out shell of the foundry and toolmakers, Harry could hear Solomon's distraught sobs. A single plume of smoke was rising from the ruin, beside which the boy was lying beating the ground with his fists. All thoughts of the smashed coops fled as Harry's heart went out to him. Hunkering down beside him, he spoke softly.

'Solomon, it's me, Harry Higgins from the school.' The boy stilled, his sobs muffled as he tried to bury his head into the hardened mud. Harry waited.

'Go away,' the child muttered eventually.

'Afraid I'm here for the duration,' Harry murmured gently.

Silence, then a sniff.

'Why do you use them fancy words?'

'Probably because I'm a schoolmaster,' Harry replied easily. 'Always had a liking for words and their meanings.'

'Suppose you've come to give me a rollicking for ruining them coops. Well, you can save yer bref 'cos I don't care.' The boy's attempt at bravado was spoiled by a hiccup.

'I see,' Harry replied, and lapsed into silence. Experience told him to hold his tongue. The silence lengthened until eventually there was a soft rustling sound as the boy sat up and peered at Harry through the darkness.

'Ain't you cross?'

'Yes.'

'That all yer got to say?' Solomon asked.

Harry shrugged. 'Words won't change what you've done. Besides, I'll have my job cut out explaining to the others that their hard work has been in vain. It's a shame because they've been looking forward to keeping hens and collecting fresh eggs for breakfast.' This was met with silence. 'Of course, I'll also have to tell Farmer Jim that we won't be able to help him by taking some of his poultry. Your actions will affect a lot of people.'

'I didn't mean to destroy them,' Solomon muttered. 'It's just that I was cross and once I started I couldn't stop.' Harry remained silent. 'They all looked happy banging away and didn't care I was 'urting and upset.'

'I know you've had a nasty shock, Solomon, but the others have suffered ordeals, too.'

'That Bunter was right snotty,' Solomon muttered, wiping his nose with his sleeve.

Harry ignored it. 'He can be a bit bossy,' he agreed. 'But then he has his reasons. He had to stick up for his sister when his stepfather took the smoothing iron to her.'

'Blimey, what 'appened?'

'The man came home worse for drink and took it out on the poor girl. Bunter tried to defend her but . . .' He let his voice trail away.

'You mean the brute did her in?' Solomon gasped.

'Yes. He was locked up, of course, but Bunter blamed himself for his sister's death.'

'My father never drank. He was a good man,' he whispered. Then, overcome by grief once more, he began sobbing. This time, though, when Harry went to comfort him, he didn't move away.

'That's it, old fella, you let it out,' he murmured, patting the boy's back.

'They wouldn't let me go and see 'im,' he wailed. 'I wanted to say goodbye. I needed to speak to 'im,' he cried, becoming agitated again.

Harry pulled him close. 'Probably better to remember him as he was when you last saw him.'

The boy stiffened. 'That's what Mrs Daws said.'

'Well, we can't both be wrong, can we? Now I'm perishing sitting on this cold ground. What say we go back to Red Cliffs and have a hot drink?' he suggested.

Solomon shook his head vigorously.

'You don't have to come back with me if you don't want to, but you can't live there,' Harry added, pointing to the still smoking rubble that was all that remained of the foundry. 'Do you have any friends you could stay with?'

The boy shook his head. 'The likes of us don't have friends,' he murmured.

'How old are you, Solomon?' Harry asked, as a thought occurred to him.

'Eleven years and three months,' he announced, puffing out his chest.

'Well, in that case, if you don't want to come back with me, it will probably mean the workhouse,' Harry said, getting to his feet.

'I ain't goin' to no workhouse. I'm almost growed up and can look after meself, I'll stay here,' he declared, crossing his arms defiantly. Just then an owl hooted as it

27

swooped low in front of them. The boy jumped then crumpled. Seeing the look of terror on his face, Harry held out his hand.

'Come on, old chap.'

'But what about the damage I done? The others will kill me when they find out.'

'They will certainly be cross at first but I don't think they'll go as far as killing you. As far as I'm aware we've never had a murder at Red Cliffs. Of course, you'll need to apologize and offer to help them rebuild the coops. You could even promise to make them finer than they were in the first place.' He smiled so that the boy realized he was trying to help.

'How can I do that?'

'By offering to lend them your tools. I take it that's what's in there?'

'Well, yes, but . . .' He frowned, clutching his bundle to him once more.

'Our school funds don't run to fine tools, Solomon, and the ones we've been managing with are rusty, leaving ugly marks on the wood. Some of our edges are quite wonky as well,' Harry laughed.

'Well, I could put that right, I suppose,' Solomon replied, patting his bundle. Then, as the threatened sleet began to fall, he put his hand up to his shaved head and grimaced. 'Those blinkin' women haven't left me any 'air and me 'ead's freezin'.'

'Here, put this over you,' Harry said, removing his muffler and winding it around the boy. 'Come on, it's time we headed back. That's if you want to return to Red Cliffs, of course.'

'Yeah, all right,' Solomon sighed. They walked in silence for a few moments.

'You know, Solomon, it's good to have friends around you when you lose someone as special as your father,' Harry said.

The boy looked at him in surprise. 'You sound like you know.'

'I do, old fella. Admittedly I was older than you when my father died but it still hurt terribly. It's true that time does ease the pain somewhat. I never believed it when people told me that, but as the months roll by you find yourself remembering the good times you shared.'

'Yeah, but that's just it. I bet you was always good when 'e was alive,' Solomon muttered.

To his surprise the master chuckled. 'I lost count of the number of times he threatened me with a hiding.'

'Really?' The boy stopped and stared at him in amazement.

'Yes, really. I thought he was bluffing until the time he caught me trying to erase a blot from the page of his dictionary. It was his prize possession and I was forbidden to use it unless he gave permission. Goodness, was he cross; I couldn't sit down for days,' he admitted.

'Makes you sound 'uman. Yer know, yer all right for a teacher,' Solomon muttered.

'Just remember that's what I am, Solomon, your schoolmaster,' Harry said gruffly. 'And in class you're a pupil and will receive the same treatment as everyone else.'

'Yes, sir,' he murmured, trying to execute a salute through the wool of the muffler.

*

Although Harry had tried to warn the boys about the mess they would find in the workroom, there was such an outcry he had to intervene.

'This just ain't blinkin' fair,' Black cried, dark eyes glinting as he gestured towards the smashed coops. At nine years old, he might be mischievous but he couldn't understand this act of blatant destruction.

'All that bloomin' work for nuffin',' eight-year-old Brown growled, his cheeks red with indignation. 'If I get me 'ands on the culprit I'll kill 'im.'

'We was goin' to get the chicks on Saturday, too,' Luke murmured, his eyes filling with tears.

'Who would 'ave dun such a terrible thing?' Bunter exclaimed.

'Someone very unhappy, I think,' Harry replied. He was about to add more when Solomon spoke up.

'It was me and I'm sorry for what I done,' he admitted. The boys stared at him in disbelief. 'I don't know what came over me. One minute I was angry about me father dying the next . . .' He shook his head and gestured to the splintered wood littering the tables and floor.

'Well, at least you've had the courage to own up,' Harry said. 'That can't have been easy.'

'I'd like to help rebuild them,' Solomon told the boys, who were all silent for once. 'I got me tools here,' he added, holding up his bundle. 'They're real good ones and you can use them if you want.' Eagerly he untied the string and laid out his hammers, various chisels, files and a small shovel. 'Oh, and I got a saw, too,' he added, unfolding a longer implement that was wrapped in thick cloth.

'Blimey, they're the real job,' Luke marvelled, reaching out and running his fingers over the smooth handles.

'So what do you say, boys? Shall we accept Solomon's apology and offer of help?' Harry said, quick to sense the change in mood.

'Guess it was 'orrid for you losing your father,' Bunter admitted. 'Sorry I called you Sniff.'

'It really hurts in 'ere, don't it?' Luke agreed, tapping his chest.

'Yeah, and we know what it's like being orphaned, too,' Black and Brown agreed, serious for once. 'All right, we'll use those tools to make more coops,' they agreed, eyes now wide with excitement.

'Good, I was hoping you'd say that, boys. Right let's get on and see if we can have the new ones ready by Saturday,' Harry said briskly. 'Put that saw down, Black. It's sharper than the one we've been using and you need to be careful.'

Harry suppressed a sigh. Although he was relieved the boys had accepted Solomon's apology, the wood was so badly splintered he would have to use the last of his supply. He only hoped there was enough; the school didn't have the funds to purchase any more.

Meanwhile in the classroom, Sarah was helping the girls to sort through the donations for suitable items of clothing to adapt. Having spent a long, anxious night waiting to find out if Solomon was safe, she'd slept fitfully and woken with a thumping headache. When Harry had asked if she minded switching the time of her sewing lesson, she had been grateful for the opportunity to abandon her paperwork in favour of an easier morning.

'Coo, I loves this yellow floaty one, miss,' Kitty gushed, dragging Sarah back to the present as she held up a full-skirted dress complete with petticoats. 'Imagine wearing something like this; you'd feel like a princess.'

'That voile will be a bugger to work on,' Edith pointed out, then put her hand to her mouth when Sarah stared at her. 'Pardon my French, miss.'

'I would prefer you not to use such language, Edith. It really isn't necessary.'

'Sorry, miss,' she muttered, paying more attention to the clothes than Sarah.

'As you are finding that donations box so riveting, perhaps you would like to select garments that would be suitable for us to work on,' Sarah suggested.

'Me?' Edith gasped.

'Yes, you seem to know quite a bit about it and if you share your knowledge, it will save us all time in the long run.'

'Well, I did use to watch me old gran, unpicking old things. She were the Queen's personal seamstress afore she died and . . .'

'Then I'm sure you'll be happy to show the others what you learned,' Sarah interrupted quickly before the girl's imagination ran away with her further. 'Now, as April is unable to join us today, you can help Maggie get started on her dress. The rest of us will watch as you demonstrate how to unpick and remodel. And you can give us a running commentary using your best language.'

'Cripes, I mean, I can?' she squeaked.

'Indeed, Edith.'

The girl squared her shoulders. 'Like I said, me gran told me you gotta choose your material carefully. You need somefink easier to work on than that flimsy voile. This would be good,' she announced, brandishing a long robe in checked cotton. You unpicks the seams then spread out the material. Using your measurements, you then pins the shape . . .

'Oh, rabbit's bol . . .' Kitty cried, then stopped as the room fell silent.

'Is something wrong, Kitty?' Sarah asked, walking over to where the girl was trying to hide the yellow dress beneath the table.

'Kindly show me what you've been doing when you should have been watching Edith.' There was a pause. Then, looking guilty, Kitty held up the voluminous yellow dress.

'Perhaps you would like to tell us how this got here?' Sarah asked, waggling a finger through the large hole in the front of the bodice. 'Or perhaps it was already there when you took it out of the donations box?' She paused and could see Kitty was tempted to take the easy way out. Then she swallowed and shook her head.

'The scissors slipped, miss,' she admitted.

'And why were you using scissors instead of this?' she asked, holding up the silver unpicking implement.

'I thought it would be quicker, miss.'

'Well, clearly it wasn't. Apart from the fact you should have been watching the demonstration like the rest of us,

I don't remember giving you permission to even have that dress, let alone begin taking it apart.'

'But it's so pretty and I really, really wanted it, miss,' Kitty wailed. 'When Edith said it would be a bugger to work on, I just knew you wouldn't let me have it so I thought whilst you was all busy watching, I'd show you what I could do.'

Seeing the girl's look of abject dejection, Sarah's heart went out to her. Most of these girls had never had anything beautiful of their own before, yet she knew she couldn't ignore the use of expletives.

'First, may I remind you that we do not use language like that at Red Cliffs. There are enough adjectives in the English language to express an attribute of something.'

'What?' the girl blinked.

'Right, everyone,' Sarah said, turning to the others. 'Who can give me a suitable adjective to use instead?' she asked. As they stared blankly back, her heart sank. Surely Master Higgins had touched on this?

'Well, who can tell me what an adjective is then?' Sarah persisted.

'I doesn't know no jectives,' seven-year-old June lisped.

'Perhaps one of you older girls can enlighten June?' Sarah suggested. 'Maggie?'

'Search me,' the eleven-year-old shrugged.

'No good looking at me, miss,' Edith added.

'Right then, girls, gather round now and we'll finish this morning with a lesson on English grammar.' Ignoring their groans, Sarah smiled and began explaining suitable words they could use to better express themselves.

'Still don't see what's wrong with "bugger",' Kitty muttered, ten minutes later when they were dismissed. 'I mean, it described that voile all right, didn't it?'

4

Having dismissed the girls from their lesson and with her head still thumping, Sarah decided to forgo luncheon and catch up on her paperwork. She couldn't believe she'd had to make the girls learn adjectives rather than continue with the dressmaking they'd been so excited about. She understood they all had their own way of speaking, but the continued use of expletives wasn't something she was prepared to put up with. She wanted to raise the standard of teaching at Red Cliffs and when the new schoolmistress was appointed, she would make her aware of this.

Sifting through the pile of envelopes that had been neatly placed on her desk, she saw one was from Mr Fothergill, her solicitor. Eagerly, she slit the seal but her heart sank as she read the contents.

Lady Chorlton appreciates that you are keen to meet with her, but regrets this is not possible at present as she is in mourning for our dear late Queen. She sends her apologies and will advise when she is available to receive you.

Disappointment surging through her, Sarah tossed the letter aside and rested her head in her hands. Apart from being curious about her godfather's close friend, she had discovered that last night's bad weather had brought yet more wet in through the roof, albeit in a different place.

Knowing the money in the bank account was dwindling fast, she'd been hoping their benefactress might be able to help. Although it went against the grain to have to ask for more support, she could think of no other way of securing funding in the short term. Clearly she now needed to make other arrangements, but what? Her musing was interrupted by a brisk rap on the door.

'Come in,' she called. As the schoolmaster stepped into the room, she stared at him in surprise.

'Goodness, Harry, you don't normally wait to be invited in,' she joked. He didn't return her smile, just stood there looking so stern she could feel the anger emanating from him. 'Whatever is the matter?'

'I have come to tender my resignation,' he informed her stiffly.

'What do you mean?' she asked, taken aback at the coldness in his voice.

'It would appear my teaching methods leave much to be desired. I hear from the girls you have seen fit to give them a lesson in the proper use of adjectives.'

'Oh, that,' Sarah laughed, waving her hands dismissively. 'I thought for a moment there you were being serious.'

'But I am, Miss Sullivan. To go above my head and teach my pupils without the courtesy of prior consultation is unforgivable, not to say darn right unprofessional.'

'But, Harry, it was barely a quarter of an hour at the end of the sewing lesson and only came about because of Edith's use of expletives. As proprietress of Red Cliffs it is my duty to . . .' she began, but his hazel eyes darkened and he refused to let her finish.

37

'I would remind you that I am the schoolmaster here, the only one trained and qualified to teach.'

'And as I was saying,' Sarah continued, annoyed by his pomposity, 'I am the proprietress of this school. It is my desire the children learn to speak without resorting to swearing. In fact, I'm finding their continued use of expletives unacceptable,' she explained.

'As you obviously consider this to be more important than their feelings of security and stability, I won't stand in your way. Good afternoon, Miss Sullivan.'

'Oh, Harry, that's ridiculous,' she began, but she was talking to thin air. 'Nuts,' she muttered, realizing she had wounded his pride but before she could go after him, there was another knock on the door. Fighting down her frustration, she took a deep breath.

'Come in,' she called.

'Ah, Miss Sullivan, Mr Wise, the verger, wonders if you can spare him a moment?' Mrs Daws asked pleasantly enough, whilst managing to convey to Sarah that she wasn't happy with her. She might have realized the master would have confided in the housekeeper and she would take his side.

'Of course, Mrs Daws, do show him in,' Sarah replied, hoping the man wouldn't stay long. As if picking up on her thoughts, the housekeeper ushered the man into the room then smiled cordially.

'Would you like a cup of tea, Verger?' she asked.

'Well . . .' he hesitated, glancing at Sarah for approval.

'Bring us in a pot of tea and some cake, please, Mrs Daws,' Sarah replied sweetly. Not for one moment would she give the housekeeper the satisfaction of seeing she was annoyed her authority as hostess had been usurped. Besides, a cup of tea might help ease her throbbing head.

'If you're sure, that would be grand,' Jack Wise replied, giving Sarah an appreciative smile that restored her equilibrium as well as doing wonders for her morale.

'Now how can I be of help, Mr Wise?' she asked.

'Jack,' he corrected her with a smile. 'The vicar asked me to call. Well, no, actually that's a fib. The vicar wants to know if you would lend Sally to us and I offered to come and ask.'

'You want to borrow Sally, Mr W . . . Jack?' Sarah frowned.

'Yes. Her voice, that is. Well, her along with it, of course.' Cheeks flushing, he drew to a halt. 'What I mean is, we have noticed that Sally has the most beautiful voice and wonder if she might be permitted to sing in our choir.'

'Trills like a lark, does young Sally,' Mrs Daws said, pushing the door open with her behind as she came in bearing the tea tray. 'You should hear her on the piano. Not that Red Cliffs has one, of course.' She paused and glared at Sarah as though this was her fault. 'The deaconess, now, she has a beautiful baby grand at her school and Sally used to play that,' she added, passing the verger his tea with a slice of shortbread alongside. 'Sorry there's no cake only the school timetable has been turned upside down today and I didn't get my usual help in the kitchen.' The housekeeper shot Sarah another disapproving look before sweeping from the room.

'Oh dear, have I come at a bad time?' Jack asked.

'No, not at all. It's just that we've had a few problems these past two days.' She went on to tell him about Solomon's arrival and the smashed coops.

'Nasty business, that fire,' Jack sighed. 'If we can help in any way with the young fellow then do let us know, Sarah. St Nicholas' is here to be of service.'

'Thank you, Jack.'

'Forgive me for mentioning it, but you are looking rather peaky,' Jack remarked. 'Can I be of assistance at all?'

'Well, you could rob a bank,' Sarah laughed.

'What?' the verger spluttered, so that his tea sloshed into the saucer. Sarah sighed inwardly, wishing she'd phrased it differently for she'd forgotten how he took everything literally.

'Don't mind me, Jack. It's just that the roof needs repairing sooner rather than later and . . .' She shrugged.

'You need to raise funds,' he finished for her. He took a sip of his tea then broke into a smile. 'It just so happens I have a couple of ideas. St Nicholas' is planning to hold a choral evening to celebrate Easter. If young Sally was in the choir, she'd naturally be part of it and, of course, we could always include the other pupils. Perhaps Master Higgins could tutor them in a suitable festive hymn? The vicar thinks you do a wonderful job here and I'm sure he'd agree to sharing the proceeds between the church and the school.'

'Goodness, what a marvellous idea, Jack,' Sarah enthused. Then she remembered Harry had tendered his resignation. Honestly, that man and his principles. Still, he was hot-headed and bound to come to his senses when he'd calmed down, she thought, sipping her tea.

'With Easter Sunday being the 7th of April, we were thinking of holding the concert the evening before. The good ladies always decorate the church with flowers for the day's celebratory service so it would set the scene beautifully.'

'April?' Sarah gasped, thinking of their immediate need for finance. The share of the money they'd receive would be merely a trickle in the pond but yet they had to start somewhere, didn't they? Seeing he was waiting, she forced a cheery response.

'That's a brilliant idea, Jack, and kind of you to think of involving Red Cliffs. I didn't realize you held a concert at Easter.'

'We don't usually but it's been a miserable few weeks, what with our Queen's demise and the passing of our own dear Mrs Knight, so the vicar asked what the Church could do to cheer people up.'

'It's certainly been upsetting and unsettling,' Sarah agreed. 'And her granddaughter returning to live with her parents, whilst understandable, has left us short staffed. Amelia was an admirable schoolmistress.'

'Ah, you're having to teach the girls as well as run the school,' Jack guessed, his eyes softening. 'No wonder you are looking . . . well, er, I mean you're looking as pretty as ever, of course, but . . .' His voice trailed away and he sat there, embarrassed.

'Oh, Jack, you're good for my morale even though I know I'm looking frazzled.'

'I should imagine running this place is demanding,' he said, glancing round the cluttered room. 'Perhaps if you had a man to look after you, it would . . .'

'Jack Wise, this 1901. Are you really suggesting I should become a little woman at the beck and call of her husband?' she cried.

'No, well, yes. I mean it would be an honour to have someone as wonderful as you to care for,' he muttered, his cheeks growing hotter by the moment.

'Thank you,' she replied, fighting down her irritation. How many times did she have to refuse him before he got the message? Maybe her gentle hints should be replaced by overt statement, yet he was a sensitive man and she didn't want to hurt him. 'However, before I can even think of myself I have the pupils here to consider. You see, Jack, it is important to me that the girls especially realize their potential so that when they go out into the world, they can earn a good living and stand on their own two feet.'

'Very commendable,' he agreed, taking a bite of his shortbread. 'Hmm, Mrs Daws is a good baker.'

'She is,' Sarah agreed. 'And the girls learn well under her direction, too. Now, going back to what I was saying, I actually intend applying to become a member of the School Board and, as soon as time permits, attend meetings of the National Union of Women's Suffrage Societies. Miss Harmon, one of the school inspectors, told me they are active here in Torquay.'

'Indeed, they are,' he frowned.

'You disapprove of the idea of women voting in Parliamentary elections?'

'Not at all. However, I rather think you have your hands full already, what with taking the girls for their lessons as well as overseeing the running of the school.'

'Yes, well, that's only until the new schoolmistress is appointed. In the meantime, I have already made a start on the girls' sewing. Mind you, their use of expletives needs curtailing. Why, only this morning I brought them to heel over their rough language.'

Jack stared at her sadly. 'You make them sound like little puppy dogs. I would have thought their main requirement is for love and understanding,' he said.

'I agree, and that is, of course, our main priority,' Sarah replied quickly. 'However, it is also our duty to prepare them for life outside the school,' she added. 'Anyway, I'll certainly speak to Sally about her joining the choir. Do you have any idea what you would like the pupils to sing?'

The verger shook his head and got to his feet. 'No, I'll leave that up to Master Higgins. He knows best what they're capable of. Their rendition of carols at Christmas was very, er, enthusiastic,' he said, smiling once more. He opened his mouth, then hesitated.

'Was there something else, Verger?'

'Actually, yes. You might not be aware, but because of the mild winter so far, some of our parishioners with large gardens have a glut of vegetables – turnips, leeks, potatoes, etc. – which they don't want to see go to waste.'

'That's very kind, Jack, but the school has its own supplies from the garden,' Sarah told him.

'Oh dear, I'm making a ham fist of this. Let me start at the beginning. Since the demise of Mrs Knight and her sewing bee, the good ladies have been at a loose end. In fact, between you and me, the vicar is desperate to find something else for them to become involved in. They mean well but are . . . well, let's just say it's easier all round when they are gainfully occupied. I believe I am right in saying that being full to capacity here, Mrs Daws is rushed off her feet.'

'Indeed, she is and that's something else that worries me,' Sarah sighed.

'Well, it seems to me that if you put the good ladies together with that glut of vegetables they could make soup for those urchins you feed on Sundays.'

'Goodness.'

'We understand how Red Cliffs prides itself on helping the less fortunate and wondered if the pupils could serve the soup in the church hall after Sunday service for a while. Mrs Daws can help, too, of course, although I rather think she may welcome the break – not that she's said anything,' he added quickly, seeing Sarah frown.

'Do you know Jack, that would be such a godsend, if you'll excuse the pun,' she laughed.

'Well, if it's made you smile again then I'm pleased. Thank you for the refreshment, most welcome. Now I'll bid you good afternoon.'

Talk about manna from heaven, Sarah thought, pushing her paperwork to one side. Mrs Daws' increased workload had been playing on her mind and this would relieve the housekeeper from some of her duties. And, if the good ladies were happy to make the soup for the Sunday urchins using vegetables from elsewhere, then the school's supplies would last longer. Gathering up the tea tray, she hurried along to the kitchen where the housekeeper was rolling out pastry while April stirred a huge pot of meat in gravy.

'Something smells good in here,' Sarah said brightly.

'We're making the master's favourite pie to cheer him up,' April said, without looking up.

'Well, I have some news for you,' Sarah smiled.

'Hope it's good, for those poor girls and the master were downright miserable at luncheon,' the housekeeper sniffed, using her rolling pin with unnecessary force. Sensing the atmosphere, Sarah decided that perhaps it would be better to square things with Harry first.

'Where is Master Higgins?' she asked.

'In the classroom, of course. Where else would a dedicated teacher like him be? He's not the sort just to walk out and leave his pupils high and dry, whatever the provocation,' the woman puffed.

'The girls were really upset at their noontime meal, Miss Sullivan,' April added. 'We's not posh round here and speaks like we always have. Even Amelia just suggested we say our H's at the beginning of our words.'

'I was only trying to encourage them not to use expletives,' Sarah explained. Then seeing the girl's blank look, added, 'Swear words.'

'Well, they's taken umbrage, like, and no mistake. We thoughts you liked us as we was,' she said, her hand straying unconsciously to the scar on her cheek.

'Oh, April, I do,' Sarah cried, mortified that was how she'd come across. 'It's just that I know how people judge by appearances, and that includes speech, and I just wanted to help you all get on in the world,' she said, going over and putting her arm around the girl's shoulder.

'Well, they didn't see it like that,' April murmured, staring at Sarah sadly.

'Then I'd better explain, hadn't I?' she said softly. 'You must understand that I just want to raise the standards of our school.'

'Like April just said, we are what we are, Miss Sullivan. The dear doctor never expected us to be anything else,' the housekeeper sniffed.

'And nor do I. You are all very dear to me and I shall go and make that clear to everyone right this minute.'

5

Oh dear, what have I done? Sarah thought, throwing her shawl around her shoulders and hurrying to the school room. The pupils were just filing outside and the girls shot her a wary look.

'I have to speak with Master Higgins, but I'll see you all at supper,' she called to them.

'Not if we see you first,' Kitty muttered.

'Harry . . .' she began just as he appeared in the doorway. Despite the challenging gleam in his eyes, the sight of him set her pulse racing. From the moment they'd met he'd had an effect on her, she thought, sighing as she recalled the disparaging look he'd given her the first time she'd stepped into his classroom. He'd thought her some do-gooder and she'd been determined to prove him wrong. Now it seemed she needed to do the same again.

'I was about to lock up,' he said curtly.

'About earlier, Harry. Please may I have a word?' she asked, trying to keep her voice even as she saw they were being observed.

'You'd better come in,' he sighed. 'On your way, you lot,' he shouted to the group of pupils who were obviously hoping for a showdown. As she followed him into the school room the *Love Never Faileth* motto above his desk caught her eye. He followed her glance. 'That was your godfather's aphorism and the principle he tried to abide by.'

47

'Which you think I have not,' Sarah replied. 'Believe you me, I really thought I was doing the best for the girls correcting their expletives. I thought if I showed there were better ways for them to express themselves, they'd stand more of a chance of getting on when they leave here.'

'But it's no good teaching them words way above their comprehension. To express an attribute, indeed,' he mocked. 'Why not just say an adjective is a describing word?'

'Well, you have no qualms in using fancy words, Master Higgins,' she retorted, hating the way he persisted in wrong-footing her.

'That's different, I'm a schoolmaster. Fancy words will hardly help these girls when they apply to become kitchen hands or dairy maids.'

'But that's just it. I'm hoping that with guidance they will aspire to better jobs than that,' she protested. He stared at her for a few moments then let out a long breath.

'Your heart may be in the right place, but if you think we can turn these rough diamonds into fine jewels then you're kidding yourself. They have been saved from a life on the streets or at best, the workhouse, and they are grateful for food and a roof over their heads. If we can provide them with a basic education, then that is more than they would have had.'

'But I . . .' Sarah began, then remembered her mission. 'Look, Harry, I apologize if I've acted out of turn but I really do have the girls' best interests at heart.'

He arched a brow cynically. 'Theirs? Or is it about your dream of furthering Red Cliffs, because if it's the latter then I would remind you this is a ragged school set up to help waifs and strays.'

'Yes, I understand that, but surely it doesn't mean we should encourage them to say "bugger me" this and the "rabbit's bollo . . ."'

'Really, Miss Sullivan,' he cut in, trying to look suitably shocked. However, his twitching lips betrayed him. 'Look, I appreciate you want to help. However, you need to understand that if you try to teach them things beyond their ability they either switch off or worry. Poor Monday and June have been muttering about "pletivs" and "jectivs" all afternoon, while Kitty's been chortling over your "stern mam" manner.'

'Oh,' Sarah murmured, feeling like a scolded schoolgirl herself. Despite her best intentions, it seemed she'd got things very wrong.

'I wasn't kidding when I said you need to be trained how to teach, especially children like these. It's a case of working to the lowest level most of the time or you end up losing their interest completely.'

'Don't you find it frustrating?' she asked, her curiosity piqued despite herself.

'Sometimes, but then you see one of them suddenly grasp what you've been trying to drum in for ages and, well, pow, you get that tiny tingle of success.'

'You love it here, don't you?' she replied, noting the spark of satisfaction in his eyes. He stared around the room with its makeshift desks, slates that were scratched and worn, the dwindling fire in the grate.

'I enjoy the feeling of a job well done. However, I am not the type of man who tolerates having his authority in the classroom usurped, Miss Sullivan.'

'I can only apologize if it appeared that way and I promise

49

it won't happen again.' She held her breath, realizing how much his answer mattered, and not only to the school.

'I'll let you have my decision in the morning. I've promised Mother I will dine with her tonight so Pip will be supervising the boys over supper. I've asked him to keep a special eye on Solomon. Although he was happy enough whilst helping the boys rebuild the coops, as soon as we'd finished he became dejected and has been morose all afternoon.'

'Well, I shall be supervising the girls at supper and will also keep an eye on him. Poor chap, the realization that his father's dead is probably only just sinking in.'

'I've a hunch it's more than that. Anyway, I'll see you tomorrow. Oh, and by the way, there's no need to change the wording of grace at the table. As far as I'm aware it contains no expletives.'

'Funny, ha ha,' she grimaced. 'I'll leave you to lock up then. Remember me to your mother.'

'I will. We shall certainly have much to discuss over the supper table.'

Sarah slept badly that night. Her conciliatory overtures to the girls hadn't been altogether successful and she was mortified her good intentions had been misunderstood. Although they'd listened and nodded at her explanation they'd left the table as soon as they could. Later, when she'd outlined the verger's proposal for the Sunday soup kitchen to Mrs Daws, the housekeeper had said she couldn't contemplate any changes until she knew what the master was doing.

Outside the wind was howling like a banshee and Sarah

hoped none of the tiles would blow off. Finally, unable to stand it a moment longer, she lit a candle and dressed. Creeping out of her room, past the deserted kitchen and down the corridor, she let herself into the sanctity of her office.

Shivering in the cold of early morning, she set light to the fire Pip had laid the previous evening, then settled at her desk. Ignoring the pile of invoices and letters requiring her attention, she drew out Mrs Knight's book, hoping to draw some inspiration from her pearls of wisdom. As she flicked through the pages, one in particular seemed to jump out at her.

Fifth Principle (a): Never Assume You Know Best
 Ascertain the requirements of people using your business and endeavour to fulfil them. It is no good providing a goodly stock of the finest silk if they only have the means to purchase muslin.

Like her trying to teach the girls words beyond their capabilities, Sarah realized. How had she not seen it herself?

Fifth Principle (b): Gaining Trust
 Gaining trust takes time and requires the client having total confidence in your recommendations. Strive to meet their requirements and never presume you know better. By all means suggest an alternative if you truly think it will serve their needs. BUT only do this if you know it to be suitable and not beyond them. A blouse sewn in sateen might look more stylish for the evening than cotton, but only if the person has the capabilities to master the more difficult material.

Like Edith and her pointing out the voile would be hard to work on, she remembered. Banishing thoughts of the disastrous lesson of the previous day, she read on.

Fifth Principle (c): Keeping Trust

Once gained, work hard to maintain the client's trust. Their satisfaction is paramount and will see them eager to return. Take an interest in them, remember what you have recommended and reassure them you will always be here if they should need any help.

Sarah put her head in her hands. She'd spent the last four months or so gaining the girls' trust and yet they'd left her in no doubt they were not looking forward to her next lesson in 'proper speaking', as they called it. Well, she'd just have to try to get the balance right, she determined, turning the page.

Sixth Principle: Gaining Confidence

Once you have gained their trust consolidate this by gently instilling their confidence in you. This ensures that should anything go wrong they will feel comfortable talking to you, thus giving you the opportunity to rectify the situation. It takes years to build your good reputation yet only one dissatisfied client to ruin it in a moment.

As a vision of the girls' despondent faces surfaced, Sarah groaned. Yet again she wondered how she could have been so stupid as to try to teach them the way she had. Well, she would do her best to rectify the situation. Pulling her notepad from the drawer, she wrote herself a list:

1. Never assume you know best – remember to work at the girls' level.
2. Regain their trust – teach them something they'll understand.

3. Ask questions and ensure they are not struggling with anything.
4. Confidence – build their own and let them know they can ask about things they are not sure of.

She was just wondering if there was anything she could add when there was a knock on the door. Recognizing it as the schoolmaster's, she felt her heart begin thumping in her chest. Had he reached a decision? Red Cliffs without Harry was unthinkable.

'Come in,' she called briskly to hide her nerves.

'Good morning,' Harry said, towering over her desk in the grey dawn light. She looked up, trying to ascertain his mood but his expression gave nothing away.

'Do take a seat,' she said formally. Without saying anything he straddled the seat in his usual manner. 'How is your mother?' she asked politely.

'She's cross, actually,' he replied, looking down at the desk. That the woman should be annoyed with her came as no surprise.

'I'm sorry,' Sarah sighed.

'So am I,' he muttered. 'She's been going on all night. As you know, Mother was fond of the doctor, and Red Cliffs is a cause close to her heart. She says such foolishness is futile.'

'I agree and can only apologize again for my stupidity,' Sarah replied.

'What?' he cried, staring at her in surprise.

'I agree I have been foolish and . . .' Her voice trailed off as he held up his hand.

'Not you, me,' he spluttered. 'Mother pointed out running this place is a full-time job in itself, without having to take the girls' classes until a new schoolmistress is appointed. She told me that, as the master, I should have given you a run-down of each of their capabilities.'

'Goodness,' Sarah murmured, marvelling at this turn of events. 'Does this mean you'll stay?'

'I got a right flea in my ear for tendering my resignation,' he admitted, looking shamefaced. 'So, Miss Sullivan, I'd be grateful if you would consider it rescinded. Really, I was just letting off steam but things got out of hand.' He leaned his elbows on the desk and stared at Sarah in a way that quite unnerved her. As a mixture of relief and emotion flooded through her, she smiled for the first time that day.

'Oh, I see,' she replied, frowning as she considered her next words. 'I'm sorry . . .'

'I'm really sorry . . .' he began at the same time. They stopped, stared at each other and then burst out laughing.

'What are we like?' Sarah said, just as the door opened and Mrs Daws came in carrying a tray.

'Heard all the mirth and thought as you'd both come to your senses you could have your early morning tea in here. Even made you some toast,' the housekeeper sniffed virtuously. 'No doubt you've got a lot to discuss so April and Pip can supervise breakfast,' she added, giving them one of her knowing looks.

'Mrs Daws, have I ever told you what a wonderful woman you are?' Harry asked, jumping to his feet and throwing his arms around the woman's shoulders.

'No need to go overboard,' she muttered, but Sarah could see by the flush on her cheeks that she was pleased. 'Anyway, being as how you says the soup kitchen's to be moved, I thought I'd ask if I could take some time off each Sunday. This weather makes my legs play up something chronic and some extra rest would help.'

'Of course, Mrs Daws, you do quite enough as it is,' Sarah assured her. 'I'll let you know the exact arrangements when I've confirmed them with the verger.'

'Thanks, Miss Sullivan. Well, this won't get the porridge served,' she muttered.

As the door closed behind her, Harry looked askance. Quickly she outlined the details of the verger's proposal to relocate the soup kitchen to the church hall.

'That would certainly make life easier,' Harry agreed. 'I do worry about Mrs Daws' workload. She never seems to stop.'

'I know and I think we should get the older children helping more. But only if you, as schoolmaster, think that would be appropriate, of course?' she asked, her lips twitching.

He raised his brows but instead of smiling looked serious.

'So much is changing, I think we need to devise a new timetable. However, first things first,' he said, proffering the plate of toast.

Suddenly realizing how hungry she was, Sarah took a slice. Mrs Daws had been generous with the butter and she licked her lips appreciatively and stared at the fire. It had taken hold and the glowing coals made the room warm and cosy. As the two of them munched in contented silence, Sarah found herself relaxing.

'What's that?' Harry asked, screwing up his eyes as he tried to decipher what she'd written on her notepad.

'Oh, just a few things I jotted down,' she replied. Not wishing to admit she'd been gathering inspiration from Mrs Knight's principles, she slid it into her drawer along with the book. 'We really need to talk finances, I'm afraid.'

'What's new?' he asked, raising his brows.

'As you know the roof's leaking again and we need to get it repaired as soon as possible. I hate resorting to Lady Chorlton but needs must. I was hoping she might help with the funding but I've heard from Mr Fothergill that she's in mourning for our late Queen and can't see me yet so . . .' She stopped as the door opened with a sudden bang.

'It's the new boy, miss,' Pip cried. 'He's covered in red spots and groaning like he's in pain.'

6

Sarah hurried upstairs and into the boys' dormitory. The curtains were still drawn, although the material was so faded the daylight penetrated enough for her to make out the bed Solomon was in. He had the cover pulled up over his face, but she could tell from his irregular breathing he wasn't asleep.

'How are you, Solomon?' she asked softly. There was no response although his body stilled. Gently she eased back the cover.

''Ere, 'ands off, you're a woman,' he protested.

'It's Miss Sullivan. I've come to see how you are,' Sarah told him, ignoring his protests. 'Pip told me you have a rash and I need to see it, so please open your nightshirt.' He glared at her warily but she stared back at him, and he grudgingly did as he'd been asked.

'Goodness, you are certainly smothered in spots,' she cried, staring down at the livid red rash that covered his body.

''Tis all up me arms, too,' he said, holding them up for her to see. 'I feel 'orrible and 'ot,' he moaned. Sarah reached out and felt his forehead. It didn't feel overly warm to her, and although he was still looking at her warily, she saw that his eyes were clear. As if sensing her doubt, he groaned and frantically began rubbing his body.

'I'll send April to get Dr Hawkins,' Sarah told him, pulling the cover back over him.

'It's probably something catching so you'd best send me to the infirmary straight away.' A prickle of fear crept up her spine. Supposing he was contagious and the others had already been infected?

'Don't fret, Solomon. I'll go and consult with Master Higgins and see what he thinks,' she told him, patting his hand.

'No! Got to go to the infirmary now,' he cried.

'I'll get Mrs Daws to make you a hot drink to calm you,' she added quickly.

'Don't want no drink,' he protested. 'Just get me to the infirmary. You'll be sorry if I die.' Swallowing down her fears, Sarah hurried to the kitchen.

'How is he?' Mrs Daws asked, looking up from the pot she was stirring.

'Covered in spots and scratching. He doesn't appear to be running a temperature, though. I said I'd get the doctor to look at him but he insisted on being taken to the infirmary immediately,' she murmured.

'Never known a child ask to be taken to hospital before,' the housekeeper muttered. 'Hope it's nothing infectious, though, 'cos things go through here like a dose of salts.'

'Precisely, and that's why we can't be too careful,' Harry said, coming into the room. 'Send April straight down to the surgery,' he instructed. He waited until the door had closed behind her, then turned to Sarah. 'We must be careful not to alarm the pupils, but until the doctor has diagnosed the rash, they must stay on the premises.'

'But April can go?'

'She's had the usual childhood ailments so should be all right. However, I'll instruct Pip only to let Dr Hawkins through the gates. Heaven help us if it's something serious,' he sighed.

'Will you still be taking their lessons this morning?' she asked.

'Yes. Better to keep to their routine. No point in alarming them until we know what it is.'

'I can take the girls for sewing this afternoon instead of their normal lesson with you, if you like,' Sarah offered, desperate to do something useful.

He frowned. 'We'll play it by ear, I think. If Solomon is carrying something contagious, Dr Hawkins will need to examine everyone. Let me know when he arrives.'

'Of course . . .' she began, but he was already marching towards the school room.

'April's gone for the doctor so I'll make Solomon one of my tinctures,' Mrs Daws said, bustling back into the room.

'That's kind,' Sarah smiled.

'Poor little mite. Suppose his system's all upset after losing his father like that. Still, like I said, in all my years I've never known a child ask to go to the hospital.'

'Well, I'm sure Dr Hawkins will tell us if that is necessary,' Sarah said. 'With April busy, you'll need some help in here, Mrs Daws, so what can I do?'

'I'm thinking a nice nourishing broth will go down well, so if you would get some vegetables and prepare them for the pot, I'd be grateful, Miss Sullivan.'

Although Sarah was quick, by the time she returned

from the store shed, Mrs Daws had already prepared her potion.

'I'll take this up to Solomon and sit with him till the doctor arrives. Just hope he's not busy. I told April to say it was urgent but . . .' The woman shrugged, then hurried away.

As Sarah scraped and diced the carrots and turnips, her thoughts were a jumble. Being a new arrival Solomon had possibly brought something unpleasant with him. What illness took so long for the rash to emerge, though? She thought back to the days she'd helped her father in his surgery in Plymouth, yet couldn't recollect ever having seen anything similar. Those spots were a vivid red and all differing shapes and sizes. It was most odd. And the boy wasn't running a fever either.

She'd just covered the prepared vegetables with water and put the pot to simmer when the pupils came surging in for their morning drinks.

'How's Solomon, Miss Sullivan?' Sally asked, setting out the beakers in a neat line.

'We're still waiting for the doctor to call. However, Mrs Daws is sitting with him,' Sarah reassured the girl.

'Hope 'e ain't brought nuffink catchin' with 'im,' Kitty muttered, reverting to her old way of speaking.

'Might be the plague,' Brown announced delightedly.

'Or that scarlet whatsit,' Black shrieked.

'I'm sure it's nothing serious,' Sarah said, frowning at the boys.

'What if wes gets it?' Monday asked, staring at Sarah in horror.

'I'm certain all will be well. But if we were to catch

something, Dr Hawkins, being a clever man, will make us all better,' Sarah reassured them quickly.

'Dr Hawkins will be here as soon as he's finished bandaging his patient,' April announced, coming into the room.

'Coo, 'as someone broken somethink?' Brown cried.

'Who wants one of my special biscuits?' April asked, ignoring him. As the children clamoured around her excitedly, Sarah gave thanks for the girl's perception and kind heart.

'As the weather's nice, you can eat them in the fresh air,' Sarah said, shooing them outside.

It was noon by the time the doctor arrived. Harry showed him upstairs, telling Pip to supervise the children, who were filing into the dining room for their meal.

'Well, Solomon's still insisting he be taken to the infirmary. It was the first thing he said to Dr Hawkins. I must say, he's very vocal for someone so poorly,' the housekeeper said, carefully setting the empty cup down on the table. 'Drank that like a fish, then asked for food, would you believe? Why bless you, Miss Sullivan, you've got lunch all prepared.'

'I was pleased to help. Now, the children are waiting so shall I dish up?' Sarah asked.

'If you wouldn't mind. Then while you're doing that, I'll start on making young Solomon a nice sponge. Happen he'll appreciate a little treat.' Sarah looked at the housekeeper in surprise. Surely the boy wasn't up to eating cake? However, not wishing to question the woman's ways, she began ladling the broth into the serving dishes. April and Pip had just carried them through to the tables when Mrs Daws bustled back from the pantry.

'Either I'm getting senile and forgetting where I put things or there's a thief about,' she muttered, placing eggs and flour on the scrubbed table.

'What do you mean, Mrs Daws?'

'I thought I'd make the poor boy one of my marble cakes. A bit of colour always tempts the appetite. Oh well, he'll have to make do with a plain one,' she muttered, reaching for her mixing bowl.

Sarah was just wondering what to do next when she heard footsteps coming down the stairs. She hurried out to the hallway where the doctor was talking to the master.

'How is he, Doctor?' she asked anxiously.

'Insisting he be taken to the infirmary straight away,' he replied. 'And I've a good mind to send him there.'

Sarah exchanged a bewildered look with Harry. 'He's that poorly?' she gasped.

'No, Miss Sullivan, he is not. In fact, he's not ill at all.'

'But those spots?'

'A clever bit of artistry,' he replied, holding up a little bottle and a twig.

'Cochineal!' Harry cried.

'Indeed, Master Higgins,' the doctor grimaced. 'Who would have thought colouring obtained from the common beetle could wreak such havoc. I could almost find it funny if he hadn't taken me away from a surgery of people who really do need my attention.'

'I'm so sorry, Dr Hawkins,' Sarah murmured. 'If only I'd inspected those spots more carefully.'

'Well, you had no reason to suspect him, did you? Although in future, it might pay to check the back of the body and not just the front,' the doctor pointed out, not unkindly.

'I'll kill the boy,' Harry roared. 'I've spent this morning making contingency plans in case he had something infectious and we had an epidemic on our hands.'

'At least it hasn't come to that. However, when Solomon found out his plan had failed, he got quite hysterical. I've given him a sedative, Miss Sullivan, and here's another one in case he should need it,' the doctor said, passing Sarah a twist of paper. 'When he's recovered, no doubt you will impress upon him the error of his ways, Master Higgins.' Doctor Hawkins picked up his Gladstone bag to leave, but hesitated at the door. 'You might like to find out why he was so desperate to be taken to the infirmary, though.'

'I certainly will, Dr Hawkins,' Sarah replied, although a suspicion was already forming.

'I can't help thinking about that poor little mite, Solomon,' Mrs Daws said, stretching her legs out in front of the range. The children had gone to bed and they were relaxing after the traumas of the day. 'He must have been desperate to see his father to go to such lengths.'

'Poor chap didn't realize he was no longer at the infirmary. When I explained, he went berserk and I had to give him the other sedative,' Harry sighed. 'He'll probably sleep until morning now, but Pip has promised to keep an eye on him.'

'I suppose it's normal he should want to see his father's body but why didn't he just ask?' Sarah said. 'Or why didn't I guess?'

'The same could be said of me,' Harry added. 'Solomon did say he wanted to go and see him the night he ran away but in view of the state of the man's body, I told him it was probably best to remember him as he was,' Harry admitted. 'Perhaps I was wrong.'

'Me and all,' the housekeeper replied. 'I suppose he needed to see to accept. Say goodbye, as it were. Still, at least I know I'm not going senile,' she chuckled, holding up the nearly empty cochineal bottle. 'Though if it's all right with you, Miss Sullivan, I think I'll get Bert to put a lock on the pantry. I can't risk any more of my baking ingredients going walkabout.'

'Indeed, we can't risk upsetting our pistoriophile, can we?' Harry said, grinning at the housekeeper.

'What's that when it's at home?' the woman asked.

'It's someone who loves baking, Mrs Daws,' he explained.

'Well, why didn't you just say that then? You and your weird words,' the housekeeper scoffed, getting to her feet. 'Now I'm going to have a wally before bed.'

'A what?' Sarah asked.

'One of my pickled gherkins.'

'Now who's using weird words, Mrs Daws?' Harry chuckled.

'At least we've settled Bert's invoice,' Sarah said, stifling a yawn. 'Goodness, I'm tired. Oh, we never did get round to drawing up the new timetable,' she cried, staring at Harry in dismay.

'Well, we are certainly not going to do it now. I'll come in early tomorrow. By the way, Kitty said she would prefer to go to the farm on Saturday rather than do any more sewing.'

'Oh, she did, did she?' Sarah asked. 'She made a right mess of the dress she chose to work on so she needn't think she's getting out of putting it right.'

'I said I would check with you but she assured me you were adamant girls should be treated the same as boys so it was bound to be all right.'

'Sharp as a tack, that one,' Mrs Daws said, biting into her pickle.

'Hoist by your own petard, I think, Miss Sullivan,' Harry chuckled, and Sarah couldn't help but join in.

It was Saturday evening, and Sarah and Harry, having escaped the confines of Red Cliffs for a few hours, were enjoying their fish supper in a nearby restaurant. This being bath night, Mrs Laver and Mrs Daws had seen to the children, giving Sarah time to get ready for their date. Having become adept at making the most of the cast-off clothing that regularly arrived at Red Cliffs, she had put together an outfit suitably smart for the occasion. Her forest-green dress with its frilled sleeves set off her colouring, and the amber stone brooch pinned at the throat added the final touch. Even her usually wayward hair, tamed by vigorous brushing, now sat in a neat chignon.

'. . . And then Kitty told Farmer Jim that she hoped the hens were on the point of lay,' Harry grinned, seemingly oblivious to the pains she'd taken with her appearance.

'Poor Farmer Jim,' Sarah murmured. 'I should think he was affronted at having a young girl telling him his job.'

'Not a bit of it. He was impressed by her knowledge and said we'd have to wait a little longer in that case. While the others were mucking out the stables, he asked lots of questions about the farm they were raised on. Luke came to life and replied enthusiastically as well. Jim and Bess would have loved children of their own, but it wasn't to be. Anyway, while Kitty helped Bess skin the rabbits ready for the pot, they had a good old natter about how to care for the poultry.'

'Obviously the girl is more cut out for farming than sewing,' Sarah chuckled.

'There's nothing wrong with that. She might even end up becoming a farmer's wife,' he pointed out, spearing a chip with his fork.

'Or even have her own farm,' Sarah threw back quickly.

'Now that's hardly likely, is it?'

'No, I guess not. It's not fair that women are still beholden to men in this day and age,' Sarah said.

'We're not all tyrants, you know,' Harry smiled. 'In fact, some of us would love a woman to cherish and care for,' he added, his eyes softening as he stared at her meaningfully. 'Especially one who looks as beautiful as you do tonight.' As he continued gazing at her, Sarah looked down at her plate, toying with her fish. 'Don't you ever dream of having a man to look after you?' he persisted.

Carefully, she put down her knife and fork.

'Jack Wise asked the same thing only the other day.' He frowned and she went on quickly, 'I told him I was far too busy looking after Red Cliffs and that my ambition is to help the pupils reach their potential so they can secure good jobs.'

'That's commendable, but you also have your own life to consider,' Harry advised.

'I know, and just as soon as a new schoolmistress is appointed I intend spending more time on the people and issues that are dear to my heart. In fact, I received a letter this morning from the Local Authority confirming they have found a suitable candidate and will be sending her along for an interview later this month.'

Harry smiled at her delightedly. 'We shall have to make some plans then.'

'We? Why, Harry, I hardly think you'll be interested in attending meetings of the National Union of Women's Suffrage Societies,' she laughed. 'It's time women had a say in what happens in Parliament, time we were eligible to vote. I understand the movement is very active round here and I intend helping them further their cause.' Looking at her impassioned expression, Harry felt his heart sinking. She seemed like a different woman from the one who arrived at the school all those months ago, more detached somehow, but then she was ambitious. Well, there would still be free time for them to walk out together, wouldn't there?

'So, what about . . . ?' His voice trailed off as she held up her hand.

'I know you are going to ask about the School Board. Well, don't worry, Harry, I intend applying for membership of that as well.'

Hastily Harry swallowed the last of his drink. That wasn't what he'd meant at all. Perhaps it was time to let her know how he felt.

'I had thought that we could spend the time getting to know each other better again, walking out, making plans for . . .' he began.

'And we will, Harry,' she assured him, covering his hand with hers. 'It's just that I have things I must do first.' Although she wanted to spend time with him, he needed to understand that these issues meant a lot to her.

'Come on, let's go down to the harbour,' she suggested. 'We can take a stroll by lamplight.'

But for Harry, the light had gone out of the evening.

7

It was the middle of February when Sheena O'Reilly arrived at Red Cliffs, bringing with her the first real cold snap of the year. She shivered, pleased she'd wrapped up well in a cherry-red woollen hat and matching muffler that cheered up her charcoal coat.

Her green eyes sparkled with excitement as she stared at the substantial house with its reddish-grey stucco walls and elaborate quoins. What a place, she marvelled, ready at last to take on the new challenge that lay ahead. She rang the bell beside the gate then as she waited for someone to admit her, noticed a young boy with the darkest eyes she'd ever seen staring sullenly through the iron railings.

'Hello, there,' she called brightly but he glared silently back at her. Then a stooped young man hobbled towards her. 'Good morning, I'm Miss O'Reilly and I have an appointment to see Miss Sullivan,' she told him in her lilting voice.

'Right-ho,' he said cheerfully, but as soon as he'd turned the key in the lock and pulled back the heavy gate, the other boy launched himself at the opening. 'Steady on, Solomon,' he said, restraining the flailing boy. 'Let the lady enter.'

'Goodness, what a firecracker,' Sheena chuckled, only to receive another scowl.

'Don't worry he's still getting used to the place, aren't you, Solomon? Lessons are about to begin so you'd better get yourself over there before Master Higgins sees you here again.'

The boy sighed deeply, then trudged off towards the classroom.

'I'm Pip,' the young man grinned. 'I'll show you to Miss Sullivan's office.'

She followed him up the gravel path and through the front door, which, although badly in need of redecoration, sported a highly polished brass letterbox and bell.

'Miss O'Reilly to see you, Miss Sullivan,' he announced, showing her into the office.

'Well, would you look at that,' she remarked, staring up at the motto above Sarah's desk. '*Love Never Faileth*, now is that just not a wonderful sentiment, Miss Sullivan?'

'It is indeed, Miss O'Reilly, and one my late godfather endeavoured to live by,' the woman in front of her replied, smoothing down the skirts of her navy-blue dress. 'Would you care to take a seat?' she added, gesturing to the chair opposite.

'This is a wonderfully cosy room, is it not?' Sheena said, perching on the edge of the seat and staring around the room. Sitting down was the last thing she wanted to do; she was jumpy as a flea.

'Thank you, although, as you can see, it is in need of some updating. Now, perhaps we should start with your testimonial?'

Sheena scrabbled around in her bag and handed it over. Then while the woman carefully perused it, she took another peek around.

It was true the furnishings were a bit threadbare but the high ceiling was decorated with an ornate cornice and the sash windows on two sides flooded the room with light. A fire was burning brightly in the grate and she longed to go over and warm her frozen hands. Just then the door opened and a motherly-looking woman entered carrying a tray of tea.

'Thought you might like a nice warm drink after your walk, dearie.'

'That is so kind of you, missus,' Sheena cried, jumping up. 'Here, let me help.'

'Don't you worry yourself, dearie. I can manage. Kind of you to offer, though,' the woman smiled before pouring the amber liquid carefully into two cups edged with tiny red rosebuds.

'This is Mrs Daws, our housekeeper,' Miss Sullivan said. The woman nodded, then bustled out again. 'Your character looks in order although the detail seems a little sparse.' Feeling herself scrutinized by two clear brown eyes, Sheena answered with a bright smile.

'I only had one position before coming to England, Miss Sullivan,' she explained, holding the woman's gaze and hoping she wouldn't probe further. She wanted the past to remain firmly where it belonged.

'Yet you are twenty, are you not?'

'I am indeed and the eldest of seven siblings.'

'Ah, then you are obviously used to young children,' Sarah replied, looking relieved. 'I see your previous position was as schoolmistress in a female establishment. I take it the Local Authority have outlined what will be required of you at Red Cliffs?'

71

'To be sure they have, Miss Sullivan,' Sheena chirped, happy to be on safe ground once more. 'Three afternoons taking the girls for needlework, handicraft, good morals, manners, that kind of thing. Of course, I'd be happy to teach them anything you want,' she smiled.

'Tell me, Miss O'Reilly, do you believe girls should be given the same opportunities in life as boys?' From the way she said this, Sheena sensed her answer was important.

'I most certainly do,' she cried. 'The female brain is just as intelligent as the male, capable of absorbing facts and applying them in the same manner.'

'Indeed, that is my theory, too. What prompted you to come here, if you don't mind me asking?'

'Of course not. When my grandmother took a bad tumble and broke both a leg and an arm, she asked if I could help. It was meant to be a temporary arrangement but I don't want to leave her. I love it here in Devonshire and decided to stay, hence my seeking employment.'

'And will you be working at other education establishments as well?'

Sheena frowned, wondering if this was a trick question.

'No, Miss Sullivan. This would be my only employment whilst I continue to care for Nanna. She hates being cooped up indoors and likes me to keep her company, read to her and assist with her embroidery. Do you know, she insisted on learning to use her left hand? Isn't that truly marvellous? Although her stitches went aslant to begin with. She kept at it, though, until she'd mastered a way that worked for her.' Aware that she was gabbling, Sheena drew to a halt.

'I think perseverance is key to many things,' Sarah smiled. 'We have one girl here who, being left-handed, gets frustrated for the very same reason.'

'We discovered it's the way you hold the material. I'd be happy to show her the trick. Sorry, that's always assuming you decide to engage me, of course.'

'That will also be up to Master Higgins to decide. He teaches the children here full time, with the exception of the girls' subjects, of course. Ah, I can hear they have broken for morning break, so if you'll excuse me I'll ask him to join us.'

Left by herself, Sheena quickly took off her hat, unwound the muffler then shook out her long hair. She'd been getting increasingly hot during the interview but hadn't liked to ask if she could make herself comfortable. Miss Sullivan, although not much older than herself, looked so poised and confident in her smart dress, she'd felt quite the country bumpkin beside her.

No sooner had she sat down again than Miss Sullivan returned, followed by a tall, serious-looking man.

'This is Miss O'Reilly,' Sarah said, indicating Sheena. 'Miss O'Reilly, let me introduce Mr Higgins, our illustrious schoolmaster.'

The man studied her for a moment then held out his hand. As Sheena gripped it enthusiastically, she noticed his brows lift slightly and wondered if he thought her too young for the position. She lifted her chin, determined to prove her suitability.

For the next quarter of an hour, Sheena answered the questions they fired at her before being asked to wait in the hallway whilst they conferred. Catching sight of herself in the glass on the wall, she grimaced. Her face was flushed as red as the tumble of wayward curls. In fact, she looked more like an excited schoolgirl than the sophisticated mistress she'd hoped to portray. If only she'd taken a moment to prepare herself before entering the house but she'd taken so long watching the activity of the boats in the harbour, she'd only made her appointment on time by a gnat's breath. She was just rearranging her hair, when she noticed a young girl, holding a bundle of bed linen, eyeing her curiously.

'Goodness, you gave me a fright,' Sheena said, smiling. 'Is something wrong?' she asked when the girl continued staring.

'Sorry, miss, but your red hair's so pretty, I can't help looking at it.'

'I see you are also a fellow scarlock,' Sheena laughed.

'Eh?'

'You also have curly red hair,' she explained.

'Scarlock? I never heard that name before. Beats April,' she said, her free hand going to her head. 'Have to have mine cut short and wear a cap, it's the rules,' she sighed.

'Ah, that's a shame. You're still very pretty,' Sheena replied.

'Now you're having a laugh,' April snorted, her hand straying to the scar on her cheek.

'Not at all. Anyway, you can get powder and things to cover that if it makes you feel self-conscious.'

April's eyes widened in amazement. 'Really?'

'Sure. In fact, my nanna has a pot and if I am lucky enough to be taken on here, I'll bring you some.'

The girl beamed, but before she could answer, the door opened and Sheena was called back into the office.

'Wish me luck,' she whispered to April.

'Master Higgins and I have decided we would like to engage your services, Miss O'Reilly. You did say you were free to start straight away?'

'Indeed, I am,' Sheena cried. 'So, this position will be until the end of May, then?'

What makes you say that?' Harry asked, looking at her sharply.

'The Local Authority admitted they couldn't guarantee the school would be staying open past that date. Something about another inspection?' Sheena replied.

'Ah,' he said, understanding dawning.

'We have every confidence that the issues raised in November will have been addressed by then,' Sarah told her. 'They found nothing wrong with the teaching, I hasten to add. It was more about the condition of the property.'

'Well, that's grand then,' Sheena smiled. 'I'll look forward to meeting the pupils. The one I saw earlier was trying to escape.'

'Ah, that'll be Solomon, no doubt. We call him our Tuesday child as that was the day he came here. Poor chap, he lost his father in a terrible fire,' Harry explained.

'Oh, no,' Sheena cried, covering her face with her hand as she remembered calling him a firecracker. She really must be more careful.

'It's a difficult time for him but we're keeping an eye on his welfare. Now, I really must be getting back to the classroom.' Harry hesitated. 'Would you like to sit in on my lesson for the rest of the morning?' he offered. Sarah stared at him in surprise. He was usually so precious about his work and had only invited her to join him just before the Local Authority inspectors were due to pay a visit. But then she wasn't a teacher, was she?

'That would be grand,' Sheena enthused, smiling at him warmly. He beamed back so eagerly, Sarah nearly fell off her chair in surprise.

She couldn't fault Miss O'Reilly's passion, Sarah thought, watching them leave. If only she could summon the same enthusiasm for the paperwork on her desk.

Amongst the usual clutch of bills in that morning's mail was another letter from Mr Fothergill, but before she could open it there was a knock on the door. Would she get nothing done today, she thought, forcing down a sigh of exasperation.

''Xcuse me, ma'am.' She looked up to find a swarthy man dressed in dirty overalls, leering at her from the doorway.

'May I help you?' she asked, suppressing a shudder.

'More a case of me who can help you,' he grinned, revealing tobacco-stained teeth. 'Been asked to take a look at yer roof.' He whistled and shook his head. ''Tis in a right sorry state, from what I can see, and that temporary patching looks suspect. Lots of tiles need replacing on the southern side where the winds lifted 'em and then there's the . . .'

'Perhaps you could just give me an idea of what it will cost?' Sarah asked, interrupting what promised to be a litany of defects.

'Think I'd better talk to the boss. I mean, a pretty thing like you don't want to worry about filthy lucre.'

'Lucre?' she frowned.

'Lolly,' he grinned. 'Brass.'

'Oh, money. Well, Mr . . . ?'

'Tyler,' he chortled. 'Good name for a good roofer, eh?'

'Well, Mr Tyler, I am Miss Sullivan, the boss, as you put it,' she informed him, fighting down her irritation when she saw the astonishment in his eyes. 'I took over when my godfather, Dr Lawrence, died last year. Perhaps you'd like to send me an estimate for the work you perceive necessary,' she added briskly.

The man whistled. 'Never done that afore. The doctor just let me get on with things, then paid me the damages. You won't find a fairer or better worker than me, Miss Sullivan.'

'I'm sure I won't, Mr Tyler, and I'm not questioning your integrity,' Sarah told him, crossing her fingers. 'However, before I can agree to any work being done, I have to secure the necessary funding. In order to do that, I need to have the "damages", as you put it, in writing. Is that a problem?'

The man scratched his head. 'Not for me it ain't, but it could be for you, being as how they're sayin' we're in for sleet and snow showers.'

Sarah stifled another sigh. Melting snow would get in through gaps in the broken tiles. Pip and April already worked hard to clear up any leaks and she couldn't expect them to keep on mopping up puddles and drying out bedding. However, there simply wasn't enough in the school's bank account to pay for replacement tiles and goodness only knew what else.

'I can't risk the pupils getting wet this cold weather so

could you just patch up the gaps again until we have the money?' she asked hopefully.

'I could,' he agreed, staring at her thoughtfully.

'Thank you,' she cried.

'Cors, it will cost more that way, it having to be done twice, like,' he began, scratching his head.

I might have known, she thought, staring down at her desk

'If snow is forecast, it appears I have no choice, Mr Tyler,' she replied. 'When can you start?'

'Just so happens I'm free today,' he grinned. 'I'll take a proper look around, then go and get the necessary materials.'

'Thank you, Mr Tyler,' she replied. 'I'll show you upstairs.'

'No need to get up, missus. I know the way,' he said, giving her a mock salute and disappearing outside.

What a repugnant man, Sarah thought. Had she done the right thing allowing him to start work before she had the money, she wondered, fighting down a prickle of unease. Yet she really had no choice, did she? The children's welfare came first. She'd have to worry about the bill when it came in.

Catching sight of the letter she'd abandoned earlier, she snatched it up. As she read the contents, all thoughts of Mr Tyler vanished. Lady Chorlton would receive her at 3 p.m. on Thursday 28 February. Apparently, she resided at Hesketh Crescent, which wasn't an address Sarah was familiar with, but no doubt Mrs Daws would know. Getting to her feet, she caught sight of the motto on the wall and smiled. *Love Never Faileth*. It would be the perfect opportunity to thank their benefactress for all her previous assistance and mention funding for the roof. Of course, she'd explain they were trying to raise the necessary money themselves but it was a mammoth task and not one they could manage without something short of a miracle.

'That new mistress seems nice,' Mrs Daws commented as soon as Sarah entered the kitchen. 'Saw you were busy so she popped in here to say hello. I asked her to stay for luncheon.'

'After all you said about Miss Green cadging free meals, I'm surprised at you, Mrs Daws,' Sarah replied, remembering how the housekeeper had taken exception to the thin-lipped, grasping woman who had been the previous travelling mistress.

'I just thought it would be a friendly gesture. Make her feel welcome, like,' the housekeeper muttered, slamming the lid on the pan with a clatter. 'Anyhow, she had to go and get her grandmother's luncheon. Said she'll be back for afternoon lessons.'

'Miss O'Reilly is so pretty,' April gushed, looking up from the pastry she was rolling out.

'Goodness, she does seem to have made a good impression,' Sarah laughed.

'Especially with the master,' April giggled. 'He couldn't take his eyes off her.'

8

When Sheena entered the classroom, she found the girls staring out of the window.

'A very good afternoon, everyone,' she called cheerily. 'It's certainly a nippy old one out there,' she added, unwinding the bright muffler and pulling off her cap.

'How did you get here? We didn't see you walk past the window,' Kitty asked.

Sheena laughed. 'To be sure, I arrived by shanks's pony.'

'You've got a pony?' Monday gasped, her eyes widening.

'I likes that name – Shanksy,' June whispered.

'Well, actually . . .' Sheena began.

'I said she were different, didn't I?' Kitty cried, clapping her hands delightedly. 'Where've you put him? By the big tree down the end of the garden, I bet. Will he be all right by himself?'

Seeing their faces glowing with excitement, Sheena hadn't the heart to disillusion them. Besides, didn't a little magic brighten the day?

'The little people will look after him.' The words were out of her mouth before she'd had time to think.

'What little people?' Edith asked.

Sheena hid her dismay. Hadn't it been her runaway tongue that had got her into trouble before?

'Those lovely pint-sized folk who care for good people

and animals,' she said quickly. 'Now take your seats, my angels, and we'll begin our lessons.'

'Can we learn more about the little people?' Monday squealed excitedly. 'I've never heard of them before.'

As they all stared at her expectantly, Sheena realized she'd boxed herself into a corner.

'Tell you what,' she said. 'If you pay attention to your lessons I'll tell you a story about the little people afterwards.' To her relief this satisfied them and with much scraping of stools on the stone floor, they took their seats.

'Now, my angels, in order to help me get to know you, I've made some little badges on which I'd like you to write your names.'

As she walked around distributing them, Kitty asked, 'Aren't you going to wear one, miss?'

'Well, there's only one of me so you'll be sure to remember my name now, won't you?'

'You speak differently to us, Miss O'Reilly. All singsong like the birds.'

Sheena looked at the name on the girl's badge and smiled. 'Well, Sally, I come from another country called Ireland and it's how we talk there.'

'Never heard of it,' Kitty shrugged.

'Ireland is separated from England by a large expanse of water called the Irish Sea, and although it is a long way away, Ireland is still part of the United Kingdom.'

'The what?' Edith frowned.

'Have you not heard of the United Kingdom?' As they all looked blankly at her, she chuckled. 'I'm thinking we'll have a little geography lesson then. Now listen here, my angels, the United Kingdom is made up of four countries, Scotland, England, Wales and Ireland.'

'Blimey, I only knows about Devonshire. Where are all these other places, then?' Edith cried.

'Devonshire is a county, Edith. Lots of counties make up a country and these four countries make up the United Kingdom,' Sheena explained. Seeing their perplexed looks, she began worrying she'd pitched the impromptu lesson too high. Then Monday smiled and took something from her pocket.

'My dadda works on the sea and he brought me this globe. It's got all the countries in the whole world on it.'

'That's wonderful. Might I borrow your globe to show everyone exactly where these countries are, please, Monday?' The little girl proudly handed it over and they watched in fascination as Sheena pointed to each one in turn.

'I expect Dadda's been to them all,' Monday said.

'Then he's a lucky man, for travel is a wondrous thing,' Sheena smiled. 'Now I'll write the names up on the blackboard,' she said, picking up the chalk. 'Each country has a symbol called an emblem to represent it. Would you like to know what they are?' When they nodded eagerly, she drew a thistle alongside Scotland, a leek next to Wales, a rose next to England, and a shamrock next to Ireland.

'I never heard of a shamrock afore,' Ellen said.

'It is similar to a clover plant,' Sheena explained.

'And we all knows what they are, 'cos they cover the fields the cattle are in,' Kitty laughed. 'You know, miss, this is quite interesting for a lesson.'

'It's great you think that way, Kitty, because if you enjoy

what you're learning it will stay with you. Now, I believe you usually do sewing today, my angels?'

'Worse luck,' Kitty groaned, rolling her eyes.

'You don't like needlework?'

'I love it,' Edith sighed.

'But I don't,' Kitty grumbled.

'So, what do you like to do?' Sheena asked.

'I prefer being on the farm skinning rabbits to being cooped up in class,' Kitty stated.

Seeing the spark of challenge in her eyes, Sheena smiled. 'Being able to prepare food for the pot is a good skill to have and will ensure you never go hungry.' Seeing the girl's grudging admiration, Sheena decided to push home her advantage. 'However, you will also need to learn other skills to get on in life.'

'Like what?' Kitty muttered.

Aware her answer would determine whether she'd be perceived a mistress worth listening to, Sheena smiled brightly.

'Well, why don't we decide between us exactly what we need to know?'

'You mean you're interested in what we have to say?' Edith gasped.

'Of course, Edith. When you leave here you will all need to earn a living, won't you?' They murmured in agreement. 'Then let's discuss the possible positions that interest you and what skills you'll need. So much of your time will be spent working, it's worth thinking about what you'd enjoy doing. Then when you marry and have your own family you will be able to use those skills to run a good household.'

'Do you enjoy teaching, miss?' Edith asked.

'Indeed I do, but I had to work hard at my lessons.'

'Yeah, but that ain't goin' to be much use when you 'ave a family,' Kitty snorted.

'You think?' Sheena asked. 'Well, why don't we start with you, Kitty? What would you like to do when you leave Red Cliffs?'

'I want to work on a farm, make butter, cheese, that kind of thing. Not do needlework,' she added.

'We'll write that down,' Sheena said, taking up the chalk again. 'Kitty needs to learn how to make butter and cheese. Edith, how about you?'

'That's easy, I want to be a seamstress to a rich lady.'

Smiling at the girl's positivity, Sheena wrote that down next to her name, then moved on to the others. By the time she'd asked them all the left-hand side of the board was full.

'Now, my angels, we need to decide which of these skills will be useful to run your own household. Kitty wants to make butter and cheese. Will she need those for her own home?'

'Yes, 'cos we has butter and cheese at luncheon,' Monday said.

'That's right, Monday. And what about sewing?'

'Yes,' they chorused. ''Cos we'll have to make clothes and turn sheets.'

'Baking bread and cakes?'

'Yes, so we can eat them with the cheese,' Monday cried. And so it went on until finally they reached Maggie's name.

'I want to teach like you, miss,' she said.

'Like I said before, that ain't goin' to be much good

when you wed, is it, girl?' Kitty snorted. 'I've yet to hear a man listen to anything a woman says.'

'That's as maybe,' Sheena smiled. 'But what about sums? A good household needs to run to a budget and that is a skill any man would appreciate in a wife. Besides, what about children?' Sheena asked. 'Teaching them to read and write would give them a good start in life, would it not?'

'Here, you've been bloody clever, miss,' Kitty cried, almost beside herself. 'All them columns go together, don't they?'

Sheena smiled, deciding not to dampen the girl's enthusiasm by correcting her language. That could wait for another day.

'Well spotted, Kitty. The skills you learn in school will not only help you gain good positions, they will ensure you are able to run a household within budget and enable you to give your children a good start in life.'

'Except I ain't never going to marry,' Kitty declared.

Taken aback by the girl's vehemence, Sheena endeavoured to keep her voice neutral. 'You'll still need to know how to run a home, though, Kitty. Or are you intending to stay at Red Cliffs all your life?'

'Cors not. Although this is the best home I ever had since Mother left Father and took up with that . . .'

'Yes, I can see Red Cliffs is a splendid place,' Sheena cut in quickly. 'Now, my angels, you have done very well this afternoon, so gather round and we'll have that story before the bell goes.'

The girls were lively at supper and Sarah had to remind them to finish their meal before talking. She was dying to

85

ask how the lessons with the new mistress had gone but knew it was important to keep order at the table. As soon as they'd finished eating, though, it was April who asked about their lessons.

'Did you enjoy your afternoon with Miss O'Reilly?'

'It was great fun,' Ellen told her.

'She came on her horse,' Monday cried.

'Really?' April asked. 'I didn't see any horse.'

'He's called Shanksy and he's looked after by the little people,' June sighed. 'We had a story all about them.'

'You didn't do your sewing?' Sarah enquired.

'No, thank 'eavens,' Kitty replied.

'What did you learn then?' Sarah persisted when she saw the master taking an interest.

'Well, we didn't really do lessons as such,' Edith said.

'Miss told us about Ireland, that's where she comes from. It's part of the United Kingdom,' Sally said.

'And we found all the countries on my globe,' Monday said proudly.

'We also learned their emblems,' Sally added. 'Miss O'Reilly is really good at drawing.'

'And she told us why learning is important. If we take it seriously we'll get good positions and everything we learn will help us when we have our own homes as well,' Maggie added.

'Oh? How?' Sarah asked, frowning.

''Cos knowing sums will help us balance the budget,' Edith explained.

'Well, you can't argue with that,' Mrs Daws said, as she collected up the serving dish. 'It sounds to me as if you've had a good afternoon's learning, lessons or no. Now, how about putting some of it to good use in the kitchen?' For once the girls followed her without moaning about the chores they had to do.

'They certainly sound as though they covered a lot of ground,' Harry said, coming over to the table with his cup of tea.

'But what about their sewing?' Sarah couldn't help asking. 'The whole idea is to teach them how to become self-sufficient so that they can get good jobs and earn a decent wage.'

'Plenty of time for that, surely? It's obvious Miss O'Reilly has captured their imagination, which means they'll listen to what she has to say.'

'But a pony called Shanksy? What was that all about?' To her surprise, Harry threw back his head and laughed.

'Oh, Sarah, you're priceless. Have you never heard the expression "shanks's pony"? It refers to someone who walks everywhere.'

Irked by his teasing, Sarah stirred her tea vigorously. In spite of her annoyance, she was pleased the girls had taken to the new mistress so well. It left her free to tackle the administration here and meant she could attend the Women's Suffrage Society meetings. That women should be taken seriously was important to her and she couldn't wait to make her voice heard.

As for the new mistress, no doubt if she spoke to her about the importance of the sewing classes and her wish to have every girl wearing their new outfit by Easter, Miss O'Reilly would ensure her timetable was adhered to. After all, she was still in charge, wasn't she? Which reminded her about her concerns for the new boy.

'Has Solomon settled any better? I noticed he was still scowling at everyone and everything over supper,' Sarah asked.

'The only time he wasn't angry was when he was helping rebuild the coops. I'm hoping another visit to the farm might help. There's something about being out in the fresh air, don't you think?'

'Not in this cold weather,' Sarah shivered. 'Which reminds me, I had a visit from Mr Tyler this morning.'

'Who?'

'Tyler. He claimed he was the best roofer in the business.' Harry eyed her sceptically and she hurried on. 'Anyway, he said as snow was forecast, he'd be happy to patch up the roof until we can afford to have it done properly.'

'At some extortionate price, no doubt.'

'He did say it would cost more that way, but as we can't afford to have the roof retiled and the weather's changing, I didn't have any choice. Coincidentally, I had a letter from Lady Chorlton inviting me to visit at the end of the month and . . .' She trailed to a halt. 'Why are you frowning, Harry? You know I've been dying to meet her.'

'It's not Lady Chorlton I'm worried about. It's this Tyler. Can you remember what he looked like?'

'Swarthy, yellow teeth and there was something about the way he leered . . .'

'Tell me you haven't given him the job?' he interrupted, looking worried.

'Well, he hasn't actually done anything yet. He said he'd take a look around upstairs, then go and get the materials he needed.'

'Did you get Pip to go up with him?'

'No. Tyler said my godfather always let him get on with the job, then paid him when it was done.'

Harry let out a long sigh. 'That man is called Slater and your godfather wouldn't even let him inside the building, Sarah.'

'But he definitely said his name was Tyler and he offered to help . . .'

'Like he offered to help the vicar with the church roof. Except the only one he helped was himself – to all the lead. He's been in gaol these past three years.'

'You mean I've been duped?'

'I'm afraid so,' he said, leaning forward and patting her hand.

'To think I've allowed a criminal near the children,' Sarah cried, her hand flying to her chest.

'Oh, Sarah, don't upset yourself,' Harry said, crouching down beside her and putting his arm around her shoulders. 'It's really not your fault. You're not from round here so you weren't to know that Slater's a con man. With luck, if he didn't get any money from you he might have decided the job wasn't worth wasting his time on. You didn't give him any, did you?' he asked, his eyes searching hers.

'No, the cash box is completely empty.'

'Well, no harm done then,' he said, smiling at her reassuringly. 'However, I will have a word with Sergeant Watts, put him on his guard, so to speak.' She relaxed back against him, relieved to have someone share the burden and was just revelling in the warmth of his touch when they heard Pip cry out.

'Here, the gong and candlesticks have gone walkabout.'

9

'Let's go over this again,' Sergeant Watts said, glancing around the kitchen table where Sarah, Harry and Mrs Daws sat gloomily staring into their cups.

'You say you gave Mr Slater, alias Tyler, permission to go upstairs and look at the roof, Miss Sullivan?'

'Yes, Sergeant, he introduced himself as Mr Tyler and said he had carried out work here before.'

'And you didn't think to check with Master Higgins, you being a wom . . . er, I mean being new to these parts?' he hastily amended, seeing Sarah's frown.

'No, I didn't,' Sarah said, guilt making her speak more sharply than she'd intended. 'The man sounded plausible, saying he needed to check what materials were required in order to effect a temporary repair.'

'Hmm,' the sergeant replied, managing to lend an air of disapproval to the word. 'And you heard nothing, Master Higgins?'

Harry shook his head. 'I was in the classroom for most of the day, which as you know is accessed from outside.'

'And I never knew the man was in the house. Knew nothing till I went to sound the gong for supper and it weren't there,' Mrs Daws cried. 'The kids were in one of their excitable moods, frolicking around all over the place like blinkin' puppies, so I thought they were playing one of their pranks. Wouldn't be the first time they've hidden it. Anyhow, I yelled at the top of me voice that if they didn't get to their seats pronto the food was goin' for pig swill. That soon shifted them.'

'I can imagine.' Sergeant Watts gave a small grin. 'Now do we know exactly what's missing?' he asked, his pencil poised.

'Pip and April have taken a good look around and are in the front room making a list,' Harry told him.

''Tis wicked stealing from folks who don't have much,' Mrs Daws declared. 'If I get my hands on that ruddy roofer, I'll throttle him.'

'Now, now, Mrs Daws, to be fair we don't know for sure it was him. Although the evidence does seem to point that way,' the sergeant replied. 'Ah, come in.' He beckoned to April and Pip, who were hovering in the doorway.

'We've made that list, sir,' Pip said, handing over a sheet of paper to the sergeant.

'Well done,' he said, scanning it quickly. 'I'll get my constables to check out the markets and other places these villains use for a quick sale. Now, I had to ring the bell on the gate to gain entry, so presumably someone had to let Slater in?'

'Yes, the gates are kept locked for the pupils' safety,' Harry agreed. 'Did you let Mr Slater in, Pip?'

'Yes, he told me he had an appointment with Miss Sullivan,' Pip replied.

'And you showed him to Miss Sullivan's office, of course?' Harry said.

Pip looked uneasy and stared at Sarah. 'I would have, but as soon as I opened the gate Solomon tried to do

91

another runner. By the time I caught up with him, the man had left his barrow and gone inside. I'm sorry, miss, I didn't think much of it 'cos he used your name.'

'It's not your fault, Pip,' Sarah sighed. 'It's mine for taking the man at his word.'

'Dangerous thing to do that, Miss Sullivan, if you don't mind me saying,' the sergeant replied. 'And what's this about escaping pupils?' he asked, turning to Harry.

'We don't usually keep anyone here against their will, Sergeant, but you might remember Solomon's the boy who lost his father in the foundry fire. He's taken it extremely badly and hasn't settled at all.'

'Ah, bad job, that. They don't even know what caused it, you know! Now back to the case in hand. Did you let Mr Slater out again, Pip?'

The boy nodded. 'Yeah, he followed that new mistress out. Waved and said, "Thanks, young man." He were all polite; you'd never think he were a villain.'

'Well, appearances can be deceptive. Now did he speak with this new mistress?'

'Not that I saw, but then as soon as they'd gone through the gates, I locked them quickly in case Solomon was lurking.'

'And the name of this new mistress?' Sergeant Watts asked, turning to Harry.

'Miss O'Reilly, but I'm sure she'd have nothing to do with a scoundrel like Slater.'

'Well, you never can tell,' the sergeant replied, snapping his book shut and getting to his feet. 'I think that's all for now. Thanks for the tea, Mrs Daws. Don't worry, I'll get my men out looking first thing in the morning.

In the meantime, don't go letting any more strangers onto your premises, Miss Sullivan.'

As if she would, Sarah thought. She felt humiliated enough as it was without his condescending attitude.

'Don't worry, I won't, Sergeant,' she said emphatically. 'Thank you for coming out so promptly.'

As the sergeant opened the front door, he was buffeted by a burst of hail.

'Can't say the man didn't know his weather, though. 'Night, all.'

'I'll get the gates for you, Sergeant,' Pip said, hobbling after him.

'Poor Pip, he feels dreadful,' April murmured.

'He has nothing to blame himself for,' Sarah sighed. 'Which is more than can be said for me.'

As Sheena was hurrying towards the classroom, trying her best to avoid the huge hailstones that were falling, she heard her name being called. Looking up, she saw Miss Sullivan beckoning her from the front door. Today the woman was dressed in a smart olive-green dress with an ivory lace collar at her throat. Wishing she had something as smart to wear, Sheena tugged her coat down further over her brightly coloured patchwork skirt and smiled warmly.

'Good afternoon, Miss Sullivan,' she said, beaming brightly. However, the woman stared so soberly back, Sheena's heart fell. Whatever could she have done wrong?

'Good afternoon, Miss O'Reilly. Do step inside out of this dreadful weather. I hope you have settled in well to Red Cliffs. How are you getting on with the girls?'

'I have, thank you, Miss Sullivan, and the angels are just grand.'

'Angels? Well, I've never heard them referred to as angels before. I hope your horse — Shanksy, isn't it — is being safely looked after?'

'Ah . . .' Sheena blushed. So that was what had annoyed her. 'To be sure, it was just a joke but then the girls wanted a story about him at the end of lessons and I didn't see any harm in it.' Seeing the woman frown, Sheena couldn't help adding, 'It's just a bit of fun and finishes the afternoon on a happy note.' Sarah opened her mouth to disagree, then, recalling the principles in Mrs Knight's book, bit her tongue.

'I'm sure you know best, Miss O'Reilly,' she conceded. 'How is their sewing coming along? I'm given to understand that at your last lesson you were debating the skills they might require in order to gain suitable employment. Bearing in mind their ages, wasn't that a little presumptuous?'

'I'm sorry if you don't approve, Miss Sullivan. In my opinion it's never too early for pupils to start thinking about their future. Sort of focuses the mind, I think. Besides, it was my way of getting to know each of them as a person. It's much easier to teach pupils when you understand what makes them tick. However, I will ensure this afternoon is spent on their needlework.'

'Thank you. While I agree the children need to think about their futures, at this moment raising funds for the school is our priority, which is where our deadline comes in. They will be representing Red Cliffs as well as earning some much-needed money at a concert, which is why their new outfits must be ready to wear by Easter.'

'I shall make sure they are,' Sheena assured her, keen to please the woman. When she still didn't smile, Sheena wondered what on earth could be amiss. If she'd done something wrong, she wished she'd hurry up and say. She really didn't want to be late for lessons.

'Pip informed me that you left the premises the other day at the same time as a man wearing overalls, Miss O'Reilly. May I ask if it was someone you were acquainted with?'

Sheena frowned and tried to remember.

'There was a man pushing a barrow but I didn't pay much attention to him. Pip asked me to hurry in case that poor Solomon tried to do another runner. He surely must be a very unhappy little boy, Miss Sullivan.'

'He is, Miss O'Reilly, and we can only hope that when he comes to terms with his father's death, he'll settle down. In the meantime, can you confirm that you didn't know the man who was pushing the barrow?'

'I never saw him before then, Miss Sullivan. Why?'

'We thought the man was carrying out work on the premises but after he left we found some of our household items were missing.'

'I hope you aren't implying that had anything to do with me,' Sheena snapped. 'Because I can assure you it did not.' Aware that panic had made her voice shrill, she stared down at her boots.

'There's no need to get alarmed, Miss O'Reilly,' Sarah replied, puzzled by her reaction. 'Naturally the police have been informed, but if you see anybody suspicious lurking around the premises, perhaps you would let either myself or Master Higgins know?'

'Of course, Miss Sullivan,' Sheena muttered, relief searing through her. 'I hope they didn't take anything precious?' she asked.

'Candlesticks, brass lamps, trinkets, but most importantly to Mrs Daws, her dinner gong. Anyway, I won't detain you any longer,' Sarah said, opening the door again. 'Oh, I can see the girls peering out of the classroom window; no doubt they're looking for Shanksy,' she added with a ghost of a smile.

She really would have to be more careful about keeping her feelings under control, Sheena told herself as she hurried back to the classroom. Panicking like that had caused Miss Sullivan to give her a curious look and the last thing she wanted was to raise her suspicions. Obviously, the girls having their new clothes ready for Easter was an important issue so she'd do as she'd promised and ensure they spent the afternoon sewing. As she stood in the doorway, shaking the melting ice from her clothes, Master Higgins called to her from the workshop.

'Good afternoon, Miss O'Reilly. I've heard such excellent reports about your last lesson, perhaps I should get you to teach the boys about the United Kingdom and its emblems.' Sheena gave him a searching look lest he was teasing, but he seemed serious.

'I love geography so I'd be glad to, Master Higgins,' she replied. 'Although I have been directed to get the girls progressing their sewing this afternoon.'

'Well, good luck with Kitty, then. I understand from her it's an evil punishment from the devil,' he grinned.

'But there again perhaps it's the devil's punishment for the mistress.'

Sheena chuckled and made her way into the classroom.

'Still no sign of Shanksy,' Monday sighed.

'Come away from the window, girls,' Sheena said, hanging her coat, muffler and hat on the peg. 'Now haven't I told you he's being well looked after?'

'Yeah, by them little folk,' Kitty chortled. 'Perhaps you could ask them where the thief's taken the school's things?'

'To be sure, the man's sins will come back and haunt him,' Sheena replied.

'Coo, are these little people ghosts as well then, miss?' Maggie asked.

'Sure, they can spot someone rotten at a thousand paces. Now let's get on with our lessons.'

'So, what we doing this afternoon then, miss?'

'Needlework, Kitty. I understand from Miss Sullivan she wants you all to have your new dresses ready to wear for Easter.'

'Yeah,' Edith cried. 'Shall I get our things out?'

'Yes, please, Edith,' Sheena replied, watching as the girl skipped over towards the big old cupboard in the corner of the room and began taking out parcels of materials.

'You needn't look so blinkin' 'appy, Edith Cordy,' Kitty groaned.

'Right,' Sheena said, clapping her hands. 'I'd like to see what you are all making, so please set out your work on the desk in front of you.'

Sheena circled the room, looking at each girl's materials and wondering how they were going to turn the shapeless used garments into wearable outfits. Still, they seemed to be quite happy repinning the cloth. Apart from Kitty, who was glaring at the material in front of her.

'Oh dear,' Sheena muttered, following the girl's gaze.

''Tis a blooming mess, ain't it?' Kitty sighed, holding up the yellow floaty voile with the hole in the bodice.

'Perhaps it's a bit ambitious to start with voile, Kitty. It's not the easiest material to work on.'

'Told you,' Edith called. 'But you knew better, clever clogs.'

'Thank you for your advice, Edith,' Sheena smiled. 'Now, Kitty, let's have a good look at our work.'

'Mess, more like,' the girl snorted, waggling her finger through the hole.

'Tell me, why did you choose this dress?'

'I liked the big skirt and petticoats. I thought it would make me feel like a princess. God knows what I was thinking, though, 'cos I wouldn't wear it in a month of frig—'

'Right, I think we should start again from scratch,' Sheena butted in quickly. 'This cotton dress has a lovely big skirt, too, and would be easier to work on. The bands of blue and pink would suit your colouring a treat.'

'You reckon?' Kitty asked doubtfully.

'I do, my angel. Better than that yellow, which would make your lovely skin look quite sallow,' Sheena said firmly. 'Now, do you need any help unpicking the seams?'

'Nah, I can manage that.'

'As long as she uses the unpicker,' Edith laughed.

'Right, well, nobody is using it, Kitty, so you can make a start. Remember, girls, the success of your sewing depends on accurate measuring and checking the structure of the garment you have unpicked against the shape of your own body.'

'What's stuctor?' June whispered.

'You mean structure, June,' Sheena gently corrected. 'And it means the way the dress has been put together. But don't worry, I'm here to show you what to do every step of the way. You are all going to look beautiful, my angels.'

She was interrupted by the door bursting open and April rushing into the room.

'Am I too late?' she asked breathlessly. 'Mrs Daws said as soon as I'd finished scouring the pots, I could come and work on my dress, as long as it's all right with you, miss?'

'Why of course it is. We've only just started so why not collect your sewing from the desk at the front and show me what you've done so far?'

'I wasn't at the last lesson, miss, so I haven't started anything yet,' she said, looking worried.

'Then let's go through the clothes box and choose you something to work on,' Sheena said enthusiastically.

However, when the girls realized that making their dresses wasn't going to be as easy as they'd thought, their excitement turned to frustration. Although Sheena gave guidance and endless words of encouragement, she could see it was going to take every lesson between now and Easter to make the dresses anything like wearable. While Miss Sullivan's intentions were commendable, they were at the very least, ambitious.

By the time the shadows lengthened, the girls were despondent. Keen to cheer them up, Sheena lit the lamps and told them to put their sewing things away.

'Now gather round the fire and I'll tell you what the little folk have been up to,' she invited. Whoops of excitement replaced sighs as they quickly formed a circle on the rag rug. April looked at the clock and her face fell.

'I'd love to join in, miss, but Mrs Daws said I had to be back in time to cook the vegetables. She's been in a right old paddy since her precious gong was taken, so I daren't be late.'

Knowing how hard it was to miss out on anything, Sheena's heart went out to the girl.

'That's all right, my angel, you run along. I haven't forgotten your face powder. I'll put some on for you later,' she promised.

'Coo, April, that's what them women of the night wear. Are you goin' to become one of them?' Kitty cried.

'No, I am not,' April gasped, then promptly burst into tears.

'That wasn't very nice, Kitty,' Sheena said, putting her arms around April's shoulders.

'That's a horrible thing to say to someone,' Edith shouted, glaring at her friend.

'Oh my Lor, I was only joking,' Kitty gasped. 'I didn't mean to upset you, April.'

10

'Is everything all right in here, only the bell's gone for the end of lessons?' Harry asked, appearing in the doorway. Seeing the sobbing girl, he quirked a brow enquiringly at Sheena. 'Problems?'

'Just a misunderstanding, nothing that can't be sorted,' she replied, trying to look more composed than she felt.

Harry gave her a knowing look. 'Right, you little lot, take yourselves off to the kitchen,' he ordered.

'But we haven't had our story yet,' Maggie protested.

'Well, it's too late now. Hurry up, it's snowing and you don't want to freeze in your tracks, do you?' he said, shooing them outside. 'You, too, Kitty,' he added as she stood there hesitating. With a last despairing look at April, she slunk from the room.

'Need any help?' he mouthed.

Sheena shook her head. 'April and I are just going to have a little chat. Perhaps you'd be good enough to tell Mrs Daws we won't be long?'

He nodded and followed after the girls.

'Sorry, miss,' April murmured, her sobs turning to hiccups.

'Well, now, that was a very naughty thing Kitty suggested, but as she said, she only meant it as a joke.'

'I know,' April whispered. 'But with me face like this,

'no fella's ever going to be interested in me, even like that, are they?'

'Any man would be very lucky to walk out with you, April. You're a very pretty young lady, both on the inside and out. No, don't look at me like that. I mean it.'

'Miss Sullivan said that, too.'

'Well, then, we can't both be wrong, can we?' Sheena asked, smoothing the hair back from the girl's forehead. 'Now, I'm guessing that when you look in the mirror your eyes go straight to your scar?'

'I try and avoid looking in the glass other than to check me cap's straight.'

'It might surprise you to know, but to others it is hardly discernible. However, you know it's there and it obviously bothers you so let's see what we can do with this, eh?' Sheena reached into the pocket of her skirt and drew out a little pot. Taking off the lid, she lifted a fabric pad and sprinkled on some of the fine powder. Then she gently dabbed it onto April's face, paying extra attention to blend it along the jagged line.

'Now take a peek,' she said, passing over a little pocket mirror. April glanced at herself, her eyes widening in surprise.

'But you can hardly see it, miss,' she cried. 'I can't believe that's me.'

Sheena smiled at the girl's delight. 'Better pop this in your pocket then,' she said, holding out the pot.

'I can't take this, miss. I've got no money to pay you.'

Sheena chuckled. 'You can show me how to make those feather-light dumplings of yours that Mrs Daws was telling me about. Mine always sink to the bottom of the pan.'

'Really?' April asked.

'Truly,' Sheena replied. 'Now come along, before she thinks I've kidnapped you.' Throwing her coat around her shoulders, she ushered the girl from the room.

Outside huge fluffy flakes were falling, cloaking everywhere in a silvery white blanket.

'Jeez, it's cold. Here, you wear this,' Sheena said, handing over her muffler.

'I hope Shanksy's all right,' April laughed, wrapping it around her.

'You don't believe in Shanksy?' Sheena gasped, clutching her hand to her chest.

'Mrs Daws explained what shanks' pony means, but don't worry, Miss O'Reilly, your secret's safe with me.'

Pleased to see the girl happy again, Sheena patted her shoulder. 'Just don't let the little people hear you say that,' she winked.

As they opened the door to the kitchen, huge clouds of steam billowed out. Mrs Daws was juggling pans on the range and two of the older boys were busy counting out forks and knives from the dresser.

'Something smells delicious,' Sheena said, sniffing the air appreciatively.

'Ah, there you are,' the housekeeper said. 'April, you go upstairs and check on the dormitories, please?'

'But surely you need help in here?'

'I'd prefer it if you made sure the beds are dry, dear. You know what these scallys are like – any excuse to delay going to bed – and I'm dying for some peace and quiet.' Seeing the girl dither, Sheena gently nudged her towards the hallway.

'I'll help here,' she murmured, shrugging off her coat again. 'Right, Mrs Daws, give me an apron and tell me what needs doing,' she added, walking over to the range.

'If you're sure, dearie, the spuds are ready for mashing.'

Moments later, a vast pinafore covering her clothes, Sheena stood at the table, happily pounding a huge bowl of potatoes.

'Gosh, this takes me back to my mother's scullery, Mrs Daws,' she cried.

'And where would that be exactly, Miss O'Reilly? I understand you are from Ireland.'

'I am indeed, from the south-west. Ten of us to a weeny cottage in a wooded hollow Father grandly called Dingle Dell,' Sheena laughed.

'Ten, you say? No wonder you're used to preparing large meals, Miss O'Reilly. And by the way you've taken our April under your wing, good at caring for people, too.'

Sheena smiled at the approval in the woman's voice.

'That's why when Nanna had her accident they asked me to come and look after her. Although I reckon they thought it was a good opportunity to get me away from . . .' her voice trailed off.

The housekeeper waited but when Sheena said no more she went back to her pan.

'What was the problem with April, if you don't mind me asking? Master Higgins just said Kitty appeared to have upset her.'

'Well, she didn't mean to, of course. Just hit a raw nerve, so to speak. Anyhow, I hope it's all right but I've given April some powder to tone down the redness of her scar.'

'That's kind of you. She's right fixated about that,

though I tell her no one notices. Still, it's what she sees, I guess.'

'To be sure, it is. Why, hello,' Sheena said, turning to the boy who was glaring at them from the doorway. 'Now you'll be Solomon, I'm thinking?' she asked brightly.

'What's it to you?' he growled.

'As we're both the new ones here, I was hoping we might be friends. Help each other find our way around.' The boy narrowed his eyes and Sheena continued her mashing.

'I knows my way round already,' he grunted.

'Well, you must be cleverer than me then,' she replied without looking up. 'I was telling Mrs Daws that I come from a weeny cottage and this place has so many rooms it's easy to get lost.'

The boy snorted. 'Couldn't be that small 'cos you've got an 'orse.'

Sheena heard the housekeeper smother a laugh. 'Ah, but it's a teeny tiny one.'

'Well 'ow'd you ride it then with a big bottom like that?'

'Solomon Smith!' Mrs Daws cried.

'Ah, but I fear he's only telling the truth, Mrs Daws. Did my mother not tell me I'd regret forever sampling her cooking before she'd dished up,' Sheena sighed down at the bowl and waited. 'But that was the bit that always tasted the best.' Sure enough the boy inched closer.

'I likes mash,' he said, eyeing her hopefully.

Sheena scooped a small mound onto a spoon and held it out. 'Now, I'd be pleased to know if I've added enough salt.' In a flash he'd whipped it from her hand and gobbled down the contents.

''S good,' he announced. Then before Sheena could reply, he ran from the room.

'The young scally,' Mrs Daws muttered. 'Ah, April, everything all right upstairs?'

'Yes, all dry, Mrs Daws.'

'Good. Perhaps you'd call everyone in for supper, dearie. I'm lost without my gong, I don't mind telling you.'

'Grub up. Come and get it,' April bellowed. Moments later there was a stampede as children appeared from seemingly nowhere.

'Gawd love us, they're just like a herd of blinkin' elephants,' Mrs Daws muttered as they swarmed through to the dining room, jostling and pushing in their haste to get to the tables.

'We'll supervise, shall we, Mrs Daws?' April asked as Pip appeared. 'Miss Sullivan and Master Higgins said they'll serve themselves later as they've got something important to discuss,' she added, lifting one of the big serving dishes.

'Them spuds look nice and creamy,' Pip said, licking his lips.

'Well, you can thank Miss O'Reilly,' Mrs Daws told him. 'Just let me take this through then we'll have a cuppa before you leave,' she said, turning to Sheena.

'I'll pour,' the teacher insisted, noticing the housekeeper looked weary.

'Let's put our feet up for two minutes,' Mrs Daws said when she returned. 'Well, April's looking right pleased with herself thanks to her new powder. And do you know that's the most Solomon's said since he's been here? Seems you have the knack of getting on with children, Miss

O'Reilly. I do hope you'll be staying.' Sheena let out a sigh. 'Oh my, you're not thinking of moving on already?' the housekeeper cried, setting her cup down with a clatter.

'I do hope not, Mrs Daws.'

'But?' the woman asked, eyeing her shrewdly.

'I'm not sure I'm up to the job. Miss Sullivan wants the girls to have their new outfits ready in time for Easter, and with their limited skills . . .' she shrugged. 'Adapting clothes to fit properly takes time.'

'But you can sew?'

'Goodness me, yes, with all my younger siblings, hand-me-downs were the norm and always needed altering.'

'Well, the girls sounded keen when they came in.'

'They are. Well, most of them,' she laughed. 'The trouble is they need a lot of help and supervision. I'm not sure that three afternoons a week will be enough. I don't want to let Miss Sullivan down. Perhaps I should just resign now,' she said sadly.

'That would be a shame, Miss O'Reilly,' Mrs Daws said, picking up her cup and sipping thoughtfully. 'Miss Sullivan has high standards and wants the children to be a credit to Red Cliffs, which is admirable,' she said finally. 'However, she is realistic. I'm sure if you explain your worries she'll come up with a solution. She'll not want to lose a good mistress like you.'

'Oh, Mrs Daws, you've made me feel a lot better,' Sheena cried. She looked up with a start as the little clock chimed the hour. 'Goodness, is that the time? I should have been home ages ago.' Jumping to her feet, she threw on her coat, then almost collided with Harry in the doorway.

'Goodness, Miss O'Reilly, what are you still doing here?'

'She's been helping me, Master Higgins,' Mrs Daws called.

'You're not walking home by yourself?' Harry asked.

'It's a lovely clear night so I'll be fine,' Sheena smiled.

'I'd feel better if you'd allow me to accompany you,' he said.

'Thank you but there's no need.'

'I insist,' he said, snatching up his coat. 'Tell Miss Sullivan I'll see her in the morning, Mrs Daws.'

They walked together down the road, their feet crunching on the thick white carpet. It had stopped snowing and a bright moon lit their way.

'Nature's diamonds,' Sheena cried, staring up at the velvet sky where myriad stars twinkled brightly.

Hearing the excitement in her voice, Harry laughed. 'Anyone would think they don't have stars where you come from,' he teased.

'Well, it rains a lot more in Ireland so the sky's not usually as clear.'

'How have you settled into Red Cliffs, Miss O'Reilly?'

''Tis a grand place. Everyone is lovely and the girls are very bright.'

'Too bright sometimes,' he laughed. 'I understand the altercation was between Kitty and Edith. They were still arguing all the way indoors.'

'Unfortunately, Kitty cracked a joke about April becoming a lady of the night, then Edith turned on her. Thought she was the quiet one, too.'

'Ah,' Harry said. 'Edith's mother was, well, one of those women. Used to lock Edith in the basement while she worked.'

'Jeez, the poor angel. No wonder she went berserk.'

'It helps to know people's backgrounds. Edith was loud and aggressive until Kitty arrived and befriended her.'

'Well, they are usually as thick as thieves, though when it comes to sewing they couldn't be more different. Edith's stitches are delightful and she's an eye for the end result. Kitty, on the other hand, has no interest. I've given her some easier material to work on but even so, she glares and mutters. Said she'd much rather be working on the farm. I take her point, mind. It's a lovely time of year with the animals preparing to give birth.'

'You like animals?'

'Ah, Mr Higgins, was I not always helping the farmer with his sheep on the hills around us?'

'Really?' he asked in surprise. 'In that case, you're welcome to join us on our weekly visit to Farmer Jim's on Saturday afternoon.'

'That'd be grand,' Sheena cried, her green eyes shining like a cat's in the darkness. Harry felt his pulse race. She really was a very attractive young lady. Lost in their thoughts, they continued down the road then turned onto the seafront.

'Would you smell that cocktail of spray and seaweed, is it not magic?' she cried. He laughed and wrinkled his nose. 'Back home we have the mountains and lakes but not all this,' she added, gesturing around the sweep of the bay. 'Why, you can even see the white horses riding the waves, and would you look at all those boats.'

'So where exactly does your grandmother live?' he asked politely, tearing his gaze away from her animated face.

'Along here past all those grand places,' she said, gesturing to the houses hugging the cliff. 'I could hardly believe it when Nanna told me they are people's holiday homes. Do you know, whole families decamp from London during the winter months to take advantage of the air?' she cried, staring at him incredulously. 'They send their servants down first with all the household goods to prepare for their arrival. Jeez, how the other half live, Master Higgins. What do they do to pass the time, I wonder?'

'Have you not seen them out promenading beside the new sea wall or on the Princess Pier in all their furs and finery?'

'To be honest, Master Higgins, I've mainly been indoors looking after Nanna since I arrived. Although now she is recovering, I hope to spend more time exploring.'

'And there's a lot for you to see. Times are changing for everyone here, Miss O'Reilly. Since the Corporation took control of local developments, the town is fractured between those anxious to preserve a genteel environment in which to reside and those determined to create a more commercially attractive and profitable holiday resort. Larger hotels are being called for and many of the big houses are being bought up by developers.'

'You sound as though you disapprove of the latter, Master Higgins. Oh, this is me,' she cried, drawing to a halt outside a house with lamplight casting a welcome over the path. 'Thank you for seeing me home. If it's all right with my grandmother, I'd love to visit the farm with you all.'

'See you on Saturday then, Miss O'Reilly.' He gave a wave and watched as she made her way safely indoors. What a delightful mixture she was, he thought, whistling happily as he wended his way home.

11

'Sergeant Watts said they've questioned Tyler, er, Slater but haven't found any of our things. When I asked if they'd searched his lodgings he muttered something about circumstantial evidence,' Sarah told Harry.

'I suppose we didn't actually catch him taking anything?' Harry murmured, peering down at the school gates.

'No, but it couldn't have been anyone else, could it? Why do you keep looking out of the window?' Sarah asked. It was half-past noon on Saturday and they'd just finished drinking their tea while the children cleared away the luncheon things.

'Just checking on the weather,' he said quickly, avoiding her eyes. 'Thankfully, the snow's almost gone so a brisk walk to the farm will do the boys good. Who knows, it might even use up some of their excess energy? I'll see you later,' he added, hurrying over to the doorway.

'Right, come along, boys,' he called. 'Time to get going.'

'And me,' Kitty cried, drying her hands on the tea towel.

'Wouldn't you prefer to stay and get on with your needlework?' Sarah teased, placing her cup and saucer beside the sink.

'Sooner pull all me teef out,' Kitty muttered. 'Besides, it gives me time to be with Luke,' she added, grabbing her brother's arm and dragging him towards the front door. 'Honestly, sir, you'd fink the world revolves around blinkin' sewin',' she said dramatically, rolling her eyes. However, Harry was too busy scanning the road for sight of a cherry-red hat and muffler to pay any attention.

'Hurry along, please,' he said, his voice coming out sharply when he could see no sign. Then, just when he'd given up, there she was, running breathlessly towards them. His heart skipped a beat.

So, that was the way the wind blew, Sarah thought, watching from the window. It seemed the new mistress was uppermost in everybody's affections these days. Still, she was far too busy to waste time on futile thoughts, she chided herself, not wishing to admit to feeling more than a little jealous.

'Goodness, I thought I was going to miss you all,' Sheena gasped. 'Nanna had to have her dressings changed and the nurse took for ever.'

'Well, you're here now,' he grinned. 'Right, let's move it,' he called, urging the crocodile of pupils down the hill.

If Harry thought he'd have a chance to talk to the mistress on the journey, he was soon disappointed.

''Ere, miss, come and walk with us,' Kitty called. 'This is Luke, me bruvver.' Smiling apologetically at Harry, Sheena went to join them.

'Hello, Luke,' she said, beaming down at the little boy. 'I hear the farm is a great place to spend Saturday afternoons.'

'Not half,' he replied, coming to life. 'It's my favourite time in all the week. We used to live on a farm, you know.'

'I've already told her that, stupid,' Kitty said.

'And jolly nice it sounded, too. Well, I'll just go and say hello to the others,' Sheena said, quickly moving to the back of the queue where Solomon was gloomily dragging his feet.

'Don't you enjoy the farm, Solomon?'

He stared at her for a moment then shrugged.

'Well, I'm looking forward to seeing the animals,' Sheena said brightly. 'Ah, look, we're at the gate now. Well, will you look at that?' she cried, pointing to the open barn where a sow was on her side, piglets squealing and jostling to reach her teats.

'Why's that one all by itself?' Solomon asked, frowning at the tiny pink body alone in the corner.

'I think it's the runt of the litter, Solomon,' she explained. 'The mother can only feed so many and the weak one is unlikely to survive anyway so . . .'

'You mean it's going to die?' he asked, tears pooling his dark eyes.

Sheena sighed and put her arm around him.

Just then Farmer Jim limped towards them, pointing with his stick.

'Best leave old Patsy be,' he muttered. 'She's right possessive of her weans.'

'Hello, Jim, this is our new mistress, Miss O'Reilly,' Harry introduced. 'Hope you don't mind but the kids have been cooped up all week so I've brought them out for a walk. Anything you'd like them to do whilst they're here?' he asked casually. The farmer gave Harry a knowing look.

'Well, they could tidy up the yard and 'appen young Kitty could 'elp the missus in the dairy. Good little worker, that one. Cors, Bess just happens to have made some of her jam buns in case you were passing, like. Come on then,' he grunted, hobbling towards the pupils who were making faces at the cows. Knowing the visit had been planned, Sheena looked at Harry in surprise.

'It's a ritual we go through. Saves his pride,' he whispered.

'Ah, got you,' Sheena smiled. 'What a kind heart you have, to be sure, Master Higgins.'

Harry beamed, his chest almost bursting with pride at her words.

'But what about that little piggy?' Solomon cried, tugging at Sheena's elbow.

'Don't fret, boy, it's nature's way. Survival of the fittest,' the farmer told him. 'Might seem 'ard, but it's better than him 'anging on then a rat goin' for his throat. You can come and 'elps with the muck. All young boys likes an excuse to get dirty.'

As Kitty disappeared into the dairy with Bess, the boys, Harry and Sheena cleaned out the stables and shippon, then put fresh bedding down for the cattle and the farm's old horse. Although Jim helped at first, he tired quickly. Seeing him struggling, Harry suggested he went indoors and had a rest.

'Make the most of it whilst we're here, Jim,' Harry told him. The man gave a token protest then nodded.

'Got some paperwork to see to, any'ow,' he muttered.

'How does he keep going?' Sheena asked, watching as, leaning heavily on his stick, he limped towards the farmhouse, faithful collie at his heels.

'Sheer determination,' Harry replied. 'With no offspring

to take over, he knows once he gives up, the farm will have to be sold.' Then seeing the boys staring in their direction, he called, 'Right, you little lot, no slacking now.'

'Come on, we'll clear the path so Jim doesn't slip,' Harry suggested to Sheena. They set about shovelling the compacted mud and ice from the track up to the farmhouse. Although the afternoon was brisk, they were soon warm from their exertions. After a while Harry stopped and smiled at Sheena.

'What are you grinning at?' she asked, resting her arms on her spade. Instead of answering, he took out his kerchief and, leaning forward, carefully wiped a smudge from her cheek. Then he removed a twig from her hat and held it up.

'I've heard of having a feather in your cap but never a twig,' he teased.

'Well, at least I've not got cow dung all over myself,' she retaliated. He grimaced down at the dark brown mess on his trousers. 'I'd better clean up before Bess calls us indoors for tea,' he said, making for the trough. Then he stopped and frowned. 'Where's Solomon?'

Sheena stared around at the group of boys who, having tidied up, were now engaged in a game of tig. Solomon wasn't with them. Remembering the pigs, she ran towards the barn and spotted the boy crouched on the straw, the tiny runt cradled in his arms.

'It's not breavin' proper,' he whispered, his bottom lip trembling. 'Make it breav, miss.'

Sheena stared down at the lifeless body. 'I'm afraid he's gone, my angel,' she whispered.

'But I wanted to take 'im back with us, feed 'im and make 'im grow strong.'

'He was never going to be strong, Solomon,' Harry said, appearing next to them and kneeling down beside the boy. As if sensing danger, the sow grunted and lumbered to her feet, weans squealing in protest.

'Quick,' Sheena cried, jumping up and pulling the boy away. With another warning grunt, the sow lunged at them. 'Come on, Solomon,' she urged, edging backwards until they were outside the barn, slamming the half-door shut behind them.

'Didn't know pigs were dangerous,' Harry muttered.

'Mother's instinct. She was just being protective,' Sheena said. 'I think we'd better see to this little chap before we go indoors,' she added, gently stroking the pink body.

Moments later they stood around a fresh hole in the earth that Harry had dug.

'Why are we putting 'im in the ground?' Solomon asked, tearfully.

'To bury the body. It's what happens when someone dies,' Sheena told him. The boy looked at the mound of earth and began trembling.

'Come on, old chap, be brave,' Harry said, putting his arm around him.

'We'll make a cross out of sticks then say a prayer to wish him a safe passage to heaven,' Sheena told him as she gently placed the body in the ground. 'Then whenever you visit you can say hello to him and tell him what you've been up to.'

Solemnly, the boy stared at the grave. 'Is that what 'appened to me father, then?'

Harry stared at Sheena then cleared his throat. 'Yes, he's been buried, too, Solomon,' he said quietly.

'So 'e's not just been dumped outside the 'ospital in the road?'

'No, he's sleeping peacefully in his grave like this little chap.' They watched as Solomon digested this information. 'So I can go and talk to 'im then? Only I got somefink I must tell 'im,' the boy muttered.

'I'll see if I can find out exactly where your father's grave is, Solomon. Now shall we say a prayer for this little fellow before we go in for tea?' The boy nodded and Harry murmured a few words. Then, each taking a hand, he and Sheena led him towards the farmhouse.

'Kitty and I saw what you was doin' when we came out of the dairy, so we brought the others in. Thanks for seein' to the little runt. At least Patsy's got six strong 'uns left,' Bess sighed, greeting them at the doorway. 'You must be hungry after all your hard work, young man. Saved you the biggest jam bun, I have,' she added, leading Solomon into the warmth of the kitchen.

'Will he be all right?' Sheena asked.

Harry stared over to where the boy was licking the jam out of the centre of the cake and smiled. 'I'm sure he will. Although when I told him his father wasn't still lying in the hospital bed, he was so upset I didn't elaborate. Clearly, I should have explained the body had been buried, albeit along with all the others in the paupers' grave,' he sighed.

'You mustn't blame yourself, Master Higgins,' she murmured, patting his arm. 'What if we make a cross and place in under the apple tree at Red Cliffs? Solomon said he had something to tell him so it would give him somewhere to do that.'

'Good idea. Then maybe he'll get whatever's bothering him off his chest.'

'Here we are, tea for the workers,' Bess said, handing them two steaming mugs. 'The boys have finished their drinks and have taken the rest of the cakes outside.'

'You spoil them, Bess,' Harry said.

'I can't tell you what a relief it is to have your 'elp, Master Higgins,' Bess sighed, and glanced over her shoulder to where Jim sat staring forlornly into the fire, his unlit pipe by his side. 'I've told him to sell up but he refuses, stubborn old fool,' she muttered, the tender look in her eyes belying her words.

'So, you're the new mistress, then?' she asked, turning her attention to Sheena.

'I am. I've only been at Red Cliffs a week, but everyone has been so kind.'

'That Miss Sullivan's a good woman, taking on the school like that,' Bess murmured.

'I was thinking, Bess,' Harry said. 'It's time these boys had a proper lesson on procreation so if you have no objection I could bring them along on Wednesday afternoon. Of course, they'd do some chores in return. That'd be only fair,' he added, then took a sip of his tea.

'You're a good man, Harry Higgins,' she murmured, patting his arm. 'Tell Mrs Daws I'll be sure to 'ave some of my best brawn and bacon for her. The 'ens are on the lay so there's some eggs for you to take today, and Kitty's got a surprise as well.'

'Them layers'll be ready for you to take back come Wednesday,' Jim grunted. 'That Kitty picked out the best for you. Knows her stuff, she do.'

'His legs might be no good but 'e's still got ears like a bloomin' elephant.'

'I 'eard that, an' all, Bess,' Jim muttered.

Kitty was beside herself with excitement as they wended their way back to the school. She was carrying a parcel wrapped in muslin but refused to say what was in it.

'I got to show Mrs Daws first,' she insisted. 'I just love it at the farm. It's like our old 'ome, ain't it, Luke?'

'Yeah, loved it there,' he agreed.

'Still, you're happy at Red Cliffs?' Sheena asked.

'Yeah, and we get fed every day,' he smiled.

'I love it there, too,' Kitty agreed. 'Apart from the soddin' sewin'.'

As Harry opened his mouth to reprimand her, the tray of eggs toppled precariously and he decided to let it go. He'd be sure to make vocabulary the first lesson tomorrow, he vowed.

'Well, I'd better be making tracks or Nanna will wonder where her supper is,' Sheena said as soon as they reached the school gates. 'I've had a wonderful afternoon,' she added, smiling up at Harry. 'See you on Monday.'

Pip opened the gates and as the boys surged through, Harry watched Sheena disappearing down the lane until her cherry-red hat was a speck in the distance.

'Hope you've had a good afternoon, Pip,' he said brightly, turning back to the school. To his surprise, the usually cheery boy frowned.

'You has a visitor in the house, Master Higgins. She's been yelling at the top of her voice this past hour and poor Miss Sullivan is at 'er wits' end.'

Mindful of the eggs, Harry hurried as quickly as he

could around the side path. He heard the screeching before he'd even opened the door.

'I tells you, them blinkin' kids is mine and they're comin' back with me now.'

'What on earth's going on?' he asked Mrs Daws.

'It's that Mrs Bawden. She says she's come to take Kitty and Luke home with her,' the housekeeper announced tearfully.

12

'Where are Kitty and Luke?' Harry asked, carefully putting the tray of eggs on the table.

'In the dining room, and I've sent the rest upstairs. I thought it best to keep everyone out of the way until you got things sorted,' Mrs Daws murmured. 'That woman's a nasty bit of work, Master Higgins. You won't let her take them away, will you?'

Hearing the anxiety in the housekeeper's voice, Harry patted her shoulder. 'I'll go and speak to her. Ask April to keep the others occupied. You know how nosy they are when they sense something is going on,' he added, raising his brows as the woman's voice became louder.

Sarah looked up in relief as he entered the office. Harry could see by her wayward hair that she'd been running her hands through it and the atmosphere in the room was frostier than the weather outside.

'This is Mrs Bawden and she's . . .' she began.

'An' you are?' the woman cut in, turning in her chair and giving Harry an insolent look. She was wearing a thick coat that was unbuttoned to reveal a low-cut top. Her lips were painted vivid red. Fighting down his distaste, he smiled back politely.

'This is Master Higgins,' Sarah introduced, a stickler for politeness at all times.

'Can't yer speak for yerself then, Master 'Iggins? Or do

you let this busybody do everything for you?' She gave a harsh laugh, her expression leaving him in no doubt as to the meaning of her words. Knowing it would do no good rising to her bait, Harry clenched his fists at his sides and counted to five.

'Good afternoon, Mrs Bawden. I understand you have come to enquire about Kitty and Luke.'

The woman gave another shrill laugh, which reverberated around the room, rattling the cups on the tray.

'There's posh. I ain't come to *enquire*,' she said, making quotation marks with her fingers. 'I've come to fetch 'em.' As she stared at him defiantly with eyes the same grey as Kitty's, his heart sank. There was no denying they were related. 'So, Master 'Iggins, what does you do here exactly?'

'Master Higgins teaches the children, Mrs Bawden,' Sarah explained.

'Oh, I gets it. He's your fella, eh? Blimey, girl, there's more to you than I thought,' the woman chuckled. 'So you gets money off the Authority for the kids, then shack up together in this grand 'ouse. Coo, nice work if you can get it.'

'That's a preposterous thing to say,' Sarah gasped.

'Yes, really, Mrs Bawden, it's not like that at all,' Harry protested, going hot under the collar.

'P'haps it's the girls you like,' the woman sniggered. 'Young flesh right on yer doorstep . . .'

Harry held up his hand. 'That's quite enough. It's Kitty and Luke we should be discussing,' he said quickly, noticing the bright colour suffusing Sarah's cheeks.

'Nufink to discuss,' Mrs Bawden snapped. 'They're my

kids and I've come to take 'em 'ome.' She jumped to her feet. 'Right now. Where are they?'

'Mrs Bawden, your children have been here for some months now. They have settled in well and made friends. You can't just abandon them and then come back here demanding their return,' Sarah replied.

'I bleedin' well can. I'm their mother.'

'But the children were homeless. I believe you and their father separated and . . .' Sarah began.

The woman narrowed her eyes. 'Well, I got a new father for them, ain't I? And a new 'ome, so go and get them or I'll 'ave the law on yer.'

'I'll ask them if they want to see you,' Harry said, edging towards the door. Quick as a flash the woman followed him and he had no alternative but to lead her down the hallway. Mrs Daws, hands on hips, stood guarding the entrance to the dining room.

'Out of my way, old witch,' Mrs Bawden snarled, pushing past her. 'There you are, me darlin's. Mummy's come to take you 'ome,' she crooned.

The two children clung to each other, eyes wide with fright.

'Well, look at you in your fancy clothes. Never seen you in a smock like that before, our Kitty, and as for that fancy waistcoat, Luke, that should fetch a few pennies. Well, come on, I ain't got all day.'

'We want to stay here,' Kitty declared, jutting out her chin defiantly.

'I said move,' the woman snapped.

'You can't make us,' Kitty cried.

'Blinkin' well can. I'm yer mother. Now come 'ere, the

pair of you,' the woman said, grabbing them both by the arms.

'But we got our lessons to learn, ain't we, Luke?' Kitty said, pulling away and turning to her brother. The boy nodded and gripped his sister's hand tighter.

'Not no more you ain't, Kitty, 'cos I got you a job.'

'I'm not old enough,' the girl retorted.

'That's where you're wrong, Kitty Bawden. Today is your tenth birthday, in case you've forgot, and at first light tomorrow you're startin' work, so come on.'

'But she's only little,' Mrs Daws cried, wringing her hands together.

'Not so little as she can't have 'er ears boxed,' the woman cried, making a grab for the girl. Kitty cowered into the corner, clutching her precious package tighter. 'An' you give that 'ere, an' all.'

'No,' Kitty cried. 'It's a present for Mrs Daws.'

'Well, it can be a present for your dear old mother now,' the woman told her, grabbing at the parcel. As Kitty desperately clung on, the paper tore, spilling its creamy contents over the floor.

'Me cheese,' the girl sobbed. 'It's me first soft cheese. I made it at the farm with . . .'

'Scoop the bloomin' thing up then you can 'ave it for yer tea,' the woman snapped impatiently. 'But for Gawd's sake 'urry up.' When Kitty didn't move, the woman stepped forward and ground the cheese into the floor with her heel. 'So much for yer precious cheese, eh?'

Scarcely able to believe her eyes, Sarah turned to Harry. 'You're not going to let someone like that take the children, surely?' she begged.

He crouched down beside them. 'Can you confirm this woman is your mother?'

'Worse luck,' Kitty muttered, staring sadly at the mess on the floor in front of her. 'Me first cheese and it's ruined.'

'You'll make another,' he assured her before turning to the boy. 'Luke?' he asked. The boy nodded. 'That's Muvver.'

Harry sighed, knowing his hands were tied.

'Look, it's nearly dark and freezing cold outside – why not let the children stay the night and come back for them in the morning?' he appealed.

The woman shook her head. 'Ain't I just said, this one starts work tomorrow. So come on, move it.' She pushed them towards the door.

Kitty stared desperately at Sarah. 'Please let me stay. I'll even do me blinkin' sewin', if you let me,' she cried. Mrs Bawden glared at her and shoved her out of the room.

'But they've not got coats on,' Sarah shouted.

'Well, they'll just 'ave to walk quickly, won't they?' the woman laughed. Then she stopped and looked at Sarah speculatively. 'Only jokin'. Where's their things, then?'

Spotting the new donations box in the hallway, Sarah grabbed a couple of thick woollens and held them out. Mrs Bawden snatched them from her and ran her hands over the material, a greedy gleam in her eyes. Harry firmly took them back from her.

'Let me help you,' he said, bending and wrapping them around the children, whispering as he did, 'You know where we are if you need us.'

'They won't,' the woman snapped. With a triumphant look, she pushed the children out into the cold night.

Harry signalled to Pip to let them out of the gate, then, trying to swallow down the lump in his throat, closed the door behind them.

'I can't believe you just let them go,' Sarah cried.

'He had no choice, Miss Sullivan,' Mrs Daws whispered, wiping her eyes on her apron. 'The law's on the side of the parents. Soon as they admitted she were their mother, that was it. We've seen it all before, you see,' she explained sadly.

'I saw Pip letting them out of the gate,' April cried, as she came into the room. 'Poor little blighters looked so sad. That woman looks a bad 'un through and through. Oh, I'm goin' to miss them little scamps.'

Sarah put her arm around the girl's trembling shoulders. 'It's not going to be the same without them,' she agreed. And goodness only knows what is going to happen to them, she thought, feeling they'd let Kitty and Luke down.

'But we have to maintain normality for the rest of the children,' Harry told them.

April nodded. 'I know, and they're getting impatient for their food. Shall I dish tonight, Mrs Daws?'

'No, I'll do it,' the housekeeper murmured. 'Best to keep busy. Ah, here's Pip,' she added as the boy hobbled into the room.

'I was tempted not to let them out,' he said, looking bleak.

'She'd only have gone for the police,' Mrs Daws sighed. 'Now you'd best call the children down for supper. I don't know, first me gong goes, now them kiddies. Is nothing sacred around here?'

'I'm going to get on with some paperwork, Mrs Daws,' Sarah said, suddenly wanting to be by herself.

'I'll explain to the children what's happened, then come and join you,' Harry replied.

The children listened to what he had to say, then took their places solemnly at the table.

'Kitty were my friend,' Edith muttered.

'And mine,' Monday whispered.

Seeing their sad little faces, Harry forced a smile. 'Still, it's good that her mother has found a new home for them,' he said cheerfully. 'We must be glad for them. Now enjoy your supper, everybody. Who knows, Mrs Daws might even find seconds for those who finish first.'

There was a buzz of excitement followed by the eager scraping of cutlery on plates.

'Well done, Master Higgins,' the housekeeper murmured, patting him on the shoulder as he passed. 'There's nothing like the promise of extra food to divert their attention.'

However, when he went through to the office, Sarah stared at him hopelessly.

'Those poor children. I feel we've let them down. Couldn't we have put up more of a fight? Is there really nothing we can do?'

Harry shook his head. 'Believe you me, if I'd thought it would have done any good, I would have. However, we are a charitable institution, here to provide for those with no one to care for them. Whatever we might think of her, Mrs Bawden is Kitty and Luke's mother and she said she'd found a home for them.'

'And a new man,' Sarah retorted. 'She also said Kitty is

to start work tomorrow. What about her education? How can we give them a good start in life if we let women like that . . . ?' Her voice trailed off as she felt tears pricking the back of her eyes.

'Oh, Sarah, we can only do our best,' Harry replied, automatically going to comfort her.

'But it's not good enough, is it?' she cried, moving away. 'Those children are vulnerable, especially Kitty, who needs the loving guidance of a woman. You can't tell me she's going to get that from her so-called mother?'

Harry shrugged helplessly. 'We can only do so much, Sarah. I'm sad at the way things have turned out but we have to move on. There are the others to think about, too. Farmer Jim said we can bring the chooks back here on Wednesday and . . .'

'Wednesday?' she cried. 'But you go to the farm on Saturdays,' she said, looking at him sharply.

'I know, but the poor man's health is failing. He needs our help more than ever. They both do, in fact.'

Sarah stared into the dwindling fire. 'I see. Well, in that case, it will be good for the boys to assist. My godfather would want that, wouldn't he?'

Harry nodded. 'I was thinking it might be a good idea for the girls to go along as well. It's still too cold to take them swimming and they'd get some fresh air and exercise. I'm sure Bess would appreciate their help in the dairy.'

Sarah nodded. 'That's a much better idea. The sea will be perishing, she added, wrinkling her nose.'

'Well, it'll soon be spring and a dip in the briny is health giving. You can come along, too, Sarah.'

She stared at him aghast. 'A woman swimming in public? How very improper, not to mention unladylike,' she replied.

'That doesn't sound like the forward-thinking Sarah I know,' he told her. Seeing his brow raised in question, she looked hurriedly away. There was no way she was letting him know she was scared of the sea. 'Something worrying you?' he asked, as ever picking up on her thoughts.

'I was thinking about the girls going to the farm,' Sarah hurriedly replied, eager to change the subject from swimming. 'When I took them for needlework this afternoon, I was disappointed to find they don't appear to have made much progress on their new outfits. Apparently, Miss O'Reilly tells them stories about the little folk at the end of the lessons, would you believe?' She rolled her eyes. 'That time would be better spent on their schooling and I shall speak to her on Monday. She does seem to be a little flighty so I hope she listens.' Even as she said it, she was aware of how petty she sounded.

'High-spirited perhaps,' Harry said, thinking of her laughing nature. 'But flighty? No, I don't think so. The children seem fond of her already and surely listening to a story occasionally is no bad thing?'

'Really, Harry, I'm surprised at you. We are meant to be preparing them for life outside the school.'

'I realize that, but children need a bit of fun as well as lessons. Besides, Miss O'Reilly admitted she's keen for the children to have their new outfits. She's just worried about having them ready in time for Easter. Perhaps if you sit down together and look at what needs to be done, you can work out a schedule. I'm sure she'd appreciate that.'

'As it's obviously important to you, I will do that on Monday,' Sarah conceded, anxious to atone for her earlier pettiness. 'After which, it is my intention to leave her in charge of the girls while I attend regular meetings of the National Union of Women's Suffrage Societies. Mrs Bawden's ignorant and ill-mannered outburst this afternoon highlighted the fact that most women still have to rely on a man to provide for them. It certainly strengthened my belief that we civilized women should have more of a say in how this country is run. We simply must ensure that future generations of girls are educated to the same level as boys in order that they can earn their own living and not be beholden to men.'

'I do understand, Sarah,' Harry replied. 'However, as I've said before, not all men expect or even want a woman who will run around after us or . . .'

'Sir, miss, we can't find Solomon,' April cried, bursting into the room. 'One minute he was at the table, the next his dish was empty and he'd gone.'

13

Could this day get any worse, Harry wondered, as he followed April through to the dining room. He stared around the tables where the children sat, unusually quiet and looking glum.

'Right, everybody, who can tell me when they last saw Solomon?'

'He were here when Mrs Daws brought out pudding 'cos he said spotted dick was his favourite,' Bunter volunteered.

The housekeeper smiled wryly. 'Though it was more dick than spots.'

'He told me he were goin' to speak to 'is father when he'd finished it,' Brown added.

'Speak to his father?' Harry repeated. Surely the boy hadn't gone in search of his father's grave, he thought, recalling the earlier incident on the farm.

'Yeah, 'e said Miss O'Reilly told 'im 'e could speak to him anywhere an' 'e 'ad somefink urgent to tell 'im,' Black said importantly.

'When did Miss O'Reilly say this?' Sarah asked, frowning.

'She came to the farm with us earlier,' Harry replied. 'One of the pigs died and we helped bury it. Poor Solomon didn't realize that's what happened when people died. Apparently he thought his father was still lying in the hospital.'

'Oh, the poor child,' Mrs Daws cried.

'But what was Miss O'Reilly doing at the farm? Saturday is not one of her working days,' Sarah frowned.

'I'll explain later. It's freezing outside and I need to find Solomon before he catches a chill or worse.' Harry went over to the dresser and lit the candle in the lantern.

'Yes, of course. I'll get my coat and come with you,' Sarah replied.

'No, you stay here and help Mrs Daws make some hot drinks. Those children look as though they need something comforting, and Solomon certainly will.' Before Sarah could respond, he was hurrying out of the door.

So Miss O'Reilly had been to the farm, had she? Obviously she had filled Solomon's mind with more of her fancy thoughts, and it seemed Harry had gone along with it. Well, for the boy's sake, Sarah hoped Harry found him soon.

Where could the child have gone, Harry wondered, swinging the lantern this way and that as he made his way carefully down the icy path. What was it Miss O'Reilly had said about communicating with a dead loved one? You could mark a certain spot as their special place then go there and talk to them at any time. That was it. Now where would Solomon choose as his particular place? She'd told him it needed to be somewhere close by so he could go there whenever he felt the need.

Harry swung the lantern again and this time the flickering light illuminated the shadow of the big tree right at the bottom of the garden. They'd buried the piglet under the old oak tree on the farm. The prickle at the back of his neck told him he was on the right track and, taking care not to slip on the frost, he made his way across the grass.

Sure enough the boy was crouched on the ground beneath the elm. He'd made a cross out of twigs and was talking to it. Not wishing to make him jump, Harry crept slowly forwards.

'So you see, Father, it were me an . . .' Solomon was saying when a twig cracked beneath Harry's shoe. The boy stopped mid-sentence and turned abruptly. 'I were just speakin' to Father. Miss said it would be all right,' he said, his dark eyes luminous in the light of the lantern.

'It is all right, Solomon,' Harry murmured, hunkering down beside him. 'Carry on, old fella.'

'Nah, can't now.'

'Of course you can.'

The boy shook his head and remained silent.

'You were telling your father it was you . . .' Harry encouraged.

To his surprise, Solomon jumped to his feet and glared down at him. 'It ain't none of your business,' he cried.

'No, fair enough,' Harry said, surprised at the vehemence in the boy's voice. He stood up, careful to stand a few paces away. 'I was only trying to help. I'll wait by the vegetable plot for you. Mrs Daws is making us a nice hot drink.'

Solomon's eyes lit up but he didn't move.

Slowly Harry made his way up the garden. An owl hooted and swooped down from the coal house roof. It was a clear night, with myriad stars, and looking up at the sky Harry was reminded of the evening he'd walked the new schoolmistress home. She was certainly lively and enthusiastic about life, but flighty? No, Sarah was wrong about that.

Remembering the way in which she'd comforted Solomon and helped him to bury the piglet, he felt a glow. And if she told the children stories about the little folk from Ireland, well, surely that livened their dreary lives. Children needed nurturing as well as nourishing.

Lost in thought, it was some moments before he realized Solomon had caught him up.

'All right?' he murmured.

'Yeah,' the boy sighed. 'I'm thirsty so I'll talk to Father in the morning.'

'Good idea,' Harry murmured, patting his shoulder. 'Now let's see if Mrs Daws has our hot drinks ready.'

'What a bloomin' day,' Mrs Daws said, easing herself into the chair beside the range.

'You're telling me,' Sarah agreed.

'At least the children have finally gone to bed,' Harry yawned. 'I'll just finish my tea and then I'd better be making tracks myself or Mother will think I've got lost.'

'Solomon didn't look quite as sullen when you came in,' the housekeeper added. 'Never seen a child generate so much anger in all my time here.'

'I think Miss O'Reilly's idea of him having somewhere to talk to his father has helped. Although I could have cursed when I trod on that twig and interrupted what he was saying. He was really opening his heart and I'm certain I nearly got to the bottom of this load he's carrying.'

'Talking of Miss O'Reilly, you were going to explain why she was at the farm this afternoon,' Sarah reminded Harry.

'When I escorted her home the other evening, she happened to mention she used to live by a farm and missed the animals. It seemed only natural to invite her along,' he replied, avoiding her gaze and staring into his cup.

'Seems to have done young Solomon good,' Mrs Daws commented. 'He was telling the others how upset he was about that runt and the farmer explaining it was better for it to die naturally than a rat getting it by the throat and . . .'

'I think we get the idea, Mrs Daws,' Sarah interrupted with a shudder. 'Well, she certainly seems to have made an impression all round. But I still can't help worrying about poor Kitty and Luke.'

'Edith will be lost without her friend,' Harry said. 'Those two were good for each other.'

'Uncle said we shouldn't get too attached, but the more you get to know them the more difficult it is, I find,' Sarah said, referring to her godfather by the affectionate title she used for him.

'I agree with you, Miss Sullivan. Even after all the comings and goings I've seen, it still upsets me when they go. Especially in circumstances like these,' Mrs Daws sniffed.

'This is not the outcome any of us wanted for them, is it?' Harry said dejectedly. 'Which reminds me, I must make a report on Kitty and Luke's record cards tomorrow. I also need to check, but I'm pretty sure Kitty should be attending school until she is twelve, and not ten as her mother said. The law changes so quickly, which is why I didn't say anything before.'

'Even so, it doesn't mean she has to attend lessons here,' Sarah replied.

'True. However, as Sergeant Watts brought Kitty to Red Cliffs in the first place, it would be only courteous to let him know her mother has removed her from our care. I'm sure he will want to keep a weather eye on both children.'

'You could have told us all this earlier,' Sarah berated him.

'Like I said, I need to check my facts,' he replied.

'You're a dark horse, Master Higgins, and no mistake,' Mrs Daws chortled, getting to her feet. 'Well, I'm for my bed. Praise be, the good ladies are preparing the soup for the Sunday luncheons. I'm not sure I'd have had the strength to chop all those vegetables tonight.'

'Well, good afternoon to you, Miss Sullivan,' Sheena greeted Sarah when she walked into the classroom on Monday. 'What do we say, girls?'

'Good afternoon, Miss Sullivan,' they duly chanted.

'We're sewing our dresses, miss,' Monday added, holding hers up for Sarah to see.

'I am pleased to see that,' Sarah said, smiling at the girl's enthusiasm while trying not to wince at the uneven stitching.

'How are things coming along, Miss O'Reilly?' she asked, lowering her voice so that the children didn't hear.

'Grand. The angels are working really hard, bless them.'

'You will have noticed Kitty isn't here . . .' Sarah began.

''Tis a crying shame the poor wee thing had to go along with her mother. Master Higgins acquainted me of the facts when I arrived,' she added quickly, seeing Sarah's surprise.

'I see. It's a terribly sad situation. We'd all become very fond of Kitty, and Luke, too, of course. Still, by your own admission, Kitty was the worst at sewing so at least you'll have more time to devote to the others. They should easily have their dresses ready for Easter now.'

'I have to admit to wondering whether their outfits will be finished in time,' Sheena frowned.

'When I saw how little progress had been made on Saturday, I was a trifle concerned,' Sarah said, giving her a worried look.

'To be sure, I'll do my very best to see they work hard but they are very young and clearly have had little tuition in remodelling garments until now. As I've said before, Miss Sullivan, they need a lot of individual attention.'

'I agree and was thinking it might be a good idea if I inspect their work every Saturday and discuss my findings with you before lessons on Monday. As I have meetings to attend to on that day, I'd be obliged if you could come in half an hour early.'

'That will not be a problem, Miss Sullivan,' Sheena assured her, making a mental note to prepare an earlier luncheon for her grandmother.

'Good. The girls themselves are so excited at the prospect of having their own dresses it would be disappointing for them if it didn't happen. Therefore I feel it would be better if each lesson be devoted to their learning and not listening to stories.'

Sheena felt her cheeks growing hot. 'Of course, Miss Sullivan. I'll see to it that they spend all the afternoon stitching,' she assured the woman. Seeing the children taking an interest in their conversation, Sarah smiled.

'I am on my way into town now to attend one of my meetings, so should you require any assistance please speak to Master Higgins. Good afternoon, girls.'

'Good afternoon, Miss Sullivan,' they muttered.

'But I likes you dories,' June wailed.

'Stories, June,' Sheena corrected. Then seeing their glum faces, she smiled and gave an outrageous wink. 'If you promise not to stop your stitching while I talk, there's no reason why we can't still have our story at the end of the lesson, my angels. After all, you hear with your ears and sew with your fingers, do you not?' The girls giggled.

'Now to work. Let's show Miss Sullivan what good little needleworkers you really are.'

Cheered by the thought of their story, the girls returned to their sewing with renewed vigour. For the rest of the afternoon, Sheena was kept busy showing them how to turn their unpicked dresses into something wearable. Only Edith and Sally could really sew competently and they stitched neatly whilst the others needed constant attention.

'Remember, accuracy is key,' Sheena kept reminding the ones who were working with more speed than skill. 'Your dresses must fit you and look good, too.'

Altering garments to match their differing measurements was no easy task and certainly bore little resemblance to the revamping of the hand-me-downs she'd done for her siblings. That these frocks were going to be on show at the concert was disconcerting, to say the least. Linings could be repaired, holes darned, but the fact remained that if the final result didn't come up to Miss Sullivan's high standards, she would get the blame or even lose her position.

Ah well, Sheena, you'll just have to be the mistress of reinvention, she told herself, as yet again, June presented her with a wonky seam.

'Now watch closely,' she told the girl. 'If you hold the material firmly in your left hand, it won't move when you stitch it.'

'But it keeps doosing it,' the girl wailed.

'Doing it,' Sheena corrected her. 'Well, let's try again, shall we?' she said cheerfully. How much easier life would be if Red Cliffs had a sewing machine, she thought. It was ironic really when that Mr Singer, who'd invented the machine, had lived in nearby Paignton.

She went around checking their work again and was impressed with Edith, who was showing a real flair for dressmaking. Perhaps there was hope yet.

'That's really good, Edith, well done,' she praised.

The girl smiled, then sighed. 'I used to think Kitty was a right pain in class but it's so quiet without her.'

Sheena patted her shoulder. 'We must hope the wee angel is happy, Edith,' she whispered.

'I don't think she will be, somehow,' Edith said.

From what the master had told her, Sheena privately agreed. However, she was saved from answering by Ellen calling out, 'Miss O'Reilly, it's growing darker and you said we could have a story.'

'Goodness, so it is, my angels. Let me light the candles so you can continue working and then I'll begin.'

'Goody,' June beamed.

'Now where did we get to?' Sheena asked, a few moments later.

'The handsome prince was searching for his sword so

he could save the princess,' Maggie reminded her. 'I wonder if he'll find Shanksy,' she added, giving Sheena a sly wink.

'Ooh, yes, I wonder if he will,' Monday cried excitedly.

'Hush now, my angels, and remember to carry on stitching whilst I'm talking,' Sheena grinned.

When the bell sounded for the end of lessons, the girls groaned.

'But we haven't found out if the prince managed to save her yet,' Edith complained.

'Or if he found Shanksy,' Monday added.

'Well, Wednesday will soon roll round,' Sheena laughed. 'Sewing and stories, what more can you ask for, my angels?' Although privately, she couldn't wait for their outfits to be finished so she could concentrate on teaching other subjects.

'Sweeties,' Monday cried, interrupting her thoughts.

Sheena smiled. 'Well, off you go then. I'm sure Mrs Daws will have something nice for you in the kitchen.'

As the classroom descended into silence, Sheena went around examining their work. Edith's was exemplary, Sally's stitching was neat but her dress didn't have the same finesse, Maggie's wasn't too bad but the rest left much to be desired. It certainly was going to be a rush against time to get them anywhere near presentable for Easter. Ah well, robes weren't made in a day, she told herself as she scurried around tidying everything away, then carefully extinguishing the candles.

'Good afternoon, Miss O'Reilly,' Master Higgins greeted her as she was leaving the classroom. 'I hope all went well with your lesson and the girls were well behaved?'

'To be sure, the little angels were enthusiastic if not efficient, Master Higgins,' she replied.

'In my experience, enthusiasm stems from the teacher, Miss O'Reilly, so congratulations.'

'Well, I just have to hope Miss Sullivan shares your sentiments, Master Higgins. She is going to inspect their work every Saturday then tell me her findings on the Monday. And I'm finding it difficult to make the required silk purses out of the sows' ears available.'

'I'm sure you'll manage splendidly,' he laughed. 'By the way, as Jim is requiring extra help, I'm thinking of taking the girls up to the farm on Wednesday afternoon along with the boys. It will give them some fresh air as well and exercise.'

'Oh,' Sheena muttered, her smile slipping.

'I know it's one of your teaching afternoons but you're welcome to join us, Miss O'Reilly,' he invited, misunderstanding her look.

'That's not the problem, Master Higgins,' she cried. 'Wednesday is one of the girl's sewing days and if I don't keep to the schedule, I'll have no chance of having their dresses completed by Easter.'

Harry stared at Sheena in surprise. The misery in her voice and despair glittering in those beautiful emerald eyes tugged at his heartstrings. As she stood there looking so despondent and vulnerable, he was seized by the sudden urge to pull her into his arms and assure her everything would be all right.

14

Sarah left the meeting of the National Union of Women's Suffrage Societies, their impassioned words ringing in her ears. It was true, with Queen Victoria dead and England moving into the new Edwardian era, it was time for women to have their say.

She made her way from the hall, down the lanes lined with Torbay palm trees, which her godfather had told her had been imported from New Zealand in the 1820s. Apparently, they lent the town a Mediterranean feel. However, having never been fortunate enough to travel abroad, she would have to take his word on that.

When she reached the harbour, it was a hive of activity with large boats loading and unloading their cargoes of slate, coal and timber. Walking on past the newly built hotel and villas converted to boarding houses to accommodate the increasing number of holidaymakers, Sarah sighed. If only Red Cliffs had the money to move with the times, she thought, trying to push the thought of the latest leak in the roof to the back of her mind.

The bay itself was busy with merchant ships transporting goods across the oceans, their 'Red Dusters' fluttering astern. She also noticed there were more naval boats than usual at anchor, with their superior White Ensign flags flying proudly, while the fishing fleet were out with their nets, ever hopeful of a catch. It hit her for the first time that this was actually a busy working port as well as being a destination for affluent tourists. What a contrast, she thought: the diligent worker and the idle rich, the latter of which there was no sign on this very brisk winter's afternoon.

She walked on until she passed the police station. Thinking it a good opportunity to apprise Sergeant Watts of the latest development with Kitty and Luke, she wove her way across the busy road, dodging the carts and dirt being kicked up by the horses' hooves.

'. . . So you see, Sergeant Watts, Mrs Bawden has taken Kitty and Luke back and I wondered if you and your men could keep an eye on them?' The sergeant snapped open his notepad. 'I mean, it was you who brought Kitty to Red Cliffs yourself in the first place,' Sarah reminded him.

The man nodded and took his pencil from behind his ear. 'Address?'

Sarah looked mortified. 'I'm afraid I didn't get an address from her – I'm sorry. It was all so sudden and the children really didn't want to go. But you'll be able to find them, won't you?' she asked anxiously.

'We'll do our best,' Sergeant Watts replied. 'Like as not she'd have given you a false address anyway, so don't worry,' he added, seeing her frown.

'Thank you, Sergeant. I do hope you find them and they are all right. Mrs Bawden claimed it was Kitty's tenth birthday and that she'd found her a job. However, Master Higgins thinks she is too young to work and should continue her schooling.'

'He could be right, but it's a hard law to enforce.

Parents give all sorts of excuses as to why their children shouldn't attend,' he said, pushing his helmet to the back of his head. 'Well, I can't promise anything, but I'll get my men to keep a lookout for them when they're out on their beat.'

'Thank you, Sergeant. Is there any news about Mr Tyler – sorry, I mean Slater – and the thefts from Red Cliffs? Poor Mrs Daws is lost without her gong.'

The man shook his head. ''Tis a right conundrum, as I said at the time. You invited the man to take an unaccompanied tour of your premises then found things missing after he left. I agree it rather looks as though he took them, but the evidence is circumstantial and we have no proof.'

'It was remiss of me not to have checked the man's credentials with Master Higgins, but it's too late now,' Sarah sighed.

'Ah, he would have done the correct thing,' the sergeant agreed. 'Still, the winds of change are blowing.' He lowered his voice and leaned towards her. 'Between you and me, Miss Sullivan, even as we speak, a new fingerprint branch is being set up in London. Of course, that's of no help to you now, but in the future, well, it could ensure hundreds of criminals are brought to justice,' he beamed, puffing out his chest as if he personally was in charge of this development.

Sarah watched the shiny buttons on his jacket strain and wobble, more out of fascination at their staying power than the man's revelation, which, although fascinating, as he rightly pointed out would be of no use to her.

'Well, thank you, Sergeant Watts, you have been most

helpful. Should you or your men find out anything about Kitty and Luke's whereabouts, perhaps you could let us know.'

'Certainly, Miss Sullivan,' he said, leaning back in his chair. 'Not like you to be out on a jaunt this time of day, and so smartly dressed, if I might say.'

Seeing the man's obvious curiosity, Sarah smiled. 'I have just been to a meeting of the National Union of Women's Suffrage Societies, Sergeant Watts,' she announced proudly. The man's smile promptly vanished and belatedly she remembered his bigoted attitude towards the female sex.

'Lot of stuck-up women talking of things they know nothing about,' he sniffed.

'On the contrary, Sergeant, we are well informed and intend making our feelings heard,' she replied.

'You'd all be better placed considering the feelings of your men,' he snorted. 'A woman's place is in the home, cleaning and cooking a nice nourishing meal for when her husband comes back after a hard day's work. If you want my advice, Miss Sullivan, you should leave it to we men to run the country. We understand these things.' He gave a patronizing smile.

'Well, thank you for the benefit of your Victorian ideas, Sergeant. Luckily, for us women, we are moving into more enlightened times. Good day to you,' Sarah said stiffly, taking herself outside before she succumbed to the urge to smack the supercilious grin from his face.

The wind had increased, making the palm trees sway, sending the dust and dirt from the road billowing in her direction, bringing with it the noxious smells of horse dung and rotting seaweed. To avoid the flying sand stinging her face, she decided to take the more sheltered path through Rock Walk. Although a desirable place for women to promenade in the clement weather, protecting them from the rays of the sun, today it was deserted.

Walking briskly past a clump of bushes, she remembered this was the very place where Kitty had hidden her brother when their mother had upped sticks and left them to fend for themselves. The boy, all skin and bones, had been burning up with fever. Poor things, what would happen to them, she wondered. It was only right the law be on the side of the parents if they were deemed responsible enough to look after their children properly. But surely not if they weren't. Unbidden the words of the school motto, *Love Never Faileth*, popped into her head.

I have to confess I find myself questioning the sentiment, Uncle. As was her wont, whenever she was stressed about anything to do with Red Cliffs, she found herself talking in her head to the man who'd bequeathed her his beloved school. *I've done my best, Uncle, but the roof's sprung another leak, Kitty and Luke have gone back to their mother and now Solomon, whom, by the way, I named our Tuesday child to remind me never to turn away anyone in need, is so unhappy he is in danger of isolating himself. Oh, Uncle, what can I do?*

As a gentle whisper on the breeze, his voice came to her. *Like the seven hills Torquay is built on, Red Cliffs has strong foundations and will survive. Stand firm in your resolve, be open to new ideas and you will thrive.*

Goodness, what a strange answer, Uncle, she replied, hurrying up the hill towards the school. The shadows were lengthening by the time she arrived.

'Afternoon, Miss Sullivan,' Pip chirped, letting her in through the metal gates.

'Thank you,' she replied. 'No disaster has befallen the school in my absence, I hope?'

'Nah, the place is still standing,' he grinned. 'The verger called by but he spoke with the master. Said young Sally was a virtuoso, whatever that is. I thought she was just singing.'

'Indeed,' Sarah smiled distractedly, for she'd spotted the master and new mistress outside the classroom. They were standing extremely close together, seemingly unaware of her approach.

'Good afternoon,' she said politely. Like naughty schoolchildren caught out, they sprang apart.

'Oh, good afternoon Miss Sullivan,' Harry replied. 'I hope your meeting proved interesting.'

'Yes, it did, thank you. I'm surprised to see you still here at this time, Miss O'Reilly. I trust all went well with your needlework lesson?' She turned to the schoolmistress, whose cheeks were tinged with pink.

'Ah, to be sure, it did, and I was just leaving,' she replied quickly.

'I've been telling Miss O'Reilly about our proposal to take the girls to the farm on Wednesday afternoon.'

'That was your suggestion, I believe, Master Higgins,' Sarah corrected him.

'Yes, and bearing in mind the way Farmer Jim and Bess are struggling, I still think it a good idea. The children all require fresh air and exercise, and helping others is what the ethos of Red Cliffs is all about, isn't it?'

'Then by all means take them, Master Higgins. You can go, too, Miss O'Reilly,' Sarah added.

'Ah, but . . .' the mistress began, looking beseechingly at Harry.

'Miss O'Reilly is worried it will take the girls away from their needlework, thus delaying the schedule you have set,' he replied.

'Which was discussed at your interview, Miss O'Reilly,' Sarah pointed out, disconcerted at the way the two teachers appeared to be ganging up against her.

'I understand that, Miss Sullivan. However, I hadn't realized then that the girls were as unskilled as they are and would be struggling with their outfits. Now, if they had more time to . . .'

'You are seeking to be paid for extra hours perhaps?' Sarah interrupted. 'I'm afraid we don't have the funding for that. With a charitable institution like Red Cliffs, we have to look at the wider picture.'

'That's it! Miss Sullivan, you're a genius,' the mistress cried. 'A picture would make a real difference to the girls.'

'What, of Red Cliffs?' Sarah frowned. 'I don't see . . .'

'No, Miss Sullivan. Of their outfits,' Sheena interrupted. 'They have no pattern to work to, and with the exception of Edith, can't visualize what the end result should be. I'll draw a sketch of each one and bring it with me to the next lesson,' she cried happily.

'At what charge to the school?' Sarah asked.

'I wouldn't want paying anything. It will be a pleasure, Miss Sullivan.'

'Oh, well, thank you,' Sarah replied, feeling she'd been wrong-footed. Judging from the way Harry was staring at her, he was thinking the same and she was overcome by shame. What was it about the mistress that brought out the worst in her? She'd never thought of herself as a jealous person, and yet ... Before she could dwell on the matter Harry was speaking.

'So will you be accompanying the girls to the farm on Wednesday then, Miss Sullivan?' he asked.

'I would love to have done, had I not been asked to attend an interview to assess my suitability for a place on the School Board,' she replied.

'Well, I can't supervise all of them. They're excited at going to the farm at the best of times, but with Jim saying we can bring the layers back with us, they'll be beside themselves.'

'Well then, I'll come along, if it's all right with you, Miss Sullivan,' Sheena replied.

'That's sorted then,' Sarah said then quickly. 'I will pop into the classroom on Friday afternoon and see how the needlework is progressing, Miss O'Reilly. Meantime, Master Higgins, I have things I wish to discuss with you.'

'To be sure, I thought I was in trouble with Miss Sullivan the other day,' Sheena told Harry. It was Wednesday afternoon and they were escorting the children up the muddy lane to the farm.

'She was just worried about the girls' outfits not being ready in time for the concert,' Harry assured her. 'It was kind of you to offer to draw pictures of them for the girls to work to.'

'I love sketching so it was fun. I'm hoping that once they see what their dresses should look like, it will spur them on. Nanna said, as they are not used to having clothes made for them, albeit with used material, it's not surprising they are finding it daunting. Apart from young Edith, of course. You know, I think she has the makings of a fine seamstress and the fitted dress she is attempting, although more detailed than the others, is already taking shape. I can see her using those skills when she leaves Red Cliffs.'

'I can't deny it will be good to see at least one of them get paid employment,' he replied, then frowned. 'Hey, Black, get back into line at once,' he called as the boy took a jump at an overhanging branch. 'Come on, Solomon, keep up,' he sighed, as the boy hung back again.

'He's still not joining in with the others?' Sheena asked.

'No, still living in his own little world. I'd hoped that once he had somewhere to grieve for his father, he might come out of his shell but he hasn't. I tell you, this lot will be the death of me.'

Sheena giggled. 'Talking of shells, Master Higgins. You make out you're so stern but underneath that tough exterior lies a soft heart.'

Harry stared at her in surprise, but they'd arrived at the farm gates and he was saved from answering.

'Afternoon, 'Arry, miss,' Farmer Jim said, hobbling slowly towards them. Today, he was leaning heavily on two sticks and his faithful collie was at his side, as if safeguarding his master. 'Didn't say ye were bringing the 'ole flippin' school with yer,' he added brusquely.

'Good afternoon, Jim. I do hope you don't mind but the girls are sorely in need of some extra exercise. I was wondering if Bess could find the odd job for them to do?' Harry replied lightly.

The farmer treated Harry to one of his old-fashioned looks. ''Appen she could,' he grunted, looking around. 'Don't see young Kitty, or Luke, for that matter?'

'Their mother was waiting for them when we returned on Saturday. Apparently, she's got a new man and home and . . .' Harry shrugged.

'That's a right shame,' the farmer sighed. 'She had the makings of a good farm girl, and were so excited about the layers, too. Well, let's get moving afore that lazy wind goes right through us. What about you, missy?' he said, turning to Sheena. 'Reckon you could 'elp Bess with that little lot in the dairy?'

Sheena grinned. 'Try and stop me. There's nothing I enjoy more than churning,' she cried.

The farmer's laugh came out as a wheeze and Harry could see he was struggling to catch his breath.

'You go on in and put the kettle on to heat while we supervise the children. What jobs would you like the boys to do?'

'Well, the pig sty needs mucking out now Patsy's used to her weans. And the troughs need cleaning and refilling,' Jim rasped.

'Right, indoors with you,' Harry urged. 'Tell Bess, Miss O'Reilly will take the girls to the dairy while I set the boys to work.'

For the rest of the afternoon Sheena and the girls helped Bess churn the butter, then patted it into neat slabs with the paddles, ready to be sold at the market. After which they collected the eggs before shutting the hens safely in their coops.

'Is this not the greatest fun?' Sheena asked the girls as they chased after an errant chicken.

'Well, blow me, if you don't get the jobs done in a quarter of the time I do these days,' Bess chuckled. 'Jim's put the layers in the barn,' she added.

'Must be hard on you, with Farmer Jim ailing,' Sheena said quietly.

The woman looked serious. 'I keeps tellin' him to give up. Don't know how we'd manage without young Harry regularly popping by with the children. He thinks we don't know his visits are planned but of course we do and we're grateful, I can tell you.' The woman put her hand to her back and winced as she straightened up. 'Time for a cuppa, I'm thinking. 'Tis a good job you just happened by, girls, as I made oaty cakes this morning.'

As they all trooped happily towards the farmhouse, Harry was running to meet them. Sheena could see by his pained expression something bad had happened.

'It's Jim, I think he's had a stroke,' he gasped.

15

'Jim needs the doctor quickly,' Harry told Sheena as Bess hurried inside.

'I'll go and get him,' Solomon offered. 'I know where his place is and I can run like the wind,' he added as Harry stared at him doubtfully.

'Let him do it,' Sheena urged, putting her hand on Harry's arm.

'Very well then, Solomon, quick as you can. Tell Dr Hawkins to come here, but you go straight back to Red Cliffs before it gets dark.'

'Like an owl's, me sight is,' Solomon scoffed before haring off down the track.

'I don't know how bad Jim is, but they shouldn't be here when Dr Hawkins arrives,' Harry said, glancing at the group of pupils who were staring anxiously at the farmhouse.

'You take them back before it gets dark, Harry. I'll stay here with Bess.'

'Are you sure?' he asked.

Sheena nodded. 'We don't know how long the doctor will be and Bess needs someone with her. Go on.'

'Very well, but as soon as they're safely indoors, I'll be back. Oh, and don't move Jim, will you?'

Sheena made shooing motions with her hands, then, leaving him to assemble the children, hurried inside.

Jim was lying on the rag rug where he'd collapsed, his faithful collie whining beside him. Bess was on her knees covering him with a blanket and Sheena could see by the rise and fall of his chest that he was still alive.

'Come on, you old fool, wake up,' Bess wailed. Knowing it was better to leave her, Sheena bent and patted the woman's shoulder comfortingly. She felt icy cold so, quickly taking off her muffler, Sheena wrapped it around her.

'Solomon's gone for the doctor and I'm here if you need anything, Bess,' she murmured but the old woman, lost in her grief, didn't reply. Sheena tossed wood into the range, stoking it into a fiery blaze. Then she looked around for the things she needed to make tea. Everywhere was neat and tidy, a plate of oaty cakes and beakers set out on the dresser for the children. The tea caddy and sugar bowl were set on a tray, along with a huge jug of milk. When the kettle had whistled to a boil, Sheena poured the water into the old brown pot and left the leaves steeping. But when she took a cup over to Bess, the woman shook her head.

'I couldn't,' she murmured.

'I do understand, but you need a hot drink to keep you going. You've got to stay strong for Jim. Come along,' Sheena added, holding out her arm and helping the woman to her feet. 'We'll sit by the range until Dr Hawkins arrives.'

Bess managed a few sips, then handed the cup back to Sheena. Then with a final look at Jim, she closed her eyes, her lips moving in silent prayer. Seeing the woman's pallor, Sheena let her be.

Taking a sip of her own tea, she glanced around. It was

a homely room, the hams and flitches of bacon hanging from hooks above the fireplace, scenting the air with a sweet smokiness. The brasses were polished, the floor swept and, apart from the things set out on the dresser, everything was tidied away. The rhythmic ticking of the long-case clock in the corner of the room sounded the passing of the minutes as they waited for the doctor to come. As the shadows lengthened, Sheena got up and lit the lamps, setting one in the window to show the man the way. She checked Jim's pulse. It was weak but at least the man was still with them.

Even before Sheena heard the sound of a cart on the tracks, the dog's ears pricked and he gave an urgent bark. Sheena hurried to the door but before she'd reached it, the latch had clicked and it swung open. As Dr Hawkins came into the room followed by Harry, Bess opened her eyes and sprang to her feet.

'We thinks he had a stroke, Doctor,' she said.

'Just sit there, while I check your husband over, Bess,' he said, pushing her gently down again. As he crouched down beside the farmer, the dog whined. 'I know, old chap,' the doctor crooned, feeling for the man's pulse.

'The doctor passed me as I was walking up the lane,' Harry explained to Sheena, taking the proffered tea gratefully. 'I see there's no change,' he added, lowering his voice.

'No,' Sheena murmured, pouring tea for Doctor Hawkins.

'You're right, Bess, I think he has had a stroke. I'll take him to the hospital and get him checked out so we can assess the damage.'

'He's not going without me,' she vowed.

'Might be better if you stayed here until we've carried out a full examination,' Dr Hawkins told her, taking his tea from Sheena with a grateful smile.

'Never. In sickness and in health, I promised, and that's what I meant,' she replied, handing the muffler back to Sheena. Then, pulling her hat off the stand, she placed it firmly on her greying hair.

'We'll come with you,' Harry said but Bess shook her head.

'I'd be obliged if you could stay and look after the animals.'

'To be sure, Bess,' Sheena assured her. 'One of us will wait here until you return.'

'Poor Jim,' Harry murmured, coming back into the kitchen after helping the doctor load the man onto his cart. The collie whined and followed him in, sad at not being allowed to go with his master. 'And poor you, old chap,' Harry added, bending and fondling the dog's ears.

'Solomon got back safely?' Sheena asked.

'Yes, he certainly rose to the occasion and arrived just after we did. I was thinking on my way back here, if we gave him some responsibility around the school it might lend him a sense of purpose.'

'That would be good. And were the other children all right?' Sheena asked, as she finished washing up their tea cups.

'A bit glum until Mrs Daws produced one of her special cakes.'

'That woman is a treasure,' Sheena declared, slumping down in a chair beside the range. 'And had Miss Sullivan returned from her meeting?'

'Yes, she was pleased they thought her a suitable candidate although they couldn't tell her when the next election would be. Then, of course, we had to tell her the news about Jim.'

'Poor Farmer Jim. I do hope he'll recover.'

Harry nodded but didn't respond.

'She's a clever lady, that Miss Sullivan. I wish I was smart like her,' Sheena added.

'She is,' he agreed. 'But it was you who showed compassion and understanding this afternoon, Miss O'Reilly.' He stared at her for a long moment, the air crackling between them until her cheeks grew hot and she had to look away.

'I really must be getting home. My grandmother is going to think I've sprouted wings and flown back to Ireland.'

'Or perhaps she'll think Shanksy has galloped you away,' he chuckled. Then he looked serious. 'I don't like the idea of you walking down the country lanes in the dark by yourself. The animals have all been seen to so I'll lock up here and escort you home.'

'There's really no need,' Sheena replied. 'It's darker than this back home.'

'All the same, I'd prefer to see you safely to your door. Anyway, I need to tell Mother I'm staying here tonight and collect my things. And what do you say to a walk?' The collie, who'd been lying in front of the warmth, pricked up his ears then lurched to his feet.

Harry watched as Sheena pulled on her cherry-red hat and wound her muffler around her neck, then opened the door. It was dark as treacle, the moon obscured by heavy cloud from which drizzle was falling. Sheena lifted up her face, welcoming the soft dewiness after the heat of the kitchen.

'You don't mind getting wet?' he asked in surprise.

'Am I not used to walking in the downpours of Ireland, Master Higgins?' she chuckled.

'You must be the original pluviophile, then,' he laughed.

'I might just well be, if I knew what one was,' Sheena retorted.

'A lover of rain,' he explained.

'Well, I am that, and I love to learn as many words as possible, Master Higgins. But now it looks like I need a whole new English dictionary.'

'I've got a spare one at home, if you would like me to bring it in for you?' he offered.

'You'll be keeping me in detention next,' she chuckled, glancing sideways at him. And the way he grinned back made her insides fizz like her mammie's home-made lemonade.

'Have you heard how Farmer Jim is?' Mrs Daws asked as Harry walked into the kitchen later than usual the next morning.

He shook his head. 'I was told not to enquire at the hospital before noon, although Dr Hawkins said he'd let me know if there were any developments before then.'

'Ah well, no news is good news, as they say. I'll go and see Bess when she's home, take her some baking so she doesn't have to bother,' the housekeeper said. 'Now I bet you've had nothing to eat so sit yourself down and have some porridge. I told April and Pip you had to feed the animals before you came here so they're supervising breakfast.'

'Is Miss Sullivan in the dining room?'

The housekeeper shook her head. 'She's in a right old tizzy. The roof sprung yet another leak during the night. Said she's going to see the bank manager about a loan.'

'I thought she tried that before,' Harry replied, his spoon poised halfway to his mouth.

'I know, but she's at her wits' end She's drawing up a list of money-making ideas to show that Mr Collings. Of course, she's still blaming herself for letting that con man Tyler have a look around unaccompanied. Me poor blinkin' gong,' she lamented, staring at the empty space where it had stood.

'I'll buy you a gold one, Mrs Daws, just as soon as my boat comes in,' Harry laughed.

'I thought I heard your voice, Master Higgins. Any news of Farmer Jim?' Sarah asked, hurrying into the room.

'Not yet, Miss Sullivan. I see you're wearing your best bib and tucker,' he said, pointing to her smart outfit.

'I thought I'd have one last try at persuading Mr Collings to lend us the money to get the roof repaired, just until I meet with Lady Chorlton, that is.'

'You seem to be setting great store by this meeting,' he remarked.

'What do you mean?' she asked, giving him a quizzical look.

'Well, you've never met Lady Chorlton . . .'

'But you said yourself, she was my godfather's good friend. Surely she'll want to continue helping his beloved school? Do you realize it is only three months until the next inspection? We have to have the roof repaired by then or . . .'

'We close,' he finished for her. 'Yes, I was explaining that to Miss O'Reilly when I walked her home last night and she said . . .'

'What, that the little people would wave their magic wands and everything would be fine? If that woman spent as much time teaching as she did telling the girls stories, their needlework might get finished,' she cried.

Harry opened his mouth to reply but she'd already stormed from the room.

'Well, that was uncalled for, wasn't it, Mrs Daws?' Harry exclaimed.

'I think we have a touch of the green eyes there, Master Higgins,' she said sagely.

Sarah stomped down the road, the early morning air cooling her temper. For some reason she couldn't fathom, that new schoolmistress really got under her skin. And Harry jumping to her defence didn't help. You'd think he'd be more concerned about the roof than Miss O'Reilly.

By the time she reached the bank, her equilibrium was restored. However, Mr Collings, although pleasant, was firm in his refusal.

'I'm sorry, Miss Sullivan,' he said, staring at her sadly. 'There just isn't the money coming into your account to allow for the repayments on a loan.'

'So you don't mind the children having wet raining down on their heads?' she retorted, glaring at him over his pile of papers.

'Yes, of course I do, but I wonder if you are looking in the wrong place for a solution,' he replied, his eyes softening. 'I understand you have received another, more substantial offer for the property.'

That must have come from Fothergill, Sarah thought, opening her mouth to protest that client confidentiality should be paramount. However, the man held up his hands in mock surrender.

'You needn't answer my question, Miss Sullivan, and shoot me if you wish. However, I knew and admired your godfather for many years and believe me, anything I or his solicitor advise is purely in the interest of the school. Perhaps it is time to accept one of those offers, and of course, my advice would be to go for the highest. Then you could find premises with a roof that doesn't leak and relocate the children.'

'Never, Mr Collings,' Sarah protested. 'My godfather built up that school from scratch. He took in the children, nurtured and educated them. Do you truly expect me to throw his life's work back in his face?' she spluttered.

'Of course not. I was merely suggesting that a solution might be for you to remove.'

Sarah swallowed and took a deep breath. 'Mr Collings, I promised my godfather I'd keep the children at Red Cliffs where they feel secure and, with or without your assistance, that is precisely what I intend to do. Thank you for your time, and good morning,' she said, getting to her feet and leaving with as much dignity as she could.

As she stood outside the bank, collecting her thoughts, she noticed the tall building opposite. Taking a chance, she called in at Mr Fothergill's office, only to be told he would be in court for the rest of the day. Thwarted for the second time that morning, she was making her way down the high street when a voice hailed her.

'Good morning, Miss Sullivan.'

Sarah looked up to see the new schoolmistress, shopping basket over her arm, smiling brightly at her.

'Oh, good morning, Miss O'Reilly,' she replied.

'To be sure, you look as though you've dropped a guinea and picked up a sixpence.' Sarah stared at the woman, wondering if she was always this impertinent. Then Sheena's smile turned to one of dismay. 'Oh, please don't tell me there has been sad news of Farmer Jim?'

'As far as we know, he is still holding his own,' Sarah replied.

'Ah, that is good then. I thought by your glum expression that you'd heard he'd . . . but no news is good news, isn't it?'

'So they reckon, Miss O'Reilly.'

'And really there is nothing as important as him making a recovery, is there? As we say in Ireland, *is fearr an tsláinte ná na táinte*,' Sheena smiled. 'It means health is better than wealth,' she added, seeing the woman's blank look.

'Well, on that point at least we agree, Miss O'Reilly,' Sarah replied hastily, not wishing to appear uncompassionate yet wishing Sheena and her breezy manner would move on. Again, she couldn't help wondering what it was about the woman that brought out the worst in her. 'You were on your way to collect some provisions?' she asked, forcing a smile as she pointed to the shopping basket.

'Yes, Nanna fancies a fillet of plaice for her luncheon and the fish around here is so fresh, isn't it? And there is so much choice. Where do you purchase yours from?'

'Well, I . . . that is to say, I don't actually do any shopping. Mrs Daws attends to our supplies.' Then seeing the woman was intent on pursuing the conversation, Sarah smiled. 'Now I must get on. Good morning, Miss O'Reilly.'

Ignoring the woman's hurt look, Sarah made her way back to the school. It must be lovely to have the morning to idle away on shopping, she thought, before remembering the teacher was actually caring for her sick grandmother. She'd make a special effort to be pleasant to her tomorrow, she resolved.

To her surprise, the doctor was just being shown out of the gates as she arrived back at Red Cliffs. His solemn look told her everything.

'They did all they could, Miss Sullivan, but he never regained consciousness. It might be of some comfort to know that had he come around, it is likely he would have been paralysed.'

'Oh, no, poor Jim – and poor Bess. Where is she now?'

'I dropped her back at the farm before coming here. She was adamant she wanted to be left alone. When I insisted she couldn't be by herself, she said that nice Miss O'Reilly would be a comfort. Master Higgins offered to call and collect her during his luncheon break.'

16

'Are you sure you'll be all right?' Harry asked Sheena, drawing to a halt outside the farmhouse.

'Of course,' she replied, jumping down from the cart then reaching for her basket. As if by magic, the collie appeared at her side.

'You've been guarding that with your life all the way here. What have you got in there, the Crown Jewels?' Harry quipped.

'No, just some chicken soup I made,' she told him. 'I doubt Bess will even think of cooking and she must eat.'

Harry smiled. 'Mrs Daws had the same idea, although I think this is vegetable broth,' he replied, retrieving a dish covered with a cloth from behind his seat.

'Great minds think alike,' Sheena chuckled, taking it carefully from him. 'Steady, boy,' she added as the dog sniffed the air and gave a bark.

'Do you need a hand with that?' Harry asked.

'I can manage. Even if Bess doesn't feel up to talking, at least I can make sure she eats something.'

'Tell her I'll be back to help bed the animals down after lessons. Now, I really must be on my way. Mrs Daws promised to keep the children busy cleaning the house but she'll probably be in need of a rest by now.'

'I love the way everyone pitches in together,' Sheena replied.

'It's the ethos of the school. The founder of Red Cliffs insisted the children had to learn they didn't get anything for nothing.'

'That's a good philosophy. Mrs Daws is a hard worker, that's for sure, and she's so loving and kind,' Sheena said. 'I'll see you later, Master Higgins.'

He watched as she made her way inside, the collie following at her heels. What a generous-hearted person she was, giving up her time to spend it with a woman she'd only recently met.

'It's only me, Bess,' Sheena called, nudging the door open with her behind.

The woman looked up and gave a wan smile. She was sitting in her chair beside the hearth, but there was no fire lit in the grate and the room that only the day before had been warm and welcoming was icy cold.

'It was good of you to come,' she muttered.

'Not at all, Bess. You need a bit of company at a time like this. Now let's get a blaze going and then I'll make us some tea.' Sheena put down her basket and Mrs Daws' soup on the table, then set about riddling the ashes and lighting a fire.

'There,' she said, a few moments later, tossing a log onto the flames and putting the kettle on the hob. 'We'll be warm in no time. Now, have you had anything to eat today?'

Bess shook her head. 'I couldn't,' she whispered.

'You need to keep your strength up,' Sheena said. 'Is there anyone you would like me to contact for you, Bess?'

'Master Higgins asked the same. I penned a note to my

166

sister earlier and he promised to see it posted. There's no one else, dear. Not being blessed with children, we kept ourselves busy and were quite happy with our own company.' She sighed and stared sadly into the fire.

'I've made you a blessings candle, Bess. Where I come from, it's usual to light one to honour our dearly departed loved one. I've decorated yours with snowdrops as they symbolize rebirth, hope and sympathy, which seemed appropriate. Nanna let me borrow one of her candlesticks.'

She set a flame to the wick but as it flared into life, huge tears began rolling down the older woman's cheeks.

'Oh, no,' Sheena cried. 'I can blow it out. I never meant to upset you, Bess.'

Bess shook her head. 'It's the most beautiful thing I've ever heard,' she whispered.

'Here, I'll put it on the mantel beside you and leave you to open your heart to Jim.'

At the warmth from the flame, the flowers gave up their perfume, scenting the air with its fresh floral notes. As Bess stared hard at the candle, Sheena poured the soup into a pan and placed it on the range to warm through. While she worked, she could hear the woman muttering quietly to Jim and knew the candle was helping her release her pent-up emotion. However, by the time the kettle was boiling, all had gone quiet and Sheena saw Bess had fallen asleep, faithful collie at her feet. Covering her with a woollen blanket, she went outside to check on the animals.

Sheena was just forking clean straw for the pigs when she heard the cart rattling up the rutted lane. Despite the sad circumstances, her heart gave a leap.

*

Sheena was just about to enter the classroom on Friday afternoon, when she saw Miss Sullivan approaching.

'Good afternoon, Miss O'Reilly. I must confess to wondering if you would turn up today. I understand you've been keeping Bess company. How is she?'

'Bess is a stalwart, Miss Sullivan. She's determined to give Jim a decent send-off tomorrow and is spending the afternoon baking for the wake. As you can see, I am here to teach the girls, after which I will return to the farm-house to help her.'

'You must let me know if I can assist in any way. We will all be there tomorrow, of course,' Sarah told her. 'I expect you've been too busy to make those sketches you were talking about?'

'Indeed, I have not, Miss Sullivan. I have them with me so shall we go inside?'

'Good afternoon, Miss Sullivan. Good afternoon, Miss O'Reilly,' the girls intoned as they entered the classroom.

'Good afternoon, girls. You may sit,' Sarah told them. 'Now, the last time I saw you was the day you were at the farm so you will have heard by now the sad news of Farmer Jim,' she began.

'Such a shame, he were a card,' Ellen said.

'No, he were a farmer, stupid,' June lisped.

'He was a fine man,' Sheena agreed. 'Bess has sent a message to say she is looking forward to seeing you all tomorrow afternoon and if . . .' She paused. 'If you all work very hard at your needlework this afternoon, she will have lots of her special cakes ready for you.'

'Yes,' Monday cried.

'That is very kind of her,' Sally replied. 'The vicar has

asked me to sing the first verse of the Psalm solo. He said Farmer Jim would have liked that. Do you think he would, Miss O'Reilly?'

'I'm sure he will, Sally, for won't he be listening from his new home up in heaven?'

'I believe Miss O'Reilly has something to show us, girls,' Sarah intervened.

'Coo, is it a present?' Monday asked. 'My dadda always brings me presents when he comes home off his ship. He's in the Merchant Navy, you know,' she added proudly.

Sheena was just taking out the illustrations she'd made when the door flew open.

'Am I too late to join in?' April asked anxiously.

'Of course not. Come in and sit yourself down,' Sheena invited. 'I was just telling everyone that I have drawn pictures of your outfits so you can see what they'll look like when they're finished.' Carefully, she spread each one out on the desks in front of them.

'That's just how I imagined mine would be,' Edith cried happily.

'Well, I hadn't got the foggiest notion,' Maggie said. 'But if my dress is going to look like this, then I can't wait to get stitching.'

Sheena stared at Sarah, waiting for her verdict.

'I have to admit that was a very good idea. Well done, Miss O'Reilly.'

Sheena beamed at the unexpected praise.

'Now there will be no excuse not to have them finished in time for the Easter concert,' Sarah continued. 'Especially as our Sally, here, is to sing a solo.'

Ah, the iron fist in the velvet glove, Sheena thought.

169

'We will certainly do our best,' she assured the woman. 'Of course, it would help if we had one of Mr Singer's fine machines,' she added hopefully.

'But alas we don't. Nor the funding to purchase one. Now I'll leave you to get on,' Sarah said briskly, and swept from the room.

'Can we start on our sewing now?' the girls pleaded.

'Indeed you can, my angels,' Sheena assured them. 'You've seen what beautiful princesses you're going to look, so remember, only the neatest stitches will do.'

'Princesses,' Monday cried. 'Can we have a story later?'

'If you're very good and work hard,' Sheena assured them.

With their pictures to guide them, the girls began sewing. Sheena went around offering help and advice. If only enthusiasm equated to expertise, she thought, unpicking another of June's crooked seams. Still, at least they were all looking happy. Apart from April, who was stretching the material between her fingers.

'Something wrong?' Sheena asked, then frowned not at her sewing but the pallor of her cheek. The girl had been so liberal with the use of her powder, she reminded Sheena of icing on a cake.

'This ain't right,' April sighed, as Sheena peered over her shoulder.

'Ah, I see what you mean,' she said, noticing the puckered seam.

'It's 'cos I use me left hand, see. When I try and sew one way the stitches point the other.'

'Try holding the material at this angle,' Sheena instructed, taking it from her and demonstrating.

'Blimey, that makes it one 'ell of a lot easier, don't it?' April cried delightedly.

'With a little more practice I'm sure you'll get on really well,' Sheena encouraged. Leaning closer, she whispered, 'I notice you're wearing your powder.'

April beamed. 'It don't half make a difference. Even Pip said he could see it.'

'Well, there's a little technique I'd like to show you, April. Come and see me when you have time.'

'Coo, I will, miss, thank you.'

The next afternoon, they buried Jim on the hill that over-looked his beloved farm. Sally sang the first verse of the Twenty-third Psalm, her dulcet tones carrying on the breeze. Then the children joined in with gusto.

'You can't fault their enthusiasm,' Mrs Daws said to Sheena, dabbing her eyes with her best handkerchief.

'To be sure, they're a credit to you all,' she replied.

When the vicar had said the last prayer, Solomon handed him a cross fashioned from sticks.

'I made this for 'im,' he said.

The vicar took it solemnly. 'May the Lord bless this cross,' he intoned, placing it on the grave.

Sarah and Harry exchanged looks of surprise.

'Maybe, he's recovering from his ordeal,' Harry whispered.

'I do hope so,' she replied.

'And now Bess would like to invite you all into her home for refreshment,' the vicar said, leading the way back down the hill towards the farmhouse.

'Just look at all that food,' Pip gasped, as they entered

the kitchen. The table was piled high with sandwiches, savouries and cakes. Jugs of cordial stood alongside beakers on the dresser.

'Now, children, remember your manners,' Sarah reminded them as they eagerly surged forward.

'Let them enjoy themselves, Miss Sullivan,' Bess said, appearing at her side. 'They're the nearest thing we had to family and Jim would have wanted them to have their fill.'

'That's very kind, Bess. How are you?' Sarah asked.

'Bearing up, thank you. Master Higgins and Miss O'Reilly have been a wonderful help. And that girl still is,' she added, nodding to the range where Sheena was busy pouring hot water into the teapot. 'They'd make a good couple,' she sighed wistfully.

Sarah stared at the woman in surprise. 'Oh?' she asked, following the woman's gaze.

'Goodness me, yes. They've both got good hearts, and the same sense of humour. The way they work together reminds me of Jim and me when we were first wed.' The woman shook her head. 'You must forgive the mutterings of an old woman, Miss Sullivan. I just like to see people happy like Jim and me were.'

'I see,' Sarah replied, not sure she did at all. Although she knew Harry and Sheena got on well, the idea of them together in that way was ludicrous. All the same, the thought of them even walking out together made Sarah's heart lurch.

'Will you be all right here now, Bess?' Sarah asked quickly, anxious to get the subject back on safer ground.

Bess nodded. 'It's going to be quiet, though.' She sighed

heavily, then glanced over to the candle on the mantel. 'Miss O'Reilly's blessings candle has certainly been a comfort.' Before Sarah could ask what she meant, an elderly woman resembling Bess appeared by their side, proffering cups of tea. 'This is Alice, my sister. She's come to stay for a few days,' Bess explained. 'Alice, this is Miss Sullivan. She runs the Red Cliffs Ragged School and, believe it or not, those smartly dressed children are her pupils.'

'Charmed, I'm sure,' the woman said, graciously. 'I see they are also wearing boots. Perhaps it's time you removed the "ragged" from the name, Miss Sullivan.'

'Goodness, really?' she asked, staring over at the children, whom Mrs Daws had scrubbed within an inch of their lives. 'But my godfather gave the school its title.'

'Ah, well, times change, don't they? Talking of which, I'm hoping our Bess will come back home with me. A break from the farm will do her good.'

'Just as soon as the livestock have been taken care of, Alice,' Bess said, smiling as Harry joined them. 'I've just been talking about the animals.'

'You leave them to me, Bess,' Harry smiled.

'My Jim must have had an inkling something like this was going to happen because he made arrangements for them to be taken to market next week. Of course, I'd been on at him to ease up for ages but he wouldn't, the stubborn old fool.'

'He was happy, though, Bess, and for that you must surely be thankful,' he said, patting her arm.

'Oh, I am, Master Higgins. Now, will you be taking them chooks back with you today?'

'Yes, Bess, the children are really excited at the thought of collecting their own eggs each morning.'

'Good job the cart's parked outside then, isn't it, Miss Sullivan?' Sheena smiled as she joined them. Sarah frowned but Sheena was looking at Bess and didn't notice. 'You're looking a bit weary, Bess. Would you like to be sitting down?' she suggested.

'That's a lovely idea, but I've my guests to attend to.'

'As you can see, they're all enjoying your wonderful food.' Sheena gestured to the children, who were happily devouring the few remaining cakes.

'Then I wouldn't mind taking the weight off my feet,' she said, letting Sheena lead her over to the fireside where she sank thankfully into her chair. 'You've been such a help, my dear.'

'Isn't that what friends are for?' Sheena asked. 'Now, you have a rest while I make us some fresh tea.'

Making her way towards the range, she heard Solomon talking earnestly to the vicar.

'But I need to get things straight. At Farmer Jim's grave, you said he'd gone to join our Father who art in heaven, didn't you?'

'Yes, my child, I did,' the vicar agreed.

'So, is that where my father's gone?' Solomon asked.

'Yes, my boy,' the vicar replied. 'That is where we all go to be reunited with our fathers.'

'But last week in church you said that the wicked would burn in the fires of hell for all eternity.'

'Only those who are guilty of some terrible crime,' the vicar assured him.

'But I'm guilty of something so terrible you'd never

believe. I'll never see my father again and I want to,' he cried.

'What can you have done that is so bad, my child?' the vicar asked.

But Solomon, distraught beyond reason, pushed past him and bolted out of the door.

17

'Not again,' Harry groaned, running after him.

'I'll go with you,' Sheena cried.

'Solomon Smith, come back here this minute,' Harry shouted, but the boy took no notice and was soon swallowed up in the gathering gloom.

'We'll never catch him,' Harry muttered, drawing to a halt. 'Suppose he'll go back to the old foundry.'

'I've an inkling what's upsetting him and it's my guess he'll be heading for his father's cross in the school garden. Didn't Pip bring Mrs Daws in the cart?'

'Good thinking, come on,' he urged.

By the time they got back to Red Cliffs, the shadows had lengthened.

'I suppose there must be a back way in,' Sheena said, as Harry jumped down and unlocked the gates. He nodded as he climbed back into his seat and urged the pony on.

Having tethered the animal to the post by the front door, they made their way around the side of the house and crept down the path. As they neared the old tree they heard Solomon's anguished voice.

'So, Father, I ain't goin' to see you again ever. The vicar says I'll burn in the fires of 'ell. I'm sorry I didn't get . . . if only I hadn't . . .' Overcome by sorrow, the child burst into tears.

'If only you hadn't what, Solomon?' Harry prompted,

inching forwards. As the boy's wailing increased, Sheena and Harry stared on helplessly. Then, unable to bear his desolation a moment longer, Sheena threw herself down on the ground and gathered him into her arms.

'Did you light the fire in the foundry that morning?' she asked softly.

'Yes,' he cried. 'I wanted to 'elp Father. 'E said I were never to light it but I did when 'e were sleepin'. I was fannin' it with the bellows when the wind blew fru from the other side. Sparks catched on the straw and 'e didn't wake up when I shouted.'

'Oh, my poor boy,' Sheena crooned, rocking him back and forth. 'And you've been weighed down with guilt ever since.'

'I needed to tell 'im I were sorry but they wouldn't let me go to the 'firmary. Then you said I could talk to 'im 'ere so I told 'im I'd see 'im in 'Eaven but I ain't goin' there so I'll never see 'im again,' he wailed.

Sheena stared helplessly up at Harry, tears making her eyes glisten like emerald pools. He swallowed and hunkered down beside them.

'Listen, Solomon. You've got it all wrong.' Solomon glowered at him.

'I knows what I did,' he muttered.

'You might have lit the fire but your father was already dead, old chap.'

'No, 'e were in 'is bed sleepin' and wouldn't wake up.'

'The autopsy showed he'd had a heart attack, Solomon. His heart had given out whilst he slept, which means he was already dead when you lit the fire. That's why he wouldn't wake.'

The boy stared at him, hope flaring in his eyes. 'It weren't my fault he died?'

'No, Solomon, it wasn't. We thought you were settling in so well we didn't want to open old wounds by telling you what the examination had revealed. If you'd told us what was worrying you, we could have spared you all this suffering.'

'Fort I'd be sent to gaol,' he mumbled. 'So does this mean I'll get to 'Eaven and see my father again?'

'If you're a good boy and learn your lessons, you certainly will,' Sheena assured him.

'I'm so pleased, 'cos 'e were all I 'ad, see?'

'To think that poor boy's been worrying all this time that he'd killed his father,' Mrs Daws murmured. 'And what a dreadful thing to be burdened with. What a day, eh, Marmalade?' she sighed, stroking the cat's ginger fur.

The children had finally gone to bed and Sarah, Harry and Mrs Daws were sitting beside the range in the kitchen, relaxing over their evening drinks.

'It has been an eventful day indeed, Mrs Daws,' Sarah agreed. 'If we'd realized Solomon was blaming himself, we could have made allowances for him.'

'He was so worried about being sent to prison, he didn't dare talk to anyone here. It explains why he's been withdrawn and not made friends with the others,' Harry replied. 'Miss O'Reilly thinks it would help him settle in if he had something of his own to look after, so Pip's agreed to let him care for the pony.'

'Well, Miss O'Reilly does seem full of good ideas,'

Sarah replied. 'Perhaps someone could acquaint her with the fact that we drive a trap, though, rather than a cart.'

Harry and Mrs Daws exchanged looks.

'A rose by any other name,' Harry murmured. 'Still, as you say, Mrs Daws, it has been quite a day. Poor Bess, she'll be lost without Jim.'

'At least she had many good years with him,' the housekeeper pointed out.

'And once the animals are sold she'll be able to take a break away from the farm,' Harry said. 'Do you know, after all that fuss with Solomon we still didn't collect the hens. By the time I'd driven Miss O'Reilly home in the trap, it was too late,' he added, emphasizing the word 'trap', but the point was lost on Sarah.

'You must know your way to her house blindfold by now,' she said, somewhat acerbically. There was an awkward silence. Mrs Daws and Harry exchanged looks again.

'Well, I think it right gentlemanly of you to see her home, Master Higgins,' Mrs Daws said. 'Now I'm away to my bed,' she announced wearily, getting to her feet. The cat gave a yowl of protest and stalked over to the door. 'Thank the Lord the good ladies still have enough vegetables stored to do the Sunday soup kitchen, for I wouldn't have the energy for all that peeling and chopping tonight.'

'Perhaps you could have a lie-in before church tomorrow, Mrs Daws,' Sarah suggested.

The woman snorted. 'Up with the cockerel, me. Always have been, always will.'

'And where would we all be without you? Good night,

179

Mrs Daws,' Harry said. As the woman made her way upstairs an uneasy silence fell.

'I must go,' Harry said, jumping up. 'Oh, by the way, Bess mentioned she had some wriggly tin in her barn that she thought might be useful for patching the roof. I could bring it back on the trap when I go and collect the hens.'

'What on earth is wriggly tin?' Sarah frowned.

'Ah, it be local name for corrugated iron roof sheets,' Harry explained, giving a good impression of the Devon dialect.

'Do you think that would do any good?' Sarah asked, ignoring his attempt to be funny.

'Worth a try, don't you think?' he replied, giving her a level look.

'My meeting with Lady Chorlton is this Thursday so perhaps we should see what she says first. I mean, if she agrees to pay for the roof to be repaired and retiled, we won't need to do any more patching.'

Harry frowned. 'Don't you think you're placing too much store on this meeting? Surely Red Cliffs should be making its own way now the good doctor has left us?'

Sarah, clucked her tongue in exasperation.

'Well, better get going. Mother will wonder where I've got to. Good night,' Harry said quickly.

'Good night,' Sarah murmured, wondering what had happened to their easy-going relationship. He'd been like a different man recently. And wasn't it reasonable to hope Lady Chorlton would want to continuing helping with funding for Red Cliffs as she had when Sarah's godfather was alive?

At least the pupils were happy, she thought, recalling

their delighted faces when they'd seen the feast Bess had prepared for them. Including their Tuesday child, who had at last been released of his terrible burden. All that remained was her meeting with Lady Chorlton on Thursday and, despite what Harry said, the more Sarah thought about it the more she was confident the benefactress would wish to continue her support by funding the new roof.

On Thursday afternoon, Sarah carefully dressed in another outfit she'd adapted from the charitable donations. Mindful that her meeting with Lady Chorlton was of great importance, she'd trimmed her hat with matching green ribbon.

It was a fair walk to Hesketh Crescent, which Mrs Daws had told her was on the east side of the bay. The weather was clement and she passed many visitors dressed in their finery, who were promenading along the seafront. Feeling dowdy by comparison, Sarah glanced down at her skirt and grimaced. Well, she'd done her best, she thought.

Arriving at the elegant crescent of four-storey houses with ornamental urns perched on the roof parapet and balconies facing the sea, Sarah gasped in amazement. She had no idea Lady Chorlton resided in such luxury. At 3 p.m. precisely, she was shown into a light airy drawing room by a maid wearing a smartly tailored black dress with snowy white apron and cap. Even the servants were better dressed than she was, Sarah thought ruefully.

'Miss Sullivan, to see you, my lady,' the maid announced.

'Thank you, Benson, you may bring tea in half an hour.' As the maid curtsied and withdrew, Sarah got her first glimpse of Lady Chorlton, a slender woman with a halo of golden curls under her house cap.

'Oh,' she gasped in surprise. Amusement sparked in Lady Chorlton's eyes.

'Am I not what you were expecting, Miss Sullivan?'

'Well, I . . .' Sarah stuttered to a halt, aware that to say the woman was much younger than she'd anticipated would be rude beyond measure. 'That is to say, it is kind of you to receive me, Lady Chorlton.'

'I am only sorry it has taken so long, but Queen Victoria's passing, coming soon after Samuel's, was almost too much to bear. He was a wonderful man, your godfather.'

'He was,' Sarah agreed. 'And I miss him, too, even though I was working with him for only a few short weeks.'

'He spoke very highly of you, Sarah. I may call you Sarah?'

'Of course, Lady Chorlton,' she replied.

'Such a pretty name. It means pure and happy, but I'm sure you know that.'

'Thank you, but it's quite ordinary really.'

Lady Chorlton's blue eyes sparkled. 'Hardly. The biblical meaning is lady or princess.'

'Really? Goodness.'

'I must confess to having a fondness for appellations. It was my dream to have a daughter to choose names for but I was blessed with two boys, so . . .' she shrugged. 'The father always gets that privilege with sons,' she sighed and stared down at her lap.

Not knowing how to reply, or indeed if one was expected, Sarah glanced out of the bay window, where beyond the immaculate lawns and flower borders, the sea shimmered.

'What a wonderful view,' she cried. Lady Chorlton, recalled from her reverie, smiled.

'His lordship liked to observe his ships as they passed, and expected me to dutifully keep watch when he was due home. However, it is not as interesting as the outlook you have from Red Cliffs. Those rocky outcrops positively glow red on a summer's day, tempting one to paint them.'

'You are an artist, Lady Chorlton?' Sarah enquired, fascinated by her picturesque description.

'I dabble, my dear. Mainly seascapes but nothing can beat the ammil.'

'Sorry?' Sarah frowned.

'It's a Devonian word for the sparkle of morning sunlight through the hoar frost,' she laughed. 'Your godfather used to love the local dialect. Now tell me, how are you getting on with managing the school, if that is not an impertinent question? Samuel was adamant there was nobody finer to run it.'

'And I certainly hope to live up to his expectations, although there has been a lot to learn,' Sarah replied.

'I'm sure Master Higgins and Mrs Daws will have been helpful in that respect.' Before Sarah could answer, the little ormolu clock on the mantel tinkled the half-hour and the maid reappeared carrying a tray.

'Ah, good, our refreshment. Do attend to us, Benson,' Lady Chorlton instructed. The maid nodded and proceeded to pour amber liquid into the finest bone-china cups Sarah had ever seen. A plate of bite-sized fancies was proffered. They looked so tempting Sarah's mouth watered. However, fearful of dropping crumbs on the immaculate Persian carpet, she declined.

'You have a lovely house,' she said, when the maid had departed. Lady Chorlton smiled.

'Thank you,' she replied graciously. 'However, what are materials things without the man you love?' She gestured around the room, with its matching Chesterfields upon which pink silk cushions were neatly aligned, the ornate fireplace with its logs ablaze, the two crystal chandeliers and the pink Regency-striped drapes at the windows.

Thinking she was referring to her late husband, Sarah said, 'I believe Lord Chorlton was lost at sea?' The woman gave a harsh laugh and Sarah was worried she'd misunderstood what Mrs Daws had told her.

'He was, but I was referring to Samuel, Sarah,' she said with a sad smile. Seeing the shocked look on Sarah's face, Lady Chorlton explained further. 'We were introduced at one of our charity soirées before my husband died, and were instinctively drawn to each other. He was so different, so selfless and devoted to helping others. Your godfather was the love of my life, Sarah. Had circumstances been different we would have married.' She lapsed into silence, a faraway look in her eyes, and Sarah was left puzzling over her words. 'I do apologize,' Lady Chorlton whispered, jerking back to the present after a few moments.

'That's quite all right,' Sarah assured her. 'But if your husband died . . .' Her voice trailed off as she realized she was in danger of appearing rude.

'Lord Chorlton and I married for family reasons. There was no love on either side, and he was a jealous and possessive man, to the extent that his Will provided continuance of all this . . .' she swept her hand around the room, 'on the condition that I never remarried.'

'Goodness,' Sarah whispered.

'If it had just been me, then I would have given it all up without question to marry your godfather. However, there were my two sons to consider and, of course, the patronage of Red Cliffs, though that had to be kept secret. I was the unknown lady,' she said with a shake of her head.

'I only learned who the school's benefactress was after my godfather died,' Sarah said, wondering if it would be indelicate to raise the subject of the school roof at that moment.

Lady Chorlton continued, 'It was a great sadness to both of us that our relationship should have to be clandestine but, better a little of something than a lot of nothing, as Samuel used to remind me.'

Lady Chorlton lapsed into silence again and Sarah sipped her tea thoughtfully. She'd wondered at her godfather's secret liaison. It seemed so totally out of character with his honest nature, but having met Lady Chorlton, she could understand why he'd been captivated by her and why he had had to keep it hidden from nearly everyone.

'Forgive me, my dear, I still find myself stricken with grief when I discuss him.'

'I understand, Lady Chorlton. It catches me unawares at times, too.'

'As I said earlier, Samuel was delighted when you told him you would take on the running of Red Cliffs, although I understand he led you to believe it would be mainly helping with the administration. I took him to task over that but, of course, he had no idea he would be taken so quickly. Now I have spoken quite enough about my past but I wanted you to know how much your godfather meant to me, and this will probably be the only appropriate occasion.'

Sarah looked askance, but Lady Chorlton didn't elaborate and she didn't like to pry.

'Anyhow, my dear, I'm pleased you have settled in well at Red Cliffs,' she said, turning her candid blue eyes on Sarah. Knowing this was her opportunity, Sarah steeled herself.

18

'Perhaps you would like me to give you an update on what's been happening at Red Cliffs, Lady Chorlton?'

The woman nodded.

'Well, I have recently been accepted as a candidate for the next election of School Board members.'

'Goodness,' Lady Chorlton said with a raise of her immaculately arched brow. 'That would certainly be an achievement for Red Cliffs.'

'I'm glad you agree for I have every intention of elevating the school's status. However, I am still waiting to hear when the election will be.'

'Yes, I understand these things can take some time. Even so, to be nominated is an achievement.'

'I was fortunate that it was actually Miss Harmon, one of the school inspectors, who endorsed my application,' Sarah explained. 'And with her assistance, Red Cliffs has been appointed a new travelling mistress to replace Miss Green.'

'More suitable, I hope?'

'Indeed. The girls have taken to Miss O'Reilly and she seems enthusiastic even if she does insist on telling them stories about the little people.'

Lady Chorlton's lips twitched. 'Well, a little make-believe never did anyone any harm, Sarah. Goodness knows, I've indulged in it myself often enough over the years.' Lady

Chorlton put down her cup and, fearing she was drawing their meeting to a close, Sarah leaned forward in her seat.

'Lady Chorlton, we do have one important issue arising from the last inspection.'

'Ah, yes, Fothergill did mention a fault had been found with the roof. I presume that is to what you are referring?'

'Indeed. Although it is more than a fault. The whole thing needs retiling and, despite trying to raise funds ourselves, we simply don't have sufficient money to pay for such a large job. That is why I am hoping you will come to our rescue, Lady Chorlton . . .' Sarah stuttered to a halt as Lady Chorlton shook her head vehemently.

'I'm sorry, my dear, but it's out of the question. As I have already mentioned, I have my sons to consider, the elder of whom attains his majority next month. He will then have a large sum settled upon him, and the second son similarly in two years' time.'

'I see,' Sarah whispered, her spirits sinking to the Persian carpet.

'Don't misunderstand me, I will still help, but regrettably, from now on, the donations will of necessity be of a lesser amount.'

As disappointment flooded through her, Sarah swallowed hard. She hadn't been expecting this.

'Don't look so glum,' Lady Chorlton continued. 'I seem to remember Samuel mentioning that a developer had offered a princely sum for the property.'

'We have now actually received three offers, but obviously I couldn't possibly accept any of them,' Sarah replied, wanting to assure the woman of her loyalty to her godfather.

'Why ever not?' she exclaimed.

188

'Because it was my godfather's home,' Sarah cried, surprised she should have to explain. 'He opened it up for waifs and strays. They love it there and rely on us to keep the school open.'

Lady Chorlton gave her a candid look. 'Of course you must keep the school open, of that there is no doubt. However, if you don't mind my saying, I think you are missing the point.'

'What do you mean?' Sarah asked, frowning.

'That house is merely bricks and mortar and if you accept one of the developer's offers – the highest one, of course – you could easily purchase another. One that didn't have a leaking roof.'

'How can you say that?' Sarah gasped.

'By your own admission, keeping the school open is what matters and if Red Cliffs fails the next inspection because of the state of the building, it will be shut down anyway, won't it?'

Sarah stared at the woman, enlightenment dawning at last. 'I've made such a mess of everything,' she cried, blinking back tears.

'You can hardly be blamed for a roof that has been leaking for some time, so there must be more to that reaction,' Lady Chorlton replied. 'What exactly have you made a mess of?' she invited.

Sarah took a deep breath. 'There was this man called Tyler who turned out to be called Slater. Anyway, he said he knew my godfather and could mend our roof for a reasonable sum.' She drew to a halt as Lady Chorlton gave a chuckle.

'I'm sorry, my dear, but really, a roofer called Tyler or Slater does take some believing.'

'Apparently, his name really was Slater but I didn't find that out before the thefts and . . .'

Lady Chorlton put up her hand. 'Thefts? I'm afraid you've lost me. Tell me about this roofer from the beginning so I can follow.'

Taking a deep breath, Sarah related the whole sorry story, including the part about Sergeant Watts saying she should have consulted with Master Higgins first.

'The police don't think there's much chance of recovering any of the items, which were not of much value anyway, but poor Mrs Daws has been lost without her gong. Oh, I feel so stupid,' she sighed.

Lady Chorlton leaned forward and patted her hand. 'You'll not be the first person to be taken in. Men like that pray on trusting women. I agree with Sergeant Watts, though. In future, you should consult with Master Higgins before employing anybody.'

Sarah stared in surprise. 'But I thought being a woman yourself, you'd understand.'

'I do understand, and I certainly believe in women making decisions. Regrettably, however, it is still a man's world. A con merchant like Slater wouldn't try it on with a man of the world like Higgins.' Never having thought of Harry as a man of the world, Sarah smiled. 'Oh, don't you underestimate him, my dear,' Lady Chorlton urged. 'Many a time he put dear Samuel right about someone trying to take advantage of his kindly nature.' The little clock tinkled the next half-hour and the woman frowned.

'I am so sorry to have taken up so much of your time,' Sarah said, jumping to her feet.

'Not at all, my dear. I have been looking forward to

meeting you. You are doing a good job at Red Cliffs so don't let a setback like this deter you. In the grand scheme of things, it is only a minor annoyance.'

'No, I won't,' Sarah assured her.

'However, I would urge you to consider accepting that offer from the developer. I think you'll find in the long run it will prove financially more viable than throwing good money after bad. In the meantime, I will instruct a deposit be placed into Red Cliffs' bank account, although alas, it won't be as much as previously.'

'Thank you, Lady Chorlton. We are all most grateful and I'll make sure every penny is spent wisely.'

'And I would hate to think of dear Mrs Daws without a gong to summon the children in for their meals, so I will send you back with mine. I prefer the gentle tinkling of a bell myself. Now, I assume you walked here?' Sarah nodded. 'Well, you can hardly carry it all that way, so I'll get Finn to drive you home in the carriage,' she said, pulling on the bell sash.

'That's most kind of you, and thank you for meeting me, Lady Chorlton,' Sarah replied, then followed the maid from the room.

As promised, Lady Chorlton's carriage stood waiting outside for her. She was about to climb onto the step when she noticed a gleaming vehicle with tan leather seats but no roof had pulled up in front.

'That's one of them horseless carriages, ma'am,' the driver said, noting her curiosity.

'I've seen a couple parading along the seafront, but nothing like that,' Sarah replied.

' 'Tis a right bobby-dazzler,' the driver whistled. 'Called

a Benz petrol car and belongs to the gentleman who's rented that house for the winter season,' he added, inclining his head towards the adjoining property. Glancing up, she saw a dark-haired man watching her from the bay window. He was dressed in a tweed shooting jacket with a colourful cravat at his neck. Catching her gaze, he waved his hand in greeting. Embarrassed at having been caught prying, Sarah quickly climbed into the carriage.

The horses pulled away and Sarah couldn't help looking up at the window where the man was still watching. As their glances locked, Sarah felt a curious *frisson* of excitement. Really, Sarah Sullivan, she scolded, staring out of the other window. Have you no shame?

However, thoughts of the stranger were soon replaced by the ever-present worry of funding. During the journey back, as the carriage rocked through the darkening streets where gaslights cast their eerie green-yellow shadows, Sarah reflected on her meeting. Lady Chorlton was charming and she could see why her uncle would have been enchanted by her. However, the fact that she would not be funding the retiling of the roof had been a bitter blow and she couldn't help wondering if Lady Chorlton would have found the money somewhere if her godfather had still been alive. It seemed to her that the lady's devotion had been of love to him rather than to the school itself and now she had to rethink her strategy. Although what Lady Chorlton had suggested made sense, Sarah had promised her godfather she wouldn't sell to a developer, hadn't she?

As soon as she'd returned home, she would sit down with Harry and go through the school's finances. Somehow they needed to raise extra money for the repairs. Her godfather's house being turned into a hotel for affluent tourists was simply not an option, and now that she'd had time to think, she was surprised that Lady Chorlton should have suggested it. At least she would stay loyal to his cause.

Before she realized it, they were pulling up outside the school.

Pip hobbled over, staring curiously at the carriage through the railings.

'It is me, Pip,' Sarah called, snapping down the window.

'Afternoon, Miss Sullivan. Didn't realize it were you in that posh coach,' he chirped, unlocking the gates.

'I've brought a surprise for Mrs Dawes,' Sarah explained.

'Oh, good. She was in a right old tizz earlier. One of the chickens escaped and got in the 'ouse. Mrs Daws threatened to wring its neck if it made any mess on her clean floor. You should have seen Master Higgins trying to catch it. Flapping around like an 'en' 'imself, he was,' Pip chuckled. Sarah smiled at the picture he painted.

'Perhaps you could help me into the house with her present then?' she asked.

'Right-ho,' he called, then nodded to the driver. The carriage moved towards the front door.

'Phew,' the driver whistled, as he jumped down and stared at the elaborate quoins decorating the house. 'This sure is some place for waifs and strays.'

As Pip helped him unload the gong, which was covered by sheeting, Sarah wondered if she should give the man anything for his trouble. What was the protocol for tipping someone else's driver? As she stood dithering, the man gave a brisk salute and called to the horses to move on.

'Well, I never, it's even got the school's initials on it,' Mrs Daws exclaimed, staring at the gleaming gong. Sarah and Harry exchanged smiles but didn't disillusion the housekeeper by telling her they were those of Lord Richard Chorlton.

'How did your meeting with Lady Chorlton go?' Harry asked, sipping his evening drink before he went home.

'She was charming and sent her regards to you both.'

'She's certainly a lady, Charlotte Chorlton,' Mrs Daws replied. 'The love of the good doctor's life. If things had been different . . .' She sighed, then looked guilty.

'It's all right Mrs Daws. Though if you all knew I do wish someone had told me before I went to visit,' Sarah said. 'Yes, Lady Chorlton explained about her and my godfather.'

'Bet she was too much of a lady to say what an obnoxious, self-centred bast— old buzzard that husband of hers was,' the housekeeper said.

'She didn't put it quite like that but I did get the message that there was no love lost between them,' Sarah replied.

'And how did she receive your request for funding of the roof?' Harry asked, eyeing her seriously.

'She agreed to make a contribution but can't spare funds for the retiling,' she explained. 'Apparently, her elder son is soon to reach his majority.'

'In other words, we can't expect any more benefactions after that,' Harry added.

'Well, we shall just have to look at the budgets again. See if we can raise some money somehow.'

'I'll come in early and we can go through the ledger; get an exact idea of our position,' Harry replied. 'I'm hoping the hens will be laying soon and we shall have our own eggs, eh, Mrs Daws?'

'As long as they don't come inside messing up my kitchen,' the woman snorted.

'I must admit, Miss O'Reilly made shutting them in for the night look much easier when she rounded them up on the farm,' Harry said ruefully.

'Well, that girl's got the knack with animals, from what I hear, and with children, too,' Mrs Daws observed. Harry nodded but Sarah, too preoccupied with her meeting with Lady Chorlton, didn't react.

'Sergeant Watts called while you were out, Sarah,' Harry said quickly. 'They've confirmed the fire at the foundry was an accident so there's no need for the site of the forge and tool shop to stay cordoned off. Apparently, the landlord thinks the old buildings were an eyesore and wants to pull them down and use the land for housing.'

'Goodness, is the whole of Torquay to be redeveloped?' Sarah exclaimed.

Harry shrugged. 'Quite apart from the tourists, the population is increasing and there is a need for additional accommodation. Anyway, Solomon has been given permission to collect any possessions that are salvageable.'

'But the blaze was so intense, is it likely anything will have survived?'

'I spoke to Solomon about that. He thinks, because they're made of metal, some of the tools might be saved.

He needs to get in there before the landlord, so I've promised to take him to the foundry in the cart after breakfast. It won't take long to see what's what, so I was wondering if you could take the children for their English lesson, Sarah?'

Remembering her fiasco trying to teach the girls adjectives, she could only nod.

'Sally has her music practice at the church first thing so I can drop her off on my way. It would be helpful if you could coach the rest in the songs they are going to sing at the concert. With everything else that's been going on, they haven't had much practice and I would like them to be word perfect so they don't have to refer to the books. Easter will be here before we know it.'

Sarah mentally ran through her timetable for the next day. 'Well, I am attending another meeting of the National Union of Women's Suffrage Societies tomorrow afternoon, but of course Miss O'Reilly should be here before I leave. And your talking of Easter reminds me I need to check how the girls' needlework is progressing.'

'Edith has been talking of nothing else,' Mrs Daws commented. 'She was showing me the drawing Miss O'Reilly's made of her outfit. Right grown up she'll look when it's finished. It's good to see her so enthusiastic, what with her missing Kitty so.'

'Speaking of Kitty, that reminds me, Sarah. We have to let the Local Authority know that she and Luke are no longer with us. It wouldn't do for us to receive funding we are not entitled to,' said Harry.

'We won't have to give any money back, will we?' Sarah groaned.

'Being as how they take so long making payment in the first place, I very much doubt it. However, we'd better check. It's a criminal offence to keep money deemed unauthorized.'

'If that happened, I'd never get elected onto the School Board,' Sarah sighed, imagining her ambitions for bettering Red Cliffs disappearing before they'd begun.

'Don't worry, Sarah, we'll run through the accounts with a fine-tooth comb. Now I'd better be getting home.'

'Good night, and thank you,' Sarah said, looking at him gratefully.

'What for?'

'For not saying I told you so. You did warn me that I was setting too much store by my meeting with Lady Chorlton.'

'You might be a touch naïve, but your heart's in the right place,' he grinned.

'Good night, Master Higgins,' Mrs Daws called. She waited until the door had shut behind him then turned to Sarah. 'It's good to see you two getting on again.'

But it wasn't Harry who filled Sarah's dreams that night. It was the dark-haired man with his earnest gaze.

19

Fragments of her strange dream were still playing in Sarah's head as the cold light of dawn filtered through the window. It wasn't like her to take any notice when a man looked in her direction. However, for some reason, the intense gaze of that dark-haired gentleman she'd seen in Hesketh Crescent had affected her. It had been as if he were memorizing her features. For heaven's sake, Sarah, she scolded herself. Get up and on. It's not as though you don't have enough to worry about.

Economy still uppermost in her mind, she ignored the lamp and lit a candle instead. Still smarting from her failure to secure funding for the retiling of the roof from Lady Chorlton, she opened her desk drawer and pulled out Mrs Knight's tome. Flicking through the pages for inspiration, her attention was caught by the words 'silver lining'. Well, that's what they needed now, didn't they?

To succeed in business, it is imperative to accept you will be knocked back in your endeavours from time to time. The key is to learn from what went wrong and rethink your strategy:

Eighth Principle (a) Apply the 5 Fs:

(i). Failure. Accept that failure is not an option, but sometimes the coat must be cut to suit the cloth.

(ii). Faith. Continue to have faith in your enterprise for if you don't have total belief, how can you expect others to?

(iii). Finance. The economics of business are such that from time to time you will need to seek additional investment/funding either to keep afloat or get a new project off the ground. If you are turned down by one source, grit your teeth and seek another. Rejection is seldom personal.

(iv). Focus. Keep your attention focused on your goal at all times. Do not allow yourself to be distracted by extraneous matters.

(v). Fortitude. Be resilient, gather your strength and look for the silver lining. You can be sure there will be one and inevitably it will turn out to be the better option.

Well, all those points were certainly relevant to Red Cliffs, Sarah thought. But why were the words 'silver lining' still chiming with her?

'White rabbits to you, O crepuscular one,' Harry greeted her, startling Sarah from her thoughts.

'Goodness, you made me jump,' she told him. 'And what's that about white rabbits?'

'It's the first of the month and saying that is meant to bring you good luck,' he admitted.

'Gracious, Harry, that's the sort of mumbo jumbo I'd expect from Mrs Daws.'

'That's probably where I heard it,' he chuckled, then shivered. 'Crikey, it's cold in here,' he added, lighting a spill and setting it to the fire.

'We're meant to be economizing,' she reminded him, as he stood holding his hands to the pitiful flame.

'There's hardly enough coal there to warm a gnat. Good reading?' he asked, nodding towards the book she'd been so engrossed in.

'One of Mrs Knight's principles caught my attention.

She refers to the silver lining, which I'm sure is relevant to our situation, but I'm blowed if I can think why.'

Harry frowned and straddled the seat in front of her.

'Could mean Farmer Jim's wriggly tin,' he replied, eventually. 'That's a sort of silver colour and could make a good lining for the roof. If you're agreeable, I'll get a chap I know to take a look and see if it would be a viable proposition?' Sarah opened her mouth to say she could organize that herself, then remembered Lady Chorlton's words.

'That would be helpful,' she conceded. 'Those recent showers have been so heavy the water found its way in through yet more tiles.'

'I'll call in and see him on my way to the foundry.'

'Poor Solomon,' Sarah said. 'He's going to find it a daunting proposition sifting through the remains of his family home and business.'

'I know, that's why the sooner it's done the better. Sergeant Watts has promised the loan of two of his constables to assist. Miss O'Reilly suggested it would help Solomon if we focus on the positive aspects of anything we can salvage.'

'Keeping focused will get the job done quicker,' Sarah replied. While privately thinking that Miss O'Reilly seemed to have an awful lot of opinions, she forced a smile. But Harry wasn't fooled.

'Miss O'Reilly comes from a large family. They don't have much money and her parents spend all their time eking out a living. Being the eldest, she was left in charge of her siblings and became adept at using her psychological skills to manage them.'

'You seem to know an awful lot about her,' Sarah replied, feeling wrong-footed again.

'We've spent time together both at the farm and here so . . .' He shrugged. 'Now, we were going to look at the Local Authority funding, weren't we? Do you have the forms handy?'

They spent the next half-hour going through the paperwork. Just as Harry had thought, the authority still owed them monies for taking in Solomon. Red Cliffs was also awaiting payment of this quarter's funding for the rest of the pupils.

'You know, if we could increase our range of trade training, we might be eligible for more,' Harry said, looking up from the form he'd been studying.

'Like what? Surely we're already teaching them everything we can . . .'

Their conversation was interrupted by the clang of the gong being sounded. There followed the thundering of footsteps down the hallway. There was a moment's silence and then the gong was banged once more.

'Mrs Daws is certainly making the most of her new toy,' Harry laughed. 'Come on, we've both got a busy day ahead so let's go and get some sustenance.'

The other choir members were already assembled when Harry and Sally entered the church.

'Good morning,' the vicar beamed, coming over to greet them. 'Well, it's March already so just over a month until our concert. I hope you are in fine voice as usual, young Sally. Run along and take your place, then we can make a start.' The girl nodded and made her way gracefully towards the others. 'I don't know why I suggested she ran, she has the makings of a young lady,' the vicar beamed. 'I'll see she's safely delivered back to the school when we've finished. Unfortunately, I am vergerless at the moment. Jack Wise has regrettably moved on to pastures new.'

'But I thought he'd settled in well here,' Harry replied.

'He had, and I shall miss him. He could twist those good ladies around his little finger.' The man sighed and lowered his voice. 'Alas, it appears we have unrequited love to blame. He was beguiled by the charms of Miss Sullivan but it would seem she was blind to his devotions.'

'Ah,' Harry nodded, remembering the man's attentions. 'Well, I'd best leave you to your practice, vicar. I'm taking Solomon to the foundry but it remains to be seen if anything can be salvaged.'

'Poor child. That was a terrible thing to have happened. I shall say a prayer for him.'

'Thank you, Vicar,' Harry replied, thinking he could do with one being said for him, too.

Back outside, Harry saw that Solomon had taken the reins and was talking to the pony. It had been a good idea to put him in charge, he thought, clambering up beside him. Solomon stared at him in surprise, then grinned.

'Come on, Thunder, get a gallop on,' he called. Harry bit down a laugh. Thunder indeed. That was a misnomer if ever there was one, for the old pony was a confirmed plodder. Thunder and Plodder, a bit like Sarah and Jack Wise, he supposed. Sarah, serious and quick to anger but well intentioned; easier-going Jack, always smiling and even tempered. Poor Jack, Sarah was so taken up with running the school and her women's meetings, she'd probably never even noticed the man's infatuation, he thought remembering his own discussion with Sarah over their fish supper, when she'd made her feelings perfectly clear. To think he'd thought they might take things further. Still, that was before Sheena had bowled him over with her bright and breezy manner. She was much more his cup of tea, or should that be his glass of Guinness?

They arrived at the remains of the old foundry to find two constables keeping watch. The smell of damp, charred timber hung heavy in the air. Seeing Solomon's earlier bravado had been replaced by an anxious hopelessness, Harry took hold of his arm.

'Come on,' he urged.

They began sifting through the debris of the thatched roof and timbers of the foundry, but found only a few blackened shovel blades. Amongst the rubble of the toolmaker's shop they came across the various implements that had been stored on shelves. Although scorched and discoloured they'd been protected from the worst of the heat by a cob wall that had collapsed onto them.

While the constables helped Harry load everything onto the cart, Solomon managed to salvage a small grindstone, which had been in the yard and escaped the fire.

'Right, that's about it,' one of the constables announced a short time later. 'Surprised even that little lot survived them intense flames, boy.' But Solomon had returned to the foundry and was still frantically searching through the remains.

'Come on, old chap, there's nothing else here,' Harry said, going over and taking hold of his arm. Solomon pulled away and continued tossing the charred wood to one side.

'But it's got to be 'ere,' he muttered, throwing himself on the ground and scrabbling in the blackened remains.

'What has, Solomon?' Harry asked, hunkering down beside him.

'Father's pocket watch. 'E always took it off and put it on the side so 'e could tell when it was time to get up. But 'e didn't wake up so it must still be 'ere.' Harry turned to the constables, who shrugged.

'Looters probably had it before we arrived,' one muttered quietly.

''E said it were the only thing 'e 'ad of any worth and when 'e died I could 'ave it,' Solomon cried.

'Perhaps he left it in his pocket when he went to bed,' one of the constables suggested.

'Yes, that's probably what happened,' Harry agreed. 'Come along, Solomon,' he added, helping the boy to his feet.

'Poor bugger,' one of the policemen murmured, his eyes bright with pity.

'Thank you for your help, Constables,' Harry called, as he helped a desolate, wet and filthy Solomon into the laden cart.

'We'll notify the landlord he can begin the demolition now. Probably be one of them new-fangled terraces of houses here before long. Good day to you, sir.' The constables tipped their helmets. Harry brushed the worst of the dirt from his clothes, wrapped an old blanket around Solomon, then called to the pony to move on.

'At least we've got some of your father's things to take

back with us,' Harry said, leaning over and patting the boy's hand. Solomon didn't reply and Harry noted his expression had regained its hopeless, morose look. He was just wondering if it would be better to keep talking or leave the boy to his own thoughts, when he caught a glimpse of a cherry-red hat ahead. His heart gave a leap and he called to the pony to get a move on.

'Good day to you, Miss O'Reilly,' he called, as they drew alongside.

'Good morning, Master Higgins. How are you?' she asked, turning to the boy. He shrugged.

'We've just come from the foundry,' Harry explained, indicating the sacks behind them.

'So you recovered some of your belongings, Solomon? That's good,' Sheena said brightly.

'No it isn't,' he muttered.

Sheena looked askance at Harry but he shook his head.

'I take it you are on your way to Red Cliffs. Would you like a lift?'

'That'd be grand,' she said, climbing nimbly up beside Solomon. 'Nanna wanted some extra shopping this morning so I'm running late. Miss Sullivan wishes to see me before afternoon lessons and I was that worried I'd keep her waiting.' She inclined her head towards him and he saw her worried expression. 'Wouldn't do to be told off by the boss now, would it? Especially as I'm still the new girl, so to speak,' she asked Solomon.

He shook his head. 'I feel out of it, too,' he replied.

Sheena stared at him, surprised at his perception. 'I thought you were settling in at Red Cliffs so why should you feel out of things, Solomon?' she asked gently.

'Well, I only got me old fings to wear. All the uvers got them posh red waistcoats,' he muttered.

Sheena and Harry exchanged a look.

'Sorry, old chap, I hadn't given it a thought,' Harry told him.

'I'm sure we can get one made for you, too,' Sheena added. 'So what did you manage to find earlier?' she asked him conversationally. He scowled.

'Tools but they're all black and their 'andles is all broke.'

'Well, that's not so bad. Tools can be cleaned, handles mended,' she chirped.

'Didn't find 'is watch, though,' Solomon wailed. 'That constable said it had probly been taken by looters. 'E fort I didn't 'ear 'im, but I did.'

'Oh, my poor angel,' she replied, pulling him close. They made their way up the lane towards Red Cliffs, silent save for the sound of hooves.

'At least it's not raining,' Harry laughed, trying to relieve the tension. 'Which reminds me, I've got that dictionary I promised you back at the school.'

'Then, to be sure, I'll be able to learn some fancy words to try out on you, Master Higgins,' Sheena smiled.

'That could be fun. Miss Sullivan finds my penchant for the lexicon quite vexing.'

'Oh?' she replied, then hearing a sob from Solomon, tucked the blanket tighter around him.

'I was thinking, Solomon,' Harry said turning to the boy. 'Those tools of yours would be really useful if they were repaired. How would you feel about the boys helping you restore them as part of their woodworking lesson?'

Solomon stared ahead but they could tell by his expression that he was mulling things over.

'Would that not be a splendid tribute to your father, Solomon?' Sheena cried. 'Every time you look at them you would remember him.' The boy's face brightened and Harry could have kissed her for her sensitivity.

As he felt his neck growing hot at the thought, he quickly said, 'It is Saturday tomorrow so we will be going to the farm in the afternoon, if you'd like to join us. The animals have been sold, but I promised Bess we would help tidy everywhere up before she leaves with her sister.'

'That's kind, Master Higgins. I'd love to see Bess before she leaves,' Sheena replied.

'Have Patsy and 'er piglets been sold, too?' Solomon asked.

Sheena glanced at Harry.

'Yes, they've all found a new home,' he said, careful not to lie. 'Well, here we are,' he announced, grateful there was no time for Solomon to pursue the subject. 'You'll find that dictionary in my desk, Miss O'Reilly. I await my first test with bated breath.'

'To be sure, I love a challenge, Master Higgins,' she assured him.

Hearing the rattle of the trap as it drew up outside, Sarah glanced out of the classroom window. She'd had a difficult morning and seeing Harry hold out his hand and the new mistress laughing down at him as she accepted his help didn't improve her mood. How could he look so cheerful when he'd taken Solomon to salvage his things, she thought. Although she had to admit the boy looked quite calm, if somewhat dirty.

'Right, children,' she said quickly. 'Are you all happy with the words you are to sing?'

'Still don't know why it's a green hill, miss,' Black muttered. 'I mean, if it had been snowing it would 'ave been white.'

'Well, it wasn't,' Sarah replied, trying to keep her voice even.

'Yeah, but why 'ave a city without a wall?' Brown asked. 'And why would you let anyone put nails fru your 'ands?'

'Well, you certainly seem to have learned the words, so well done, everybody,' Sarah said quickly. 'Now it's time for luncheon, so off you go.' She tried not to wince at the scraping of stools on the floor as they ran from the room. Who would have thought that learning a couple of hymns would be so difficult?

'Good afternoon, Miss Sullivan. You wanted to see me before the girls' needlework lesson.' Sarah looked up as the schoolmistress appeared in the doorway. The fresh air had lent colour to her cheeks and so they matched her hat, and her bright and breezy manner contrasted with Sarah's present state of mind.

'I was surprised to see you arriving with Master Higgins,' she said.

'He was kind enough to offer me a lift when he passed on his way back from the foundry.'

So, it had been a chance meeting, Sarah thought, feeling herself relax.

'Well, that was fortuitous,' she replied. 'And how was Solomon?'

'He brightened up when he realized his father's tools could be restored.'

'It will be good for him to have something positive to focus on. Talking of focus, you and Master Higgins seems to be spending a lot of time together,' she replied, then bit her lip. Despite her good intentions, she just didn't seem able to refrain from mentioning it.

20

'I can't help thinking Miss Sullivan doesn't like me,' Sheena sighed. It was Saturday afternoon and she was helping Harry escort the boys up to the farm. Although it was blustery, a weak sun was shining giving a hint that spring was just around the corner.

'Whatever makes you say that?' he asked, feigning surprise. For in truth, he had noticed Sarah's tendency to pick on her.

'I just don't seem able to meet her exacting standards regarding the girls' sewing schedule. Really I don't understand it as there's another month until Easter and they are making good progress now.'

'Well, that's not the same as not liking you.'

'It's the way she looks at me, though. Like I've crawled out of a bog or something,' Sheena tried to explain.

'Well, you're the best-looking boggart I've ever seen,' Harry chuckled, giving her a look that set her insides quivering. 'And it's kind of you to give up another afternoon for this little lot,' he added, waving his hand at the crocodile of excited children in front of them.

'It's my pleasure,' she cried. 'I've grown fond of the little angels already.' She didn't add that she welcomed the opportunity of seeing Harry, too.

'Angels?' he spluttered. 'I've seen better behaved

specimens in the circus.' He shook his head but she could tell he was really fond of his charges as well.

'Get back in line, Brown,' he called, as if to emphasize his point. 'Don't let Miss Sullivan's manner get to you,' he said, turning back to Sheena. 'That's just her way. She is so focused on raising the profile of Red Cliffs, I think she sometimes forgets there is life outside the school.'

'Well, she's taking the girls for needlework this afternoon so she'll see for herself how time-consuming the work is, especially without a sewing machine,' Sheena said philosophically, not wishing to spoil the mood of the afternoon. She watched as Solomon broke into a run in his haste to get to the farm. 'He seems brighter,' she observed.

'Yes, the promise of restoring his father's tools has perked him up no end. I just hope nobody enlightens him that his beloved Patsy has been turned into a pasty,' he murmured.

'Well, animals are reared for eating, but I agree this is probably not the best time to tell him that.' They shared a complicit look, then, feeling her cheeks growing warm, Sheena turned away.

'Is it not a glorious afternoon?' she cried, gesturing to the flowering crocuses and the daffodil buds bursting from the hedge-banks.

'Just as well it's dry for I promised to call in to see someone about the repair of the school roof yesterday morning and completely forgot,' Harry groaned.

'I expect you were too busy concentrating on Solomon,' Sheena replied. 'Or, of course, you could merely be an amnesiac,' she added casually.

'To be sure, Miss O'Reilly, you've been studying that dictionary I loaned you,' he replied in a parody of her accent. 'You'll have to do better than that, though,' he chuckled, wagging a finger at her.

'Oh, I've only just made a start, Master Higgins,' she teased. They lapsed into a comfortable silence before Sheena remembered something. 'By the way, I'm sure I saw Kitty earlier?'

'Oh? Whereabouts?' he asked.

Sheena frowned. 'Well, that's the thing. I was on my way to buy fish and thought I glimpsed her hanging around by the docks. Of course, I could have been mistaken,' she added quickly seeing Harry's mouth tighten into a line.

'Hardly. You're one of the most observant people I've met,' he frowned, vowing to look into the worrying news as soon as he had time. For now, however, there was no time to continue the conversation for they'd reached the farm gate and the boys, full of high spirits, were all racing ahead like frisky lambs.

'Be careful, boys. The place needs tidying up and there could be bits of fencing and debris scattered around,' he shouted. Revelling in their freedom, they paid little heed, though. He raised his brows. 'I don't think Jim had been in some of those outhouses for years,' he added, gesturing to the far side of the yard where run-down buildings were almost obscured by thick vegetation.

'Well, children just love to explore so I'm sure they won't come to any harm. It'll do them good to let off steam,' she laughed.

'You're right, of course. Let's leave them running wild while we go and see how Bess is. Hopefully, she'll have the kettle boiling,' Harry said as they made their way towards the farmhouse.

'Oh, you are kind, giving up more of your time, Master Higgins. You too, Miss O'Reilly. Do come on in,' Bess greeted them at the door. Although looking pale, she seemed in bright spirits. 'Alice has made the tea, if you've time for a cup?'

'Never say no, Bess, you know that,' Harry grinned. 'The warmth in here is welcome after the cold outside.'

'How have you been?' Sheena asked, when they were sat around the kitchen table. As ever, although the place was clean and tidy, it had a cosy feel that reminded her of home.

'Well, I'll not deny I'm missing Jim. Nobody to moan at, see?' she said, giving a wry smile. 'Never thought I'd miss the smell of that old pipe, or his muddy footprints.' She gave a sigh, her glance going to the fireplace.

'It must be very hard,' Sheena murmured, reaching over and patting the old woman's hand.

Bess nodded then smiled. 'Still, it was a relief to hear the livestock had all sold, and for a fair price, too.'

'That's good news, Bess. And talking of livestock, I've left the boys running through the fields,' Harry told her. 'But as soon as I've finished my tea, I'll get them tidying out the barns.'

'And I'm happy to help in the dairy,' Sheena added. 'Not that you'll have any churning for me to do, of course, but I can get started on the cleaning.'

'You're that kind-hearted, both of you. I can't deny I'd appreciate it. The whole place needs a good clean before I go.'

'When are you leaving?' Harry asked.

'As soon as we can,' Alice cried, coming into the room. 'Never seen so much muck and mess in all my born days. How you can live here, I don't know,' she told her sister.

Bess chuckled. 'You always was one for neat and order, Alice,' she said, shaking her head and bending to pat the collie's head. 'Still, at least she's agreed to let you come with me, boy.' As if he knew what she was saying, the dog whined and put his paw in her lap. The old woman's eyes misted over for a moment then she pulled herself together.

'I can't deny there's always chores needing doing here. A nice rest will be welcome.' She looked sad, though. 'All the crops and vegetables Jim planted will just have to rot in the ground, I'm afraid.'

'No need for that,' Harry replied. 'The boys and I will be keeping an eye on the place while you're away so we can tend to them as well.'

'But you've already done so much. I couldn't impose like that,' she protested.

'It will be good for the boys to take on some more responsibility,' Harry commented. 'You know the ethos of Red Cliffs, Bess.'

'I do, and it's a sound one. The good doctor certainly knew what he was doing when he started the school.' She sighed again, thinking of days gone by. 'Well, Master Higgins, if you're sure it won't be too much trouble to see to things, I'd be really grateful. And, of course, you must help yourself to any produce as it becomes ready.'

'Done deal then, Bess. Mrs Daws will appreciate the additional rations, and the rest we'll store in the barn for you. Talking of which, I'd better rally the troops. See you later,' Harry said, draining his cup and getting to his feet.

'Such a nice young man,' Alice observed, as he left.

'Yes, he is, and he's been very good to Jim and me over the years,' Bess replied.

'So would you like me to be cleaning out the dairy then?' Sheena asked, thinking it prudent to leave the women to their chat.

'If you would, dear, that would be such a help,' Bess replied.

But as Sheena drew the door shut behind her, she heard Alice say, 'That lass would make a fine wife for the master.' Her heart soared to the heavens, only to sink when she heard Bess's reply.

'That's what I thought, Alice. I said the same thing to Miss Sullivan at Jim's wake. Then I saw her expression and remembered she and the master had an understanding.'

So, that was the way things stood, was it? Stupid girl, Sheena O'Reilly, she chided. A few smiles from the master and you think he likes you.

Entering the dairy, she snatched up the broom and began sweeping furiously, all the time berating herself.

And after last time, too. Did you not learn your lesson then? Was that not why you had to resign your last post?

She swept until not a hair or speck of dirt remained, then attacked the wooden tops and utensils with the scrubbing brush.

Didn't Nanna Treasa warn you before you left home? 'Learn the lesson from this, Sheena. Men talk the blarney to get their own way.

They like to think their charms are irresistible. Let them treat you, flatter you, even fall in love with you, but do not love them back. That way disaster lies.'

Well, from now on she would treat Master Higgins as a work colleague; no more, no less.

'Have you finished in here?' Sheena jumped, for just as if her thoughts had conjured him up, there he stood large as life in the doorway. 'Goodness, this place looks like new. Bess will love you more than ever,' Harry whistled, staring around the now gleaming dairy.

'Well, if a job's worth doing . . .' Sheena muttered, rinsing the brush so she didn't have to meet his gaze.

'The boys are just finishing tidying the yard so shall we go and say goodbye to Bess and Alice?'

'I'll just finish here first,' she said quietly.

The boys were in high spirits following their afternoon in the fresh air as Harry led them back to the school. Not wishing to make conversation with him, Sheena dropped to the back of the crocodile.

'Just look at the state of them,' Harry chuckled as he urged the boys on, then fell into step beside her. 'Good job it's bath night.'

'Yes,' she muttered.

'You don't seem your usual bubbly self. Are you all right?' Harry asked. 'If you're concerned about Bess leaving the farm then don't be. I'll keep an eye on the place and the boys can burn off more of their energy tending the crops.' He frowned when she didn't answer.

'I'm just tired,' she replied. 'Tired of being taken in,' she added under her breath.

'Oh, that's a shame. Sometimes I go into town for a

fish supper on a Saturday night,' he said, looking at her expectantly.

'Well, I hope you enjoy yourself,' she said, forcing a smile. 'Now, if you're sure you can manage, I'd better be making my way home.'

'Oh, yes, of course,' he replied, disappointment replacing the hopeful look in his eyes.

As she turned towards the town, she could feel him watching her but didn't look back. She had no intention of ever being taken in again. In fact, if she hadn't become so attached to the children, she wasn't even sure she'd return to Red Cliffs.

'How are you getting on with your sewing, girls?' Sarah asked, looking around the classroom.

'Fine,' Edith replied. 'You know, Miss Sullivan, when I've finished my dress, I think I'll have enough material left to make a jacket to go over it.'

Sarah smiled. 'That's a bit ambitious, Edith. I should complete your dress first and see how it fits,' she replied, going over to the girl and studying her work. 'Your sewing is very good,' she added, marvelling at the neat stitching and the way she'd caught the line of the skirt perfectly.

'So can I make a jacket next then?' the girl pleaded.

'Jackets are very complicated to fashion, Edith,' Sarah hesitated, not wanting her to be put off if it went wrong.

'I'm sure a short-sleeved one wouldn't be too hard. I know, I'll get Miss O'Reilly to sketch me a picture of one, then I'll be able to follow that,' she replied, breezily.

'Well, that's a good idea, but as she's not here at the

moment perhaps you could concentrate on what you're currently doing.'

But Edith was holding her garment up thoughtfully. 'This shape's good, but the whole thing looks a bit dull and dated. Probably like the person who had it first,' she murmured. 'I know, I'll find some ribbon and make a sash.' Her eyes shone at the prospect.

'I wish I was clever like you, Edith. I'll never be able to make something I can wear,' April groaned, staring down at her puckered seam. 'Besides . . .' She stopped and frowned down at her work.

'Look, it just takes perseverance,' Sarah replied.

'I dosen like persevera, I likes singing,' June lisped.

'The word is perseverance, June. It means you have to keep at it,' Sarah explained kindly, seeing the girl's perplexed look.

'We could keep at it if you sang like Miss O'Reilly does,' Monday said, staring hopefully at Sarah with her periwinkle eyes.

'Miss O'Reilly sings during lessons?' Sarah asked, looking surprised.

'Yes, she says it helps set the rhythm,' Ellen replied.

'It really works, too,' Sally said.

'What does she sing?' Sarah asked curiously, but even before she'd finished the question they'd begun chanting.

Stitch, stitch, stitch, stitch, stitching. Sew a little stitch for me.
Stitch, stitch, stitch, stitch, stitching. Sew a little seam for me.

'Oh, I see,' Sarah began, but they were so caught up in their song, they didn't hear her.

Hem, hem, hem, hem, hemming. Hem a little edge for me.
Hem, hem, hem, hem, hemming. Hem a little fold for me.

'Yes, well, that's very good . . .' Sarah said, but they were off again, their little faces aglow as they sewed.

Trim, trim, trim, trim, trimming. Add a little bow for me.
Trim, trim, trim, trim, trimming. Dresses for you and me.

Sarah stared at the girls, amazed to see they were sewing as enthusiastically as they were singing. Not only that, they were working to the rhythm of the tune. Perhaps, Miss O'Reilly had something after all, she conceded, looking around the room. It was only then that she noticed April had slipped away.

The sound of laughter outside roused her from her thoughts. Looking out of the window she was surprised to see the boys already returning. Goodness, where had the afternoon gone, she wondered.

'All right, girls, leave your dresses out for me to inspect but tidy away the rest of the sewing things,' she called.

Immediately there was a flurry of activity as scissors, thread and pins were put back in the work basket. There followed a scraping of chairs and a surge towards the door.

'Now, girls, what is the correct way to end our lesson?' Sarah called.

'Good afternoon, Miss Sullivan,' they replied, then hurried from the room.

Sarah shook her head then walked around inspecting their work. Edith's was a delight and Sarah could see her wearing the dress. Sally's stitching was neat but she still had a lot of sewing to do before her garment would be anywhere near ready. As for the others, well suffice to say they would need a lot of supervision. Sarah sighed. She'd asked the schoolmistress to come up with a proposal to ensure the outfits would be completed by Easter. It would be interesting to see what she had to say at their meeting on Monday.

She was making her way towards the kitchen when she saw Harry approaching.

'Hello,' she called. 'How did you get on at the farm?'

'Very well. I've promised Bess we'll look after things whilst she's away and in return we can pick any produce we want. I've just finished helping the children shut the chickens in for the night,' he said, grimacing down at his dirty hands. 'Good job it's bath night. Those boys look like they spent the afternoon rolling in the dirt, not sweeping it up,' he laughed.

'Goodness, is it Saturday night already?' Sarah asked, feigning surprise in the hope that now good relations had been resumed between them, he might mention going out for supper. To her surprise, though, he looked uncomfortable.

'Well, better go and wash up, then get home to Mother. I promised I'd cook something nice for tea tonight. See you in church tomorrow.'

Sarah frowned and watched as he hurried over to the pump. Well, if that was how he wanted to play it, then he could jolly well get on with it.

21

For once, Harry was relieved to be away from Red Cliffs. He'd been worried Sarah was going to mention the roof repairs and didn't want to admit he'd forgotten to call into Langham's to arrange for the man to price the job. It wasn't like him to be remiss, or even amnesic, he thought with a jolt. He let out a sigh for he knew it hadn't been because he'd been preoccupied with salvaging the tools from the foundry the previous day. Oh, well, he'd just have to keep his fingers crossed it didn't rain.

Like Sarah, he was worried about the school's finances. Having given the matter a lot of thought, he'd come up with an idea of how they could obtain extra funding from the Local Authority. He just needed to write down his proposition and present it to her first thing on Monday morning.

Finally, he allowed his thoughts to turn to Sheena O'Reilly. One minute they'd been getting on really well, the next her manner had cooled. Then, when he'd mentioned that he might go into town for a fish and chip supper, she'd looked positively disdainful. He'd only been going to suggest he walk her home as it was on his way. Women, they really were an enigma.

Turning into the road that led to the seafront, he heard laughter coming from the nearby tavern. Deciding some male conversation would be welcome, he ventured inside.

*

The next morning Sarah and Mrs Daws were ushering the children from church towards the hall where they helped with the soup kitchen when the good ladies way-laid Sarah.

'Good morning, Miss Sullivan,' Miss Snooper greeted her. 'The children are all looking very smart these days. However, we couldn't help noticing that Solomon has looked a little out of place, so we've made him a red waist-coat the same as the others.' Smiling graciously, she reached into her bag and drew out a wrapped parcel.

'Oh, Miss Snooper, ladies, that is such a kind thought,' Sarah said, taking it from her. 'It is just what he needs to help him feel he belongs. Thank you so much.'

'Talking of feeling one belongs, it is such a shame Jack Wise has seen fit to leave us, isn't it?'

'I noticed he wasn't in church but didn't realize he'd actually left,' Sarah replied.

'Last week. Said he couldn't really continue when his heart is . . .' Miss Prior began, only to be dug in the ribs by Miss Middle. 'Well, we mustn't detain you; need to heat the broth for the urchins,' the woman added quickly.

'And I give thanks every Sunday for your kindness,' Mrs Daws said. 'I do so enjoy being able to put my feet up for a couple of hours after church.'

'Are you sure you don't need us to supervise the chil-dren?' Sarah asked.

The women smiled at each other and shook their heads.

'Oh, we good ladies of the Church manage perfectly, don't we, Vicar?' Miss Snooper smiled.

'Indeed you do, Miss Snooper. Those unfortunate waifs have a lot to thank you for,' the vicar replied. 'Rest assured, Miss Sullivan, I shall ensure your pupils are delivered safely back when luncheon is finished,' he said, turning to Sarah. 'No Master Higgins this morning?'

'Well, he has been even busier than normal this week helping Bess at the farm, so I expect he's spending the morning with his mother.'

'Very admirable,' the vicar replied. 'It is at times like this one needs a good friend to rely upon. Of course . . .'

'If you'll excuse us, we really must be getting back, Vicar,' Mrs Daws said quickly. 'Now behave yourselves, children, and see that you help and not hinder,' she added, waving a finger at the little group hovering behind them.

'We'll be as good as the gods,' Brown declared solemnly.

''Elpful as angels,' Black chirped.

'Cheerful as cherubs,' Edith chortled.

'Be sure that you are all those things or you'll have the devil's . . . Oh, please excuse me, Vicar,' the housekeeper blushed. 'You'll have me to answer to, children, and that will be ten times worse,' Mrs Daws warned them before turning and hurrying off down the path. With a quick nod at everyone, Sarah hurried after her.

'Are you all right, Mrs Daws?' she asked, staring anxiously at the woman.

'Already had to listen to one of the vicar's sermons this morning and I wasn't going to have my precious free time taken up with another,' she growled. 'As for those scallywags, well, I was trying that hard not to laugh at the thought of them behaving like cherubs. Ferocious as fiends, more like,' she chortled. Sarah shook her head. The usually prim and proper housekeeper could be quite incorrigible when the mood took her.

They walked on in silence for a few minutes.

'Don't mind me, Miss Sullivan. Sometimes I just need to get rid of my pent-up emotions.'

'Like Solomon, you mean?' Sarah asked.

'Something like that,' the woman agreed. 'That was real nice of the ladies to make him a waistcoat like the others. Help him to fit in, it will. The good ladies might be a pain in the backside with their pious ways, but they do come up trumps on occasions.'

'They do,' Sarah agreed, then, remembering what Miss Prior had said: 'I didn't know Jack was ill.'

'Ill?' the housekeeper looked at Sarah sideways.

'Miss Prior said there was something wrong with his heart,' Sarah murmured.

'Of course there is, but if you can't see it well . . .' Mrs Daws stuttered to a halt. 'What's the school gate doing open?' she cried.

Sarah frowned, then peered around. Hearing the sound of banging, she hurried towards the building.

'What on earth are you doing?' she called up to the figure on the roof.

The man stared down and grinned. 'Begging your pardon, madam, but from where I am the earth looks a fair distance away.'

'It's all right, Miss Sullivan,' Harry called. It was only then she saw him standing at the foot of a ladder.

'Oh, I didn't see you there, Master Higgins,' she replied.

'Won't be a minute,' he added, holding the ladder steady as the man made his descent.

'Miss Sullivan, Mrs Daws, this is Mr Langham, who has kindly offered to give us a price for repairing the roof.'

'Morning, ladies,' the man smiled. 'Shouldn't cost you much, 'Arry old fella, specially as we're using that wriggly tin,' he said. 'And after our discussion, like,' he added with a wink.

'Knew you'd see us right, Mr Langham,' Harry replied. 'How quickly do you think you can fit us in?'

The man scratched his head. 'Well, like I said, we've just finished that 'ere new terrace of 'ouses over back of Torre and we're not due to start a new one till middle of month.' He scratched his head. 'Could start first thing tomorrow, if ers like?'

'That is good news, isn't it, Miss Sullivan?' Harry said, turning to Sarah.

'Well . . .' she began, but Mrs Daws interrupted.

'Jolly well is. April and Pip have spent that much time mopping up water recently I'm surprised they've not grown webbed feet. Now, Mr Langham,' she said, smiling at the man.

'Call me Marty, Mrs Daws,' he replied.

'Well then, Marty, see you arrive about seven o'clock and I'll have breakfast and a cuppa waiting.'

'You're a treasure, Mrs D.' Marty grinned. 'See yer tomorrow then,' he said. He doffed his cap then strode off down the drive.

'I know you mean well, Harry, but surely you could have discussed it with me before agreeing,' Sarah frowned.

'Well, he doesn't look the sort to make off with me gong,' Mrs Daws commented. 'Now I'm going to put my feet up and make the most of what's left of my free time,' she added as Harry chuckled.

As the woman made her way indoors, Sarah turned to the master.

'You can take that grin off your face, Harry Higgins,' she scolded.

'I did say I'd arrange things,' he replied, rubbing his forehead. 'Now I'm going home to work on my brilliant plan for obtaining extra funding from the Local Authority.'

'Really, what plan?' Sarah asked.

But Harry's head was throbbing from his late night.

'Not today,' he added, wincing. 'We'll discuss it first thing tomorrow.'

'Feeling better?' Sarah asked when he popped his head around her office door early the next morning.

He nodded ruefully then took a sheet of paper from his pocket.

'Said plan,' he said, laying it on the desk in front of her. She frowned at the scribbled notes, so unlike his usual neat handwriting.

'This looks like one of the children's offerings,' she tutted. 'You'd better sit down and talk me through it.'

'As you know, the foundry made tools, which they sold in their workshop,' he said, straddling the chair in front of her. 'I've examined those we were able to salvage and with some judicious cleaning and repair think they should come up like the new tools most of them actually are.'

'But they're Solomon's. You can't sell them,' Sarah cried, staring at him aghast.

'Who said anything about selling them?' Harry asked, grinning in a way Sarah was finding annoying.

'Will you please get to the point?' she snapped.

Harry raised an eyebrow. 'Solomon recovered a small grindstone and, having spoken to him, I agree that we will be able to use it to resharpen the salvaged tools once they have been cleaned up, and any that are bent or mis-shapen can be hammered back into shape without the need of a forge. We can also set up a simple pole lathe to make the rounded wooden handles for some of the tools, and a shave horse to cut and shape the shafts for the oth-ers. In this way, we can teach the boys the new trades of woodturning and metalwork. As these are recognized industrial skills, this means we can apply to the Local Authority for extra funding in recognition of the boys obtaining competencies.'

'If they agree, it would certainly help with our finances as well as boosting the reputation of Red Cliffs,' Sarah smiled.

'I was thinking more about the boys' futures than the school's image,' Harry replied.

'That as well, of course,' Sarah agreed quickly.

'If, at the end of the day, we are able to sell some of the reconditioned tools, then any profit made could be shared between Solomon and Red Cliffs. We could open an account in the boy's name and the funds would help set him up when he leaves here.'

'That sounds a good idea,' Sarah said, nodding thought-fully. 'You've obviously given this a lot of thought.'

'I have,' he agreed. 'Good tools are in high demand, especially with all the new building work going on in the area.'

'Fair enough,' she conceded. 'We must remember we

are entering a new age and the school needs to move with the times.'

'Move, as in accepting one of the offers from the developers?' he asked. 'Because that was something else I was thinking about. Lady Chorlton just might have a good point about throwing good money after bad and . . .' Seeing two red spots of anger staining her cheeks, he stuttered to a halt.

'Don't even think it, Harry Higgins,' she cried. 'My godfather set up Red Cliffs here and here we are staying.'

'I was only going to . . .' he began, but his words were drowned by the sound of a cart rattling past the window.

'If you've nothing else to discuss, I see your builder has arrived,' Sarah snapped.

Monday morning and she was still in a quandary as to what she should do. Unable to stay indoors any longer, Sheena snatched up her bag and took herself for a long walk along the seafront. The weather was brisk just like her footsteps, as she pounded the pavement.

People dressed in their finery were emerging from the plush hotel set back from the promenade, intent on walking off their breakfasts. Sheena waited to cross the road, which was busy with carts transporting their goods, and carriages conveying their ladies. She couldn't help smiling as the vehicles, heedless of their passengers, kicked up dust and strands of dried seaweed in their wake. Clearly dirt didn't differentiate between classes.

As she walked, she prayed for guidance. After her previous upsetting experience, back home, she couldn't afford to make any more mistakes. Should she return to

Red Cliffs or resign her post? In the few short weeks that she'd been at the school she had grown to love the children, and her position as travelling schoolmistress offered her the chance to rebuild her career.

However, the fact remained that not only did Miss Sullivan lack faith in her ability as a teacher, she didn't appear to like her either. Then there was Master Higgins. Despite herself, her heart flipped when she thought of him. She enjoyed working with him and they'd built up a rapport. However, apparently, he and Miss Sullivan had an understanding. And that was the trouble, she admitted. Somehow, somewhere along the line, camaraderie had tipped into . . .

'Good morning, Miss O'Reilly.' Hearing her name, Sheena looked up in surprise and found herself staring into the face of Sarah Sullivan. She was dressed in her best blue outfit and was accompanied by another smartly dressed woman.

'Good morning to you, Miss Sullivan,' she replied politely.

'Miss Harmon, allow me to present our travelling mistress, Miss O'Reilly,' Sarah said, turning to her companion.

'We met before at your interview, of course, Miss O'Reilly,' Miss Harmon smiled. 'How are you settling into Red Cliffs?'

'Well, I . . .' Sheena began.

'She is doing splendidly,' Sarah replied, to Sheena's amazement. 'The children have really taken to her. I must say, Miss O'Reilly, I was pleased with the results of their needlework. To have them singing to the rhythm of a sewing machine is simply genius. I have no doubt whatsoever that they will all be wearing their new outfits for the Easter concert.'

'Really?' Sheena gasped, astonished at the woman's praise. 'I mean, I'm glad you approve,' she murmured.

'You must be on your way to Red Cliffs now, so we mustn't detain you,' Sarah continued. Sheena glanced around, astonished to find that she was nearly back at her grandmother's house. Somehow she must have reached the end of the promenade and turned around without realizing it.

Miss Sullivan was still talking. 'I have left the girls in the capable hands of Mrs Daws, so that Miss Harmon and I can exchange our ideas on suffrage over a light luncheon before our women's meeting,' Sarah was saying. 'If you could go and rescue her directly, I'd be most obliged. Good day, Miss O'Reilly.' Before Sheena could answer she turned away.

'Nice to see you again, Miss O'Reilly. So pleased you have settled in well at Red Cliffs,' Miss Harmon smiled, then followed Sarah.

Sheena stared after them for a full minute before realizing she was standing in the middle of the footway obstructing other people. Well, you asked for divine intervention, Sheena O'Reilly, and you have been given your answer, she told herself, heading determinedly towards Red Cliffs.

22

Having decided the prices in the restaurant of the hotel they'd passed would probably be beyond their means, Sarah and Josephine Harmon had ventured into the little café close by. Now they were sitting at a table in the window sharing a pot of tea along with the house speciality, Devon Chudleighs, which were light as a feather and liberally spread with cream and plum jam.

They were on their way to a meeting of the National Union of Women's Suffrage Societies later that afternoon and were debating the best way to publicize their mission. While women had made some advances in local government, the campaign for the right to vote for Parliament was moving forward very slowly. It was an exciting time and Sarah was keen to do her part to further the cause.

'Do you know that gentleman over there?' Josephine asked, lowering her voice as she inclined her head towards the right. 'Only he's been staring at you ever since he came in.'

Sarah frowned at the interruption to their conversation, but couldn't resist taking a surreptitious peek at the next table. Her eyes widened in amazement when she found herself looking directly into the bright blue eyes of the gentleman she'd seen staring out of the window in Hesketh Crescent. He nodded in acknowledgement but she turned quickly away.

'Bit of a dandy, that one – who is he?' Josephine whispered, taking another look. 'And not short of a bob or two either, from the way he's dressed. Would've thought he'd be taking refreshment in the hotel rather than here.'

'Shh,' Sarah chided, feeling her cheeks growing hot. She picked up her cup and concentrated on finishing her tea. However, she could still feel his gaze upon her and couldn't resist another look. This time he smiled warmly before returning to the notebook in front of him.

'Now what were we saying?' she said, turning back to her friend and seeing her amused look.

'You were expounding the view that women shouldn't be tied to the kitchen sink by their husbands. Saying they should have a fair say in how the country is run. In fact, you even went so far as declaring that the days of us needing a male in our lives were coming to an end.' Josephine paused for effect. 'Of course, that was before you got distracted by that handsome specimen at the next table. Who, by the way, is now staring at you as if he's committing your every feature to his memory.'

'Rubbish,' Sarah hissed, choosing to forget that was exactly how she'd felt as she'd passed by his house in Lady Chorlton's carriage. 'He's probably trying to glimpse the sea from out of the window,' she added, gesturing towards the promenade beyond, where tourists were taking the afternoon air.

'Me thinks the lady doth protest too much,' Josephine chuckled.

'If you've quite finished, perhaps we should be making

our way to the meeting,' Sarah suggested, jumping to her feet and snatching up her bag so suddenly, one of her gloves fell to the floor.

'Allow me,' a rich, well-modulated voice offered. Before she could reply, the gentleman from the next table had retrieved it and was holding it before her.

'Oh, er, thank you,' Sarah stammered.

'Absolutely my pleasure,' he replied, blue eyes twinkling. 'Bertram J. Brightling at your service.' He gave a polite bow and Sarah couldn't help but notice the incredible sheen to his dark hair. Or that he was wearing the same tweed jacket as before with another brightly coloured cravat tucked into the neck of his shirt.

Quickly taking the proffered glove, she hurried from the café. The exchange could only have taken a matter of moments and yet she felt flustered, almost as if she'd stepped off one of the gallopers at the fair. Honestly, Sarah, she chided, one look from a stranger and you're acting like a silly schoolgirl.

'Well, you could at least have had the good grace to give him your name,' Josephine scolded, joining her outside.

'Give my name to whom?' Sarah muttered, still feeling ruffled.

'To Bertram J. Brightling,' Josephine giggled. 'Some name, eh? And did you see his hair? It was slicked back with the new brilliantine that has recently come over from France. According to my brother-in-law, it costs an absolute fortune.'

Oh, so that's what it was, Sarah thought, glancing back over her shoulder. He stood watching her out of the window and raised his hand in acknowledgement. Cross at being caught out once more, she walked briskly away.

'For someone who professes to have no interest, you are acting very strangely,' said Josephine. Determined to focus her attention on the meeting ahead, Sarah pretended not to hear.

Having decided the gods had shown her the way, Sheena trudged resolutely towards Red Cliffs. She loved her job and the children, and would focus her energy on them. As for Harry Higgins, well, it would be stupid to think she could avoid him, but she would make sure that, whenever their paths crossed, she kept their dealings on a professional level. *No more giddy feelings or fancy words, Sheena my girl. You might hail from the Emerald Isle but you are no longer as green as the proverbial leprechaun.*

Having finished giving herself a strong talking to, Sheena called good afternoon to Pip and headed for the classroom. She could hear banging and whistling coming from the roof and guessed the repair work had begun. Then she noticed Solomon waiting in the doorway.

'Miss O'Reilly, Master 'Iggins said could you please sew me button on for me?' he greeted her.

'To be sure, Solomon, and may I say how very smart you're looking in your red waistcoat.'

'Thanks, miss,' he said, looking relieved. 'I was dead chuffed when Miss Sullivan gave it me. Makes me feel like the others, but then this came off,' he frowned, holding up the little bone button. 'I told Master 'Iggins I could . . .'

'Master Higgins said it needed seeing to straight away

and that you should be more careful in the future,' Harry finished for him, as he appeared from the workshop next door. Despite her resolve, Sheena's heart did its usual flip at the sight of him. 'I hope you don't mind my suggesting you would sew it back on, Miss O'Reilly,' Harry continued. 'Only these buttons the good ladies use are all matching and it would be a shame if it were to get lost.'

'That's quite all right, Master Higgins,' Sheena said quickly, ushering Solomon into the classroom and avoiding Harry's gaze. 'We've just got time before the girls appear for their needlework lesson.'

'Oh, well, I'll leave you to it then,' Harry said, looking put out by her haste.

'Fink 'e was using it as an excuse to speak to you, miss,' Solomon said, giving her a cheeky grin.

'Solomon Smith, now why would he do that?' she asked, staring at him in surprise.

'Well, you can tell 'e likes you by the way 'e looks at you. 'Sides, I said I could sew this on meself,' he chirped, holding out the button to her.

'Really? Well, Master Higgins thought it would be better done straight away so it didn't get lost,' she said, taking it from him and threading a needle.

'Then why when I told 'im first thing this morning it had come off, did 'e only have 'is brilliant idea when 'e saw Pip letting you in through the gate?' he asked, two dark eyes studying her knowingly.

She felt her insides flip. Be still, my treacherous heart, she admonished herself. Thankfully she was saved from answering the boy by the arrival of Edith and Maggie.

'We didn't see any sign of Shanksy on our way in, miss,' Maggie giggled, nudging Edith in the side. 'He's not real, is he?'

The door opened again but as the other girls swarmed into the room, Solomon put his fingers to his lips.

'Don't want to spoil the younger ones' fun, do we?' he winked. 'Got to 'ave somefink to believe in, ain't they?'

'Thank you, Solomon,' Sheena replied. 'That's very sensitive of you. Now there's your button sewn on nice and tight, so off you go.'

As he ran back to the workshop, Sheena clapped her hands. 'Right, girls, collect your work and begin sewing. I'll come round and see how you're getting on.'

'Can we sing that song you taught us?' Monday asked. 'Miss Sullivan said no when we asked, but we did anyway and she liked it.'

'That was only 'cos we said we sewed faster if we got into the rhythm,' Maggie pointed out. Picturing the scene, Sheena smiled. The girls could be very persuasive when they wanted.

'Once everyone is busy stitching, we can all sing together, my angels. Now, Edith, show me where you've got to with your dress.'

'It's almost done,' the girl cried excitedly as she held it up for Sheena to see. 'I found some ribbon and am adding a sash to brighten it up.'

'That is a splendid idea, is it not?' Sheena cried, marvelling at the girl's ingenuity.

'And,' Edith added, her eyes alight with excitement, 'as there's lots of material left, I thought I'd make a jacket. Miss Sullivan said it would be too difficult but I told her

236

you'd draw me a pattern so I could follow it. You will, won't you?'

'Let's see how the time goes,' Sheena replied diplomatically. 'You know how Miss Sullivan wants everyone to have their outfits ready for Easter.' She smiled encouragingly. Edith was certainly talented and she didn't wish to dampen her enthusiasm but neither did she want to cross Miss Sullivan.

'Me stiches is sku hiffy, miss,' June called.

'I think you mean skewwhiff, June,' Sheena corrected. 'Edith, perhaps you could help?'

'Hers probably whiff anyway,' Ellen giggled.

When everyone was finally settled to their work, Sheena began singing and before long the girls were joining in. There was no doubt it concentrated their minds and she was proud of the way they were all knuckling down. It certainly wasn't an easy task teaching to such a mix of age and ability. Then she noticed the cotton dress still sitting on the desk.

'Isn't April joining us this afternoon?' she asked.

'I expect Mrs Daws needed her. She left halfway through the lesson on Saturday,' Sally said.

'Yeah, she didn't look happy. Strange really 'cos she was so excited when Miss Sullivan said she could have the first one as she is the eldest,' Edith pointed out.

'Really?' Sheena said, frowning at the garment, which had hardly been touched since she'd last seen April.

'It's a shame, 'cos she'd look really lovely in that green cotton with her red hair,' Edith sighed. 'Wish we could grow ours.'

Sheena stared at the girl thoughtfully. Then seeing

the girls were more interested in the discussion about April than their work, she resumed singing and soon the room was filled once more with the sound of their voices.

By the time the bell went, some progress had been made. It was slow going, though, and once again Sheena lamented the fact the school didn't have a sewing machine. She picked up April's garment. If the girl really had been so enthusiastic, it seemed a shame she couldn't attend her lessons. She'd go and speak with Mrs Daws and see if they could come to some arrangement.

'Hello, Mrs Daws, do you mind if I come in?' Sheena asked, popping her head round the kitchen door. To her surprise the housekeeper was sitting at the table with her feet up on the chair.

'Of course not, dearie. Don't mind me,' Mrs Daws said, holding up her cup. 'Now the weather's better, the children can run around outside after lessons for a bit. Gives me a chance to take the weight of my feet before dishing up supper. Plenty in the pot, if you want one,' she added, indicating the cosy-covered teapot. Sheena looked around the room and, seeing no sign of April, sat down beside the woman.

'Thank you but I'd just like a quick word about April. As you know, Miss Sullivan is keen for all the girls to have their new outfits completed for Easter.'

'Yes, most insistent about that,' the housekeeper nodded.

'I understand April left Miss Sullivan's lesson early on Saturday and she didn't attend at all this afternoon. Although I understand she has her chores to do here, I'm afraid her sewing is falling behind,' Sheena explained, holding up the cotton material.

The housekeeper frowned. 'Well, she never came to help me get supper on Saturday afternoon and I certainly said she can come to all your lessons as long as she attends to anything that needs doing here afterwards.'

'There seems to be some confusion,' Sheena began just as April appeared from the hallway. Her eyes widened when she saw the mistress and she started to back out of the room.

'Get yourself in here, young April,' the housekeeper ordered. 'Now you haven't been in the kitchen helping me so what have you been doing with yourself all afternoon?'

April stared from the housekeeper to Sheena, then down at the floor.

'It's no good, miss,' she muttered.

'What's no good, my angel?' Sheena said, crouching down beside her.

April shook her head.

'Come on, girl, cat got your tongue?' Mrs Daws urged.

'I know you find stitching difficult with your left hand, but I thought we'd found a way for you to work the material.'

'It's not that,' April cried.

'Then what is it, April? Am I not a very good teacher?'

'You're the tops, miss, but . . .'

'But?' Sheena encouraged. 'You can tell me.'

'It's too embarrassing,' April whispered.

'Not as embarrassing as it will be for Miss O'Reilly

239

when Miss Sullivan finds out your new outfit's not ready to wear for the concert,' Mrs Daws snorted.

'And why would that be, April?' They looked up as Sarah appeared in the doorway. 'I saw you disappear from my lesson on Saturday so I think you owe us some answers.'

Noticing the way in which the girl was desperately glancing from Sarah to the hallway beyond and then to the back door, Sheena reached out and put her hand on her arm.

'If I'm doing something wrong, then you'd better tell Miss Sullivan,' Sheena urged.

'But it's not you, miss, it's me. I'll never fit into me dress. I must have eaten too many cakes 'cos I gone and grown too much up here,' she cried, pointing to her chest.

'Oh, my wee angel,' Sheena cried. 'That's because you're developing into a woman. It's something that happens to all girls and you should be proud of your blossoming buds.'

'Not if they mean I can't fit into me clothes,' April whispered.

'Clothes can be adapted, my sweet,' Sheena cried, her heart going out to the girl.

'Even the new dress?' April asked, hope flaring in her eyes.

'Especially your new dress,' Sheena assured her. 'If it's all right with Mrs Daws, you can come back to the classroom with me and we'll make a note of your new womanly measurements.'

'Of course, it is,' the housekeeper replied. 'I only wish I'd spotted what was happening but you can't see anything under them big blooming aprons. Never gave it a thought, Miss Sullivan, what with her knowing about her monthlies like,' she said turning to Sarah.

'That's all right, Mrs Daws,' Sarah told the woman. 'And when you've finished with April perhaps you could spare me a minute in my office, Miss O'Reilly?'

23

Sarah looked up from the pile of correspondence and smiled as the schoolmistress entered her office.

'Do come in and take a seat, Miss O'Reilly.' She couldn't help noticing that despite it being the end of the afternoon, the woman, in her brightly coloured skirt and blouse, still looked remarkably lively although there was a wariness in her eyes. 'How did you get on with April?' she asked.

'Once we'd had a little chat about how women's bodies change and why, she perked up no end. Then the poor wee angel began worrying about being behind with her sewing. I know she's only missed a couple of classes but it takes her that long to do her stitching in the first place. She began fretting about letting you down if her dress isn't ready for Easter so I . . .' Her voice trailed off.

'So you?' Sarah prompted.

'You'll probably be horribly cross with me, Miss Sullivan, but I couldn't bear to see the poor girl upset. I promised to unpick her dress at home and pin it out to her new measurements so that we could make a fresh start on Wednesday.'

'And you thought I'd disapprove?' Sarah asked, staring at the woman in surprise.

'Well, you did make it plain that you wanted the girls to do the adaptations themselves, which I quite understand,'

Sheena added hastily. 'But April is so sensitive at the moment, I thought a little extra encouragement would help.'

Sarah shook her head. Did she really come across as being so hard?

Sheena, misunderstanding her gesture, got to her feet.

'I'm sorry, Miss Sullivan, I really don't seem to be meeting your needs here, do I?'

'No, Miss O'Reilly, you don't,' Sarah replied. 'You far exceed them,' she smiled. 'Oh, I can't deny I was a little concerned about your methods at first, but having seen the girls' work and, more importantly, listened to how they feel about you, I am impressed.' She paused as the mistress gaped at her in astonishment.

'You are?'

'Yes, Miss O'Reilly, I am. However, there is something I'd like to discuss with you,' Sarah said, gesturing for her to be seated again.

Still looking stunned, the mistress took her chair.

'Since my arrival here last autumn, I have been aware that the school gives no formal instruction on girls' development and this incident with April highlights the fact that we need to put something in place. Although Mrs Daws does an admirable job of dealing with feminine issues, I feel a more structured approach to the subject would benefit the girls. How would you feel about incorporating such a lesson into your timetable?' There was silence as the mistress contemplated the idea and Sarah hoped she hadn't overstepped the mark.

'That's a really good idea. I could start with the basics, maybe tell a story of a young princess growing up, to engage the younger ones without worrying them. Then I could add more detail individually as they needed it. So many young girls have no idea of what to expect, don't they?'

'Indeed they don't. Well, if you are agreeable, I will leave it to you to encompass that aspect into their curriculum. Of course, I am here if you encounter any problems, although somehow I don't think you will. As I said, the girls have really warmed to you.'

'Thank you, Miss Sullivan, for, to be sure, I have warmed to the little angels myself.'

'As for encouraging April with her sewing, if you are happy to work on her dress at home, that would be most kind of you. I only wish we had the funds to remunerate you,' Sarah said sadly.

The mistress waved her hand dismissively. 'It will be enough to see those girls looking pretty in their new outfits at the concert,' she said, but she was frowning.

'Do I sense a but, Miss O'Reilly?'

'It is their hair, or rather lack of it. I realize for hygiene purposes they need to keep it short but could they not be allowed to grow it just a bit? Their shaven heads make them look like waifs from olden times. The girls are well looked after here but I would be happy to undertake the job of nit-picking, if it were necessary, for did I not do that for my siblings back home?'

'It's nice to know we share the same ideas, Miss O'Reilly. I will have to discuss that with Master Higgins and Mrs Daws, then let you know their views. Now, is there anything else?'

'Just one more question, Miss Sullivan. Would you have any objection to my showing Edith how to make a simple bolero? She's already finished her dress and, although she is assisting the slower pupils, I don't wish to discourage her enthusiasm.'

'By bolero, you mean a jacket?' Sarah asked.

Sheena nodded. 'A simple jacket with short sleeves. I'm happy to draw up a pattern so it would be quite easy and quick to do, but I thought I'd better check with you first.'

'You have my permission. Thank you, Miss O'Reilly, you really are going to be an asset to Red Cliffs.' Sarah and Sheena exchanged their first warm smiles, knowing they were on the same wavelength at last.

Harry hurried down the hallway, his mind on the school roof. Langham and his men had made good, if somewhat noisy progress, although he'd had the devil's own job getting the children to concentrate on their sums that morning. Thank heavens he'd had the idea of getting them to count the sheets of tin in the pile outside the classroom then devise a lesson on subtraction as they were taken away.

The afternoon had been easier, as he'd got Solomon to talk them through the various tools they'd salvaged and what they were used for. He was a bright boy with eyes like a hawk and had seen through Harry's excuse to talk to Sheena. He'd have to be more careful in future.

Now he was off to report on the progress Langham had made, before keeping his side of the bargain and sorting out the man's books. It was yet another call on his time but he had got a good price in return, he reminded himself as he knocked on the office door.

'Come in, Master Higgins,' Sarah called.

'It might not be me,' he quipped as he strode into the room. Then he saw Sheena and his pulse quickened.

'Oh, sorry, I didn't realize you were here, Miss O'Reilly.' He smiled at her genially only to receive a stiff nod in return. 'I won't keep you, Miss Sullivan,' he said turning to Sarah. 'Just thought you'd like to know Langham reckons his men should have the job finished by the end of the week.'

'That is good news. Thank you,' Sarah replied. 'No, don't go,' she added as he turned away. 'Sit down, there's something I would like your opinion on.'

'Well, in that case . . .' Sheena said, jumping to her feet, but Sarah frowned.

'Please stay, too, Miss O'Reilly. In fact, why don't you put your proposal to Master Higgins yourself?'

Harry turned to the schoolmistress and saw two bright spots staining her cheeks. 'You were going to propose to me, Miss O'Reilly?' he asked, placing his hand on his heart.

'Certainly not,' she retorted sharply. 'I merely suggested that the girls would look prettier at the concert if they were permitted to grow their hair a little.'

Harry couldn't resist raising his brows in mock horror.

'Don't tease, Master Higgins,' Sarah admonished. 'I think it's a wonderful idea, especially as Miss O'Reilly has promised to nit-pick.'

Harry almost laughed aloud at the picture that conjured up and could see from Sarah's eyes that she, too, was finding the thought funny. As if she'd sensed their amusement, Sheena stared at each of them in turn, her emerald

246

eyes turning stormy. Not wishing to upset her further, Harry pulled himself together.

'Actually, I agree that would be a good idea. Bring them into this century,' he replied.

'Good, for that was exactly what I was thinking,' Sheena said, getting to her feet. 'Now if you'll excuse me, Nanna will be waiting for her tea. Good afternoon.' Although she spoke politely, her voice had none of the warmth he associated with her and she left the room without looking in his direction.

'I hope you don't mind,' Sarah began, bringing him back to the present. 'When I met Josephine Harmon earlier, I briefly ran through the idea you had of teaching the boys to make and repair tools. She thought it could indeed bring in extra funding. However, she pointed out that the Local Authority would probably insist on a dedicated workshop being set aside for the project.'

'Hadn't thought of that,' he admitted. 'I can see it would make sense, though. I'll speak to Langham and see if he can come up with a solution.'

'Good. Is everything all right, Harry? I couldn't help noticing things seemed a bit strained between you and Miss O'Reilly earlier.'

He shrugged for in truth he still had no idea what he'd done wrong.

'I'm pleased you agreed with her suggestion of allowing the girls to grow their hair.'

'Well, the days of Victoria's asceticism are over and we should move with the times. Talking of which, it's high time I was moving, too. I'll see you in the morning, Sarah.'

Left alone with her thoughts, Sarah stretched, then

moved her seat nearer to the dwindling fire. Although it was still an ongoing battle with finances, she did feel that at last Red Cliffs was moving forward, and hoped her godfather would be proud that she was doing justice to his legacy. She stared around the room, taking in the shabby décor and threadbare rugs. *One day I shall refurbish all this, Uncle*, she promised. Half expecting him to answer, she waited, but the only sound was from the hearth as the last of the coals shifted in the grate.

In contemplative mood, she returned to her musing. Although she'd had some reservations about Miss O'Reilly, the girl's heart was in the right place and her sympathetic dealings with April's predicament earlier had proven that. She'd be the right person to teach them about their bodies, too. It was a good idea to let the girls grow their hair and she was pleased Harry had agreed. She frowned. When she'd asked if everything was all right between him and Miss O'Reilly earlier, he hadn't really given her a proper answer. Had she imagined the atmosphere between them? And where did she stand with Harry now, she wondered.

Her meeting of the NUWSS had been both inspiring and motivational. The desire for women to have more say in the running of the country was gathering momentum and with plans to spread the word to every town and village, she fully intended doing her part. She'd make it her mission to ensure the girls understood the advantages attaining the right to vote would make to their lives and insist that Harry teach the boys, too. After all, theirs would be the first generation to experience the changes. It was a thrilling time and she enjoyed supporting a cause she felt so passionate about. She'd also relished exchanging views and opinions with Josephine over tea and cake in the café.

Thoughts of the café conjured up an image of the dark-haired man with intense eyes. Bertram J. Brightling, he'd said his name was. Although she hadn't liked to admit it, Josephine had been right. He had appeared to be showing an interest in her and she felt a *frisson* of excitement tingle through her. As well as being a boost to her morale, it would distract her from her preoccupation with Harry Higgins and Sheena O'Reilly.

It was Saturday afternoon and, having driven Bess and Alice to Torquay station in the trap earlier in the week, Harry had taken the boys to the farm to see what needed doing. Sarah was supervising the girls' sewing and as she walked around the classroom, she couldn't help marvelling at the progress they'd made on their outfits.

'This is going to look right dandy, miss,' Edith cried, hopping up and down excitedly. 'Just think, me with me own outfit. I shall look like a lady, specially now we can grow our 'air.'

'Hair, Edith,' Sarah corrected although she couldn't help smiling at the girl's enthusiasm.

'Please sit quietly or you'll get that chalk in the wrong place,' she urged.

'No chance,' Edith replied. 'This pattern Miss O'Reilly's done is clear as daylight.'

'That sleeve is coming on a treat, Sally,' Sarah encouraged, moving to the next desk. 'Let me know if you need any help. Ah, April,' she said, smiling as the girl came bounding into the room.

'Mrs Daws said I can spend this afternoon sewing as well,' she cried. 'Now I know this is going to fit me,' she said, holding up the green dress, 'I can't wait to get it finished.' Sarah appraised the garment, which Miss O'Reilly had unpicked and neatly repinned. It was really coming along. 'And, as the day after Easter is my anniversary day,' April cried, 'Mrs Daws said we can wear our new dresses to my party and she'll make one of her special cakes.'

'I loves cake,' June lisped.

'Your anniversary day? Ah, that's the day you came to Red Cliffs,' Sarah guessed.

April nodded. 'Most of us don't know the day we were born on so we celebrate when we came to Red Cliffs.'

'Tell you what, April, I could make you a ribbon to go with your dress, if you like,' Edith offered.

'What a lovely idea, Edith,' Sarah said. 'Well, let's get sewing then, shall we?'

'Can we sing, miss?' Monday asked. Sarah nodded but as they began singing a movement outside caught her eye.

What were Harry and the boys doing back from the farm so early? And why was Solomon accompanied by Sergeant Watts?

'Carry on with your sewing, girls, I'll be back shortly,' Sarah said. 'April, please take charge.'

'Is everything all right?' she asked, hurrying towards the group. It was then she noticed they were carrying three sacks between them.

'We found treasure, Miss Sullivan,' Brown cried in delight.

'Yeah, and Sergeant Watts thinks it's nicked,' Black exclaimed.

Sarah stared askance at Sergeant Watts.

'Seems them old barns have been used as a store for stolen property, Miss Sullivan.'

Sarah's eyes widened in amazement.

'The boys came across all manner of stuff when they went to tidy up, amongst which were items stolen from Red Cliffs,' Harry explained.

'And me father's watch,' Solomon added, holding it out for her to see.

24

'Well, I never. To think them robbers was using the farm to hide their loot,' Mrs Daws muttered, holding up the little mallet. 'Shame they didn't find me gong as well as this, 'cos that one from Lady Chorlton's got too posh a sound for me.' She sighed and took a sip of her tea.

'Really, Mrs Daws, how can a gong sound posh?' Harry chuckled, stretching out his legs and relaxing back in the chair. 'Thank heavens it's gone quiet now. I thought those children would never settle this evening after all the excitement. Luckily it was bath night and we could leave them in the capable hands of Mrs Laver, whilst Sergeant Watts was expounding his theories. You should have heard the racket the boys made when they found the stuff. Screaming and shouting like gleeful gorillas.'

'It's a good job the farm's well away from the neighbours or that would give them something else to moan about. Josephine said the Local Authority had received numerous complaints about the banging coming from the roof here,' Sarah said.

'There's no pleasing some people,' Harry muttered. 'They moan that the state of this place is letting the street down, then complain when we do something to improve it. Damned if we do, damned if we don't.'

'Ignore them, Master Higgins. At least we've got our

candlesticks back and Solomon his father's watch,' the housekeeper replied. 'The way he was clutching it tightly to his chest reminded me of when he first arrived with his bundle.'

'Strange that it should be found along with our things, though, don't you think?' Sarah frowned.

'Not really, if the same person stole them,' Harry replied. 'Think about it: Slater coming here and the fire at the foundry happened around the same time, didn't they?'

'You mean it was all Slater?' Sarah gasped, still feeling guilty that she'd let the man roam around the house unaccompanied.

'Sergeant Watts reckoned it was, but the evidence is circumstantial,' Harry admitted.

'He always says that,' the housekeeper muttered.

'Well, when I pressed him he admitted there could be a connection and he's going to make some enquiries. We also uncovered other stolen property in the barns, some of it quite valuable, which he's getting his constables to itemize. Anyway, I've locked up the farmhouse and will keep the boys away until they've made a thorough search of the outbuildings and land.'

'Poor Bess,' Mrs Daws clucked her tongue. 'What a good job she and Alice had already left. She's had enough to contend with lately. Imagine, her property being used for storing stolen goods. Unbelievable, isn't it?'

'It's certainly not a nice thought, Mrs Daws. However, Jim hasn't been in those buildings for quite some time. Sergeant Watts reckons the thief knew that and had been stashing the goods while he found a suitable outlet for

them. Gives a whole new meaning to the word "fence",
doesn't it?' Harry said, draining his cup. 'Well, I'd better
be on my way.'

When Sheena arrived at Red Cliffs on Monday afternoon,
she found Harry wheeling a barrow across the gravel
driveway. It was loaded precariously with a wriggly tin
sheet that Solomon was trying to hold steady.

'Good afternoon, Miss O'Reilly,' he called.

'Good afternoon, Master Higgins,' she replied, trying to ignore the way his muscles rippled under his
rolled-up shirtsleeves. He put down the barrow and
gave her a warm smile. 'I see you have turned into a
builder since I was last here,' she added, quickly averting
her gaze.

'Langham reckoned there was enough tin left to erect a
shed for our new trades,' Harry told her.

'And when it's done, I'm going to help show the others
how to mend my father's tools,' Solomon said, his eyes
shining with enthusiasm. 'You'll never guess what, Miss
O'Reilly. I've got my father's watch back.' He pulled it
from his pocket and dangled it in front of her. 'It were
'idden in one of Farmer Jim's barns.'

'That's grand, Solomon. You'll be able to remember
your father every time you tell the time,' Sheena smiled.

'Aye, that's right funny, that is. Every time I tell the
time,' the boy cried delightedly.

'Perhaps you'd like to check on what the boys are doing
in the workshop, Solomon,' Harry suggested. As he ran
off, Harry turned to Sheena. 'Finding that watch has certainly perked him up. I've also filled some buckets with

sand and put him in charge of the "cleaning the tools team". At last he seems to be fitting in.' As he stood there grinning, Sheena felt her heart flip.

'It's good to see him so happy, Master Higgins,' she said quickly.

'It's a shame you didn't come with us to the farm, you missed all the excitement,' he said, his hazel eyes sparking with mischief. Forcing herself not to respond, she smiled stiffly.

'Well, Saturday is not a school day for me, Master Higgins. I did hear through the grapevine that stolen goods had been recovered from Jim's barns, though.'

'Yes, and some of it was Red Cliff's property. However, until the police have finished their enquiries the farm is out of bounds, hence starting on this project,' he said, waving his hand towards the west side of the garden where some building materials had already been stacked alongside the high wall. 'It won't interfere with your lessons, though.'

'Talking of which, I must get moving,' Sheena said, turning to go and spotting the principal heading towards them.

'Goodness, I do hope you're not being presumptuous,' Sarah cried, gesturing towards the loaded barrow. 'We've still to receive official confirmation from the Local Authority that we will get funding for the project.'

'Well, we've got the leftover wriggly tin, and Langham has kindly donated these timber offcuts and a few warped rafters for the frame, so it would be stupid to look a gift horse in the mouth. Besides, the more I think about it, the more I can see how much the boys will benefit from learning these new trades, but they would be far too messy for the workshop.'

'Well, I'm sure you know best,' she replied.

'Oh, I do, Miss Sullivan,' he grinned.

'Honestly,' Sarah chuckled, raising her brows.

Seeing their easy banter, Sheena felt her heart plummet. She'd just have to put her own feelings to one side, she reminded herself. Then she realized Sarah was addressing her.

'Let me say once again, how impressed I am with the way the girls' outfits are coming along, Miss O'Reilly. They are going to be a credit to Red Cliffs at the concert.'

'Thank you. We've been practising our singing at the same time instead of stories, you understand,' she said, looking meaningfully at Sarah.

'Good, and both Mrs Daws and Mrs Laver think your idea of letting their hair grow a good one, although they both insist it will be your responsibility to ensure they're not harbouring any unwanted visitors.'

'That is not a problem, Miss Sullivan. With Easter being so close, their hair won't have grown much anyway, but at least they'll look softer and more feminine.'

'I agree,' Sarah replied. 'Now, I'm off to the bank to ensure our money from Lady Chorlton has been safely received, then I shall be attending another meeting of the women's movement, so I'll wish you both good day.'

'And I'd better be getting into the classroom,' Sheena said quickly.

'Scurrying away again, Miss O'Reilly?' Harry teased.

'Just being assiduous, Master Higgins,' she replied.

'I can see you've been studying the dictionary. Well, you'll find yourself in good company for this morning the pupils did English comprehension and learned all manner of new words.'

'To be sure, I hope decency and rectitude were amongst them, Master Higgins,' she replied stiffly, and marched into the classroom. Although she could feel his eyes boring into her back, she didn't turn round.

Sheena was kept so busy in the run up to Easter, ensuring the girls were ready for the concert, it was easy to avoid the master. If her eyes strayed to the window when he was working on the shed, then she hastily averted them. Moral courage might be easy words to say but she was finding it incredibly difficult to put them into practice.

'Right, girls,' she said, marshalling her thoughts. 'Today is Good Friday, an exciting day, is it not?'

'Yes, we're finishing lessons early today,' Monday cried gleefully.

'Well, in that case you'd better hurry up and put on your new dresses so that I can check everything is perfect before the concert tomorrow. We'll call it our dress rehearsal, shall we?'

'Just like they have in concert halls,' Sally replied.

'This really is a Good Friday,' Maggie said, clapping her hands excitedly as the girls began to change into their new dresses.

'To be sure it is, and when I'm satisfied you all look like little angels, you can take yourselves off to the kitchen for one of Mrs Daws' special spicy buns,' Sheena told them.

'And I hope you'll be joining them,' Miss Sullivan said,

appearing in the doorway. 'We've hardly seen you in the house these past couple of weeks.'

Knowing it would be churlish to refuse, Sheena forced a smile. 'That would be grand,' she replied. 'Right, girls, line up in front of Miss Sullivan so she can see the results of all your hard work.'

There was a flurry of excitement as they began twirling around to show off their outfits. Edith stood proud in her dress and bolero and Sheena marvelled again at the girl's talent. Sally looked delightful, her delicate silk frock the perfect foil for her pale complexion. She was certainly going to look beautiful against the bright Easter floral arrangements the good ladies would have spent the morning preparing. April stood beaming beside them, the green cotton showing off her shapely figure rather than crushing it.

As Sarah took her time scrutinizing every detail, Sheena could contain herself no longer.

'Well, don't you just think our girls look pretty, Miss Sullivan?' As Sarah turned and shook her head, Sheena felt her heart plummet. What had she done wrong?

'They look absolutely beautiful. They exceed even my high expectations, Miss O'Reilly.'

Sheena laughed. 'I do wish you wouldn't shake your head when you mean yes, Miss Sullivan. It always makes me think you have found something amiss.'

'Girls, you all look lovely. You have worked very hard and are going to do Red Cliffs proud tomorrow. Now you do remember the words you are singing?'

'Yes, Miss Sullivan,' they chorused.

'In that case, change back into your smocks, lay your

dresses carefully over your desks then take yourselves off for your Easter bun and drink.'

'Can't we take our new dresses up to our dormitory ready for tomorrow, miss?' Edith asked.

'I think they would be safer in here,' Sarah replied. 'It would be a shame if they got all creased, wouldn't it?'

With the thought of their Easter treat proving too tempting, they didn't complain and as they excitedly did as she'd asked, Sarah turned to Sheena and smiled.

'Well done, Miss O'Reilly. Time for refreshment, I think. We are all gathering in the kitchen for a celebration before Mrs Daws and myself depart for Miss Snooper's. She's invited us for supper; Mrs Laver, too.'

'Oh, I, er, need to tidy away here first,' Sheena stammered, hoping to delay the moment she would have to speak to Harry again.

'Rubbish, Miss O'Reilly, I insist you come along with me now.'

Knowing there was nothing she could do, Sheena fixed a smile on her face and followed the woman to the kitchen.

'Ah, Miss O'Reilly, I thought you'd deserted us,' Mrs Daws called above the babble of excited voices. 'Now come and help yourself to an Easter bun. I found a new receipt in one of them periodicals and can't decide if it's an improvement on my usual one or not.'

With the delightful aroma of mixed spices filling the kitchen, Sheena didn't need telling twice. She smiled at the children, who were enjoying their treat of cake and juice, then helped herself.

'Oh, that's absolutely delicious, Mrs Daws,' she gasped, biting into the fragrant cake.

'Ah, we have another pistoriophile in our midst,' Harry cried, grinning at Sheena as he helped himself from the plate.

'Oh, you and your fancy words, Master Higgins,' Mrs Daws chided.

He winked at Sheena. 'Well, Mrs Daws, I can concur with Miss O'Reilly that this is the tastiest bun I have ever eaten, so in this instance your atelophobia is misplaced.'

As the housekeeper frowned, Sheena couldn't help laughing. 'Atelophobia is fear of imperfection, Mrs Daws,' she explained.

'Indeed it is, and your baking is perfection personified,' Harry agreed, catching Sheena's eye. She blushed then looked quickly away.

'Stop teasing, Master Higgins,' Sarah admonished.

'I made the blackcurrant juice, didn't I, Mrs Daws?' April announced proudly.

'And very tasty it is to be sure, April,' Sheena said quickly before the master could tease her with another long word.

'Can we go outside to play?' Brown asked.

'Good idea,' Harry replied. 'Right, you little lot, when you've finished your refreshment you can go and run off all that excess energy. No taking your beakers outside, though, and come in as soon as the gong goes because I am supervising supper tonight.'

'I must admit I'm looking forward to dining in style this evening,' Mrs Daws muttered as she began clearing away.

'I'll do that, Mrs Daws,' April said. 'You go and get your coat.'

Sarah looked at the clock on the dresser and nodded. 'Yes, that's a good idea. We should be leaving. Pip is getting the pony and trap ready and we mustn't keep Miss Snooper waiting.'

'That would never do. She is a punctilious lady, is she not?' Harry asked, humour sparking in his hazel eyes.

'She does indeed like everything to run like clockwork,' Sarah agreed, then paused in the doorway. 'And as for you, Master Higgins, you may think of us dining in elegant surroundings whilst you oversee things here.'

'Piece of cake,' he shrugged. 'However, I'm sure you will enjoy Miss Snooper's fine cuisine and suffer accordingly in the morning.'

Despite herself, Sheena couldn't help watching their lively interchange. Even if she hadn't heard what Bess had said, she would have to be blind not to see how well matched they were. Quickly, she gathered up dirty plates and beakers.

'Oh, you've no need to do that, Miss O'Reilly,' April cried.

'That's fine, April. I'll help you clear away and then be off home. Tomorrow is a big day, is it not?' She looked up in surprise to see Harry grabbing a drying cloth.

'Well, many hands and all that,' he grinned. 'Do you not think I'll make someone the perfect husband?'

Sheena flushed. Surely he hadn't guessed her thoughts?

Suddenly the back door flew open and Black and Brown stood on the doorstep, their eyes wide with panic.

'We didn't mean to do it, honest, sir.'

'No, it was a dreadful accident.'

'What's happened?' Sheena gasped, seeing their terror-stricken faces.

'What kind of dreadful accident, Brown?' Harry asked, worry making his voice sharp.

'It was Bunter. He said it would be a bit of fun to do it,' Black stammered.

'And we didn't mean to damage anything,' Brown cried.

'Calm down and tell me exactly what's damaged?' Sheena said, a horrible suspicion forming.

'We was trying on them dresses and our juice kind of got spilled on it . . .'

25

Feeling sick to the pit of her stomach, Sheena hurried after Harry. In the classroom they found Bunter desperately rubbing one of the dresses with the cuff of his shirt, purple staining a testament to his misdeed.

'You stupid cretin, Bunter,' the master cried.

'Please stop doing that,' Sheena ordered, rushing over and taking the offending garment from his hands. 'That will only make it worse,' she explained, endeavouring to keep her composure while staring at the mess in dismay.

'Wait until I get my hands on the lot of you,' Master Higgins muttered, as Brown and Black hovered in the doorway. 'I distinctly told you not to take your juice outside and yet . . .'

'Is everything all right?' Edith called, peering anxiously over the two boys' shoulders.

'Everything is fine,' Sheena said, summoning a calm she didn't feel. Knowing she needed space to think, she added, 'Perhaps you could get the girls to wash their hands ready for supper?'

'Oh, right,' Edith muttered, unconvinced. Then with a frown at Sheena, she ran to do as she'd been asked.

'Right, you boys, not a word to the girls, do you understand me?' Sheena ordered. 'They are excited about tomorrow and you are not to spoil that. If you could take the boys indoors and out of my way, Master Higgins, I'll see if anything can be salvaged from this disaster,' she hissed, biting back her frustration.

'Are you sure I . . .' Harry began.

'Please go. The sooner I can work on the stain the better,' she insisted. 'Perhaps you could ask April if there's any sour milk in the pantry and if so, would she bring me some along with a large bowl?'

He stared at her for a moment then nodded. 'Out, now,' he ordered the anxious boys.

As the door shut behind them, Sheena stared sadly at the two ruined garments, willing herself not to cry. Sally's silk had a livid purple mark to the right of her chest while Edith's dress hadn't escaped either. Fighting back the tears, she looked up to see April, clutching a bowl in one hand and a jug in the other, pushing open the door with her bottom.

'Master Higgins said you . . . oh my Lor, whatever's 'appened?' she asked, her eyes widening in horror.

'Is that sour milk?' Sheena asked, pointing to the jug.

April nodded. 'Gone off good and proper.'

'Well, keep your fingers crossed for this is our only hope. I'll explain when I've dealt with these.' While the girl stared on, Sheena draped one dress over the bowl and poured on the soured milk.

'Do you want me to rub it in, Miss O'Reilly?' April asked, eager to help.

'No, that's the worst thing we can do. We need to let the material soak and hope the milk will break down the enzymes in the fruit,' she explained, placing the garment aside while she dealt with the next. Finally, she placed them both loosely in the bowl and sighed. 'We'd best pray the saints are looking kindly upon us, April, or I don't know what we're going to do tomorrow.'

'I suppose it was those three little Bs,' April said knowingly.

'April! I know they're high spirited but . . . Oh, I see what you mean,' Sheena said, shaking her head. 'Bunter, Brown and Black. Well, to be sure, there's nothing else we can do tonight. I'll come in early and see what can be done. In the meantime, not a word to anyone. The last thing we want is Sally being too upset to sing her solo.'

'Shall I tell Mrs Daws when she gets back?'

'Only if she discovers the milk's missing. Otherwise don't say anything. She seldom gets a night off and it would be a shame to spoil it. Now off you go and see to supper.'

Sheena waited until the door had closed behind the girl, then sank into a chair and put her head in her hands. What would she do if the stains didn't come out? All that hard work and racing to meet the deadline. Why hadn't she covered the clothes or put them away in the cupboard? It was too late to make any more. What would Miss Sullivan say if the girls had to sing in their school smocks? Sally was extremely sensitive and might be too upset to sing anyway. Round and round her thoughts went, like a dolly in the washing copper, so that she didn't hear the door open again and jumped when she felt a hand on her shoulder.

'By jeez, you scared the soul out of me, Master Higgins,' she cried.

'Just wanted to make sure you were all right,' he murmured.

'Well, I've felt better,' she admitted, blinking back the tears she was determined not to shed. Sensing her distress, he kneeled down and pulled her close. Powerless to resist, she leaned in towards him, revelling in the fresh smell of his soap and the warmth of his body. Then sanity returned and she pulled away. 'Time I wasn't here, Master Higgins,' she said shakily. Disappointment flickered in his eyes, then he became the schoolmaster again.

'Pip has just returned with the trap. I've asked him to wait outside and take you home. I'd escort you myself but regrettably I'm in charge of the rabble this evening.'

Not having the strength to argue, she nodded. 'Thank you. I'll be back at first light to see what I can do with this . . . mess,' she muttered, gesturing helplessly to the bowl where the dresses were soaking.

'The boys have been severely reprimanded and will be punished accordingly, you can be certain of that,' he assured her.

Forcing her lips into some semblance of a smile, she nodded and snatched up her coat.

True to her word, as fingers of grey and pink lightened the sky to the east, Sheena let herself into the classroom. Carefully lifting the dresses from the bowl, she took them outside to the yard where she gently sponged off the now dark purple milk. She didn't dare wash the garments for they'd never dry in time. Holding up them up to the light, she surveyed the damage. The stain in both dresses had faded, but it was evident that little more could be done. Damage limitation was her only option.

Back in the classroom, Pip had already lit the fire and

Sheena spread the garments over the fireguard to dry. Then, picking up the bolero, she held it against Edith's dress. As she'd hoped, the little jacket would cover the worst of the discoloured patch. However, there was nothing more she could do to Sally's dress, for the delicate silk would pucker or worse, fray, if she wasn't careful, while sunshine would discolour the material. Why couldn't it have been one of the other dresses? she groaned. Slumping down in a chair, she pondered what on earth she could do. Then a tap on the door roused her from her thoughts. Fearing it was Harry, she swallowed hard. After her lapse last night, she didn't feel strong enough to face him.

'I thought you'd like some tea, Miss O'Reilly,' Edith said, setting a cup and saucer carefully down on the desk in front of her.

'Oh, Edith, you are an angel,' Sheena cried with a mixture of relief and gratitude. 'A hot drink is just what I'm needing.'

Edith looked at the clothes on the guard. 'Did the sour milk work?'

'You know about that?' Sheena asked, not really surprised, for word spread around the school faster than a gorse fire on the moors.

'I knew something was up and quizzed April until she told me. She swore me to secrecy, though, and I ain't told a soul. Oh bloody Nora,' she cried, spotting her dress. 'All me 'ard work gone, just like that.' She clicked her fingers. 'Them ruddy, stupid boys. Wait till I get me 'ands on them.'

'Don't upset yourself, Edith,' Sheena soothed. 'Although the stains are still visible, I'm hopeful the bolero will hide

267

the worst of yours. But poor Sally's, well, you can see for yourself. I was thinking of trying a paste of flour and water to see if that would help.'

'That silk is so fragile, though, miss, you might rub a hole in it,' Edith frowned.

'Well, I'm afraid there isn't any of the same material left to cover it either.'

Edith stared at the stain thoughtfully. 'Sally's the star of the concert so we can't let her down,' she stated, going over to the donations box and pulling out the various garments. 'You know, miss, we could use this shiny material to make one of them material cor . . . corsi, oh what's the word? You know, them flower thingys that posh people wear on their frocks.'

'A corsage, you mean?' Sheena said, looking thoughtful. Then she sprang to her feet and kissed Edith's cheek. 'My clever angel. Why, that's the very thing.'

As Sally's sweet voice resounded around the church, the congregation stood in rapt silence. Ruby rays of evening sun shining through the stained-glass windows cast a rosy aura over her fluff of fair hair and slender figure wearing the fated silk dress with its contrasting corsage. Sarah and Sheena exchanged smiles, their hearts filled with pride. Perfume from the spring flowers the good ladies had arranged seemingly everywhere mingled with the spicy tang of incense, adding to the festive atmosphere.

The children, boys wearing their red waistcoats, girls their new dresses, gave a perfect, if rousing rendition of 'There Is a Green Hill Far Away'. When June and Monday chose to give an impromptu twirl at the end, provoking a chuckle from the parishioners, the vicar gave a tolerant smile and thanked them all for their inspiring performance. A mix of songs and hymns followed, then, almost before they knew it, the organ swelled and the concert was over.

'Oh, they did look a treat,' Mrs Daws murmured, dabbing her eyes with her handkerchief as the Red Cliffs party filed out of the church.

'Ah, Miss Sullivan, may I say how splendidly your pupils sang. Sally, like a nightingale and the rest as enthusiastic as ever,' the vicar beamed. 'You will all be joining us in the hall for refreshments, I hope?'

'Thank you, Vicar,' Sarah replied.

'Splendid,' Miss Snooper cried. 'Follow me, troops,' she ordered, leading the way down the path, closely followed by Misses Prior and Middle.

'I do believe the good ladies think they are in charge of our pupils, Miss Sullivan,' Harry whispered.

'And after what I heard went on in my absence last night, they are more than welcome,' Sarah replied. 'I understand it was your quick thinking that saved the day,' she added, turning to Sheena.

'It was Edith who thought of making the corsage this morning, and helped me fashion it,' Sheena admitted.

'But you who stayed late to remove the stains, Miss O'Reilly,' Harry pointed out, giving her a warm smile.

'It all came out in the wash. Well, some of it, anyway,' Sheena laughed.

'And don't the girls look a picture in their new frocks? It's lovely to see them with some 'air an' all, even if I did have me doubts at first,' Mrs Laver said.

'If we want a chance of getting something to eat, I think perhaps we'd better get a move on. Those vultures will scoff the lot if we're not careful,' Harry cried.

The hall had also been adorned with floral arrangements, and a long row of cloth-covered trestles laden with bite-sized savouries lined one wall. The good ladies were bustling around marshalling everybody into place.

'I see they have organized the children as well as the food,' Sarah said, nodding towards the orderly queue.

'If only they'd behave like that in school,' Mrs Daws moaned.

'Yes, I was thinking after yesterday's fiasco that more discipline might be a good idea,' Sarah said, waving a finger at Harry. 'I mean things are getting very lax around here,' she added, trying to keep a straight face.

'Really, Miss Sullivan?' Harry cried. 'After all you've said about my outmoded methods, too.'

'Yes, really, Master Higgins. Honestly, you wouldn't believe how standards have slipped recently, Miss O'Reilly,' Sarah teased.

Seeing them resume their easy banter, Sheena's euphoria evaporated like dew in the sunshine. It was like a constant thorn in her side. Now that the girls had finished their new outfits perhaps it was time to seek another position.

'Ha, you wait until you see those boys emptying the privy and digging its contents into the vegetable plot, then you'll see what happens to pupils who disobey my orders.'

'Really, Master Higgins, that is not an appropriate topic of conversation for supper.'

'Supper? Why, those bite-sized morsels wouldn't even feed the little people, would they, Miss O'Reilly?' he groaned, raising his brow theatrically.

'Don't you worry, Master Higgins, knowing the good ladies set more store by appearances than appetite, I've left a nice stew cooking for later.'

'Oh, Mrs Daws, I could kiss you,' he cried. As the housekeeper flushed with pleasure, he added, 'Ah, look sharp, I do believe it's our turn to choose one of the fairy folks' portions to nibble on.'

When they'd selected their food, they made their way to chairs arranged along the other side of the hall and whilst they ate, they listened to the babble of conversation going on around them.

'I must say, it is good to see those girls actually looking like girls rather than their usual barbaric appearance,' they heard a lady dressed in fur coat and matching hat say.

'I have to agree,' her companion replied. 'Although it's still a crying shame we have to share the street with a ragged school. Have you seen their place? Gone to rack and ruin. It quite lets the neighbourhood down . . . Oh, Vicar, what a lovely concert that was,' she cooed. 'And don't the children look lovely?'

'Well, of all the hypocritical . . .' Sheena began, only to stutter to a halt as words failed her.

'Don't worry, you'll get used to it,' Sarah whispered.

'But look at all you're doing to improve conditions for them,' Sheena replied. 'To be sure, those children are a credit to you, are they not?' she asked, gesturing to where the pupils quietly sat eating their food.

'The girls are so proud of their new dresses they've

even put serviettes over their laps.' Sarah smiled as she turned back to Sheena. 'Well done, Miss O'Reilly. I know it wasn't an easy task getting their outfits completed by today, especially without a machine. I expect you're wondering what to do next?'

'Well, actually . . .' Sheena began, only to be interrupted by the sound of a teaspoon being rattled against a milk jug.

'Ladies, gentlemen, girls and boys,' the vicar cried. 'I would like to thank you all for coming to our Easter concert and supper and for making it such a success. A big thank you to all our young participants who entertained us in fine voice, and to the good ladies for putting on such a splendid feast.' There was a polite round of applause. Then, as it died away, Edith sprang to her feet.

'And we must say thanks to Miss O'Reilly 'cos she 'elped us make our dresses and came in early this morning to get the blackcurrant juice stain out of them.'

'Here, here,' Harry cried. This time the applause was almost deafening. As Sheena felt her cheeks grow hot, Sarah turned towards her.

'I think you can say your place at Red Cliffs is well and truly established, Miss O'Reilly.'

26

Sheena made her way towards Red Cliffs after Easter, her grandmother's warning still ringing in her ears. Whilst moral courage was all well and good, she'd told Sheena, it didn't mean prolonging suffering unnecessarily. And she wouldn't, she vowed, lifting her head to the late morning sun, which was surprisingly warm for early April.

The promenade was thronging with holidaymakers. Affluent gentlemen with bespoke tailored suits, frock coats and toppers, proudly escorted ladies sporting elaborate hats and fur stoles thrown carelessly over their cashmere coats. Sheena shuddered at the fox's head in front, its dark eyes glinting at her in the sunlight as it swung from the woman's shoulders. The cherry-red scarf she'd knitted was decidedly more tasteful, Sheena decided. Others were more modestly attired with capes worn over their woollen dresses, but everyone seemed to be smiling as they took advantage of the clement weather.

Squaring her shoulders, Sheena resolved to speak to Miss Sullivan about her intention of finding a new position. After all, she wouldn't be leaving a job half done, for the girls had their new dresses now, didn't they?

'Miss Sullivan asked if you would go and see 'er as soon as you arrived, Miss O'Reilly,' Pip told her as she walked up to the school gates. Well, great minds think alike, Sheena thought.

'Hope I've done nothing wrong,' she quipped as Pip hobbled over to let her in.

'Hardly, miss. Everyone seems to think you was an 'ero, the way you saved them dresses. Mind you, Master Higgins is making those boys pay for disobeying 'im, I can tell you. They've had to muck out the pony's stable as well as the privy.'

Smiling at his words, Sheena made her way up the driveway towards the front door. She could see that progress had been made on the shed but of Harry there was no sign. Probably supervising luncheon, she surmised, not sure if she was pleased or disappointed.

'Ah, do come in and take a seat, Miss O'Reilly,' Sarah said, looking up from a letter she'd been reading. 'I hope you had a pleasant Easter?'

'Yes, thank you. Nanna and I enjoyed having time to catch up on our news.' Well, that was true, for they'd spent the day discussing Sheena's future.

'Good. Now, we never finished our conversation about your next project with the girls.'

'No, we didn't, Miss Sullivan, and I would like . . .' Sheena began, but Sarah was excitedly holding out the letter for her to see.

'I have just received the most splendid news, Miss O'Reilly. Red Cliffs has been bequeathed a sewing machine and a piano. Is that not the most exciting thing?'

'Er, yes, to be sure . . .'

But Miss Sullivan, bursting to share her news, carried on oblivious.

'The sewing machine could make all the difference. As you know, Red Cliffs is still under scrutiny for the state of the building. Now the roof has been repaired – I'm hoping successfully, although we've had no real rain to test it – my remaining concern is the state of the children's bedding. I'm sure you will have noticed it is all way past its best.'

Sheena nodded. 'I have, Miss Sullivan, but . . .'

However, Sarah, still in full flood, didn't hear.

'Well, Mrs Knight, the dear lady who left us these things, has also bequeathed a large quantity of cotton material. Now in order to bring their dormitories up to the required standard, I thought you could set the girls to work on sewing new sheets and coverlets. What do you think, Miss O'Reilly?'

'It's a sound idea, but . . .'

'I know what you are going to say and I agree: you will be up against it again timewise with the inspection due at the end of next month. However, you have proven to be most capable and the girls respond well to the way you teach. So, Miss O'Reilly, do you think you could help us pass the next inspection?' As Sarah finally paused for breath and sat staring hopefully, Sheena gulped. How could she possibly let the children down, she thought, her new-found resolve disappearing fast.

'There are three dormitories, are there not?' she asked, recalling the layout of upstairs.

'Yes, and I do realize it's a tall order. However, I will, of course, do my bit when I take the girls on a Saturday afternoon, although I do have a couple of meetings coming up.' Sarah paused and frowned. 'Still, between us, I'm sure we will have the job done in time and imagine how wonderful the rooms will look.' It was then that Sheena realized the other woman had assumed she'd agreed to the project.

'Well, you'd better show me this sewing machine,' she said, forcing a cheerfulness she didn't feel.

As they made their way towards the classroom, the children, having finished their meal and lunchtime chores, were playing outside in the sunshine. Harry Higgins was supervising and his face broke into a smile at their approach. Despite herself, Sheena felt her insides tilting.

'Ah, Master Higgins, I've just been telling Miss O'Reilly about our good fortune.'

'A wonderful gesture from a very kind-hearted lady,' he said gravely. 'And I understand it is to be put to good use straight away, Miss O'Reilly,' he added, turning his gaze on Sheena.

'So it would appear, Master Higgins,' Sheena agreed. 'I understand I have less than two months to complete everything, so if you'll excuse me I'd better make a start.'

'Before you go, there is something I'd like to ask. After Easter, we always recommence the children's outdoor fitness regime. Principally this involves sea bathing and, as Miss Sullivan has declined to join us, I wondered if I could seek your assistance?'

'Mine?' Sheena frowned.

'You do swim?' he persisted.

'Of course. There is no better exercise.'

'That's debatable,' Sarah murmured. 'Well, if you're sure, Miss O'Reilly, I'll leave you to discuss the arrangements with Master Higgins after classes. I'm off to a meeting of the NUWSS and am already running late. Nevertheless, I would like to show you the sewing machine before I go.'

Sheena stared helplessly from the master to the principal and knew just how a caged bird felt.

However, when Sarah uncovered the black and gold machine with its needle already threaded, Sheena couldn't help but reach out and stroke its glossy surface.

'I can see you're as thrilled as I am,' Sarah smiled. 'Now the girls are heading this way, so I'll leave you to introduce them to the wonders of machine sewing. I'm sure they'll be excited. In fact, you'll probably have a fight on your hands as to who can have first go.'

Sheena smiled politely then watched as the woman strode from the room to be replaced by the gaggle of giggling girls.

'Good afternoon, my angels. This afternoon you are in for a treat for do I not have something wonderful here to show you?' she said, gesturing to the machine. 'With the help of this wonderful sewing appliance, we are going to turn these lovely crisp piles of material into new bedding for the dormitories. Now won't that be grand?' To her surprise, this announcement was met with looks of dismay.

'But we wanted to make a flowery thing like Sally's to go on our dresses,' Ellen cried.

'Yeth, one of them corsets,' June lisped.

'The word is corsage, June,' Sheena corrected. She stared at their long faces and felt a growing sympathy. Bedding, whilst essential, must seem very boring to them compared with fancy furbelows. 'All right, my lovelies, this is what we'll do. First of all, I'll demonstrate how to run up a seam using the machine. Then, once you've got the idea, you can each choose some material from the donations box to make a corsage.'

'Yeth!' June cried, jumping up and down in excitement.

'Me wants one just like April,' Monday said, gazing adoringly at the girl.

'Steady on, I ain't chosen my material yet,' April grinned. 'But it would be lovely if it matched this ribbon Edith made for my anniversary present,' she said, pulling out a length of green velvet that had been edged and neatly stitched.

'Why, that's lovely, April, and I'm sure we can find something similar later. Remind me at the end of the lesson that I, too, have something for you.' As April beamed, she hastily added, 'First, though, let's discover the wonders of this lovely machine that Mr Singer designed. Now has anyone used one before?'

'Nah,' Edith cried. 'Them costs a lot of money, them does.'

'Indeed they do, and this is a wonderful opportunity for you to learn how to use one, is it not? Now, you can see the cotton on the reel runs here and through the eye of the needle. Under this little flap is the bobbin, which is also threaded.'

'Why?' Edith asked.

'When it's your turn to have a go I will take you through the whys and wherefores, but if you want to have time to make your corsages, you'd better watch me demonstrate for now.' Taking up an old sheet, she carefully folded it in half and positioned it under the foot then carefully she put her feet on the treadle.

'Sounds like a train,' Maggie said. 'Only very slow.'

'To be sure, it's all modern machinery, Maggie,' Sheena replied. 'Using your feet to work the machine thus, your hands are free to carefully guide the material.'

After the initial interest, Sheena could feel the attention of the younger ones wandering. When their gazes fixed longingly on the donations box, she knew it was time to let them have their way. Hoping they'd at least grasped the mechanics of her lesson, she began covering the machine. Taking this as their signal, the girls jumped to their feet, eager to be first to choose their fabric.

'Can I have a go, miss?' Edith asked, while the others rummaged in the box for their material. Seeing the girl's hopeful look, Sheena agreed.

'Sit down here then and I'll take you through it again.' However, to Sheena's surprise, Edith had remembered most of what she'd seen and hardly needed any guidance. They became so engrossed with the machine that the chiming of the clock took her by surprise.

'Now, my angels,' Sheena said, 'have you all made your selection?'

'Yes,' they chorused, staring at her expectantly.

'Well, that's good. However, I'm afraid time has beaten us today.' As a groan went around the room, she held up her hand. 'Next lesson, though, we'll be sure to start on your flowers.' Somewhat mollified, they packed away and filed from the room.

'Now, April, did you have a lovely party?' she asked, turning to the waiting girl.

'Oh, I did, thank you, miss. Mrs Daws made me a cake of me very own. There was a big one to share with everyone and a little one for me. She's that clever. Miss Sullivan and Master Higgins gave me a silver mirror with a handle so I can see to put my powder on. It's not brand-new, of course, but I love it.'

'Well, that is grand, April, and may I say how well you are now applying it, for the powder is barely visible.'

'Now I know you're not meant to see it, I uses less. Pip said he only knows I've got it on 'cos me scar ain't so noticeable.'

Sheena smiled. 'To be sure, that's brilliant, April, for you are the prettiest girl, are you not?' At her words, April flushed with pleasure. 'Right now, shall we see what I can find for you?' Sheena said, digging into her bag and pulling out a beribboned parcel.

'Oh, miss, it's gorgeous,' she cried, staring down at the turquoise satin chemise Sheena had made for her.

'Well, you're a lovely young lady and beautiful women need pretty things to wear,' Sheena told her, taking something out of her pocket. 'Oh, and Nanna has sent you another pot of her powder.'

'That's so kind of her,' April gulped. 'I've never 'ad so many nice things before.' A knock on the door made them both jump. As the master came striding into the room, April went bright red. Hastily bundling her chemise back in the paper, she fled.

'Nice to know the effect I have on you females,' Harry quipped. 'How did you get on?' he asked, jerking his head towards the machine.

'I can't deny it will speed up the sewing although the

girls weren't exactly enthusiastic at the prospect of making bedding,' Sheena admitted.

'Ah, but what a worthwhile project that will be, especially if it satisfies the inspectors. Now, about that exercise regime. When the sea has had a chance to warm up I usually take them swimming first thing in the morning. However, the water is still too cold at the moment and, being the kind-hearted man I am, I shall settle for taking them for a nice brisk walk along the front. As we are still unable to visit the farm, I thought I'd start this Saturday afternoon. Miss Sullivan has another one of her meetings, apparently, so I wondered if you'd take pity on a poor fellow and escort the girls?'

'Oh, but . . .'

'I realize it is not within your remit or working hours and understand if you are unable to. It would be a shame for the girls to miss out, though,' he added, letting out a long sigh.

'Master Higgins, that is blackmail,' she protested, laughing despite herself.

'Corruption, extortion, call it what you will, I'll plead guilty to them all, as long as you agree.' As he stood staring at her, looking for all the world like one of the schoolboys himself, she shook her head.

'All right then, but purely for the sake of the girls' wellbeing,' she replied, ignoring the way the butterflies were skittering around her stomach at the prospect.

So much for your resolve, Sheena O'Reilly, she chided herself.

*

'I thought you weren't coming,' Josephine greeted Sarah, as she hastily slid into the seat opposite her friend in the little café.

'Sorry, I was delayed getting away,' she replied, taking a surreptitious look around.

'It's all right, he's sitting two tables to your right,' Josephine laughed.

'Who?' Sarah asked, feigning innocence as she picked up the menu.

'Bertram J. Brightling, of course, and don't pretend to be reading that when you're scanning the room over the top of it,' her friend laughed, taking the menu from her. Just then the waitress came over, pad and pencil poised, to take their order. 'We'll have our usual pot of tea with a Devon Chudleigh each,' Josephine told her, emphasizing the word 'usual'.

'After our last meeting on the founding of Parish and District Councils, I decided to look into the 1894 Act,' Sarah began.

'Makes a change from looking at that handsome fellow, who, by the way, has spent the last five minutes staring at you and is now avidly scribbling in that notebook of his. I wonder what he is writing. A sonnet, perhaps? Just imagine, "An Ode to Sarah Sullivan",' Josephine grinned and waggled her brows outrageously.

'Josephine Harmon, you have the most fertile imagination,' Sarah cried. Her reply came out louder than she'd intended, and the ladies at the next table looked at her curiously. Josephine giggled delightedly at her discomfort.

'And the man doth affect you somewhat, me thinks.'

Thankfully, however, the waitress arrived and as she began setting their cups and plates on the table, Sarah took the opportunity to look around. Just as her friend had said, Bertram J. Brightling was sitting at a table close by, writing rapidly in his book. Today he was wearing a tweed jacket in muted mauves that reminded Sarah of heather on the moors. Then, as if sensing her gaze, he looked up and smiled. Boldly she nodded back before turning her attention to her refreshments.

Josephine looked at her knowingly but didn't comment, and for the next twenty minutes or so they set to debating how, as suffragists, they could help spread the word about the movement and its aim to achieve the rights for women they both strongly believed in. Both had taken to heart the words of Mrs Thomas Taylor, who'd publicly announced: 'There are hundreds and thousands of women who do care for the suffrage; but there are millions who not only do not care, but who have, many of them, never heard of it, and certainly do not realize what it means.'

'It's a tall order but we now know exactly what our mission is, don't we?' Josephine said.

'Indeed. It is a changing world and men need to understand the days of snapping their fingers and women jumping are over,' Sarah told her friend, who instead of agreeing as usual, was grinning like the proverbial Cheshire cat. Sarah jumped as a folded piece of paper was placed on the table in front of her.

'Oh,' she gasped, looking up into clear blue eyes. But Bertram merely doffed his deerstalker politely and sauntered out of the café.

'Well, aren't you going to see what it says?' Josephine asked.

Sarah unfolded the note and scanned the contents.

'Good grief, he's invited me for afternoon tea at the Grand,' she gasped.

27

It was Saturday afternoon and Sheena was helping Master Higgins escort the children along the seafront for their constitutional. They were all excited by the outing, especially the girls, who'd been given permission to wear their new outfits complete with the corsages they'd finished making the previous day.

Although Sheena had been apprehensive at the thought of being in Harry's company, he was proving to be an entertaining companion.

'Inhale deeply of the ozone, Miss O'Reilly,' Master Higgins ordered.

Sheena nodded and did as he suggested.

'It is good to see them happy and healthy, is it not, Master Higgins?' she smiled, watching the youngsters chasing each other over the golden sands. 'Even young Solomon seems revitalized.'

'Well, Torquay is renowned for being a place of recovery,' he replied. 'In fact the motto on its Royal Charter – which, in case you're interested, was granted in 1892 – is *Salus et Felicitas*, which means Health and Happiness. Right, come along, you lot,' he called. 'Time to head back.'

While they waited for the reluctant children to join them back on the promenade, Sheena studied the large white properties hugging the cliffs.

'Isn't it funny that all those houses overlook the water, yet only some have windows to see the view?'

'Not really, Miss O'Reilly. They were built at a time when the original owners, and more recently visiting invalids, preferred residences that offered shelter from the withering south-easterly gales,' Harry explained.

'Most of the cottages where I come from have solid gables facing towards the south-west winds for the same reason,' Sheena replied.

'It's only been latterly that views have become a priority for the tourist. Of course, now you can see that the new properties popping up like mushrooms all over the place take advantage of the vista.'

'That is good, isn't it?' she asked.

He shrugged. 'For the rich, yes. However, as the demand for a sea views grows, rental prices are increasing as well. Some landladies have been known to push their poorer tenants out of their homes so that they can let the rooms to more affluent tourists.'

'But that's disgraceful,' Sheena cried. 'Where do they go?'

'Economics force them into cheaper housing, further out of town. Now, that's enough depressing talk for a sunny afternoon,' he said, seeing her look of dismay. 'To give the children fair exercise, I usually head back the long way via the Bath Saloons, then on through Rock Walk. Not that you should walk through there by night, Miss O'Reilly, for it's frequented by those ladies of ill repute,' Harry warned.

Sheena saw the colour rising above his collar and smiled to herself. So, Master Higgins was not really a man of the world, then.

286

'That was where Miss Sullivan found Kitty sheltering Luke,' he added.

'Oh, the poor wee angels,' Sheena cried. She was about to ask him about the circumstances leading up to that but the schoolmaster was already gesturing to the children to lead the way.

'Do you ever take them bathing at the Saloon?' Sheena asked, remembering his comment about the sea being too cold at this time of year.

He gave a snort. 'Our dear neighbours would have something to say about that, Miss O'Reilly.'

'Then perhaps it's time to show those charming people a thing or two,' she replied. Seeing his frown and not wishing to spoil their excursion, she went on quickly, making a sweep of the bay with her hand, 'It's great to be outside enjoying all this scenery.'

'I have to confess to be rather enjoying that myself, Miss O'Reilly. In fact, I would say the scenery appears even prettier than usual today,' he added, staring at Sheena meaningfully. She turned away and pointed to where the crocodile of children had come to a halt outside the Saloon.

'To be sure, with their hair having grown a little bit, the girls are looking quite angelic,' she said.

'Yet looks can be deceptive, can they not, Miss O'Reilly?' he replied, just as Brown and Black came running over.

'We need to go to the lavatory, Master Higgins,' Black cried.

'Desperately,' Brown added, hopping up and down for good measure.

'How amazing this always happens just as we reach the Saloon,' Harry replied. 'Perhaps we should go and make use of nature's facilities.' As he gestured to the avenue of lime trees beyond, Black pulled a face.

'But I need a number two,' he wailed.

Harry raised his brows. 'Right, boys, who needs to go to the lavatory?' Apart from Solomon, the boys all waved their hands in the air. 'Perhaps you could come and make sure they don't run off, Solomon,' he suggested, then turned to Sheena.

'Excuse us, will you?'

She nodded. 'Any of you need the lavatory, girls?' she asked.

'We're not babies, miss,' Maggie scoffed.

'No, we went before we came out,' Monday told her. 'That woman's waving to you, miss,' she added, pointing at a brightly dressed woman of indeterminate years who was approaching.

'Excuse me, ducks. I couldn't help noticing these delightful children's clothes. My, don't you all look smart?' she gushed, her sparkly earrings swinging back and forth as she waved her arm in their direction.

'Why, thank you,' Sheena replied as the girls beamed proudly.

'It's this girl's outfit that has caught my eye, though,' the woman said, turning to Edith. 'Would you mind if I asked where you purchased it, ducks?'

'I made it, missus,' Edith announced, puffing her chest out proudly.

The woman raised an eyebrow and took a closer look. 'Are you telling me this stitching was done by you? That you made these stylish garments from scratch?' she enquired, gesturing to the dress and bolero.

'Nah, we had to unpick a frock from the donations box and rework it to fit. Miss made us patterns to follow but I did all me own sewing.'

'Is this true?' the woman asked, focusing silver-grey eyes on Sheena.

'Indeed it is. Why is something wrong, Mrs . . . ?'

'Spangles, ducks, 'cos of me dangles,' she laughed, pointing to her earrings. 'Everyone calls me Sylvie, though. If what you're telling me is true, then this girl could be the answer to my prayers. I'm the costumier for the Gaiety Theatre, as well as productions at the Bath Saloons, for my sins. Anyhow, my assistant has seen fit to do a run— I mean, leave me high and dry, and now I'm frantically trying to get all the outfits ready for the cast. We open come Whitsun, see.'

'Coo, I could help you with that,' Edith cried, her eyes lighting up.

As the others crowded around to hear what was going on, Sheena smiled politely.

'Calm down, Edith,' she said gently, then turned to the lady. 'Mrs Spangles, I am Miss O'Reilly, the travelling mistress of Red Cliffs Ragged School.'

'Charmed, I'm sure, ducks. I got one of me cards in here,' she said, rummaging in her capacious carpet bag. 'Ah, here it is. Confirms who I am and where the theatre is,' she beamed.

'It's not your integrity I'm questioning,' Sheena assured her. 'Edith here is only nine years . . .'

'I'm ten in two weeks,' Edith cried. 'I've always wanted a job like that. 'Ow much would you pay?' she persisted.

The woman chuckled. 'Seems like she knows her own mind, Miss O'Reilly, and if Edith can sew like this at her tender years then she's found her vocation already. Should she want to work in the industry, she'd have no better chance of gaining experience. I'm the best in the business, even if I do say so myself. Perhaps you'd like to come and see the theatre?'

'Oh, please say yes, miss,' Edith gasped.

Sheena swallowed, undecided what to do. She had no authority, after all. To her relief, she saw Harry and the boys emerging from the Bath Saloons.

'We'll ask Master Higgins,' she said.

'Ooh, he looks nice. Is he your fella?' Sylvie Spangles asked.

The girls tittered delightedly and Sheena gave them a warning look. 'Good heavens no,' she spluttered.

'Shame, he looks a good 'un,' the woman replied, nudging Sheena in the ribs. 'You'd get on well together, ducks, if you know what I mean.'

'Is everything all right?' Harry asked, looking at Sheena questioningly.

'Mrs Spangles thought you were Miss O'Reilly's fella,' Maggie giggled.

'This is Mrs Spangles, Master Higgins,' Sheena said quickly. 'She came over to compliment the girls on their dresses.'

'And she wants me to 'elp her with the costumes for the theatre. I can, can't I, sir?' Edith begged.

'This is Master Higgins, from Red Cliffs,' Sheena said, turning to the woman. 'Pleased to meet you, Mrs Spangles,' Harry nodded politely.

'Likewise, I'm sure,' the woman grinned. 'Now this young lady here tells me she wants to work with costumes when she grows up. I need a helper and she would benefit from the experience, so what do you say to me showing young Edith and Miss O'Reilly where she'd be working, young man?'

At this the children burst out laughing.

'But thir's an old man,' June lisped.

'Thank you, June,' Harry replied. 'What do you think, Miss O'Reilly?' he asked turning to Sheena.

'Please, please, please, say yes,' Edith pleaded.

Seeing the desperation in the girl's eyes, Sheena nodded.

'If you can take the children back to the school, I'll be happy to see exactly where Mrs Spangles works. Then, at least I can report back to Miss Sullivan.'

As Harry led the children away, Sheena, with Edith hopping excitedly at her side, accompanied Sylvie Spangles away from the harbour, before turning right and stopping outside a large building with arched doorways. Large framed posters advertising the forthcoming production adorned the walls, but before they had a chance to study them, a uniformed doorman came towards them doffing his hat.

'Good afternoon, Sylvie,' he said, opening a side door for them.

'It could be now, Alf,' she replied, hurrying inside. The large domed foyer, hung with chandeliers, smelled of beeswax and tobacco. As Sheena and Edith stared around in awe, Sylvie Spangles disappeared through another door.

'Welcome to bedlam, ducks,' she called, gesturing to a large table draped with all manner of fabric, ribbons and furbelows. Wicker hampers spilling with clothes sat on the floor whilst the walls were lined with shoes and boots.

'It's always like this before a new play. Our producer's using a new writer and he's a perfectionist; insists the devil's in the detail. Anyhow, he's changed the leading lady's outfits at least three times. I can't deny it gets frantic but you'll never get better experience of putting costumes together, ducks,' she told Edith.

'I think it's all wonderful. When can I start?'

'Wait a moment, young lady,' Sheena cautioned, trying not to smile. There was no denying Edith was already in her element. 'You say you put together costumes, Mrs Spangles, so what exactly would Edith be required to do?'

'Well, most of them actors hire their outfits these days and it's my job to see that all their costumes are tailored to fit . . .'

'Like we did at school, miss,' Edith cried.

'Of course, we have to be careful not to cut material unless we really have to. It's more a case of adapting the shape by resewing seams, taking up or letting down hems. When I worked in Shaftesbury Avenue, we had to remember the three Rs: rework, recolour, reworn, which just about sums everything up. Of course, the fun is in adding the sparkle and glitz, but there's the boring side, too. Actors and actresses are notorious for ripping something just before the curtain goes up.'

'I don't mind what I do!' Edith cried. 'I can work with Mrs Spangles, can't I?' Edith asked, turning to Sheena.

'You'd have to continue your schooling,' Sheena reminded her.

'I'll work extra 'ard, promise. Not that it'll do much good 'cos I'm useless at English and 'rithmetic,' she sighed. 'Still, I won't need them if I'm to work here, will I?'

'Now that's where you're wrong, ducks,' Sylvie Spangles smiled. 'A good costumier keeps a book of all her customers' measurements so you'll need to be able to write names and numerals clearly.'

'Well, I will work extra 'ard in class then,' Edith promised.

'Perhaps we could agree on the young lady working some afternoons and at the weekend so she can continue her lessons?' Sylvie suggested.

'I'll have to discuss it with Miss Sullivan, and I'm sure she'll want to meet you, Mrs Spangles, but in principle I can't see why it couldn't work. As you say, the experience would be invaluable for Edith's future.'

'And I'll get paid?' Edith asked anxiously.

'You'll get a fair wage, young lady,' Mrs Spangles assured her. 'Perhaps Miss Sullivan would like to bring Edith here to see what she'll be doing and I can discuss money with her then?'

'Thank you,' Sheena replied. 'Come along, Edith, I'm sure Mrs Spangles has work to be getting on with, and we need to speak with Miss Sullivan.'

Having attended a lively meeting of the NUWSS, Sarah and Josephine were walking back along the seafront.

'Well, you must have worked up an appetite after all that,' Josephine grinned, stopping outside the entrance to the Grand Hotel.

'I really can't decide whether to go in or not,' Sarah confessed, staring nervously at the elegant building.

'What! You can't tell me you put on your best dress for the benefit of a group of women,' Josephine scoffed.

'Well, I . . .' Sarah stuttered to a halt. In truth, she'd been wavering ever since she'd read the note from Bertram J. Brightling. On the one hand she found him fascinating and was keen to get to know him better, on the other she felt it would be too intimidating entering such a plush place. Still undecided, she had dressed carefully, yet here she was, dithering. Before she knew it, her friend had opened the door and pushed her inside.

'No,' she protested, but it was too late. A uniformed man had approached and was smiling askance.

'Oh, I'm meeting a Mr Brightling for afternoon tea,' she told him.

'Of course, madam. You may leave your coat in the cloakroom over there,' he replied. Knowing there was no going back, she nodded her thanks and walked briskly through the door he'd indicated. The room was larger than their lounge at Red Cliffs and plushly carpeted in deep burgundy. After having handed over her coat to the attendant, she hastily tidied her hair then, heart thumping like a drum, made her way through to the dining room. She just had time to take in the far-reaching views over the bay before a waiter approached and escorted her to a table where Bertram was waiting.

'I am delighted you could join me,' he said, getting to his feet As Sarah stared into Bertram's earnest blue eyes, she could see his sincerity and began to relax at last.

'It was kind of you to invite me,' she replied. Suddenly

she was looking forward to finding out more about BJ, as she and Josephine had nicknamed him. She was also eager to experience first-hand the splendid cuisine the hotel was renowned for.

'It's a delightful place,' she added as soon as the waiter had poured their tea. She took a sip and tried not to stare longingly at the finger sandwiches of smoked salmon adorned with slivers of cucumber, or the dainty fancies artistically arranged on a tiered glass stand in front of them. Should she help herself or wait to be offered, she wondered. Deciding the latter would be polite, she took a discreet look around the room while she waited.

A man in white jacket and bow tie was playing the piano at one end of the room, and the atmosphere was genteel. The other tables were discreetly placed a respectable distance apart, and the ladies, partially hidden by the huge potted ferns that seemed to predominate, were elegantly coiffured and wearing stylish afternoon frocks. Sarah hoped she didn't look out of place in her navy dress with its lace collar. Feeling his gaze upon her, she turned back to her host.

'Miss Sullivan, or would it be too forward to call you Sarah?' Bertram asked.

'Sarah will be fine,' she replied.

'Sarah, I have to confess to having been fascinated since the first time I saw you,' he confessed, looking somewhat awkward and ill at ease. He cleared his throat. 'You are like no other woman I have met before, with your English rose complexion and . . .' His voice trailed off and, seeing the colour creeping up his neck, Sarah looked politely away.

She sat sipping her tea and watching people in their finery promenading along the front, casting her mind around for something to say in return. Suddenly she gave a gasp and hastily put down her cup. Ignoring Bertram's puzzled look, she snatched up her reticule, mumbled her apologies and hurried out of the hotel.

28

The road outside the hotel was thronging with cabs drawing up and porters waiting to help unload their passengers' trunks. Desperately Sarah scanned the promenade through the gaps in the passing traffic, but of Kitty there was no sign. She dashed across the road and hurried in the direction of the harbour, the way she'd been sure she'd seen her heading. After walking for some minutes without another glimpse, she was just wondering if she'd dreamed seeing the girl when someone called her name.

'Miss Sullivan, wait.' Looking up, she saw Edith running towards her, Miss O'Reilly hot on her heels.

'Edith, Miss O'Reilly, what are you doing here? Is everything all right?'

'Miss, it's the bestest thing ever,' Edith cried. 'I've got a job and you can come and see where I'll be working.'

Sarah frowned then looked askance at Miss O'Reilly.

'Edith, you're so excited, it would probably be better if you let me explain things to Miss Sullivan,' Sheena smiled, but as she began telling Sarah about their meeting with Sylvie Spangles, the other woman frowned.

'Forgive me, Miss O'Reilly, but I have something important on my mind right now. Can we speak back at Red Cliffs?'

'But, miss, this is really important,' Edith cried, tugging at Sarah's arm.

'Very well,' Sarah sighed, knowing she had no chance of catching up with Kitty now, always supposing it had been her she'd seen. 'You were saying, Miss O'Reilly?'

'That I told Mrs Spangles I had no authority, and would have to discuss things with you, Miss Sullivan,' Sheena explained. 'But the woman seems a genuine soul and it would be a wonderful opportunity for Edith to gain experience in costume making.'

'And I'd be earning some good lucre so could 'elp you with the running of the school,' Edith added sagely. 'The theatre's just beyond the end of the prom, so please, please, say you'll come and see her now?' Edith begged.

Before casting one more desperate look round for Kitty, Sarah looked into the girl's shining eyes and nodded.

'Very well, show me the way then. But I'm not making any promises, mind,' she told them. As she assumed the mantle of proprietress once more, all thought of Bertram J. Brightling disappeared from her mind.

'To think, come Monday our Edith is going to be working as an assistant costumier,' the housekeeper murmured, cup of tea balancing on her lap as she sat with her feet up beside the range.

'I rather fear she'll be more of a runner, Mrs Daws,' Harry replied. 'Although I have to say from the brief conversation I had with the woman, she did strike me as being genuine. A colourful character, but sincere.'

'I was sceptical at first but when Mrs Spangles explained how important it was for Edith to continue learning her arithmetic and English, I could see she had the child's best interest at heart. Miss O'Reilly thought it a good idea, too,' said Sarah.

'So Edith will still attend my lessons?' Harry asked.

'Most definitely. It was agreed that she will work at the Gaiety three afternoons a week and longer on Saturdays. I shall take her there on Monday to satisfy myself all is well, then Pip can run her back and forth in the trap each time.'

'The Gaiety, eh? Long time since I've been there. Mrs Laver and I used to go to the odd matinée when the good doctor was still alive.'

'And I'm sure you can again, Mrs Daws,' Sarah told her. 'With Edith not available to help, Miss O'Reilly has kindly offered to come in an hour earlier on each of her days as she will need the extra time for sewing the bedding. I had to point out we couldn't reimburse her, but she is happy to do it for the sake of the school.'

'That girl has got a heart of gold,' Mrs Daws murmured. 'The least we can do is give her luncheon, then.' At the thought of seeing more of Sheena, Harry smiled and the housekeeper shot him a knowing look.

'Oh, by the way, Sergeant Watts called in whilst you were out. Said to tell you his men have had a tip-off about them burglaries and the net was closing in.'

'Did he elaborate?' Harry asked.

The housekeeper shook her head. 'You know what he's like. Just stood there telling me how important this operation was that he'd mounted. Anyway, he said you're to stay away until he gives you the all clear. Though you needn't worry about the farmhouse itself, 'cos he's keeping an eye on that, an' all.'

'That won't help with Bess's crops, though, will it?' he sighed. 'Oh, well, it's time we were planting our own here so I'll get the boys onto it tomorrow afternoon. Pip can supervise whilst Solomon and I continue with the new shed.'

'Ah, another Sunday rest to look forward to,' Mrs Daws sighed contentedly.

Sarah smiled fondly at the woman. 'You deserve it, Mrs Daws.'

The housekeeper returned her smile, then turned to Harry. 'I see Solomon follows you round like a willing slave, hanging on to your every word. A bit of hero worship there, Master Higgins, I think.'

'Well, I have some paperwork to catch up on before I turn in,' Sarah said, getting to her feet.

'And I've some invoices in my desk that need paying,' Harry grimaced. 'I'll just go and get them.'

'First thing tomorrow will do,' Sarah told him. To her surprise, he looked uneasy.

'I might not be in until later. When we were out with the children, Miss O'Reilly mentioned their back door was sticking so I offered to take a look.'

'Fair enough. I'll see you in a few moments, then,' Sarah called as she made her way down the hallway.

'Solomon's not the only one with a bit of hero worship, then,' the housekeeper teased, giving Harry another of her looks. As he promptly fled outside, her chuckle resounded around the room.

Although the fire was still burning, the office felt cold after the warmth of the range. By the time Sarah had lit the candles and stoked the flames, Harry had joined her.

'Well, the April showers have arrived,' he announced, brushing raindrops from his jacket. 'Let's hope that wriggly tin does its job, especially as one of these is from Langham.' He passed a sheaf of papers across the desk.

'Are you sure this is right?' Sarah asked, quickly scanning the first invoice. 'It doesn't seem very much considering the amount of time those men put in.'

'Well, we already had most of the materials,' Harry shrugged.

'Even so, Langham and his men were here for best part of a week,' Sarah frowned. 'We can't accept charity, Harry.'

'The fact is, Langham got in a muddle with his accounts. In fact, they were in much the same state as Red Cliffs' were, so I've been helping him bring his books up to date.'

So, that's where he'd been scurrying off to each night, Sarah thought.

'That's an admirable thing to do, Harry, and I'll see the invoice is paid first thing. Oh, on another matter entirely, you do think I've made the right decision about Edith, don't you?'

'I do. She's nearly ten years old and whilst not the brightest in the classroom, knows what she wants to do when she leaves here. It will give her the opportunity to see what sewing for a living entails and, who knows, might even give her the incentive to pay attention in class.'

That's pretty well what Miss O'Reilly said,' Sarah agreed, trying not to smile as he cleared his throat.

'We should make a record of any earnings she gets and the amount Red Cliffs deducts for living expenses.'

'You mean we should charge her for her food?' she frowned.

'I do, Sarah. As you pointed out just now, we are not a charity. Teaching pupils the value of money has always been a priority here. They know you don't get anything for nothing and if Edith makes a contribution to our funds, we can put the rest aside for when she leaves here.'

'Yes, I can see how that fits with our ethos. I knew Edith was a good seamstress but it seems she has a talent worth cultivating.'

'It will certainly give her a rung on the ladder, and don't forget it is our job here to prepare the children for the outside world,' he smiled. His words triggered an earlier memory.

'You know, Harry, I was certain I spotted Kitty in town today,' Sarah said. 'However, she'd gone by the time I got outside. And then, of course, I was detained by Miss O'Reilly and Edith insisting I go and see Sylvie Spangles so I had no chance of following. I can't help worrying about Kitty; Luke, too. Is there really nothing more we can do?'

'I worry, too, you know,' he admitted. 'Although our head tells us not to become too attached to the pupils in our care, the heart has other ideas. I'll have another word with Sergeant Watts when I go into town and see if any of his men have found out anything. By the way, talking of the town, I hear you were seen coming out of that swish hotel on the front. Going up in the world, are we, Miss Sullivan?'

Not in the mood for his banter, she gave him a stern look. 'I attended a very important meeting of the NUWSS earlier and women are indeed going to be rising up in the world, Harry Higgins, so you'd better watch out.'

'You've got me quivering in my boots, Miss Sullivan,' he teased. 'You mean a man won't come home to find his dinner on the table and his wife waiting to do his bidding?'

Sarah gave a most unladylike snort. 'Well, this one certainly won't be doing anyone's bidding. I can't imagine what possesses a woman to waste her life running round after a man.'

Seeing her outraged expression, Harry sighed inwardly. How had he ever imagined they were on the same wavelength?

'All right, Sarah, keep your hair on. I wouldn't want a woman running round after me in any case. A cosy home and family would be nice, though,' he replied wistfully.

However, Sarah was already pulling out the ledger from her drawer. As she did her hand brushed against Mrs Knight's book of *Principles for Trading and Profit*. Thinking she'd do well to refer to the wise lady's words, she put it to one side.

'A little light reading?' Harry enquired. Home and hearth were obviously not on Sarah's agenda, he realized, wondering how he'd ever thought they would be.

'Anyway, talking about going up in the world,' she said ignoring his comment, 'with the inspection due at the end of next month, we need to bring our books up to date ready for them to be audited. Help me enter these invoices so we can at least make a start.'

''Tis slave labour, O mistress,' he muttered, but did as he was told.

With her new system in place, it didn't take long for them to work out that, although Red Cliffs' funds were improving, expenditure still outstripped income.

'It's an uphill battle just keeping this place running, isn't it?' Sarah said, pushing the ledger aside and rubbing her eyes. 'Even with Lady Chorlton's kind benefaction, we still have a deficit. I just hope the Local Authority hurry up and approve your application to run the boys' toolmaking classes. That extra funding will assist greatly.'

'Can't see why they shouldn't,' he replied. 'Let's look at the positives. Thanks to the good ladies running the soup kitchen, we've still got vegetables left in the shed and the hens are laying well. It's a shame we're unable to get to the farm's produce, though.'

'It sounds like Sergeant Watts will soon catch those thieves and then you will,' Sarah pointed out.

'I'm hoping the roof will hold up and the building will pass the inspection but . . .' He looked at Sarah seriously, hardly daring to voice what was on his mind.

'But what, Harry?' she urged.

'What will you do if Red Cliff fails, Sarah? The Local Authority have made it quite clear this is our last chance for keeping the school open.'

'Harry Higgins, I'm surprised at you. That's defeatist talk,' she exclaimed.

'Defeatist or realistic? Perhaps you should consider accepting one of those offers from the developers.' She gave him such a glare, he sprung to his feet. 'Well, I must be on my way.'

As the door closed behind him, Sarah sat back in her chair. Harry knew how she felt about keeping her godfather's legacy going. How could he even suggest she do otherwise? Although he was a good master, he really wasn't turning out to be the man she'd thought he was.

Her glance fell on Mrs Knight's tome but as she flicked through its pages, hoping again to find some inspiration, it fell open at the same page as before.

Eighth Principle (a): Apply the 5 F's:
(i) Failure. Accept that failure is not an option, but sometimes the coat must be cut to suit the cloth.

Well, she knew failure was not an option. Hadn't she just told Harry the same? As for the coat . . . Her hand flew to her mouth. Her coat! In her haste to catch Kitty, she hadn't collected it from the cloakroom of the hotel. Worse still, she'd left Bertram sitting alone at the table in the restaurant. Good heavens, whatever must he think of her?

Although the rain was still coming down in sheets, Harry whistled happily as he made his way towards the address Miss O'Reilly had given him. Sheena, he thought, his heart beating wildly. Now there was a real woman. Having stopped to check the number on the gate of the little terraced house she was staying at, he walked up the path. The garden was small but neatly tended, daffodils bobbing brightly in the breeze. He saw that the door and frames were freshly painted and the windows gleamed. It was obviously a home well kept.

'Come in, Master Higgins,' Sheena greeted him, pulling open the door before he'd had a chance to ring the bell. 'Nanna has gone to church with our neighbour, but

I'll show you the sticking door that's been driving her wild.'

He bent to remove his boots but she shook her head.

'No need, Master Higgins. I'm sure the job won't take long,' she said, leading the way through to a cosy kitchen where a kettle was singing on the range. 'I'll make a pot of tea whilst you're working.'

He set to, making the adjustment to the door. It was a simple enough job yet the sight of her flitting around the room in her brightly coloured skirts distracted him. When he'd finally finished, she set a mug of tea and a scone-like cake on the kitchen table before him.

'There, take a seat and eat, as Mammy always says,' she invited. He didn't need telling twice, and pulled out a chair with a bright red cushion in the same material as the cosy covering the teapot. It was a cheerful room, and as she relaxed in the chair opposite, it was all he could do not to gaze into her emerald eyes. Not wishing to appear a half-wit, he took a bite of his scone. It was meltingly light and like nothing he'd ever tasted before.

'This is delightful,' he murmured, taking another bite.

'Oh, it's only a potato cake,' she replied, colour tingeing her cheek.

He sniffed the air appreciatively. 'Something else smells good, too.' He saw her glance towards the pot simmering on the stove and then at the clock on the wall. 'Irish stew for luncheon. Nanna's invited her neighbour to join us and I'm afraid there's only enough for the three of us. Still, to be sure, you'll have other arrangements anyway,' she said quickly.

Disappointment flooded through him for he'd been

hoping to have the opportunity of getting to know her grandmother. He nodded politely, wondering if he dared invite her for a stroll along the seafront after she'd eaten.

'Do you not worship with your grandmother?' he asked, to break the awkward silence that had fallen between them.

'My faith has been called into question recently, Master Higgins,' she told him, taking a gulp of her drink.

'Oh?' he asked. Her eyes clouded but seeing that she wasn't going to be drawn, he hurried on. 'But you have settled well into Red Cliffs?'

She nodded and smiled but didn't reply.

Determined to find out more about her he continued, 'You were a schoolmistress back home, weren't you? What did you teach? I don't believe it said on your testimonial.'

He just had time to register her frown when they heard voices in the hallway. Her eyes widened in alarm as the door opened and a sprightly woman in a bright green jacket and skirt entered.

'Oh, Sheena dear, I didn't realize you had company,' she said, her lilting voice a clear indication they were related. 'Well, aren't you going to introduce me?' she added pleasantly.

'This is Master Higgins, Nanna,' she whispered.

Immediately the woman's smile froze. 'Is it indeed?' she replied. 'And pray what are you doing sneaking into my house to see my granddaughter when she's all alone?'

'It wasn't like that, Nanna,' Sheena gasped. 'I mentioned that your back door was sticking and Master Higgins kindly offered to take a look.'

'As long as that's all he was looking at,' the woman replied sharply.

'Indeed it was, Mrs . . . ?' he began, taken aback by the woman's icy manner. However, she continued staring stonily at him but didn't respond. 'Well, it's all fixed now so I'll be on my way,' he said quickly. 'Good day to you,' he said, hurrying past the surprised-looking neighbour in the hallway.

29

'The rain has stopped at last,' Mrs Daws announced as she busied herself preparing the children's breakfast on Monday morning. 'And from what April tells me, the roof hasn't leaked. Mind you, the racket on that tin was enough to give a person an 'eadache if you was that way inclined.'

Sarah smiled at the housekeeper's expression. Since coming to Red Cliffs the previous autumn, she'd only ever known the woman have one headache, which, with everything she undertook around the place, was a blessing.

'I know there's been some water damage to some of the rooms upstairs, so I'll take a good look around and see what needs fixing. We must have those dormitories spick and span for the inspection,' she replied.

'I know you've got a lot to do with Edith starting her new job today so I can check them over, Miss Sullivan,' April offered, looking up from the bread she was cutting.

'That would be a great help,' Sarah smiled. 'Oh, good morning, Pip,' she called as the boy hobbled into the room clutching a large parcel tied with an elaborate red bow.

'This was dropped off at the gate by some swell driving an automobile,' he exclaimed. 'He were wearing a deer-stalker and tweed jacket with goggles that covered 'is face. Spoke all posh, like, and said I must be sure to deliver it straight into your own fair 'ands,' he mimicked, bowing low as he ceremoniously proffered the package.

'Goodness,' Sarah gasped, taking it from him. 'I'll be in my office if anyone wants me,' she added quickly. Then ignoring their curious stares she hurried from the room.

Closing the study door firmly behind her, she tore at the ribbons and found her coat nestling in layers of tissue paper. How kind of Bertram to deliver it personally, although she wished he'd called in to see her; then she could have thanked him and apologized for her behaviour. She shook her head, still unable to believe she had left him high and dry in the hotel. Having thought long and hard how to atone, she'd decided to write him a note explaining her reasons but in the end, worried this would look too forward, she had decided against it.

Knowing she'd need her coat to wear that afternoon, she shook out the folds and only then noticed the envelope pinned onto the lapel. The paper was expensively crisp and crackled as she unfolded it, and the note was penned in the same green ink as his previous one.

Dearest Sarah Sullivan,

I beg your forgiveness for my crass behaviour at our meeting last week. Overwhelmed at being in the company of such a beautiful lady, I regret my tongue failed to engage with my brain, resulting in that outlandish outpouring of gibberish. No wonder you ran away as fast as your dainty feet would take you.

If you could find it in your heart to take pity upon this repentant fellow and grant him another chance, he would be forever obliged. I shall be waiting at the same table on Saturday afternoon at three thirty in hopeful anticipation.

Your humble servant,
Bertram J. Brightling

Sarah reread the note, then frowned. She'd been so in awe of the plush surroundings and stylish ladies, she'd hardly paid attention to what he'd said. Yet if he thought it had been his behaviour that had caused her to run away then that excused her actions, didn't it? She sighed, knowing her conscience wouldn't permit her to take the easy way out. Still, he had given her the perfect opportunity to meet him again, she thought, her spirits lifting at the prospect.

Sheena's heart was heavy as she tramped up the driveway. If only she hadn't offered to come into work early. Now, there was no way she'd be able to avoid bumping into Harry. Besides, decency decreed she apologize for her nanna's curt manner, although what she could say if he asked why the woman had taken against him, especially after fixing their back door, goodness only knew.

The children, having finished morning lessons, were busy in the grounds, the boys digging over the vegetable plot, the girls cleaning out the chicken coops. Noticing Harry was still working on the new shed, she hurried inside.

'Ah, there you are, Miss O'Reilly,' Mrs Daws said, looking up from the big pot she was stirring on the range. 'Now sit yourself down, dear, and have a bowl of potage before them gannets come in and devour the whole ruddy lot.'

'That's very kind, but I'm here to work, Mrs Daws,' Sheena replied quickly. 'I just came in to let you know I was here.' The woman took no notice and ladled broth into a bowl and placed it on the table.

'I told Miss Sullivan that if you was doing longer hours

then the least we could do was feed you,' the housekeeper declared. As the woman stood there, hands on hips, Sheena smiled for the first time that day and sat down to eat.

'Miss Sullivan has already left with Edith. My word, you should have seen that girl. Squealing like a pig in . . . well, she were that excited,' Mrs Daws said, as she began cutting slices of bread. 'Dressed in her new outfit with that big flower on, she looked right grown up. It's her birthday next week so we'll have to have a party for her.'

Determined to finish eating before Harry came in for his meal, Sheena let the housekeeper chatter on. However, she was just getting to her feet, when he strode into the kitchen. From his slicked-back hair and the droplets of water glistening on his face, it was evident he'd just taken a wash under the pump. He looked so fresh and handsome, Sheena felt her pulse quicken.

'Miss O'Reilly,' he acknowledged. His manner was polite enough, but his eyes were wary.

'Master Higgins,' she replied, her voice hoarse.

The housekeeper glanced their way, shook her head, then went over to the range.

'I, er, would like to . . .' Sheena faltered, then took a deep breath. 'To thank you for fixing Nanna's door. She is very relieved not to have to use her bottom any more.' No, that didn't sound right, she chided herself. A spark of amusement gleamed in Harry's eyes but he didn't respond. 'And, er . . .' she trailed to a halt.

'And?' he prompted.

'You're early, miss,' April cried, bounding into the room. She looked from Sheena to Master Higgins and giggled. 'Oops, sorry, am I interrupting something?'

'Of course not, April,' Sheena replied, trying not to show her frustration. 'Well, I'd better get on or the girls will be wondering where I am,' she said quickly.

'Hardly, miss. They're still seeing to the 'ens.'

'And they'd better not bring any of that mess into my spotless kitchen,' the housekeeper warned, shaking her wooden spoon at them.

'Don't worry, Mrs Daws, they're all off rinsing their hands and I've reminded them to wipe their feet on the mat outside. You can sound the gong, April,' Harry said, and without glancing in Sheena's direction he went through to the dining room.

'I'll be in the classroom when they've finished,' Sheena muttered, just as the gong sounded and the hungry hordes surged inside.

While the children were having their luncheon, Sheena uncovered the sewing machine and set out the new material along with pins, scissors and thread. Having been told they would need to make at least fifteen sets of bedding, she knew there was no time to waste and she decided to make a start. However, as her feet worked the treadle and the machine whirred, so did her thoughts. She'd had the perfect opportunity to apologize and had messed up. You stupid, silly girl, she scolded.

'Did you say something, miss?' Maggie asked.

Sheena jumped as she saw the girls staring enquiringly at her. Lost in thought, she hadn't even heard them enter the room.

'Good afternoon, my angels,' she called brightly. 'Come in and we'll get started.'

'Was you telling Shanksy off?' Monday asked.

Seeing her earnest expression, Sheena set aside her own thoughts and smiled.

'If you all work well, my angels, I'll tell you a story at the end of the lesson,' she promised. Mollified by this, they took their seats and listened as she explained what needed to be done.

'I have already made a start here so, Maggie, as the eldest, you can take over and work on the machine. Sally, you can pin the hems, while the rest of you tack the seams.'

'Mrs Daws said you might like some help,' April said, bounding enthusiastically into the room. 'I don't like sewing much but I can easily do them big tacking stitches.'

The room fell silent as the girls set about their tasks but it wasn't long before they began fidgeting.

'This is so boring, miss,' Ellen sighed.

'I doesn't like this cloth, it's all bare,' Monday moaned.

'It's all right for the sheets,' Sally observed. 'But our dormitories will look very plain without any colour. Still, I'm sure we are grateful for having new bedding,' she added sweetly when she saw Sheena frown.

'You know, my angels, you do have a point,' she said, staring down at the cotton fabric. It was good quality but very stark. No wonder the girls were uninspired. 'I've had a thought,' she cried, staring at the brightly coloured clothes in the donations box. 'Where I come from, we make cottage quilts.'

'What's them, miss?' Maggie asked, looking up from the machine.

'Covers made of strips of material sewn together and backed with material, just like this,' she told them, holding up the sheet she was hemming. 'Why don't we sort through the contributions the good ladies have left for us and see what we can find?'

'Yes,' they chorused, and descended on the battered box, pulling out garments willy-nilly.

To be sure, you're a glutton for punishment, Sheena O'Reilly, she told herself, for did this not mean she'd be spending hours each evening sewing by candlelight? Then she looked at their faces and smiled, for their sulks had been replaced by ecstatic excitement.

'If you each choose your favourite colour or pattern and put it on my desk, I'll make sure the fabric is cut into strips ready for your next lesson,' she told them.

'It's dory dime,' June lisped, pointing to the clock.

'Story time, June,' she corrected. 'And you are right, my angel.'

'Will you tell us why you were telling Shanksy off?' Monday begged.

Sheena smiled. 'I will if you settle down and resume your sewing.'

The girls did as they'd been bid and were soon lost in the magic of make-believe so that the ringing of the bell took them by surprise.

'Off you go, my angels. I'll tidy away,' she told them, shooing them outside.

Once she was satisfied the room was ready for classes the next day, she made her way towards the kitchen. Spotting Harry Higgins heading in her direction, her heart lifted. Fixing a bright smile on her face, she determined to finish apologizing properly for her grandmother's rudeness the previous day. However, as soon as he saw her, he veered off the path and disappeared behind the new shed. Cursing under her breath, she went on her way.

As Sheena entered the kitchen, Mrs Daws looked up from pounding a huge dish of potatoes.

'I don't know how you do it, Miss O'Reilly. One minute those girls were all moaning they had to make boring sheets, the next they're chatting away like magpies about cottage quilts. There's tea in the pot if you want a cup, but you've just missed Master Higgins. Seems a bit out of sorts today, he does.'

'Thanks, Mrs Daws, my throat's parched as a dried-out ditch,' Sheena murmured, setting a cup down on the table.

'Everything all right?' the housekeeper asked, giving Sheena one of her knowing looks. Sheena nodded and concentrated on pouring her drink. 'Hmm,' the woman murmured, pounding the potatoes harder. Sheena sipped her tea then, unable to settle, prowled the cosy room. She was aware of the housekeeper darting her puzzled looks and, sure enough, it wasn't long before she spoke.

'Now, you can tell me to mind my own business, but it seems to me that if two normally happy people are going around with faces as miserable as sin, then something must be wrong. Cors, you might not want to talk to a daft old woman . . .' She left her sentence hanging in the air.

'Mrs Daws, anyone less daft than you would be hard to find,' Sheena cried. 'But you're right, I am miserable. I do like it here but . . .' The housekeeper continued pounding the potatoes but didn't say anything. Finally, unable to keep her fears to herself any longer, Sheena shared what was worrying her.

'It's this understanding between Master Higgins and Miss Sullivan,' she burst out.

The housekeeper looked up in surprise then dropped her spoon into the bowl. Sinking into a chair, she patted the one beside her.

'Sit down and tell me what you are on about, dear,' she invited.

Taking a deep breath, Sheena explained what she'd heard at the farm. The housekeeper frowned. 'You sure that's what Bess said?'

Sheena nodded dismally. 'Surely you must have heard about it?' she asked.

Mrs Daws' frown deepened. 'Can't say as I have, but then I'm only the housekeeper so not privy to everything that goes on around here.'

'Since I found out, I've tried not having much to do with him, but Master Higgins is so clever and funny and kind . . .'

'My, my, you have got it bad,' the housekeeper sympathized, reaching out and patting Sheena's hand. 'Have you spoken to Master Higgins about it?'

'No. As soon as I found out I tried to avoid him but . . .' Sheena shrugged helplessly. 'Then we took the children out and got on so well. He offered to help with my nanna's door but I'd already told her . . . Oh, Mrs Daws, I expect you think terribly of me,' she cried.

The woman clucked her tongue. 'I can't deny some of what you've told me has been a surprise,' she admitted. 'Still, I'm sure if you talk to Master Higgins, he'll have a better understanding of how you're feeling.'

'But how can I when he's avoiding me?' Sheena cried.

'Men can be dull-witted, dear. Sometimes they need showing the way, a signal so to speak. Of course, in my day a lady would drop her handkerchief to attract his attention, but I'm sure we could think of something,' she said peering around the room. 'Ah, the very thing,' she said, picking up a copy of the parish periodical the vicar had left. 'Can never resist a read of this, can't the master,' she winked, placing it in Sheena's hand.

'You think?' Sheena asked.

'Oh, I don't think, dear, I know. Now I've got supper to prepare, so off you go,' she urged.

'Thank you, Mrs Daws,' she cried, jumping up and kissing the woman on the cheek.

Walking back down the path, Sheena saw the master was still working. Venturing as close as she dared to the new tool shed, she dropped the magazine and carried on walking.

30

'Miss O'Reilly,' Harry called. 'Miss O'Reilly,' he shouted louder, but still she didn't appear to hear him. Sighing, he picked up the periodical, thinking to take it back indoors for her to collect. But then his inherent good nature overcame his annoyance at the events of the previous day, and he hurried after her.

'You dropped this,' Harry explained, holding out the magazine as he caught up with her.

'Really?' she cried, her eyes widening in surprise. 'Why, thank you, Master Higgins,' she added demurely. As she took it from him their hands touched, sending a tingle up his arm. She must have felt something similar for he saw she was trembling.

'My pleasure,' he murmured. 'It's a lovely afternoon, isn't it?' She peered around as if checking what he'd said was true, then nodded. Knowing this was his opportunity to get to the bottom of what had been puzzling him, he said casually, 'And it would be criminal to waste the last rays of the day, so if you've finished work for the afternoon, would you object to my walking you home?'

She hesitated for a moment then nodded. 'I'll just collect my things and be right with you.'

They sauntered down the street, an awkward silence between them. Although he could have reached out and touched her, she seemed as distant as the rocks at the far end of the harbour. As Harry pondered on how to phrase his question without causing offence, Miss O'Reilly seemed lost in her own thoughts. Finally, he could stand it no longer.

'I didn't know you read the parish periodical, Miss O'Reilly,' he said.

'Mrs Daws thought I might find it useful,' she replied.

'Really?' he asked in surprise. 'Did she have any particular piece in mind?'

'Oh, no, just the thing as a whole,' she said quickly. Then she stopped walking and turned to face him. 'I really must apologize for my grandmother's rudeness yesterday, Master Higgins.'

'I've been thinking about that, Miss O'Reilly,' he replied. 'Now at the risk of sounding like some latter-day saint, having just done her a favour, I cannot for the life of me think what I could have done to provoke such hostile a reaction.'

Colour stained Sheena's cheeks and she stared down at her boots. 'It's because she thought I was becoming too fond of you,' she finally admitted.

'And that would be a problem?' he frowned.

Sheena nodded.

'May I ask why?'

'Because of your understanding with Miss Sullivan,' she cried, before taking off down the street as if the devil was after her.

Harry stood there trying to take in what she'd said, then hurried after her.

'Miss O'Reilly, you cannot come out with a bald statement like that and run away. Perhaps you would be good enough to tell me more about this understanding I'm supposed to have with Miss Sullivan.'

'Supposed?' she cried, turning to him in dismay. 'Surely the matter of an arrangement to marry Miss Sullivan is not so trivial it could have slipped your mind?'

Realizing they were attracting the interest of passers-by, he took her by the arm and led her to a bench in the park.

'I think we need to get a few things clear, Miss O'Reilly, so let's sit down and discuss this properly, shall we?'

Sarah perched on a stool and watched as Sylvie Spangles, wearing her shiny blouse with cameo brooch at the neck and fingerless lace mittens, showed an excited Edith where all the costumes for that day's fittings were hanging. The dressing room was draughty and she pulled her coat tighter around her. Seeing her shiver, the woman chuckled.

'Don't mind Marlin, ducks.'

'Marlin?' Sarah frowned, peering around to see who'd come in.

Sylvie laughed delightedly. 'He's our resident ghost. A true thespian, he was; couldn't bear to leave the theatre behind when he passed.'

'Passed? Oh, you mean, died,' Sarah replied, trying not to shudder.

Edith beamed. 'A real live ghost,' she cried delightedly. However, before Sarah could point out that what she'd said was a contradiction in terms, the girl went on, 'Is this not the finest place ever, Miss Sullivan?' Her arms made a sweeping gesture encompassing everything. 'It smells magical.'

Sarah wrinkled her nose, thinking the place smelled musty.

'Ah, you've got it, Eedie ducks. Knew it as soon as I set eyes on you,' Sylvie replied, nodding her head so that her earrings swayed back and forth. 'Now, we've got ten minutes until the first one comes for his fitting, so come over here and I'll show you my bible.'

Sarah frowned: surely this was no time for prayer? Then she realized the woman was opening a brightly coloured book bound with ribbons and explaining to Edith how she kept track of all the costumes.

'This column is for their names, their measurements and what role they are playing. Then I note down all the costumes they'll need and what adaptations have been made to them. On this page, I mark down the cost of the rental, how much they've paid up front and if it's not the full amount, show how much they'll need to give me each week to clear their debt.'

Edith was quiet for a moment. 'But if they don't pay the full cost at the start, they'll end up owing loads more by the end,' she frowned.

Sylvie chuckled delightedly. 'Spoken like a true businesswoman, Eedie. That's how Sylvie Spangles makes her money, see? Cors, there's a lot of hard work goes into getting their costumes just right, so believe you me, that money is well earned.' She was interrupted by a knock on the door. 'Come in, Ollie,' she called, smiling affectionately at the middle-aged man who minced into the room. He was wearing a lilac shirt with red silk scarf knotted at the neck and trousers so tight it was surprising he could walk in them.

'I come to be clothed,' he announced, affecting a bow. Sarah had to stifle a giggle as the grandiose statement came out as an effeminate squeak.

'Now, Ollie dear, this is my new assistant, Eedie, and her teacher, Miss Sullivan,' Sylvie told him.

'Hello, there,' he greeted them cordially. Then he frowned and took a second look at Sarah. 'But we have met before, have we not?'

'I don't think so,' Sarah replied, certain she would have remembered such a spectacle.

'Ollie Burns never forgets a face, love,' he replied. 'It will come to me, never fret.'

'Right, Eedie, time for work. Pass me the whistle and flute off that rail, and we'll see how it fits.' Eager to please, Edith scurried over to where Sylvie was pointing, then frowned. 'Hurry up, ducks, we haven't got all day,' she said, snapping her fingers impatiently.

'But there ain't no whistle, or no flute come to that,' Edith cried.

To her astonishment Ollie burst out laughing. 'Now ain't that the funniest thing you ever heard?' he chortled, tears running down his cheeks.

'I don't think . . .' Sarah began.

'Don't mind him, ducks,' Sylvie said. 'Control yourself, Ollie. Anything less like an English gentleman and more like a constipated penguin I've yet to see. Now, Edith Curdy, you just pass me that navy and cream striped suit, there's a good girl.'

'But you said . . .' Edith began, feeling stupid.

'Sorry, ducks, it's how we speak in London. Whistle and flute, suit, see?'

Edith brightened and passed over the garments. 'This is going to be such fun.' She watched as Sylvie took out her tape and measured the man, meticulously recording her findings in her book.

'How's your lines coming along, Ollie?' the woman asked.

The actor rolled his eyes theatrically. 'Don't even ask,' he sighed. 'Still, it's a good play. This new producer has got some swell ideas. He showed me the posters earlier. They're being put up as we speak, but will only show the leading lady bit by bit. He's saving the big reveal until opening night. Quite a wheeze, eh?' he said, holding out his arms obediently for Sylvie.

'I'd like to be a leading lady,' Edith sighed, draping a fur stole around her shoulders and parading up and down. 'And 'ave a catchy name like yours. Is Sylvie Spangles your real name?'

'Remember your manners, Edith,' Sarah chided.

'That's all right, ducks,' the woman smiled, through a mouthful of pins.

'Well dressed like that, you could be Eedie Ermine,' Ollie suggested. 'I've got it,' he said, snapping his fingers so that they all jumped. 'You're that lady on the posters,' he cried, turning to Sarah. 'Said I never forget a face.'

'I don't think so,' Sarah laughed. 'Well, Edith, it's time we were getting back to Red Cliffs,' she said, squinting at the tiny travelling clock on the table.

'Oh, miss,' Edith cried. 'I ain't hardly done nothing yet.'

Making a mental note to ask Miss O'Reilly to begin teaching the girls correct pronunciation, Sarah got to her feet.

'I've got to make sure Ollie's trousers fit now, so you'd better run along, ducks,' Sylvie said. 'Tell you what, you've been such a help you can take that bit of fur with you,' she added, pointing to the stole Edith was still sporting.

'Cor, really? Ta ever so,' Edith cried, stroking the fur lovingly. 'I can't wait to come back again.'

''Bye, Eedie Ermine,' Ollie called. 'You, too, Miss Sullivan,' he added, eyeing Sarah thoughtfully.

'Good day, Mr Burns. In future, Mrs Spangles, Pip will be conveying Edith in the trap so she can spend whole afternoons with you. Though I'd feel easier in my mind if you would see her safely back onto it at the end of her working sessions.'

'Cors I will, ducks,' the woman said, giving Edith a wink. 'You leave it to me.'

Out in the street, Edith hopped up and down excitedly as she studied the bills advertising the forthcoming play.

'Coo, look, miss, that man was right, you can only see 'er feet,' Edith cried, but, glad to be outside, Sarah was already striding down the street, breathing in the fresh, salty air.

Thinking a good walk would calm the girl's high spirits and clear her own head, Sarah decided to return to the school via the seafront. What an afternoon, she thought. Whilst she'd wanted to see Edith settled into her new job, she'd spent the time mentally running through all the tasks awaiting her return. The inspection was only six or seven weeks away and she had so much to do beforehand. Thank heavens Miss O'Reilly had offered to work longer hours. Sarah glanced at Edith swanning regally down the road in her fur stole and smiled.

'I take it you enjoyed your time at the theatre today, Edith?'

'Not 'alf, miss. I just loves Sylvie Spangles,' she sighed. 'She's so glamorous. I'm going to wear clothes and sparkly dangles just like 'er when I leave Red Cliffs and becomes a costumier. I had a good idea, an' all. From now on everyone can call me Eedie Ermine.'

Sarah hid a smile. She could just imagine what Master Higgins would have to say about that.

'Look, miss, there's Master Higgins with Miss O'Reilly,' Edith cried, pointing towards the park. Sarah look up and sure enough the pair were emerging from the tree-lined walk ahead. They were deep in conversation and walking very close together. Then, as Miss O'Reilly looked up, laughing at something he said, Sarah saw him lean forward and kiss her gently on the lips. A feeling she couldn't describe seared through her body and, taking Edith by the arm, she ushered the girl away.

Having spent a restless night, Harry made his way to work earlier than usual the next morning. He'd lain in bed, reliving the events of the previous afternoon and the feel of Sheena's velvety lips on his. How relieved he was to find out the reason for her grandmother's frosty reception of him. Where Bess had got the idea that he and Sarah still had an understanding or arrangement was beyond him. He was just drifting off to sleep when a thought struck him. Did Sarah think the same?

He'd gone back over the relationship they'd had since Sarah had taken over Red Cliffs. First there had been animosity between them, then as they'd began working together, friendship, then deeper feelings had developed. For a while recently he'd hoped to rekindle their thwarted romance, and he couldn't deny there had been occasions when he'd felt she'd expected something more again. But then she'd become so remote lately, making it clear that her priorities were Red Cliffs and furthering the cause of that women's movement she supported. It seemed there was no room for him in her life as anything more than a good colleague. Women – they sure took some working out. Still, at least he had a better understanding of himself now. Whilst he admired Sarah's selfless devotion to both causes, he wanted a wife who shared his desire for a home and family. When he finally fell asleep, it was Miss O'Reilly who'd filled his dreams. But she was running away from him and, no matter how fast he ran, he couldn't catch up with her.

'Morning, sir,' Pip called, swinging the gate open for him. 'Cor, you looks like you lost sixpence and found a farthing. Miss Sullivan wants to see you as soon as you arrive. She's looking miserable, an' all.'

'Thank you, Pip,' he replied, his heart sinking. After his musings of the night before, he had wanted to check Sarah saw their relationship the same way as he did, but if she was in a mood it was hardly the time to clear the air between them. Seeing Pip waiting to close the gate behind him, he forced himself back to the present. 'If I'm still busy when the children have had their breakfast, can you get them planting out the rest of the seeds? We need to have our produce in the ground so that when we get the all clear from the farm, we can tend to Bess's crops.'

'Heard someone tipped off that burglar and 'e's done a runner,' Pip sighed.

'How on earth do you know that?' Harry asked, but Pip just grinned and tapped the side of his nose. 'Word on the street.'

Shaking his head, Harry made his way towards the office where Sarah greeted him by thrusting a letter under his nose.

'I cannot believe this,' she cried.

He stared at her dishevelled hair and clothes that looked like she'd slept in them, and frowned. 'Whatever's happened?'

'Well, they've given us notice of their intention this time, but really, is it our fault Whitsun falls at the end of May?'

'Sorry?'

'Sorry? Is that all you can say. The Bank Holiday means the inspection will be earlier than expected. Not only does this give us less time to prepare, they've given us a long list of things they want to check on. It will mean searching through all those,' she cried, gesturing towards the boxes that still lined the wall. 'As if I haven't got enough to do.'

Harry opened his mouth to ask what Sarah was on about but she was like a dragon breathing fire.

'Not only that, when I arrived back yesterday, the girls were babbling on about Miss O'Reilly's latest bright idea. She's only gone and promised they could make cottage quilts for their dormitories instead of the plain bedding I stipulated. As if we have time or the extra material that will entail. I mean, just think of the added expense. Oh, it's all just too much,' she cried, throwing the letter down on the desk and sinking her head in her hands.

Having tried hard to follow her disjointed diatribe, Harry snatched up the letter and scanned the pages.

'We knew the inspection was looming,' he reasoned.

'Yes, but we thought we had until the end of next month,' Sarah cried.

'It's only a week earlier, though,' Harry said, checking the date.

'But have you read all the things they intend looking at? So much still needs doing, there's no way we'll be ready in time,' she groaned.

31

Thinking Sarah was overreacting, Harry sat and read through the letter, item by item. By the time he'd finished his spirits had sunk lower than the school funds. She was right, they had an almost impossible task ahead of them.

'Well, faint heart never won fair lady,' he cried, endeavouring to cheer Sarah up.

'Or a red-headed one, I suppose,' she muttered.

He stared at her in surprise. Choosing to ignore her remark, he snatched up pencil and paper from the desk. 'Right, let's draw up a plan of action.'

'Hey, that's my role,' Sarah smiled, rallying at last. She took back the letter and read down the list. 'Let's prioritize. Item one. "Inspection of Roof". None of those heavy showers we had penetrated the wriggly tin, or anywhere else, so that should be all right. But we need Pip to whitewash the areas in the rooms where the rain came in.'

'Good idea, disguise the evidence and all that,' Harry said.

'Item two is your province,' Sarah said. '"Application for New Skills Funding. A request has been made for funding for tuition in additional skills, principally woodturning and metalwork. Before this can be granted the inspectors will require sight of the new facilities and witness the demonstration of a typical lesson."'

'Although the tool shed is nearly completed externally, there's a heck of a lot that needs doing inside before that can happen,' he groaned.

'What happened to faint heart, etc.?' she reminded him, staring sternly over the top of the letter. 'Item three. "Licence. The Local Authority wishes to see sight of the original documentation granting Red Cliffs a licence to run the premises as a school. Normally this is displayed in a prominent place but at the last inspection it was noted that this document was not in evidence,"' Sarah read. 'I don't remember that being mentioned before. Do you know where this licence is, Harry?'

'No. Never seen such a thing myself.'

'I'll have to make a search, then,' she replied, staring dismally at the row of boxes. 'Maybe Mr Fothergill will have it,' she added hopefully.

'You could ask him,' Harry agreed.

'Item four. "Tuition". This is also your area, but doesn't need any attention. "Demonstrate typical lessons in reading, writing and arithmetic."'

'That's easy enough,' Harry nodded. 'As long as I tell the children what to do and not involve them in discussion, like I did last time,' he added ruefully, remembering the inspector's previous comments.

'Item five. "Health and Wellbeing". Mrs Daws will get everyone giving the house an extra-special clean and I'll ask April to pay particular attention to the dormitories. As there's a lot to do in such a short space of time, perhaps we can get Mrs Laver to help when she has finished her laundry duties. I will also speak to Miss O'Reilly about concentrating the girls' efforts on making the simple bedding only, and she will have to demonstrate the girls' skills for that as well.'

'That shouldn't be a problem,' he replied, trying to ignore the way his heart skipped at the mention of the mistress's name.

'And the last item, the "Audited Accounts",' Sarah groaned. 'I will get on with sorting those out before anything else.'

'That's divided the tasks up,' Harry said, ticking off his list. 'Pip the painting, Mrs Daws the house, Miss O'Reilly the bedding, you the paperwork and me getting the tool shed up and running. Though how I'm going to learn enough about toolmaking in a few short weeks, goodness only knows,' he sighed, running his fingers through his hair.

'I'm sure Solomon could help you there,' Sarah pointed out.

'You're right. Phew, that's a relief,' he cried, wiping his brow with his hand theatrically. Then he saw Sarah was frowning again.

'What's wrong now?'

'I'm just surprised about my friend, Josephine Harmon — you remember her?'

Harry nodded. 'The inspector. Nice woman, from what I recall.'

'Precisely, so why didn't she tell me the inspection was being brought forward?'

'Perhaps she didn't know,' Harry shrugged. 'Anyway, if she's one of the inspectors we're halfway there, aren't we?'

'That makes me feel better,' Sarah told him, putting down the letter and relaxing back in her chair.

'No time for slacking, Miss Sullivan,' Harry said,

jumping to his feet. 'Sooner we start and all that . . .' The rest of his sentence was drowned by the gong being sounded for breakfast. 'I suppose we couldn't send the children somewhere for the next few weeks so we can concentrate on our tasks? Just think how much easier it would be to get things done if the school was empty.'

'Now you know you'd miss them, Master Higgins,' Sarah smiled.

'Like a hole in the head,' he muttered. 'And talking of empty, my stomach thinks my throat's been cut. Let's go and get some sustenance before we begin.'

Sheena arrived at the school on Wednesday afternoon, her bag heavy with the material she'd spent the past day cutting into strips. Humming happily to herself, she divided them into piles then set out the cotton fabric and sewing things the girls would need to make their cottage quilts. She'd only just finished when they came swarming into the room, their faces lighting up when they saw the coloured material they'd selected, ready and waiting.

'Why, my angels,' Sheena beamed at them, 'it's grand to see you so keen.'

'We wants to sew the pretty stuff you was getting ready for us,' Monday cried.

'Yeah, we want thomefink nice to thow Edif,' June lisped.

'She's been prancing around with a fur thing round 'er neck saying we gotta call 'er Eedie Ermine now,' Maggie scoffed. 'She's gone right la-de-da since she went to that Gaiety place.'

'Well now, Edith's been given a marvellous opportunity

333

so we should be pleased for her, my angels,' Sheena told them. 'Settle down and I'll show you the strips I have prepared for you to attach to the sheeting,' she added, ushering them to their chairs.

'Can we have a dory later,' June lisped.

'No, you may not have a story,' Miss Sullivan snapped, striding into the room.

'Is everything all right, Miss Sullivan?' Sheena asked, guessing from the woman's stony face that it was not.

'Girls, I want you to begin stitching your sheets while I have a word with Miss O'Reilly,' Sarah told them.

'But miss was just going to show us how to use our pretty stuff for quilts,' Ellen cried.

'Do as I say, please, Ellen,' Sarah said brusquely. The girls stared at her in astonishment but did as she said. 'Perhaps you would step outside,' Sarah said to Sheena.

'Of course, Miss Sullivan,' she replied, following her from the room. 'Be good for me, my angels,' she called.

'Did I or did I not give clear instruction as to what the girls should be making for their dormitories, Miss O'Reilly?' Sarah asked once they were standing on the path away from the class.

'To be sure you did, Miss Sullivan, and they are.'

'So what is this I hear about cottage quilts?'

'After the pretty material the girls used for their dresses, they found the cotton plain and, well ... boring, so I thought if they chose some of the more colourful fabric from the donations box, I could cut it into strips for them to add to the sheeting,' Sheena explained.

'Once again, Miss O'Reilly, you presumed to take something upon yourself without authority from me.'

'I'm sorry, but you weren't here to ask and . . .' Sheena began but Sarah cut her off mid-sentence.

'Miss O'Reilly, I set this task specifically so that the dormitories are fitted with new bedding for the inspection, no small feat when this was scheduled for the end of next month. However, owing to Whitsun falling then, the inspection has been brought forward. Now, Miss O'Reilly, you are required to have all bedding finished by the seventeenth of next month so that I may check it beforehand.'

'Oh, I see,' Sheena gulped.

'What's more, with April busy helping Mrs Daws prepare the house and Edith working at the theatre, you will be short-handed. There will be no time for frills and furbelows so whatever promises you have made those girls will have to be unmade, Miss O'Reilly. Do I make myself clear?' Seeing the woman's resolute expression, Sheena knew it would be futile to argue.

'Yes, Miss Sullivan,' she replied.

'Good. I take it you will manage to have the bedding completed in time?' The woman waited, staring challengingly.

So, she was throwing down the gauntlet, was she, Sheena thought. Summoning all her self-control, she smiled sweetly back.

'Of course, Miss Sullivan. Even if I have to take sewing home with me like last time.' Sheena saw that this had hit home.

'Yes, well, I look forward to seeing the finished results next month. Obviously, there will be no time to waste on stupid storytelling,' Sarah added, before stalking back to the house. 'Oh, and Master Higgins is going to be extremely busy, too,' she threw over her shoulder.

Feeling her hackles rise and wanting to make her own feelings known, Sheena called to the woman, 'We all are, Miss Sullivan, and in any case, I wish to make it clear that I take my duties as schoolmistress very seriously.'

Slowly the woman retraced her steps and Sheena wondered if she'd overstepped the mark.

'And I take my duties as proprietress of Red Cliffs seriously, too, Miss O'Reilly. It is my responsibility to ensure the school passes the inspection in order to stay open.' Then she forced a smile. 'Shall we work together to make that happen?'

'To be sure, that would be in the children's best interest,' Sheena agreed. 'Would you object to my promising the girls they can add strips of coloured material to the plain sheeting after the inspection, Miss Sullivan?'

'No, Miss O'Reilly, I would not,' Sarah replied, her voice softer now. 'I quite see that it would make their bedding brighter as well as being warmer; it was just the time constraints,' she conceded. 'Oh, and one more thing. If you could encourage them to pronounce their hs and say "is not" instead of "ain't", I would be most grateful. They did it for a while but then . . .' She shrugged then walked away. As Sheena watched her go, a voice behind her made her jump.

'Mutiny in the camp?' Harry asked.

'Jeez, Harry, sorry, I mean Master Higgins, you fair startled me. Miss Sullivan sets such high standards.'

'You mean she's a perfectionist?' he asked.

'I was thinking more an obscurantist,' she grinned.

'Miss O'Reilly, I do believe you've swallowed my dictionary,' he teased.

'To be sure that'd give me indigestion, but it does make for compulsive reading.'

'Perhaps you would permit me to escort you home after school? I could carry your books and we can discuss this further, Miss O'Reilly.'

'That would be grand. Although with the extra sewing I need to do, it will be my bag of bedding you'll be carrying.'

'Then a packhorse I'll be,' he grinned.

'Well, no peace for the wicked so back to the grind.' Smiling to herself she made her way back into the classroom.

'Coo, I fort you'd be cryin',' June lisped.

'Yeah, Miss Sullivan looked in a right old strop,' Maggie said. 'Was you in trouble?'

'No, my angels, Miss Sullivan just wants everything to be grand for the school inspection. Now who would like to help make that happen?'

As their hands shot up, Sheena smiled.

'How can we be of help, Miss O'Reilly?' Sally asked, in her well-modulated voice.

'Now this jolly old inspection is to take place earlier than planned, so we won't have time to sew all these strips onto our new bedding beforehand.'

The girls groaned.

'Don't sound jolly to me, miss,' Ellen said.

'But all is not lost, my angels,' Sheena told them, 'for I'm going to put them in the cupboard, ready for afterwards. I know you're disappointed but sometimes in life we have to accept these things as part of growing up.'

'Has you had to cept fings you ain't wanted, miss?' June lisped.

'Oh, yes, I most certainly have,' Sheena cried, thinking back to her job in Ireland. 'However, do you know what?' She paused and stared at each of them in turn. They shook their heads. 'Everything turned out better than it would have done, so is that not the most wonderful thing?'

'But Miss Sullivan said we couldn't 'ave any more stories,' Ellen cried.

'She's mean,' Maggie grumbled.

'Realistic, Maggie. Now, whilst you are sewing, my angels, I thought we could sing. You remember how it gets you into the rhythm?'

They nodded enthusiastically.

'We are going to make a game of it. So, while Sally sings us the first verse, I want you to listen very carefully to how she pronounces the words. And then, it will be your turn to copy her. Who can manage to do that and sew at the same time?'

All their hands shot up again.

'Then that is what we'll do. And, what's more, we'll make Miss Sullivan proud of us all.'

As instructed, Pip was waiting outside the Gaiety when Edith came out of the theatre escorted by Sylvie Spangles.

'You can tell your Miss Sullivan you've been a right help this afternoon, Eedie,' the woman said. 'Hello, ducks,' she called to Pip. He waved and waited until Edith had climbed up beside him, then pulled on the reins.

'See you on Friday, Sylvie,' Edith called, as the pony began to move. 'Coo, I've 'ad a great afternoon, Pip,' she said. 'I've been really busy but I also had time to pin these jewelled things in my 'air. It don't 'alf make a difference to 'ow I look. Sylvie says they'll look even better when it's grown a bit more. Sylvie says the devil's in the detail, you see.'

'Oh, does she now?' he replied affably. 'It's good you've had a nice time but do you think you should be calling her by her first name?'

'Oh, yes, ducks, that's what we do in the theatre, you know,' Edith said, with a toss of her head. 'Do you know I had to check all the costumes for holes in case the moths had been at them and . . . 'ere, why are we going this way?' she asked as they turned towards the station.

'Master Higgins asked me to collect a parcel off the four thirty train. Come along, Thunder, get a giddy up,' Pip urged.

'That Solomon's sure got a funny sense of 'umour, ain't 'e?' Edith chuckled.

'Maybe, but this old pony here gave him a shoulder to cry on when he needed it,' Pip said, serious for once. 'Anyway, hopefully he'll get us there in time and then we can go home for supper.'

'Good, 'cos I'm starving. They don't seem to eat at the Gaiety. When I asked what they lived on, that Ollie said fresh air, can you believe that?' she exclaimed.

Pip smiled as he brought the cart to a halt and handed Edith the reins.

'Won't be a mo,' he called as he hobbled into the office by the side of the station. Edith stared around at all the passengers who'd alighted from the train. Some were dressed in everyday clothes, others in their finery. She was just deciding which of the ladies' outfits she would have chosen when a familiar voice made her start.

32

Peering around to see where the voice was coming from, Edith spotted a bundle of rags crouched by the station entrance.

'Spare a coin, mister?' the girl cried.

Her suspicion confirmed, Edith jumped down from the cart and, fearful of scaring her away, crept closer.

'Spare a coin, miss?' the girl begged, turning towards Edith. Then, seeing who it was, her hand flew to her mouth in horror. 'Oh 'ell,' she muttered.

'Kitty, is it really you?' Edith gasped. 'Cor blimey, you looks awful,' she added, taking in the girl's tattered clothes and mud-spattered face.

Kitty stared at Edith in dismay then looked frantically around for a way of escape. But Edith was too quick for her, grabbed her friend by the arm and hung on for dear life. To her relief she saw Pip coming back, a large parcel under his arm.

'Pip, over 'ere,' Edith shouted.

Seeing Kitty, his eyes widened in surprise and he quickly dropped the package into the back of the cart and hobbled over.

'Cor love us, look at the state of you,' he muttered. 'And what's wrong with your face?' he added, gesturing to her swollen cheek.

'What the 'ell's 'appened to you, girl?' Edith asked,

glaring at the passers-by who'd slowed to see what was going on. Kitty shook her head and stared down at the ground. Following her gaze, Edith gasped. 'Blimey, girl, you ain't got nothing on your feet and they're all cut to bug . . . Right, you're coming back to Red Cliffs with us,' she told her, pulling the girl towards the cart.

'I can't go back looking like this,' Kitty muttered, finding her voice at last.

'You blinkin' well can,' Edith told her. 'Come on, up you get,' she said, helping her friend into the seat. 'Mrs Daws is bound to 'ave the supper on,' she added, climbing up beside her. Kitty stared at Edith, then burst into tears. Putting her arm around the girl's shoulders, Edith pulled her close.

'Think we'd better get back to Red Cliffs as soon as we can,' Pip said, urging the pony on. As Kitty sobbed her heart out, Edith and Pip exchanged troubled glances.

'What on earth can have happened?' Pip asked.

'I dunno,' Edith replied. 'But sure as 'ouses, I'm goin' to find out.'

Sarah put her hand to her aching back and pulled herself into an upright position. What a day it had been, she thought, tucking stray tendrils of hair back into its bun. She felt grimy and out of sorts, for having ascertained Mr Fothergill was not in possession of the school licence, she'd spent the best part of the afternoon searching through battered boxes. If only she'd got around to sorting them earlier, she mused, but there were always more pressing things to attend to. Smiling wryly, she recalled her godfather saying the very same thing.

Hearing the trap rattling up the driveway, she guessed Pip had collected Edith from the Gaiety. The girl had really taken to her job and would no doubt regale them all with stories of the latest happenings in theatreland over supper, she thought, smiling as she went over to the window. Then her eyes widened in surprise and she flew from the room.

'Kitty, is that really you?' she gasped, arriving in the kitchen just as Edith was helping her distraught friend through the back door.

'We found her begging on the station steps,' Edith explained, cuddling the trembling Kitty closer. 'She weren't sure about coming back but she was in such a state, me and Pip insisted,' she added, staring anxiously at Sarah.

'You did the right thing, Edith,' she replied. 'It's good to see you again, Kitty,' she added, frowning as the girl avoided her gaze and stared down at the floor. She was filthy and her hair, which had grown since she'd left the school, clung to her head in matted clumps. The pitiful sight tugged at Sarah's heartstrings and, wanting to comfort the girl, she opened her arms. However, Mrs Daws shot her a warning look.

'Well, young Kitty, it's good to see you back and no mistake. But just looked at the state of you,' the housekeeper chided, snatching a towel from the pulley. 'April, bring that kettle of hot water out to the wash house,' she ordered. 'Now, young Kitty, a nice warm soaping is what you need. You've chosen a good day to visit 'cos there's rabbit stew for supper. Cors, if you'd come a bit earlier you could have skinned the thing for me. Never seen anyone do it as quick as you.'

As the girl smiled for the first time, the housekeeper ushered her back outside, closely followed by April.

'Good old Mrs Daws,' Edith muttered. 'She always knows what to say and do.'

'Sit down and tell me exactly what happened, Edith,' Sarah said, sinking into a chair and patting the one beside her.

'Pip had to collect a parcel for Master Higgins, and when 'e went inside the station, I heard this girl begging coins from the passengers. It was Kitty, miss. She had a wild look in her eyes and kept staring this way and that. Right scared, she were, and did you see her feet? All caked with blood and mud and she's got a right old bruiser on her cheek . . .'

Edith's voice shuddered to a halt and seeing she was in shock, Sarah poured tea from the seemingly ever-full pot, added two spoons of sugar and placed the mug before her.

'Drink this, Edith. It'll make you feel better.'

'Ta, miss. I never seen Kitty like that, not even when she first came 'ere.' She took a sip then scratched her head. 'Something terrible's 'appened, ain't it?'

Sarah reached out and patted the girl's shoulder. 'Don't worry, we'll take care of her. It's almost time for supper so I'll go and get Master Higgins to supervise,' Sarah said, getting to her feet.

'He ain't 'ere, miss. We saw him walking with Miss O'Reilly when we was on our way back. Looked right 'appy, they did. He were carrying 'er bag and they was chatting away so 'ard they never even saw us. Just like when we clocked them the other day, 'cept without that kiss,' she grinned, the colour returning to her cheeks.

'I see,' Sarah replied, pursing her lips. 'Well, if you've finished your drink you can go and tell the others to wash their hands and faces while I dish up supper. Ah, April,' she said as the door opened. 'How is Kitty?'

'She's in a bad way, miss,' she replied, shaking her head. 'I got to put the kettle on to heat again and then go for Dr Hawkins.'

'And what about Luke? Is there any news of him?'

'She didn't mention him but then she's not really with it,' April sighed.

'Ah well, happen we'll ask her when she's recovered, then.'

The children had just sat down to supper when April reappeared with an anxious-looking Harry.

'The doctor's finishing with a patient and then he'll be here,' April panted. 'I ran all the way and literally bumped into Master Higgins, didn't I, sir?'

'Yes, you did,' Harry agreed. 'Now you go and get yourself something to eat and I'll see Dr Hawkins when he arrives.'

'It's criminal. I've never heard anything so appalling in all my life,' Sarah muttered, staring into her mug.

'It happens, dearie,' Mrs Daws sighed. 'Poor Kitty. Let's hope that stuff the doctor gave her makes her sleep. Rest is what she needs. It was good of you to let her have your room, Miss Sullivan. Although you'll have to check your bedding for lice. Riddled, she was. What would we do without carbolic, eh?'

Sarah grimaced. 'I couldn't persuade Edith to leave her. Cuddled up together like Siamese twins, they are.'

'Well, Kitty looked out for Edith last year so I guess she feels it's her turn to repay the favour. Makes you realize we're getting something right at Red Cliffs, anyway,' Harry smiled. Then his expression darkened. 'But if I ever get my hands on that brute, I swear I'll throttle him or worse.'

'I can't get over it,' Sarah sighed. 'What man climbs into a child's bed and tries to ... to ...' She shuddered, unable to finish her sentence.

'Luckily Kitty was able to escape before he could ... well, you know. Apparently, she gave him a right good kicking in his ... er ... private bits, which was when he retaliated by punching her in the face,' Mrs Daws glowered.

'Dr Hawkins said he'd tell Sergeant Watts what's happened, so no doubt he'll be here to take a statement tomorrow morning,' Harry said.

'Well I hope they catch that, that ... monster,' Mrs Daws replied, shaking her head.

'It's not likely if he's already scarpered. I can't understand how Kitty's mother, knowing what he'd done, ran off with him. What possesses a person to even think of being with a man like that?'

'Some women need a man, any man,' Mrs Daws said, shaking her head.

'But surely it's better to be by yourself than with someone like that. The sooner women win the right to vote and have a say in how things are run, the better. You'd think she'd have stayed and looked after her daughter,' Sarah cried.

'At least she's got us to take care of her, eh, Marmalade?' Mrs Daws said, stroking the cat's fur.

'Well, it's been a long day and I'd better get home to Mother before she wonders where I've got to,' Harry said, getting to his feet.

'I guess the tool shed must be coming along well, for I hear you had time to walk Miss O'Reilly home,' Sarah said, giving him a searching look.

He nodded. 'I offered to carry her bag for her. She realizes how important it is for the new bedding to be finished for the inspection and has taken it upon herself to do some of the sewing in her spare time.'

'She's a fine woman, that Miss O'Reilly,' the housekeeper commented.

'That is good of her,' Sarah agreed. 'But what about the shed and all those dirty tools? You know it's vital to have everything ready for the inspectors to observe a sample lesson if we're to secure that funding.'

'Don't worry, everything's in hand. While I was finishing off the outside of the shed earlier, Solomon got the boys cleaning the worst of the tools with dry sand, while he and Bunter cut and trimmed a long branch to make the lathe. That boy's been a real help. It was he who pointed out that working with metal can't be done in the same place as woodworking, due to flying sparks, so we are going to clear out the empty stable as well. We can't go up to the farm at the moment so we'll spend Saturday afternoon doing that. Gosh, just talking about it all has made me tired,' he yawned.

'Me, too, Master Higgins. When I thinks of all the cleaning that needs doing round here, I feel like Annie Domino,' Mrs Daws chipped in.

'Annie who?' Sarah asked, collecting their used mugs together.

'You know, that friend of the doctor he was always going on about when he were fatigued.'

'I think you mean Anno Domini, Mrs Daws, and the doctor meant he was getting older,' Harry pointed out.

'Exactly,' Mrs Daws said. 'Everything takes me so much longer these days. It's a good job April's so willing. She'll be taking over before I'm much older.'

'Oh, Mrs Daws, I do hope we're not working you too hard,' Sarah cried.

'Well, this place takes a fair bit of running, Miss Sullivan. Right, Marmalade, it's time you went out for the night, then I'm away to my bed.'

'I'll sleep in here tonight, then I can hear if Kitty needs anything,' Sarah said.

'And I'll report for duty bright and early,' Harry replied, giving her a mock salute.

The next morning, although pale, Kitty was more like her normal self.

'The resilience of youth,' Mrs Daws commented when Kitty insisted on answering Sergeant Watts' questions straight away.

'Go easy on her, Sergeant,' Sarah whispered as they gathered around the table. Mrs Daws set cups of tea in front of them, then took her seat.

'So, young Kitty, you didn't like this man your mother had, er, moved in with?' he asked, his gaze sharp behind his glasses.

'He were 'orrible,' Kitty replied. 'Kept giving me sly winks and making rude remarks when she weren't there. I'd have left sooner if it weren't for Luke.'

'She took your brother with her?' he asked. Kitty nodded. 'And left you to fend for yourself?' Kitty nodded again.

'When your mother came to collect you, she said she had a job lined up for you, Kitty,' Sarah prompted.

'If you can call being nice to that creep's customers a job,' Kitty snorted.

'What exactly did this man do?' Sergeant Watts asked, pencil poised.

'Sold things,' she muttered.

'And do you know where these things he sold came from?'

Kitty gave him an old-fashioned look. 'Stole 'em.'

'That's a serious allegation, Kitty. Can you be certain of that?' Sarah asked.

'Cors. I mean, do you know any shops that sells things during the dead of night? All 'is punters came to the 'ouse to pick up their stuff. 'E'd steal to order, see. Some of it were expensive things yet they got it for a song. It were my job to get them to up their prices.'

'But how could you do that?' Sarah frowned.

Kitty gave a long-drawn-out sigh then looked at her pityingly. 'You don't know much about life, do you, Miss Sullivan? I 'ad to smile and be nice,' she said, making quotation marks with her fingers when she said 'nice'. 'Lousy creeps. 'Ands like flamin' octopuses.'

'Have a drink of your tea, Kitty. It'll make you feel better,' the housekeeper urged, two spots of anger staining her cheeks.

Kitty grinned, giving a glimpse of her former self. 'Dear Mrs Daws, that's your answer for everything.'

'You've been very helpful, Kitty,' Sergeant Watts said. 'I don't suppose you could give me a description of this man.'

'Cors I can,' she snorted. 'He 'ad skin like a leather belt and always wore stinkin' overalls. Me mum refused to wash them they were so filthy. 'Is teeth were all yellow 'cos he always had a fag hanging out the corner of his mouth and 'e leered like a loony. Gave me the creeps.'

Sarah frowned at this description. Surely it couldn't be . . . ?

'Don't suppose you know his name?' the sergeant asked.

'Cors I do,' Kitty spluttered. 'Honestly, Sergeant, you must 'ave forgotten what a good memory I've got. Mostly called 'imself Slates but sometime he used Tiles. Used to think it funny, for some reason.'

'Not Slater or Tyler?' Sergeant Watts asked.

'Nah, it were definitely Slates or Tiles. Still, it's close, ain't it?'

'It is indeed,' he agreed, glancing at Sarah.

'Now, Kitty, you've been most helpful but I think that's enough for one day,' Sarah told her.

'Yes, you come with me, young lady, and I'll settle you into bed,' Mrs Daws said, getting to her feet.

'But it's daytime,' Kitty said, trying to stifle a yawn. 'Besides, I can see to meself,' she grumbled, but let the housekeeper lead her away.

'Well, that links neatly with my findings,' Sergeant Watts said, frowning down at his notes.

'Do you think it's the man who robbed us?' Sarah asked, voicing her suspicions.

'Could well be, Miss Sullivan.' The sergeant got to his feet. 'It all ties in, along with the fact that the robber who was stashing things up at them barns did a runner before my men could apprehend him. Cors, it's only circumstantial evidence at this moment in time, you understand.'

'Of course, Sergeant. Well, thank you for coming. I'll show you out.'

'Don't you worry, Miss Sullivan. No stone will be left unturned, no lead not followed up. Sergeant Watts will see this man brought to justice,' he assured her, puffing out his chest so that his shiny buttons strained alarmingly.

Sarah was just about to shut the door after him, when Edith came into the room.

'Shouldn't you be in class, Edith?' Sarah asked.

'Master Higgins sent me to see you 'cos I been scratchin' my 'ead all morning,' she sighed. ''E finks I might 'ave caught somefink from Kitty.'

'Sleeping like a little lamb, she is,' Mrs Daws said, bustling back into the kitchen. 'Shouldn't you be in lessons, young lady?' she asked, frowning at Edith.

'Master 'Iggins said you should check me 'air 'cos I been scratchin' like one of them 'ens.'

The housekeeper exchanged looks with Sarah, then with a deep sigh snatched up her comb with the tightly packed teeth.

'Come outside, young lady, and I'll take a good look.'

'Yes, it's nits,' she pronounced, a few moments later.

Sarah's thoughts flew to the forthcoming inspection. 'All the children will have to have their heads shaved immediately,' she said.

'I can't have me 'ead shaved,' Edith wailed. 'Francesca's goin' to show me how to dress me 'air like she does.'

'Who?' the housekeeper frowned.

'Francesca, she's the star of the show and . . .'

'Sorry, Edith,' Sarah interrupted. 'I know it's terrible timing for you, and if there was any other way . . .' she shrugged.

'Miss O'Reilly did promise to check everyone's head, Miss Sullivan,' the housekeeper reminded her.

'But she won't be in until tomorrow afternoon, Mrs Daws. Edith already has nits, and we can't risk them spreading. Every pupil is to have their head shaved before luncheon.'

33

Edith was still sulking about her hair when Sarah escorted her to the Gaiety on Saturday afternoon.

'Would you like me to come in with you and explain exactly why we had to take action?' she asked.

'I've already told them,' Edith snapped. 'And Sylvie and Francesca feel sorry for me,' she added, rolling her eyes.

'Well, have a good afternoon, and don't forget Pip will be waiting in the trap to take you back,' Sarah reminded her. Edith sighed dramatically then, without a backward glance, stalked towards the side entrance. Sarah noted the girl's theatrics and couldn't help wondering if this job was a good idea after all.

Hurrying towards the hall where the women's meeting was being held, she pondered on the last couple of days, which had been difficult, to say the least. As well as the children's heads being shaved, all the bedding had needed washing, necessitating Mrs Laver putting in an extra day's work. Although the woman was willing and a great help to Mrs Daws, it had still meant an added expense. Miss O'Reilly telling them she had heard you could now get powder to treat head infestations hadn't helped either.

'Gracious me, Sarah, you look ready to do battle,'

Josephine Harmon said, catching up with her as she waited to cross the street.

'I am, believe you me,' Sarah replied, dodging between the cabs and carts.

'Well, it won't help the cause if you get yourself killed. I've heard that the women working in the mills in Lancashire are getting up a petition to bring to London. As there are over twenty-nine thousand of them that should make some impact, don't you think? And it's rumoured the ladies from Yorkshire are to do the same, so word's definitely spreading.'

'Talking of spreading the word, you could have warned me the inspection of Red Cliffs was being brought forward,' Sarah said, turning to face her friend.

'I had heard something about that but didn't know a date had been set,' Josephine replied, looking embarrassed.

'It's to be on Monday 20th May so be sure to put it in your diary,' Sarah told her.

'Ah,' Josephine replied, looking extremely uncomfortable now.

'What do you mean, ah?' Sarah asked, staring at her friend. 'I'm counting on your support.'

'Well, that's just it, Sarah. As we are now friends it could put me in an awkward position, so another inspector has been assigned in my place.'

'What? You mean you're not coming as well?' Sarah gasped.

'Here we are,' Josephine said quickly as they arrived outside the red-brick building. 'Gracious, look at the turn-out,' she added, gesturing inside the packed hall. 'Should be a lively meeting.'

But, shocked at her friend's announcement, for once Sarah's mind wasn't on the women's cause.

Just as her friend had predicted, the meeting had indeed been animated but Sarah was distracted by what Josephine had said. She even toyed with the idea of forgoing afternoon tea with Bertram J. Brightling even though she'd been looking forward to it so much. But she really needed to apologize for leaving him in the lurch at their previous meeting, so determinedly pushing all thoughts of Red Cliffs aside, she made her way to the plush hotel on the front.

Entering the opulent building with its sparkling crystal chandeliers and rich-pile carpet that made her feel as though she was walking on air, she couldn't help feeling a thrill of excitement. It was like a different world. The contrasting atmosphere between the musty hall and heady fragrance of the rose petals and clove pot-pourri in the cloakroom was astonishing. Checking her appearance in the gilt-framed mirror, she patted her hair in place and then headed for the restaurant where gentle music was playing. As a waiter led her to the table where Bertram was waiting, he got politely to his feet and smiled.

'I am so pleased you agreed to meet me, dear lady,' he said, giving a small bow. He was dressed in his customary tweed jacket with yet another colourful cravat at his neck, yet his eyes were wary.

'I must apologize for my hasty departure last week, Mr Brightling,' she began.

'Bertram, please,' he reminded her. 'And I, too, must express regret, dear lady, for my loquacious outpouring. I don't know what you must have thought of me, rambling on like a blithering idiot.' He paused, as the waitress approached.

Sarah watched as she placed a silver stand, artistically arranged with finger sandwiches and iced fancies topped with delicate frosted flowers, on the lace cloth between them. The sandwiches with their crustless edges revealed an array of tempting fillings, and as the aroma of smoked salmon and cucumber wafted her way, Sarah's mouth watered. Although, she couldn't help feeling Mrs Daws would lament the waste of good roughage the crusts would have afforded.

'Let us partake of this delicious fare,' Bertram said, as the waitress withdrew. 'There is nothing finer than Earl Grey with lemon for whetting the appetite, don't you think?'

Sarah nodded and duly took a sip of the fragranced pale liquid. It wasn't really to her liking but she smiled politely then nibbled at a dainty sandwich. Goodness, she could eat the whole lot, she thought, and, fearful in case she might, promptly folded her hands in her lap and concentrated on the music.

'The Spring Concerto from Vivaldi's *Four Seasons*,' Bertram said, noting her interest. 'Of course, he composed it for the violin really. "*Spring has arrived with joy. Welcomed by the birds with happy songs*,"' he trilled, waving his hand in time to the beat.

'"*And the brooks, amidst gentle breezes, Murmur sweetly as they flow*,"' she added. He beamed delightedly, all awkwardness between them gone. 'You, too, are an aficionado, Sarah? Sorry, that was forward of me, but kindred spirits should be on first-name terms, don't you think?' As he stared hopefully at her, blue eyes sparkling like Sylvie Spangles' dangles, Sarah felt something stir inside her.

'I do indeed, Bertram,' she agreed. 'And, yes, I am a devotee of Vivaldi. He is so descriptive. *"The goatherd sleeps. His faithful dog beside him,"* conjures up such a peaceful scene, does it not?' Encouraged by his enthusiastic nod, she continued. 'And then the contrast of black skies, thunder and lightning, the birds falling silent. It's such powerful imagery, it almost makes one want to pick up a pen and write.'

'It certainly does,' he replied, glancing down at the table. For the first time, Sarah noticed the notebook at his elbow.

'You are a wordsmith, Bertram?' she guessed.

He shrugged apologetically. 'Sometimes I feel the urge to put my feelings down on paper.'

'Oh, that reminds me,' Sarah said, scrabbling in her reticule and drawing out an envelope. 'I wonder if I might beg a favour of you, Bertram. You see, I penned a letter to Lady Chorlton, which I quite neglected to post. As you live next door, I wonder if I could prevail upon you to see that she gets it?'

His expression darkened and Sarah frowned, worried she'd overstepped the bounds of propriety.

'I regret to say Lady Chorlton no longer resides in Hesketh Crescent,' he told her.

'Oh goodness, I do hope nothing untoward has happened to her?' Sarah cried.

'Her son secured ownership of the property on his majority and . . .' he shrugged. 'There is no nice way to put this, I'm afraid, dear lady. He insisted she leave.'

'You mean he threw her out?' Sarah gasped. 'But that's terrible. She has been so good to the school, I would really like to help. Do you know where she's gone?'

Bertram took a discreet look around.

'Have you finished, sir?' the waitress asked, misunderstanding his gesture. Bertram nodded and Sarah, all thought of hunger gone, waited impatiently while the woman deftly stacked her tray with crockery and the remains of their afternoon tea. As she bustled way, he leaned forward.

'My housekeeper, whom I inherited along with the lease, was friends with Lady Chorlton's maid.'

'Then she could pass on my letter,' Sarah said, holding it out.

'I'm afraid not, dear lady. You see,' he glanced from right to left, then continued in hushed tones, 'she, too, has left. This son made unwelcome advances, if you get my meaning. According to my housekeeper, who has served at the house for a long while, he is just like his father. Anyway, he made the poor girl's position untenable and she fled.'

'That's awful,' Sarah frowned, recalling the pleasant young girl with her smartly tailored black dress and pristine white apron. 'And poor Lady Chorlton,' she sighed, returning her letter to her bag. 'Do you know where she has gone?'

Bertram shook his head. 'All I know is that she was seen leaving in the family carriage taking one small bag with her. I'm led to believe the son has inherited his father's estate, and she has been left virtually penniless.'

'How could he be so heartless?' Sarah whispered. 'Surely, he has a duty to see she is provided for?'

'As I said earlier, Sarah, it would appear he takes after his father. Now, it was not my intention to pour cold water upon our meeting, so let us change the subject forthwith. When I returned your coat, I noticed the Red Cliffs Ragged School sign on your gates. I found it intriguing imagining what goes on in that big house so why don't you enlighten me?' he invited.

Pushing thought of Lady Chorlton to the back of her mind, Sarah proceeded to tell him about inheriting the house from her godfather. And with gentle prompting from a clearly interested Bertram she gave an account of the day-to-day running of the school.

'It's a full-time job but one I wouldn't swap for all the world,' she finished.

'Your godfather sounds like a wonderful, selfless man, and you, dear lady, obviously share his ideals.'

'What about you, Bertram? Apart from a love of music and words, what do you do?'

'Actually, they are intrinsically entwined and the reason for my removing to Torquay for the season.'

'How fascinating. Do tell me more,' she urged.

His eyes lit up, sparkling like the chandeliers overhead. 'Indeed, dear lady, I can't tell you just how fascinating it has been. You see, I had this idea in my head that just wouldn't go away. Then I was presented with this marvellous opportunity, but the trouble was, no matter how hard I tried, I couldn't get the features of the leading lady right.'

'You mean you're writing a play?' she gasped, her eyes widening.

'Written, actually,' he beamed. 'You see, almost as soon as I arrived here, I found the perfect muse and my character came to life before my very eyes.'

'How wonderful. And does your play have a name?' she asked excitedly.

'Oh, yes, it came to me one afternoon,' he said, giving her a tender look. Then he frowned and looked around the room. 'The pianist has ceased playing and, regrettably, I think that's a signal we should be leaving,' he sighed.

Sarah, enthralled by his story, could have cried with disappointment.

'Perhaps I could offer you a lift home in my automobile, dear lady?' he said, getting to his feet and holding out a hand.

Sarah's heart almost flipped with excitement. She'd never been in a motor car before.

'Oh, I can walk,' she suggested, taking his proffered hand, whilst keeping the fingers of the other tightly crossed.

'I wouldn't hear of it, dear lady,' he assured her. 'Whilst you retrieve your coat, I'll bring my car round.'

As he negotiated the driveway, Sarah sat back in the leather seats, her pulses tingling with exhilaration. She wondered at the popping noises coming from the vehicle and was slightly perturbed that there was no horse in front of them. They drove along the seafront, people turning to watch as they passed. Soon she became accustomed to the openness ahead and marvelled that everything rushed by at such a speed. She felt as if she were flying and didn't care a fig about the wind tugging her hair from its knot. All too soon, though, Bertram was drawing up outside the gates of Red Cliffs.

'What a charming house,' he exclaimed. 'I noticed the stunning quoins and elegant façade last time. And what a vista, too,' he added, peering through the iron railings. 'It's just the kind of property I would buy.'

'Really?' Sarah laughed. Then she frowned as a thought occurred to her. 'You're not a property developer as well as a writer, are you?'

'Heavens, no, although I'm not just a wordsmith, I . . .'

'Cripes, Miss Sullivan, is that you sat in that automobile?' Pip cried, as he pulled open the gates. 'Oh, 'ello again, sir,' he added, noticing Bertram behind the wheel.

Sarah turned to Bertram. 'I'd better jump out here,' she told him. 'Otherwise you'll have all the pupils coming out to inspect your car. Much as I love them, they're a nosy lot and you don't want sticky fingermarks spoiling your shiny paintwork.'

'I'm sure it wouldn't matter,' he replied. 'However, I do have an appointment later this evening, so better be making tracks and all that. Erm . . .' He paused, looked awkward, then seem to gather his strength. 'I was wondering if you would be free to join me next Saturday afternoon?' he asked, his words coming out in a rush. 'We could share more of our thoughts on Vivaldi perhaps?' As he looked at her hopefully, Sarah's heart skipped.

'That would be lovely. Summer perhaps. "*A gentle breeze blows but Boreas . . .*"' she began, but he shook his head and nodded to where Pip stood glaring at them.

'Winter might be more appropriate. "*To hear leaving their iron-gated house, Sirocco, Boreas and all the winds in battle,*"' he intoned.

'Yes, you could be right,' she laughed. 'I've had a wonderful afternoon, Bertram. Thank you so much.' He beamed delightedly and she watched as he drove off down the street.

'Coo blimey, miss, thought you was never goin' to stop yappin',' Pip moaned, shutting the gate behind her. 'You goin' up in the world, ain't you?' he added, eyeing her curiously.

'Did you collect Edith all right?' Sarah asked, ignoring his remark.

'Oh, yes, miss. Swanned out of that Gaiety like she was a flipping actress. Had this funny thing on her head, an' all,' he told her, raising his brows.

Knowing it was supper time, Sarah went straight through to the kitchen to see if Mrs Daws needed any help.

'No, that's all right, Miss Sullivan. Kitty's been helping me whilst April supervised the girls' sewing. 'Been having a nice old natter, haven't we, dear?'

Kitty grinned. 'Yeah, anything's better than doing stupid stitching,' she replied.

'And how are you today, Kitty?' Sarah asked, noting the girl had a better colour and that her eyes had lost their glazed look.

'I'm fine. It's that Edith you need to worry about,' she muttered.

'Did you have a good time at your women's meeting, Miss Sullivan?' the housekeeper asked.

'Women's meeting,' Pip chortled, coming into the room. 'It weren't no lady driving her 'ome in that posh auto-car, I can tell yer.'

Sarah felt her cheeks blaze as they turned to her in astonishment.

'Something smells good, Mrs Daws,' she said quickly. 'I noticed the children were rinsing their hands ready so I'll just take off my coat while you sound the gong, Kitty. I'll supervise supper tonight.'

After saying grace, Sarah stared around the tables, checking that everyone was happy. The boys, having been served by Pip, were already tucking into their food. The girls, however, were all staring at Edith in fascination.

'What is that on your head, Edith?' Sarah asked, staring at the black scarf-like creation.

'It's me twinkly twurban, miss,' she said proudly.

'You mean turban,' Sarah replied.

'No I don't. It's definitely a twurban,' Edith glared. 'I told you Sylvie was 'orrified at the state of me 'ead so she made it for me. And she found me this brooch to put on it so I can twinkle like 'er. Sylvie said me sewing's so good I can 'elp her accessyrise Francesca's costume tomorrow. Sylvie says we will be the mistresses of creation and reinvention and that . . .'

'For God's sake shut up, will yer, Edith? All I've 'eard since I come back is Sylvie this and Sylvie that,' Kitty cried.

'You're just jealous 'cos I can sew and you can't,' Edith snorted.

'That's enough,' Sarah snapped. 'Eat up and be quiet, the pair of you.'

As Kitty and Edith stared at her in surprise, she stared quickly down at her plate. She'd been thinking about Lady Chorlton and was in no mood for their bickering.

Ignoring the incredulous looks the girls were giving her, she resolved to contact Mr Fothergill first thing on Monday.

Despite her concerns, however, when she fell into bed that night it was dreams of Bertram that punctuated her sleep.

34

When Harry popped his head around the office door early the next morning, he found Sarah humming softly to herself.

'Someone's happy,' he said, noticing the smile playing around her lips. 'You know you should do that more often.'

'Do what?' she asked.

'Sing like that. It makes your face look softer somehow,' he said. Then he went hot, worried in case she took his words the wrong way. To his relief, her smile widened.

'Why, thank you, Harry. Actually, it was a tune from Vivaldi's *Four Seasons*.'

'Oh,' he replied, taken aback. 'That's, er, nice.'

'What music do you like, Harry?' she asked, staring at him curiously.

'Can't say I've given it much thought,' he shrugged. 'Usually I'm thankful for a bit of peace and quiet after the hullabaloo of the classroom.'

Sarah gestured to the corner of the room where the piano Mrs Knight had bequeathed the school stood. 'You know, Harry, it might be nice for the children to have a singalong at the weekends.'

'Really?' he muttered, wondering if Sarah was feeling all right.

'Sally could play for them. She hasn't had a chance to practise since coming here, has she?'

He shook his head. 'We've been too busy to think of music, apart from that concert at Easter.'

'Well, to work,' she said briskly, reverting to the Sarah he knew. 'I was ticking off some of the items on my list when you arrived. That's always satisfying, don't you think?'

'I certainly do,' he replied, relieved to be back on safe ground. Digging in his pocket he produced his list with a flourish. 'The tool shed is now built, tick. The boys cleaned out the stable, tick. That reminds me, whilst you were out yesterday, Sergeant Watts called to check something with Kitty. Then he gave the all clear for us to go up to the farm.'

'Was Kitty all right?' she asked, remembering the girl's surliness at supper.

'She was fine. Said the sooner they caught the bast— er, that man, the better,' he said.

'I couldn't agree more,' Sarah replied. 'That's good news about the farm.'

'Yes, and in fairness to Bess, I thought it better to check the place over sooner rather than later. If it's all right with you, I'll take the boys up there this afternoon. Solomon told me we need a big tree stump, so we'll look for that as well.'

'Whatever do you want a stump for?' Sarah asked, staring at him in disbelief.

'To put a steel plate on so we can hammer the bent tools back into shape, of course,' he chuckled. 'I tell you, Sarah, that lad's knowledge is invaluable. We can take the cart in case we find a suitable one.'

'I agree it would be a good idea to take the trap,' she said, giving him a reproving look. 'And when they return from helping the good ladies with the soup kitchen, I'll set the girls to their sewing. Right, my list now,' she said, glancing down at the paper in front of her. 'I've brought the ledger up to date, tick. Pip can drop it off at the offices of Calculus and Arithmica tomorrow after he's taken Edith to the Gaiety. I'm hoping that will give them plenty of time to get the accounts audited.' Then she frowned. 'I still can't find that blooming licence so I'll have to resume my search after church. Oh, and guess what?'

'Someone's popped their clogs and left us a fortune,' he teased.

'Harry, really,' she cried. 'Although under the circumstances, that would be a help. I heard yesterday that Lady Chorlton was ordered from her home.'

'What? By whom?' he asked, sinking into the chair opposite.

'By her elder son. Apparently on reaching his majority he inherited his father's estate, along with his money.'

'Poor old Lady Chorlton,' Harry whistled. 'Samuel would turn in his grave, if he had one.'

'I'll ignore that tasteless comment, Harry,' she retorted, back to her formal self. 'After all the help Lady Chorlton has given us, the least we can do is try to reciprocate. I therefore intend contacting Mr Fothergill to offer our assistance.'

'Good idea,' Harry agreed.

Sarah sighed. 'It's a bitter blow for Red Cliffs, though. When she said she would have to cut back on her benefactions, she didn't mention we wouldn't be getting anything at all.'

He shrugged philosophically. 'From what you said earlier, it sounds as if she didn't know either. Don't worry, Sarah, we'll manage.'

'I don't know how you can stay so calm,' she cried, staring at him in that way she had of making him feel like he didn't understand things.

'Look, Sarah, let's just concentrate on getting everything ready for the inspection. Goodness knows, I've got enough to do if we want to secure that extra funding from the authorities.'

'You're right, of course, Harry,' she said, tossing her list onto the desk and sitting back in her seat. 'At least the weather's warmer so we don't need to have the fire lit,' she added, nodding to the empty grate.

'We'll have to be careful the spirits don't take up residence in the chimney, though,' he joked.

'You've been spending too much time with Miss O'Reilly,' she groaned, although she was smiling inwardly at the sudden flush on his face. She'd recently come to realize that Harry and Sheena were a good match and was surprised to find it came as a relief.

'Actually, I was going to speak to you about that,' he said, determined to seize the opportunity of discussing what had been worrying him. 'We, er, that is, I have asked her to walk out with me, Sarah.' He paused and waited for her reaction. To his amazement, she smiled.

'Whatever took you so long?' she quipped.

'You mean you don't mind?' he asked, relief flooding through him.

'Why should I? Oh, I know we once thought we might . . . well, you know. But you and Miss O'Reilly are far better suited.' When he quirked a brow she went on: 'Well, you both enjoy using those funny long words, for a start,' she told him.

'I suppose it does save me from having to explain them to you,' he grinned. 'Right, if there's nothing else, I'd better get on.'

'And I'd better hunt down this blooming licence. What the . . . ?' She stopped as she heard a thud followed by Edith shrieking.

'I 'ate you, Kitty Bawden. It's your fault I look like this.'

Hurrying to the door, Harry pulled it open to see the two girls scrapping in the hallway.

'Kitty, Edith, get yourselves in here, this minute,' he ordered. 'Now tell me what on earth is going on.' The two girls stood staring down at the floor. 'I asked you a question, so do me the courtesy of answering,' he persisted.

'I was makin' another twurban to wear to the theatre and she snatched it and ripped it apart,' Edith wailed, holding up two pieces of material, now frayed at the edges.

'Theatre, theatre, theatre. That's all you go on about these days,' Kitty snapped.

'Just because you can't sew . . .' Edith began, but Sarah interrupted.

'That's enough, girls. Give those to me, Edith, then go get yourselves ready for church.' Sarah held out her hand and Edith reluctantly handed over the pieces of fabric. 'You will both spend the afternoon in the classroom sewing sheets with me.'

'I ain't . . .' Kitty began.

'I said that's enough. Now go.' As the door closed behind them, Sarah turned to Harry. 'I'm worried about those two.'

'Kitty's been through a traumatic time,' Harry reminded her.

'And Edith has let this new job go to her head. I'm seriously thinking of stopping her from going to the theatre.'

'She'd only resent you, Sarah. This is Edith's first venture away from Red Cliffs so she's feeling all grown up and finding her feet. She's a good kid, really. I mean, she didn't even want to celebrate her birthday when she found out what had happened to Kitty.'

'But we've got to do something, Harry,' Sarah said, getting up and going over to the window. 'Goodness, the children are already lining up ready for church. We'd better get our skates on.'

'Actually, I've got so much to do, I think I'll skip the vicar's sermon.'

'Harry!'

'You can say a prayer for me,' he grinned, then looked serious again. 'Going back to Kitty and Edith. It might be better to separate them for a while. Kitty's let us know in no uncertain terms that she hates sewing so why don't I take her up to the farm this afternoon?'

'But I won't be able to accompany her,' Sarah frowned.

'No, but Miss O'Reilly will,' he winked. 'She loves it up at the farm and is happy to give up her Sunday afternoon. Seriously, Sarah, we have to think what's in the children's best interests, don't we?'

*

Harry whistled as made his way to the new shed, pleased to have cleared the air with Sarah. Although he'd once thought they were on the point of rekindling their relationship, Sheena's arrival had changed everything. Almost immediately, he'd realized that Sheena was the woman for him. Of course, poor Bess couldn't be expected to know that. He admired Sarah hugely but Sheena was good fun and, well, more womanly, he thought, smiling as an image of her swam before him.

Forcing his thoughts back to the present, he assessed the new building. It was open at the front to accommodate the lathe pole Solomon had cut from a long branch. Together they'd set it in the ground outside and angled it up into the roof. Next week they were going to build a wooden frame for the lathe along with the shave horse. They could then begin the woodturning lessons. His intention was to have wood sawn into basic shapes so the inspector could watch them being turned into rounded handles or shaped into axe handles. Satisfied everything was in order, he went into the classroom to set the next week's lessons.

It wasn't easy balancing the requirements of their different ages, but with time spent planning and not a little ingenuity he prided himself on giving them the best education possible. It was easier said than done, though, and, head bent over his papers, he let out a long sigh.

'Tribulations on the Sabbath, Master Higgins?' He looked up to see Sheena standing in the doorway and grinned. She was wearing a dress in the same cherry red as her hat and with her hair cascading in curls over her shoulder, had never looked more beautiful. His heart did a somersault.

'Just setting the little darlings a history test,' he replied. 'Do you know Bunter said King Alfred couldn't possibly have burned the cakes because baking was women's work? Miss Sullivan would kill me if she heard such bigoted talk.'

'She is right to insist the girls have the same opportunities as the boys. However, this woman has done some cooking so if you're hungry there's a pan of soup heating on the range,' she told him.

'Beauty and broth, what more can a man want?' he asked, slapping his hand to his chest. 'I certainly won't say no to dinner *à deux*, Miss O'Reilly,' he replied, waggling his brows suggestively.

'I'm afraid you'll have to make it dinner *à quatre* because Miss Sullivan and Mrs Daws are joining us,' she chuckled. 'Although, if you're interested, Nanna has invited you to luncheon when you're not so busy, to atone for her behaviour.'

'And would that meet with your approval, fair lady?'

'Any excuse to stop stitching endless lengths of sheeting meets with my approval, Master Higgins,' she quipped.

With Harry leading the pony and cart and the excited boys alongside, the little group headed along the lane towards the farm. Seeing Kitty hanging back, Sheena waited.

'What's wrong, Kitty?' Sheena asked. 'I thought you'd be excited at the prospect of an afternoon away from sewing.'

'I am, an' being away from that Edith, an' all,' she muttered.

'Oh? But I thought you two were friends?' Sheena said, trying to keep her voice light.

'Not no more, we ain't. Said she wished she'd left me and me lice begging on the station steps.'

'Edith doesn't really mean that, Kitty.'

'But I wish she 'ad, an' all, miss. I ain't no use at stitchin', in fact I ain't no good at nofink.'

Hearing the despair in the girl's voice, Sheena reached out and pulled her close. 'Now that simply isn't true. Why, I'm relying on you to help me check over the dairy and farmhouse whilst the boys help Master Higgins in the fields.'

'Are yer?' Kitty replied, staring at Sheena in surprise.

'To be sure I am, Kitty, for am I not an old scaredy-cat when it comes to empty buildings?'

'Don't you worry, miss, I'll look out for yer,' the girl replied, squaring her shoulders. 'You should see some of the doss 'ouses I bin in. 'Ere we are, so you just stay close to me,' she added, as the boys gave a yell and swarmed through the gates. They made their way up the drive, which was already overgrown with weeds, and stood looking around the yard.

'It looks all darlict, sir,' Brown cried, looking around.

'You mean derelict,' Harry corrected, letting the pony loose on the grass. 'It doesn't take long for things to go to pot when you don't tend them. Now you can appreciate how hard Farmer Jim and Bess had to work to keep the farm going.' He saw Solomon's crestfallen gaze taking in the big barn where the pigs had slept, and clapped his hands.

'Right, first of all I want you boys to tidy up the yard and weed the drive. Solomon, you come with me, we'll take a look in the barns that thief used, then check the crops in the fields. We'll keep an eye open for that stump while we're at it.'

'Miss and me is goin' to make sure everything's all right in the farm'ouse and dairy, ain't we, miss?' Kitty told him.

Harry looked askance at Sheena, who nodded.

'To be sure, we want everything to be spick and span for when Bess returns,' she assured him.

The house felt cold and dismal without the heat from the range, and a fine layer of dust had settled over all the surfaces. It was a far cry from the cosy home Bess had prided herself on keeping.

'Right, Kitty, you grab a cloth and give everywhere a wipe over. I'll lay a fire so the range will be ready to light when Bess comes back.'

'Do you think she'll want to live here again now Farmer Jim's gone?' Kitty asked.

Sheena stared at the girl in surprise for hadn't she just voiced her own thoughts?

'I'd just love to live somewhere like this,' Kitty added, gazing around wistfully.

'Well, it is a lovely home and Bess has left most of her things, so she must be intending to return at some stage. We'll make it nice for her, shall we?'

Once the house was sparkling again they took themselves into the dairy. Sheena shivered, remembering the last time she'd been here. Having heard Bess and Alice discussing the arrangements between Harry and Sarah, she'd been so miserable, she'd scrubbed every surface to within an inch of its life.

'Come along, Kitty,' she urged, suddenly wanting to be outside. 'Everything is fine in here. Let's go and see how the others are doing.'

'Good news and bad,' Harry said, when they joined him. 'We've found a suitable stump for the metalwork but the crops in the fields are choked with weeds. It's going to take a lot of work to get the fields back to how they were.'

'But we got some veggies for Mrs Daws,' Solomon grinned, pointing to a pile of potatoes, cabbages and leeks.

'To be sure, that puts me in mind of my mammy's colcannon,' Sheena smiled.

'Well, climb up into the cart and you can tell me about it on the way back,' Harry invited. 'You little lot, on your way.'

'What about Kitty?' Sheena began, but Harry pointed to where she and Solomon were deep in conversation.

'Looks like she's found a new friend,' he smiled. 'Now tell me about what this colcannon is?' he invited, urging the pony on. Sheena sat back in the seat and did as he'd asked.

'So it's a bit like our bubble and squeak, then?' he replied.

'Only much more sophisticated,' she teased.

'You looked really happy when you were talking about your home. I know you came to Torbay to look after your grandmother but what prompted you to stay here?' Harry asked.

Sheena's heart lurched and she turned away from him.

'To be sure, we're back at the school already,' she said. Then as they waited for Pip to open the gate, she jumped from the cart. 'It's been a lovely afternoon but Nanna will be waiting for me.'

Before Harry could reply, she'd taken off down the street as if the devil was after her.

35

When Sheena reappeared the next afternoon, Harry was engrossed in setting the stump on the cobbled floor of the stables. Looking up briefly, he gave a wave, then went back to his task. He was determined to have the tool shop up and running by the end of the day and wasn't going to stop until the task was completed.

Once the steel plate had been secured on top of the stump to act as an anvil, he went through to the old school workshop, where Solomon was supervising the boys.

'Right, Solomon, we know time is too short to train everyone so I've decided to draw up a plan of action.'

'Good thinking,' he agreed, then dropped his voice. 'If you are going to give everyone their own task then Bunter, being large, would be best for hammering the bent tools back into shape.'

Harry nodded and wrote that down. 'We'll make a list so everyone knows what they're to do. And, Solomon, I'm relying on you to give a demonstration to the inspector.'

'I can do that,' he agreed. 'Mind you, I don't know what he'll say about her being in the class,' he grinned, jerking his head to where Kitty was deftly smoothing down a piece of wood with a plane.

*

The next weeks passed in a frenzy of activity and before they knew it the day of the inspection was upon them.

'I have to say, Miss O'Reilly's done a wonderful job getting all this bedding finished,' Mrs Daws said, as she and Sarah gave the dormitories a final check.

'With the girls' help,' Sarah replied, thinking of all the hours they'd spent sewing.

'Yes, but it's been Miss O'Reilly who's been taking all that work home to make sure it's done in time and up to standard. Why, she even had to cancel Sunday luncheon with Master Higgins.'

'Oh, I see,' Sarah frowned. 'Only having taken the girls for sewing a couple of hours each week, I didn't realize they were behind.'

'She's not one to blow her own trumpet, and I know you've been very busy, too, Miss Sullivan,' the housekeeper said quickly.

'Fingers crossed we've done enough to satisfy the inspectors,' Sarah replied, staring around at the freshly whitewashed walls and sparkling windows with satisfaction. Then she saw Pip open the gate and let in a smartly dressed man wearing a bowler hat.

'Here we go,' she said, smoothing down her best navy dress and hurrying down the stairs.

'Good morning and welcome to Red Cliffs,' she said, smiling brightly.

'Miss Sullivan?' he asked. She nodded. 'Mr Mahon, from the Local Authority,' he announced. His voice had a slight lilt and his manner was pleasant.

'Do come into my office,' she invited him. 'Can I get you some refreshment?'

'Thank you, that won't be necessary,' he said, drawing a file from his leather briefcase and placing it on the desk before him.

'There's only one of you?' Sarah asked in surprise.

'Yes, and I don't think this re-inspection will take long. I see the school has applied for extra funding for the tuition of, er,' he referred to his notes, 'wood and metalworking. Naturally, I will be wishing to see a demonstration on that. I also wish to have a word with Miss O'Reilly.'

'Miss O'Reilly teaches in the afternoon, Mr Mahon,' Sarah told him.

'Perhaps you would ask that she sees me as soon as she arrives. First, I will check your books – your accounts have been audited?'

'Yes,' she replied, passing the ledger across the desk.

'You need not wait, Miss Sullivan. I will call you if I have any queries. Oh, and I need sight of the school licence?'

'I'm afraid I haven't been able to find it, Mr Mahon. I've searched everywhere,' she explained.

He glanced at the row of opened boxes but didn't comment. 'Perhaps you could tell Master Higgins I will be sitting in on his lesson in . . .' he frowned and consulted his pocket watch, 'twenty minutes. Then I will take a look around the premises by which time Miss O'Reilly should have arrived. When I have spoken with her I will want to see a demonstration of toolmaking. After which we will have another meeting. Thank you, Miss Sullivan.'

As he bent his head over the ledger, Sarah hurried to the classroom.

'Excuse me, Master Higgins,' she said, careful to remain in the doorway, out of earshot of the pupils.

'Everything all right?'

Quickly she relayed the inspector's requests.

'Well, that all seems straightforward,' Harry shrugged. 'I'll just go and bribe that little lot to be on their best behaviour. I don't suppose your Bertram has dropped any more candy off for them?'

Sarah smiled, remembering the large box that had been delivered after their last meeting.

'I'll see if there's any left,' she promised. 'Good luck.'

True to his word, the inspector, having sat in on Harry's lesson, then proceeded to take a look around the property. He politely declined Sarah's offer of a guided tour then refused Mrs Daws' invitation to luncheon.

'It's my best cottage pie,' she told him.

'Although it sounds delicious, Mrs Daws, regrettably I must decline.'

'That Mr Green always scoffed as much as he could,' the housekeeper added.

'But he is no longer with us. However, talk of your *cottage* pie has jogged my memory about the school's future, and for that I thank you.'

'Well, he's a real gent,' Mrs Daws said to April, mollified by his words. 'Oh, there you are, dear,' she added, looking up as Sheena entered the kitchen. 'Miss Sullivan says you're to go straight through to her office.'

'Sounds ominous, Mrs Daws,' she said.

'Oh, don't you worry, dear, that inspector's a right nice man,' the housekeeper assured her.

Quickly taking off her hat and coat, Sheena hurried down the hallway and knocked on the door.

'Come in,' Sarah called. 'Mr Mahon, this is Miss . . .'

'We already know each other, don't we, Miss O'Reilly?' he said.

Sheena gulped as the familiar grey eyes stared challengingly at her.

'I am surprised you managed to secure a position here in view of your past record. Tell me, Miss Sullivan, did you not request a character from Miss O'Reilly?'

'Yes, of course,' Sarah replied, looking from Sheena to the inspector in dismay.

'And did it not state that this woman was a marriage wrecker and thief to boot?'

'What?' Sarah gasped. 'Now, Mr Mahon, there must surely be some mistake.'

'No mistake whatsoever, is there, Miss O'Reilly.'

'I am not a thief, Mr Mahon,' Sheena replied, her voice coming out as a whisper. 'And as for . . .'

'We have discussed this before, Miss O'Reilly, 'he snapped before turning back to Sarah. 'Miss Sullivan, did Miss O'Reilly not tell you she had been dismissed from her previous situation?'

Sarah shook her head.

'But you did check her character?'

'Yes, of course I did,' she spluttered. 'Although . . .'

'Although, Miss Sullivan?'

'It was very sparse in detail,' Sarah admitted.

'I would be failing in my duty as inspector if I didn't advise you to dismiss this woman on the spot. As proprietor of Red Cliffs, responsibility for the moral welfare of your pupils lies with you. It is your decision, of course, but I do have my report to make.' He shrugged but left Sarah in doubt as to his meaning.

'Well, I . . .' Sarah began, then turned to Sheena. 'Do you have anything to say in your defence, Miss O'Reilly?'

'I am not a thief,' she replied.

'But your character, it was sparse, was it not?' Sarah persisted.

'I omitted some detail,' Sheena admitted. Then she squared her shoulders. 'Don't worry, Miss Sullivan, I'll be on my way.'

Sarah watched helplessly as, head held high, she left the room. Surprisingly, she'd become quite fond of the mistress and didn't want to see her go like this.

'Was that really necessary?' she asked the man.

'A word to the wise, Miss Sullivan,' said the inspector. 'Whenever you engage staff, be sure to check their credentials thoroughly. Now, I believe it is time to see this demonstration of toolmaking. No, don't get up,' he added, as Sarah made to move. 'I know my way.'

He walked briskly from the room, leaving a stunned Sarah staring after him. Then, realizing the girls would need supervising, she hurried through to the kitchen.

'Could April look after the girls for an hour or so, Mrs Daws?' she asked.

'What's wrong with Miss O'Reilly? Isn't she supposed to be watching them?' the housekeeper frowned.

'She's had to go home,' Sarah said quickly, unwilling to divulge the inspector's bombshell until she'd spoken to Harry.

'Good afternoon, Mr Mahon,' Harry greeted the inspector outside the new shed. 'Children?'

'Good afternoon, Mr Mahon,' they intoned.

'Right, everyone, let's show the inspector what we have learned so far. Solomon, perhaps you would like to start.'

'Sir,' he said, going over to the pole lathe. 'Brown will assist me in turning some billets of wood into rounded handles,' he explained.

As they worked, the pole bobbing up and down, Solomon turned to the inspector and said, 'You might find it interesting to take a look outside, sir, for if we are doing this properly it will look like a nodding donkey.' The man raised his brow but duly did as Solomon suggested. When he returned, Harry noted he was smiling.

'Now we will demonstrate the shave horse, sir. We use this for forming wood into irregular shapes such as axe handles. Black here will demonstrate how we do this using a draw knife,' Solomon said.

The inspector watched closely then turned to Harry. 'I'm impressed with what you've taught them so far, Higgins. But what is that girl doing here?' he asked, pointing to Kitty.

'She requested to learn this craft in preference to needlework, Mr Mahon.'

'Isn't that irregular?' the inspector asked.

'Miss Sullivan is keen that, where practicable, the girls should be given the same opportunities as the boys,' Harry explained.

'Indeed?' the man replied. 'Well, perhaps she would like to give me a demonstration of metalworking now,' he challenged.

'Come along then,' Kitty said, leading the way to the converted stable.

'Can you tell me why this is in a different building, young lady?' he asked.

'To keep the sparks away from the wood shavings,' she told him. 'Now, Master Higgins has shown me how to hammer bent tools back into shape but you'd better stand back.'

To Mr Mahon's amazement, Kitty picked up the hammer and began bashing it skilfully.

'What else do you do?' the man asked, when she held up the straightened tool.

'Polish the steel part with dogfish skin. Then Solomon and Bunter are going to show you how to get the tools ready for use by grinding a keen edge on 'em.'

'I see. Well, thank you, Master Higgins, that is quite enough,' he said, turning to Harry. 'Perhaps you could join me in Miss Sullivan's office in . . .' he consulted his pocket watch, 'twenty minutes.'

Sarah looked up anxiously as Mr Mahon re-entered the office.

'Everything all right?' she asked.

'Most interesting. Now . . .' he said, opening his file again. 'Your accounts, while up to date, don't show much in reserve, do they?'

'No, but we have lots of plans to address that,' she told him. He raised a brow but didn't comment. 'We have applied for funding for the tuition of . . .'

The man held up his hand. 'I know and would like to discuss that when Master Higgins joins us. Now, to his academic teaching. He is proficient, his lessons well put together. The pupils, both girls and boys, were attentive and smartly dressed. My tour of the property revealed well-kept rooms, clean bedding and no evidence of water ingress. The steps you have taken to remedy the roof defect have clearly worked. Mrs Daws keeps a well-stocked larder and is obviously a good and efficient housekeeper.' As he paused for breath, Sarah let out a sigh of relief.

'However, there are a couple of things that concern me, Miss Sullivan. First, the licence.'

'I know, and I have searched everywhere.'

'Our records don't actually show one was ever issued. Can you confirm the previous proprietor, Dr Samuel Lawrence, was granted a licence to open Red Cliffs as a school?'

'He must have been,' Sarah stammered.

'But you cannot actually confirm that is the case?'

'Well, no. I mean, my godfather died last year so . . .' she shrugged.

The man wrote something on his file and then looked directly at her.

'The main other concern here is the lack of modern plumbing. It is now a requirement for schools with residential accommodation to have water piped into the property and internal water closets installed.'

'Really?' Sarah replied, her heart sinking.

'A costly expenditure, I know,' he nodded. 'Ragged schools have had their day, Miss Sullivan.'

'What? But what about the pupils?' she cried.

He sat back in his seat and studied her for a moment.

'The thinking now is that orphans and deprived children benefit hugely from a more, how shall we say, homely environment. They are known as cottage schools or homes and . . .' He was interrupted by a knock on the door.

'Come in, Master Higgins,' Sarah called.

'You either see through wood or you know the person about to enter very well,' the inspector smiled. 'Ah, indeed it is Master Higgins,' he confirmed as Harry hovered in the doorway.

'Come and sit down,' Sarah invited. 'Mr Mahon has been going through his findings.'

'All good, I hope,' Harry smiled, but Sarah could see the anxious look in his eyes.

'I was impressed with your teaching of the woodturning and metalwork, especially as you had the pupils demonstrating their skills.'

'Oh, that's good,' Sarah replied, relief flooding through her. But the inspector hadn't finished.

'However, in order to agree funding, I need you to tell me what benefits the children will gain from this. I mean, they won't all go on to use these trades, will they?'

'I have observed the children working and believe the repetitive work plus the need to concentrate while using sharp tools on both the pole lathe and shave horse make them calmer and less disruptive,' Harry explained. 'The heavy work hammering the steel blades and turning the grindstone helps build their physical strength as well as leading to a stronger mentality. They are also growing in confidence as they realize they are now doing a man's job.'

'Even the girls?'

'I feel strongly that girls should receive the same opportunities as boys, Mr Mahon,' Sarah explained. 'In years to come, who knows what jobs will be open to women?'

The inspector quirked his brow in that way she'd come to recognize meant he wasn't about to be drawn.

'Well, thank you both for your co-operation and a very interesting day here at Red Cliffs,' he said, snapping his file shut and getting to his feet.

'You will receive my official report in due course and in the meantime I will inform the Local Authority that you are in need of a new travelling mistress, Miss Sullivan. I'll see myself out. Good afternoon to you both.' With a quick nod, he left the room.

'What did he mean about needing a new travelling mistress?'

'He told me I should dismiss Miss O'Reilly on the spot, Harry. Apparently, he knew her before and she was accused of theft and, er . . . he also called her a marriage wrecker,' Sarah told him uneasily.

'What? I don't believe that,' he cried, springing to his feet. 'I'll go to the classroom and speak with her.'

'It's too late, Harry. She's already left.'

36

Harry rushed down the street, his mind whirling like falling sycamore leaves. Why hadn't Sarah stood up for Miss O'Reilly? Worse still, why had she let her go? And why had Sheena left without discussing it with him? Reaching her grandmother's house, he hammered on the door.

'She's gone, lad,' the woman said, staring sadly at him.

'Gone? Gone where?' he demanded.

'Just packed her bag, said she'd be in touch and left.'

'The inspector said she'd been accused of theft . . .' he began.

'My granddaughter is no thief, Master Higgins,' Sheena's grandmother retorted, green eyes glittering. 'Night after night she spent stitching that bedding for the school and yet you choose to think the worst of her. Knew you were out to take advantage of her, first time I clapped eyes on you. On your way,' she cried, closing the door.

'If you hear from her, please tell her she's welcome at Red Cliffs anytime,' he pleaded but he was talking to fresh air.

When Edith came out of the theatre she could hardly contain her excitement.

'Come and look at this,' she called to Pip, who was waiting patiently in the cart.

Seeing the girl's flushed face and the way the turbanlike thing on her head wobbled alarmingly as she jumped up and down, he sighed good-naturedly, climbed down and hobbled over to see her pointing at a poster advertising the new production opening that weekend. 'They've done the final reveal, and look,' she squeaked.

'Well, I'll be,' he muttered.

'It's Miss Sullivan to a T, ain't it? Look, they've even captured that snooty look she's got.'

'It certainly looks like her,' Pip admitted. 'Didn't know she 'ad dainty feet, though.'

'That's the name of the play, silly. Still, we can check them out when we get back. It's funny, when we was dressing Francesca – that's the leading lady, yer know,' she told him.

Pip nodded indulgently. 'Yer's only mentioned it about a thousand times,' he grinned.

'Well, when me and Sylvie was checking her costume, Francesca put me in the mind of miss, but I thought it was 'cos she was sticking her nose in the air.'

'Can't see Miss Sullivan with a cigarette holder, though,' Pip sniffed. 'Now come on, or you'll miss supper.'

'I can't wait to tell Miss Sullivan her face is on them posters,' she cried, climbing into her seat. 'How did that inspection go?'

'Don't ask me, Edith. All I know is Miss O'Reilly went running down the drive without her coat on,' he replied. 'Didn't even speak when I opened the gates for her.'

'Oh Lor,' Edith muttered.

Trying to put all thought of the inspector's visit and the way Harry had glowered at her to the back of her mind, Sarah went through to the kitchen to see if Mrs Daws needed any help.

'Is Miss O'Reilly all right now?' the housekeeper asked. 'Only I was wondering if she's staying for supper being as how her coat's still on the peg.'

'I'm afraid she's had to leave us, Mrs Daws.'

'Oh, has her grandmother been taken poorly? Such a caring girl. Shouldn't have gone without her coat, though. She might catch a chill,' the housekeeper fussed.

'I'll explain later,' Sarah said quickly as she saw the children washing their hands at the pump outside. 'Now, what can I do to help?'

The housekeeper gestured to the plates of bread and scrape. 'You can take them through, if you would, while I dish up the soup. That inspector man seemed quite nice compared to pompous Mr Green,' she added, going over to the range and taking the lid off her big pot.

'Hmm,' Sarah replied non-committally.

'Edith and Pip are back,' April said, coming into the room. 'I'll sound the gong,' she added, giving it a resounding whack. 'Doesn't have the same boom as your old one, does it, Mrs Daws?'

'No, it doesn't. It's a shame they never found it amongst all that loot,' Mrs Daws sniffed. 'I still think that one sounds too posh for this place.'

Hiding her smile, Sarah took the plates through to the dining hall and waited while the children filed in and took their places. Once she'd said grace and dished up supper, she looked around the room to make sure all was well. As usual the boys were tucking in oblivious to anything other than their food. Then she noticed Edith was looking under the table.

'Have you dropped something, Edith?' she asked.

'No, miss,' the girl replied, quickly straightening up.

'Well, eat up and then you can tell us about your day,' she urged.

'We 'ad a great time,' Kitty told her. 'Solomon showed the inspector how to work the shave horse and the pole lathe, and I banged some blades straight on the anvil. He was right impressed, I can tell yer.'

'Well, Sylvie and me had to check the costumes for the dress rehearsal and . . .'

'Finish your meal, girls, and then you may talk,' Sarah told them. As Kitty and Edith raised their eyebrows at each other, Sarah hid a smile. It seemed they were in cahoots again.

As usual the food disappeared faster than early morning dew in the sun. Sarah was helping to clear the tables when she saw Edith and Kitty pointing at her feet and muttering to each other.

'Is something wrong?' she asked.

Shaking their heads, they nudged each other and giggled. Then Sarah noticed Pip glance down as he passed her.

'Pip, perhaps you could explain this sudden interest in my feet,' she asked, aware that the others had stopped to see what was going on.

'*Dainty Feet*,' he mumbled, his cheeks flushing the colour of the soup they'd just eaten.

'You think I have dainty feet?' she asked, staring down at her buttoned boots. The words chimed at the back of her mind but she couldn't think why.

'That's the name of the play at the Gaiety, miss,' Edith spluttered. 'You know I said they were doing this great reveal?' Sarah frowned. 'I told you, miss. Each week they uncovered a bit more of the leading lady on the posters. Well, today it was the final reveal and guess what?' she squeaked.

'I cannot imagine,' Sarah replied.

'Well, she was you,' Edith announced triumphantly.

'Now, now, Edith,' Sarah chided, shaking her head at the girl's imagination.

'But it was you,' she insisted. 'Pip thought so, too.'

'Must be a coincidence then,' Sarah smiled. Then a thought struck her. 'When you said uncovered, you don't mean she was unclothed, I hope?'

'Oh, miss, you should see your face,' Edith squawked. 'No, you're all right, she's wearing a right bobby-dazzler of a dress.'

'Thank heavens,' Sarah murmured. 'Well, everyone, excitement over, so perhaps you could get on with helping Mrs Daws clean up the kitchen. Oh, and by the way, well done to all of you. The inspector was most impressed by your good behaviour in class.'

'Why didn't Miss O'Reilly take us this afternoon, miss?' Ellen asked.

'We likes April, but she doesn't dell dories,' June lisped.

'Stories, June,' Sarah corrected. 'Now, girls, Miss O'Reilly has had to leave us for a while,' Sarah told them. Hearing their cries of dismay, she went on quickly, 'But don't worry, I'll be taking you for needlework lessons.'

'But you don't tell stories of Shanksy either,' Monday cried.

'Can we make our quilts now?' Maggie asked. As they all stood looking at her hopefully, Sarah swallowed hard.

'Are you sure you're ready for such complicated work?' she asked.

They nodded enthusiastically.

'Miss said we could do it if we concipated,' June lisped.

'You mean concentrated,' Sarah automatically corrected. 'Well, we'll give it a go then, shall we?'

At last the children were in bed and Mrs Daws and Sarah were settled at the kitchen table with their late evening pot of tea. Sarah had just finished explaining about Miss O'Reilly when Harry reappeared. Seeing his dejected face, the housekeeper sighed.

'Not good news then, Master Higgins?'

He shook his head and slumped into a chair.

'Have a cup of tea, dear. It'll make you feel better.'

He nodded his thanks as the woman slid a mug in front of him.

'Her grandmother said she'd packed her bag and left. Claimed she didn't know where she'd gone. But I don't know . . .' he shrugged. 'I can't believe you just let her go like that.' The accusing look in his eyes left Sarah in no doubt that he placed the blame firmly at her feet.

'What could I do?' she cried. 'Mr Mahon made it clear my moral duty was to the pupils.'

'I, for one, don't believe that kind, sweet girl could be a thief or that she would . . . well, do that other thing either,' the housekeeper muttered. Harry realized that was the thing that disturbed him the most. Had she played him for a fool?

'At least Mr Mahon was complimentary about your teaching, Master Higgins, and your housekeeping, too,

393

Mrs Daws,' Sarah said, trying to lighten the atmosphere. 'Let's hope we get that funding.'

'Sounds as if everything else went somewhat better than expected this time around, then,' Mrs Daws said, sipping her tea. 'Even if he didn't want any of my cottage pie. The good doctor must be looking down and smiling that his precious school has been saved.'

'I'm afraid that was the good news, Mrs Daws,' Sarah sighed. 'Mr Mahon pointed out that Red Cliffs requires water piped into the house and internal water closets installed.'

'Nobbly Nora,' the housekeeper muttered, 'that'll cost a fortune.'

'Precisely, Mrs Daws,' Sarah sighed. 'He also said that cottage schools were thought to be better for orphans and deprived children, although I'm not sure what that involves exactly.'

'Maybe they have to eat cottage pie all the time,' the housekeeper suggested.

Harry looked up from his mug and gave a ghost of a smile.

'That could only be good if it were your cottage pie, Mrs Daws. I believe cottage schools have married couples looking after the children in houses, usually on the school grounds. Don't know any more than that, though,' he said, sipping his tea and staring moodily into the range.

'I'll ask Josephine to explain what's involved when I meet her on Saturday. Being Whitsun weekend, there's no women's meeting so we'll have time for a good talk. In the meantime, it seems I'll be taking the girls' classes. They want to begin making their quilts so I'll get them started and perhaps April could supervise on Saturday afternoon, Mrs Daws?'

'I'll be busy making my Pentecost cakes, dear, so it'll be good to have the kitchen to myself. What about you, Master Higgins?' she added, trying to rouse him from his reverie.

'The vegetable plot's been a bit neglected while we've been concentrating on the new workshops, and the coops need a good clean out, so I'll get the children seeing to that after classes this week. Then I'll take the boys, plus Kitty no doubt, to the farm. I don't know how long Bess is staying with her sister but I don't want her returning to find her fields looking like a jungle.'

It had been a hectic week and, for once, Sarah was pleased to be away from the school. Having turned out all the papers in the boxes, to her consternation she still hadn't found the missing licence and was beginning to wonder if the inspector had been right and her godfather had never applied for one.

Although the girls had been enthusiastic at the thought of making their quilts, getting them forming a pattern on the sheeting with the brightly coloured strips had proved challenging, to say the least. Whilst Harry had been polite, there was a distance between them and Sarah could tell he still blamed her for letting Miss O'Reilly leave. She felt bad about the way the mistress had been dismissed and had to admit to missing the woman and her cheery ways. Then, in the dark hours of night, her fears for the future of Red Cliffs surfaced, keeping her awake until dawn. There was no way they'd be able to raise the necessary capital to have internal water closets installed. To add insult to injury, only that morning she had received a letter from Fothergill informing her that one of the developers had raised his offer to an eye-popping amount.

Now, walking briskly along the seafront, she breathed deeply of the salty air and raised her face to the sunshine. The promenade was thronging with visitors, and paddle steamers were busy plying their trade. As seagulls screeched overhead and children played happily on the sands, Sarah felt her spirits lifting.

Josephine was already waiting at their usual table in the window of the little café. Mindful of her meeting with Bertram later, Sarah ordered a pot of tea but declined anything to eat.

'Goodness, Sarah, it's not like you to refuse a Chudleigh,' Josephine remarked, as she spread cream liberally over her cake.

'Actually, I've been invited to afternoon tea at the Grand Hotel later,' she admitted.

'Not with Bertram J. Brightling, by any chance?' Josephine asked. As Sarah felt the colour rush to her cheeks, her friend laughed. 'Why that's wonderful. You do know he's the writer and producer of that new play opening at the Gaiety tonight?' Sarah stared at her friend in surprise, but she was in full flow. 'It's called *Dainty Feet*, and do you know what?'

'What?' asked Sarah, her cup still poised mid-air.

'The woman on the poster poses a remarkable resemblance to you.'

'Really?' Sarah replied, recalling Edith had said the same thing. She'd been meaning to take a look but Edith had sought permission to go to the theatre early to help with last-minute alterations, so Pip had dropped her off in the trap. Before she could ask any questions, her friend had turned the conversation to the inspection.

'I hear that you had to dispense with your travelling school mistress.'

'Yes, and I do feel bad about that. I admit Miss O'Reilly's testimonial was sparse in detail but I still find it hard to believe she was a thief. Master Higgins is adamant I shouldn't have let her go.'

'From what I hear, Mr Mahon didn't leave you much choice. I must admit, I find the accusations that have come to light quite at variance with the opinion I formed of her. I could make some enquiries, if you like?'

'Oh, would you?' Sarah cried. 'That would be helpful. The children love her and none of us can believe what has been said about her. On another matter, Mr Mahon mentioned cottage schools. What can you tell me about them?'

'They're based on a family principle with groups of orphans living under the supervision of house parents. It has been proven that children thrive better in a home-like environment, which gives them a free and more natural mode of life than all being under one roof. Oops, sorry, no reflection on Red Cliffs. You do a wonderful job in strained circumstances.'

'Thank you and I take it you are referring to our lack of internal facilities?'

Josephine nodded. 'I would be lying if I didn't admit to finding out how your inspection went.'

'Going back to cottage schools, surely it is expensive employing all those teachers?' Sarah frowned.

'Oh, they're not all teachers, Sarah. House parents are employed to run the homes and receive a modest wage as board and lodging is provided. The idea is for the children to receive nurturing in a family environment. The schoolmaster and mistress still take lessons in the normal way. I can dig out some details if you're interested.'

'If you would, I'd be most grateful.' Sarah glanced at the clock on the wall and frowned. 'I'm so sorry, I must dash. Thank you so much for your advice.'

'My pleasure. I'll bring that information to our women's meeting next week. Now hurry along, you mustn't keep the illustrious Bertram waiting,' she grinned.

37

Harry watched as the children weeded the rows of vegetables that Jim had planted before he died. Although the sun was shining from a cloudless sky, his heart felt leaden and he couldn't help remembering the last time he'd been here. Everything had seemed brighter with Sheena by his side.

'I'm just going to check on the house,' he called. 'Solomon, take charge.'

'Will do,' he grinned. 'You 'ear that, Kitty? You got to do as I say,' he teased.

'More chance of 'ell freezing over,' she snorted, rolling her eyes. Despite himself, Harry couldn't help smiling at their banter. They'd struck up the most unlikely friendship, which had helped them both recover from their traumas. Solomon was a far cry from the surly, unhappy lad he'd been when he'd first arrived at Red Cliffs and Kitty had regained her strength and lost her haunted look, although she had no idea where her brother was and fretted about him.

Deep in thought, Harry arrived at the farmhouse almost without realizing it. He was just taking a look around the empty rooms when he heard hooves and the rattle of wheels. Looking out of the window he saw a cab draw up outside. As the driver jumped down to help the passenger, a collie gave a joyous bark.

'Welcome home, Bess,' Harry said, throwing open the door.

'Thank you, Harry. And what a lovely surprise.' As the driver carried her things inside, the collie circled the room excitedly. 'Silly old fool,' she muttered.

'Sorry, ma'am?' the driver said.

'Not you, the dog,' Bess laughed, handing over coins for her fare.

'Right obliged, ma'am,' he replied, tipping his hat.

When he'd left, Harry turned to Bess. 'How are you?' he asked.

'Mustn't grumble,' she smiled, staring around the kitchen. 'Though truth to tell, I can't decide if coming back was a good idea. My memories are here yet I feel just like that blessings candle Miss O'Reilly made me. The wick's there but the flame's gone out,' she sighed, patting the collie's head.

Harry nodded, knowing what she meant.

'How about you, Harry? I saw the children busy in the fields when I passed by. They seemed happy as larks but I have to say you're looking a mite peaky.' She eyed him anxiously.

'It's been a busy time, what with the inspection and things.'

'Go well, did it?' she asked, collapsing into her chair by the range and patting the one alongside. As he sank into it, he shook his head.

'Still waiting for the official report but it appears Red Cliffs needs internal plumbing installed if we're to stay open.'

'I never appreciated what a difference modern

conveniences could make until I stayed with Alice. It was bliss not having to go outside for water and you know, but I guess it's an expensive business,' she said sagely.

'You've hit the nail on the proverbial head, as always, Bess,' he replied. 'Anyway, I need to tell you what's been going on here in your absence. I regret to say that your barn was used to store stolen goods and . . .'

'I know, lad. Sergeant Watts was waiting at the station,' she interrupted him. 'Pompous little man made out he'd single-handedly ensnared a notorious gang of thieves who'd stolen the crown jewels. By the time I winkled the true story out of him it was something of an anticlimax,' Bess chuckled. 'Heard you got your things back, though.'

'We did, although not Mrs Daws' precious gong. Solomon's father's watch was retrieved, though. You wouldn't believe the difference it made to the boy.'

'Real treasure is priceless,' Bess replied. 'And I'm glad for him. To lose his father and home like that was terrible. Still, if any other gems come to light I'll donate them to the Red Cliffs' convenience fund,' she said, patting his hand.

As rays of the afternoon sunlight filtered through the window, they lapsed into companionable silence. Then Bess stared around her room again.

'I can't believe how spotless everywhere is. You must have worked hard.'

'Can't take credit for in here, Bess. That was down to Miss O'Reilly and Kitty.'

'That's kind of them. Is that lovely Miss O'Reilly with you . . .'

'Bess, Bess, you're home.' The door flew open and Kitty came bounding in, followed by the others. 'We saw the cab and picked these to welcome you,' she added, holding out a bunch of wild flowers.

'Why, thank you,' Bess whispered.

'Miss laid the fire for you. Come on, Solomon, you light it while I put these in water. Brown and Black, you go and fill the kettle; I'm sure Bess is parched. Bunter, you set the tray.'

'My, my, Kitty, I see you're back and haven't you grown up?' Bess laughed. 'You'll find provisions in my bag on the table, dears. Alice sent me off with a goodly supply of her spiced biscuits.' Their faces lit up and, as they sped about their tasks, Bess turned to Kitty. 'I must thank you for keeping my home so spotless.'

'Miss and me did the dairy, too. It'll just be me 'elping now miss has gone.'

As Bess frowned and looked askance at Harry, he turned to the children.

'Right, you lot, we'll get Bess settled then we must be getting back. I'll explain another time, Bess,' he added quietly.

She gave him a knowing look. 'I'd like to thank you and Miss Sullivan for all you've done whilst I've been away, so perhaps you'd both like to come to supper, say on Thursday? I'll cook something nice and we can have a chat then.'

'Good afternoon, dear lady,' Bertram greeted Sarah with his customary bow as she slid into the chair opposite. 'You are looking as charming as ever.'

'With my dainty feet, you mean?' she asked, suddenly recalling why Edith's words had struck a bell.

'I mean all of you,' he smiled. 'Now, I hope you don't mind, but as I have a rather important engagement later, I've taken the liberty of ordering.'

As if on cue, the waitress appeared with a tray of afternoon fare. Sarah waited until she'd poured their tea and departed before turning to Bertram.

'It seems to me you've taken rather a lot of liberties lately.' He furrowed his brow uncertainly. 'I've been told the posters of that new play, *Dainty Feet*, bear a resemblance to myself,' Sarah said.

'Ah, dear lady, have I not been trying to explain that it is you who has been my muse? The moment I first set eyes upon you, I knew you were the one.'

'You did?' she gasped, nearly spilling her tea in surprise.

'I have thought about you, dreamed about you, poured out my innermost thoughts onto the page. You have changed my entire life, dear lady.' As his ardent speech came to an end, Sarah was struck dumb. Then, realizing he was waiting for her to say something, she pulled herself together.

'Goodness, I had no idea,' she finally managed to say.

'Well, I'm too excited to eat a morsel right now,' he replied. 'I've been wanting to share this with you for an absolute age, and now we really should celebrate.'

'We should?'

'Of course, dear lady. Look, if you don't want anything more, why don't I drive you home? You can make yourself beautiful . . . er, I mean change into something more glamorous and we'll paint the town red after the show.'

'Oh, but . . .' she began, her mind spinning like crazy.

He smiled and put up his hand. 'I know you're desperate to see the play. And, you will, I promise. However, first nights are nerve-racking as it is, and knowing you were in the audience, I wouldn't be able to concentrate on a single thing. So please bear with me, dear lady,' he said, getting to his feet and proffering his arm.

Sarah didn't notice a thing on the journey home. She couldn't stop thinking about Bertram's declaration. Then he was drawing up at the gates.

'That is such a property, Sarah, and it would make a lovely home,' he said, staring at her hopefully.

'Even if it requires water to be piped inside and internal water closets fitted?'

'I am prepared to pay the same, if not more than the highest offer you have received. I can just picture us in it,' he sighed, staring at the house once more.

'What? You can?' Sarah gasped, staring at him in surprise.

He nodded, then collected himself. 'Now, dear lady, I must away. The show must go on,' he cried, waving his hand in the air theatrically. 'Whilst you were retrieving your coat, I took the liberty of reserving a table in the restaurant so we can celebrate in style. Could we meet there?' he asked.

Still stunned by what he'd said, she shook her head, then noticed he was frowning. 'Sorry, Bertram, there's so much to take in,' she murmured.

'Well, when Bertram makes up his mind about

something, then he makes it happen, just like that,' he replied, snapping his fingers.

'I see,' she said, her eyes widening as she took in his determined look. 'I'll use the trap,' she added, trying to pull herself together.

'In the meantime, I beg you to give my proposal favourable consideration, dear lady.'

'Rest assured I shall be able to think of nothing else,' she assured him. 'Now, break a leg, isn't that what you say in the theatre?'

Smiling at the thought of the evening ahead, Sarah made her way through to the office. An official-looking envelope had been placed in a prominent place on her desk. Recognizing the writing, she sank apprehensively into the chair and scanned the contents.

Dear Miss Sullivan,

Please find below the findings of the inspection carried out on Monday 20 May:

1. Condition of the temporary repairs to roof and fabric of building satisfactory.

2. The teaching and welfare of the pupils satisfactory.

3. Miss O'Reilly's terms of employment unsatisfactory and revoked.

4. The new workshop facilities satisfactory and funding is hereby granted for the additional skills training of metalworking and woodturning.

5. In line with Local Authority standards, you are hereby granted twelve months to arrange for water to be piped into the property and the installation of water closets.

An inspection of the new facilities to be arranged nearer the time.

However, failure to produce the licence granted for use of the premises as a school is a serious matter. As proprietress of Red Cliffs, you are required to make an appointment to attend the premises listed above at your earliest convenience.

Yours sincerely,

K. Mahon, Esq.

Chief Inspector

Sarah sat back in her chair and reflected on the letter. They'd been granted the extra funding so Harry's hard work hadn't been in vain. Everything apart from the licence had proven satisfactory. Surely that was a matter that could be easily rectified? They would have to employ another travelling mistress, but in the meantime, she was happy teaching the girls. Money for the installation of new facilities, however, was another matter.

Of course, Bertram had mentioned purchasing the property and if she accepted, then that would undoubtedly solve that problem. Yet his proposal coming out of the blue like that had taken the wind out of her sails and she'd hardly had time to think things through. An image of his piercing blue eyes and the special way he looked at her surfaced and sent butterflies skittering round her stomach. That the dashing Bertram J. Brightling should be interested in someone as ordinary as her was astonishing. Closing her eyes, she tried to imagine Red Cliffs as an updated home. She wouldn't be selling to a developer and the house would still operate as a school, of course. Added to that, the pupils would benefit from the modern facilities. Surely her godfather would approve?

But what about you, Sarah? His voice came out of the blue and her eyes flew open in surprise.

Perhaps we could turn a couple of rooms into a private suite, she replied.

You always did run before you could walk, Sarah. Remember the motto.

Love Never Faileth? *Well, that's appropriate, isn't it?* Sarah smiled.

It is, Sarah, believe you me, it is. Think everything through very carefully, Sarah. Very carefully indeed. The whispered voice faded away.

Uncle? she called. But there was no reply and she knew he'd gone.

Frowning, she went back over the detail. Of course, she would have liked more time to get to know Bertram better before his sudden declaration. But that could only mean he was sure of his feelings. As for her own, well, fondness could turn deeper with time, couldn't it? And if she were to accept, the future of the school and its pupils would be assured. They hadn't discussed arrangements for the pupils whilst the work was taking place but she could ask Bertram about that tonight. And, of course, he would have to understand that acceptance of his proposal would not mean her turning into the little wife at home. Her belief in women's rights meant too much to her for that.

As she was placing the letter safely in her drawer, her hand brushed against Mrs Knight's tome. Perhaps she could glean some words of wisdom from it. A glance at the clock on the mantel showed there was just time for a quick read before getting ready for her dinner date. As she flicked through it, just as she'd come to expect, the page fell open at a certain page.

'I'm sure you're guiding me, Dorothy Knight,' she murmured.

Twelfth Principle: Loyalty

There is no place in business for misplaced loyalty. What worked in the past may not be the best way forward at this juncture. Should suppliers be complacent in their dealings with you, ask for better trading conditions and if these are not forthcoming, take your custom elsewhere. Customers expect to receive the best service and you should, too.

Thirteenth Principle: Reassessment

Follows on from the previous principle. No business can thrive without reassessment. No matter how busy, you cannot afford not to take the time to review your current practices and ensure you have moved with the times. Do not remain in the past.

Fourteenth Principle: Trust Your Instinct

If something seems too good to be true, then it probably is. Proceed with caution. Ask questions, listen to answers but always keep your powder dry.

What a strange thing to write, she thought as the clock tinkled the hour, jolting her back to the present. Realizing she hadn't checked all was well with the pupils, she hastily slid the book back into her drawer. 'Sorry, Dorothy, I don't think you've helped me this time. I don't even wear powder,' she murmured.

'Something smells delicious, Mrs Daws,' Sarah said, sniffing the air appreciatively, as she entered the kitchen. Having eaten nothing at both luncheon and afternoon tea, she was starving.

'Eggs and bacon, no less,' the housekeeper said proudly.

'Smells divine, and what a treat. Has everything been all right whilst I've been out?'

'It has. I made my Pentecost cakes for tomorrow. The children are all eating. Goodness, Miss Sullivan, you should see those boys' appetites when they return from the farm. Ah, here's Master Higgins. I was just saying they're eating us out of house and home,' she added, nodding her head towards the dining hall. 'Good job you got them 'ens. I don't know what we'd do without the extra eggs.'

Harry and Sarah exchanged amused glances.

'Good afternoon?' he asked.

'It was until I read the letter from Mr Mahon,' she sighed. 'The good news is that the new workshops passed muster and funding's been granted for the new training.'

'And the bad?'

'We've twelve months to have water piped in and the internal water closets installed.'

'Well, we expected that,' he shrugged philosophically.

'Yes, but the crux of the matter is that I've to see Mr Mahon about not being able to produce the licence,' Sarah said.

'I've been thinking about that licence issue,' Harry replied. 'Surely it would have been granted to Samuel in his name. Now you're proprietress, they probably require you to have one in your name.'

'I hadn't thought of that,' Sarah replied, her spirits

lifting again. 'Thank you, Harry. That's made feel a whole lot better.'

'Good. Never say die and all that. By the way, Bess is back.'

'How is she?' Sarah asked.

'Feeling a bit lost, I think. Anyway, she wants to thank us for looking after things while she was away and has invited us to supper on Thursday.'

'How kind. It will be nice to see her again. Talking of food, I'm dining at the Grand tonight and will be taking the trap.'

'The Grand, eh?' Harry whistled. 'Well, you'd best go and put your glad rags on.'

'I must admit to being excited,' Sarah smiled, her insides glowing at the thought of the celebration ahead. 'Especially as when I return, I shall probably have some news for you.'

Bertram was waiting in the comfortable lounge when she arrived. His face was flushed and she guessed the play had gone well.

'Sarah, dear lady, how charming you look,' he said, rising to his feet. 'Will you join me in a glass of champagne before we dine?' Sarah noticed the bottle in the ice bucket was already half empty and concluded he'd begun celebrating before her arrival.

'Thank you,' she replied, and paused whilst the waiter poured. 'Your play was a success, I take it?'

'It was,' he cried. 'And now, dear lady, we must celebrate. Here's to us,' he added, raising his glass and clinking it against hers. Sarah smiled and took a sip. She'd never tasted champagne before and wasn't sure if she would like it.

'Now, I do hope you have thought over my proposal,' Bertram continued, leaning closer to her.

'Indeed, I have. Before I accept, though, I need to clarify your intentions regarding the pupils.'

'Sorry, dear lady, I don't quite understand,' he replied, frowning.

'You must understand that the welfare of all the children at Red Cliffs is paramount and before I can accept your marriage proposal, Bertram, I need to . . .' She came to a halt as he nearly choked on his drink.

'Marriage? Who said anything about matrimony?' he spluttered, looking at Sarah as though she'd grown an extra head.

'But you said your life had changed since you met me and that Red Cliffs would make a lovely home,' Sarah replied.

'My dear lady, you have completely misunderstood me. Look, I think you're wonderful and you have provided the perfect muse. However, when I said I had met someone special, I was referring to a fellow thespian. My proposal was for purchasing Red Cliffs so that my new friend, Ollie, and I could set up home. You see . . . well, we . . . marriage between us is out of the question.' As she remembered the effusive actor she'd met in the theatre's dressing room, everything clicked into place. Feeling mortified, she jumped to her feet.

'If you wish to purchase Red Cliffs, Bertram, then you may contact my solicitor. However, you will have to prove you intend living in it. Red Cliffs is not for sale as a development project. I promised my godfather on his deathbed that his precious home would never be turned into a hotel and I intend to honour that,' she said, opening her reticule and taking out a card. 'Here are my solicitor's details. Now, if you'll excuse me, I must be going.'

38

'There's a letter for you, Master Higgins,' the housekeeper said, when he came out of the dining hall with Sarah on Tuesday morning.

'Thank you, Mrs Daws,' he replied, holding out his hand.

'It's got all fancy writing on the envelope and "c/o" in front of "Red Cliffs Ragged School". Here, we ain't gone all co-operative like the shops, have we?'

'No, Mrs Daws, we haven't,' Sarah assured the woman.

'Well, Mrs Laver was saying a whole bunch of them girls are coming down to Torquay for a holiday later this year. Fancy that, eh?'

'Tourism is certainly booming around here. Perhaps we're in the wrong line of business, Master Higgins,' Sarah said, turning to Harry, but he was frowning at the envelope in the housekeeper's hand.

'"C/o" stands for "care of", Mrs Daws. Now please may I have my letter?' Harry asked, trying to curb his impatience.

'Well, I hope it's good news 'cos you've been going round with a face like sour cream since Miss O'Reilly left,' she said, shooting him a knowing look as she handed it over.

'I'll be in the school room,' he replied, ignoring her comment.

'Well, charmed I'm sure,' the housekeeper sniffed. 'And you're not much better, Miss Sullivan, if you don't mind me saying.'

'Lots to think about if we're to keep this place going, Mrs Daws,' Sarah replied, gesturing around the room. In truth, she was still smarting from her altercation with Bertram, but felt too stupid to discuss the matter with anyone. She only hoped it wouldn't deter him from putting in an offer for the property, though. Loath as she was to sell, she was beginning to realize there was no other way for the school to survive. There was absolutely no possibility they could raise enough money to pay for the new facilities required. At least this way she could keep her promise to her godfather that his house wouldn't be developed into a plush hotel. 'I'll be in my office,' she added, as the children swarmed into the kitchen ready to help with the day's chores.

—

Shutting the door behind him, Harry tore open the envelope. He'd recognized the writing and now his heart was hammering like a steam train.

Dear Harry

Please forgive me for leaving without saying goodbye. When the inspector placed Miss Sullivan in that awkward situation, my first thought was to spare her any further embarrassment.

To my shame, I admit my testimonial had more holes than Mammy's knitting. But there was a reason for this, one which I should have sorted before leaving Ireland. I like to think I would have done, had Nanna not had that fall. But I have to be honest and admit that, being as green as the hills of home, I may have taken the easy way out.

Anyway, I am now returned to Ireland to rectify this, better late than never, I hear you say. When my name is cleared, and only then, I will return and give you the explanation you deserve.

In the meantime, dear Harry, please do not think too badly of me for I find myself missing you so very much.

Yours most sincerely,

Sheena O'Reilly

She misses me! She's coming back! Harry's heart flipped at the thought. Sheena hadn't just disappeared and left him dangling like a spare rope.

His musing was interrupted by the door opening. Solomon peered in then beckoned to the others, who, mindful of the master's recent mood, filed quietly into the room.

'Good morning, girls and boys. Is this not a grand day?' he greeted them.

'Cripes, he sounds just like Miss O'Reilly,' Kitty murmured.

Sarah stared at the plaque on the wall.

Love Never Faileth, eh, Uncle? Well, we certainly need some of that. I can't think of any way to keep this place running now we have to update the facilities. I'm sorry, Uncle, for I know how much this old house meant to you, but times have changed. Be assured I'm still determined not to sell to a developer. A place that's been used as a refuge for waifs being turned into some fancy hotel for the idle rich is too ironic to bear. I'm hopeful that Bertram will purchase Red Cliffs so that it can stay a family home, although his meaning of 'family' is somewhat different to ours. Oh, Uncle, please show me this is the correct way forward, she pleaded.

There was a brisk knock on the door. 'Blimey, that was quick,' she whispered.

'Can I come in?' a bright voice asked.

'Goodness, Josephine, what are you doing here?' Sarah asked, staring at her friend in surprise.

'Mrs Daws let me in. I've dug out some information on cottage schools and . . .'

'Here we are; thought a cup of tea might go down well, Miss Harmon,' the housekeeper said, depositing a tray on the desk. 'Hope you're not here to do another inspection,' she asked, giving the woman a curious look.

Josephine laughed. 'This is purely a social call, Mrs Daws, but that cup of tea will be very welcome, thank you.'

'Sorry about that,' Sarah said, when the housekeeper had left. 'She does like to know what's going on.'

'That woman is a treasure,' Josephine replied. 'Besides, she has every right to wonder what's going to happen to her job.'

'I know. It's such a responsibility,' Sarah replied.

'I'm sure Master Higgins will help, but before getting too depressed, I should read through this information,' Josephine said, handing over a sheaf of papers. 'Oh, and I found out why Miss O'Reilly was dismissed from her last post.'

'So, her employment *was* terminated?' Sarah groaned. 'It seems I make a habit of taking people at face value.'

Josephine quirked a brow enquiringly.

'It would appear Bertram J. Brightling only used me as his muse. He has alternative love interests,' she said, making quotation marks with her fingers.

To her astonishment, Josephine hooted with laughter. 'I'm sorry,' she spluttered, 'but I can't say I'm surprised.' Seeing Sarah's indignant look, she went on quickly, 'Now do you want to hear about Miss O'Reilly or not?'

'Yes, of course,' Sarah replied, taking a sip of her tea.

'When Mr Mahon knew her previously it would seem she was having a fling with a married school teacher . . .' Josephine began.

'What?' Sarah cried, spraying her drink over the blotting sheet.

'As you can imagine, when the Local Authority were informed, they took an extremely dim view, and in the moral interest of the children she was removed from the school straight away.'

'Goodness!' Sarah exclaimed, replacing her cup on the tray and quickly wiping up the mess. 'It would seem Master Higgins had a narrow escape. Hold on a minute, though, Mr Mahon said she'd been accused of theft.'

'That, too. Apparently when the "affair" came to light, the wife reported her gold bangle missing. It was found in Miss O'Reilly's desk.'

'Really?' Sarah replied. 'Surely not?' Then she recalled the day Miss O'Reilly had been seen leaving the school at the same time as Mr Slater. But that had been coincidental, hadn't it? She wasn't the sort to take other people's property, was she? But in light of Sarah's recent misunderstanding about Bertram, who was she to make a judgement about anyone's character? She frowned. 'It all sounds a bit convenient, though. Did she admit to taking it?'

'She denied it, then ran away,' Josephine said, then glanced at the clock on the mantel. 'Time I wasn't here,

I'm afraid. I hear the NUWSS are becoming quite vociferous so we should be in for a good meeting on Saturday. Shall we meet at the café beforehand?'

'Yes, and this time I'm having a Chudleigh with lashings of jam and cream,' Sarah replied, lamenting her missed afternoon tea the previous weekend.

'You look happier than you've been for a while,' Sarah told Harry as they made their way to see Bess on Thursday evening. He smiled and tugged on the reins. The pony obediently turned into the driveway leading to the farm. 'Must be something to do with that letter,' Sarah persisted.

'You can't have been busy if you've had time to waste pondering my affairs, Miss Sullivan,' he murmured.

Sarah turned towards him then saw the smile playing on his lips. The word 'affair' jangled her memory, but the farmhouse was looming ahead and she decided to tell him what Josephine had said on the journey back.

'I'll have you know, I've been occupied studying the notes about cottage schools, Master Higgins,' she retorted.

His smile broadened to a grin but there was no time for further discussion as the door opened and the collie ran out to greet them.

'Come in, my dears,' Bess greeted them.

They stepped into the warm kitchen where a delicious aroma wafted their way.

'It's lovely to see you again, Bess,' Sarah said, handing over the bag of freshly baked rolls Mrs Daws had sent.

'Something smells good,' Harry said. 'And it looks as if I'm not the only hungry boy here,' he chuckled as the dog stared hopefully at the pot on the range.

'Don't know what I'd have done without his company these past few days. Funny, he was always Jim's dog before,' she sighed. 'Anyhow, you must be hungry so sit yourselves down while I dish up. How's them lovely kiddiewinks doing?'

'Lovely?' Harry snorted, but they knew his word belied his fondness for them.

'You'd be lost without them,' Bess commented as she placed plates of mouth-watering casserole in front of them.

'Yes, we would,' Sarah agreed, realizing it was true. For all the headaches they gave, she would hate not to have them around. 'Edith's been working in the costume department of the Gaiety these past few weeks. She's an expert little seamstress.'

'Kitty's taken to woodturning and metalworking, Bess.'

'And to young Solomon, if I'm not much mistaken,' the woman laughed.

'Really?' Sarah gasped. 'Goodness, we'll have to keep an eye on that.'

'Well, they are growing up, dear.'

'But they're only ten and eleven,' Sarah protested.

'In years, maybe, but in experience . . .' Bess shrugged.

While Sarah mulled that over, Harry told Bess what had been done on the farm whilst she'd been away.

'Now if you've finished with your casserole, dears, I've a nice apple pie for afters,' she said, getting to her feet.

'I'll clear these,' Sarah said, taking their plates over to the sink.

'You're spoiling us, Bess,' Harry said, as she poured thick custard over his pie.

The woman smiled. 'It's nice to have someone to fuss over. Who'd have thought I'd miss cooking for a hungry farmer, eh? Now, who wants a nice cuppa? I hear they serve coffee after their evening meal in those fancy hotels, but give me a good cup of Rosy Lee any day.'

'I'm with you there, Bess. But let me make it.' As Bess demurred, Sarah got to her feet. 'It's the least I can do after you've cooked us that splendid meal.'

'I wanted to thank you both for looking after the farm. Not just while I've been away but over the years. Jim and I knew only too well, you didn't just happen to be passing each Saturday afternoon, Harry.'

'Well, I, er . . .' he began. 'The truth is the children love coming here and I do, too.'

'And Miss O'Reilly, too. You started to say something when those little pitchers with big ears arrived,' Bess prompted.

'She's had to return to Ireland to sort something out,' Harry explained, ignoring the look of astonishment on Sarah's face.

'Oh, I see. Well, I hope she hurries back,' Bess said, leaning back in her seat. 'Now, dears, I want to thank you for all you've done,' she went on, looking from one to the other.

'You've already done that, Bess. And that was a splendid meal,' Sarah assured her.

'That's not what I mean, my dears. As you know, Jim and I were never blessed with children and having you all coming here cheered us up no end, as well as helping with

420

the chores. Poor Jim could never have kept going so long without that. Anyhow, this was always a happy place.' She sighed and stared around the room. 'Now Jim's gone, it's like an empty shell.'

'You must come and share supper with us,' Sarah said quickly.

'The truth is, I've decided to sell up and go and live with Alice. We can share living costs and chores as well as keep each other company.'

'We'll be sad to see you go, Bess, but it makes sense. I'll keep the fields and yard tidy till you find a buyer,' Harry assured her.

'You misunderstand me, lad. I'm offering this place to you both for a nominal sum. I know it will need some renovating but if you sell Red Cliffs, you'd have enough and more besides to do the work.'

'But . . .' Sarah began, then stopped as Bess held up her hand.

'If you don't want to give up Red Cliffs, Miss Sullivan, then you could sell here and keep the bulk of the money. It would certainly be enough to install those internal facilities or whatever. All I require is sufficient money to pay my share of the bills.'

'That's an extremely generous offer, Bess,' Harry murmured, overwhelmed. 'But sleep on it, eh? You really must make sure you've thought everything through.'

She patted his hand. 'You're a good man. Jim and I spoke about this a while ago, so I'm already sure. A shroud has no pockets so I can't take anything with me, can I? Besides, what with you two having an understanding, it will help set you up.'

'Sorry, Bess. I don't know what you mean,' Sarah replied, feeling her face growing hot.

'That's all right, Miss Sullivan, old Bess can keep a secret,' she grinned and gave a sly wink. 'I've already seen my solicitor, so no doubt your Mr Fothergill will be in touch shortly. Now, my dears, if you'll excuse me, I must away to my bed.'

'I don't know what to say, Bess,' Sarah cried, choked by the women's selfless generosity. She threw her arms around her, 'My godfather said you were the salt of the earth and he was right,' she whispered.

'Well, I don't know about that. Whatever option you choose, it will give me a good feeling to know I've gone some way to repaying your kindness,' the woman smiled. 'And I'd be mighty glad of your help until this place is signed over to you, whatever you decide to do with it,' she added, turning to Harry.

'I don't know what to say,' Sarah murmured as they rattled their way back down the driveway.

'It's an extremely generous offer,' Harry replied. 'What will you do?'

'Me? Bess made it clear it was to be a joint arrangement, although I don't know what makes her think we have an understanding.'

'Ah,' he muttered.

'Harry?' she cried. 'You're keeping something from me. Stop the trap this instant.'

He did as she said. Then, looking over the darkening fields, he relayed what Sheena had told him.

'So everyone, apart from me, thinks we have an understanding.'

'Not now they don't,' he said, turning back to face her. 'Apart from Bess. I was so stunned by her generosity, I hadn't the heart to explain,' he finished. 'We'll have to tell her, though; that's only fair. But you know, somehow I don't think she'll be surprised. When Miss O'Reilly returns, we'll go and see her together.'

'She's coming back?'

'Yep. As soon as she's cleared her name. I always knew she wasn't a thief,' he stated.

Sarah opened her mouth to ask about the other allegation then snapped it shut. He looked so happy and, after all, it was only a claim.

'I knew that, too.'

'You did? I thought you hadn't taken to her,' he said, in surprise.

'My instinct told me she was an honest person, but the responsibility for who cares for the children lies heavy, Harry.'

'I can see that and you don't do a bad job, for a woman,' he added, groaning as she jabbed him in the ribs. 'I suppose you won't sell Red Cliffs so it'll have to be the farm.'

'This hugely generous offer from Bess, coming out of the blue like this, has knocked me for six. I think we need to ensure she has thought everything through before we take things further.'

'It sounds like she has, especially as she said she and Jim had discussed it,' Harry replied.

'Well, there's also a lot for us to consider, Harry. We'll need to go through everything in fine detail with Mr Fothergill before accepting. Come on, let's go back to Red Cliffs and sleep on it.'

As Harry took up the reins, Sarah couldn't resist peeking back at the farmhouse and surrounding outbuildings. It would be just perfect, she thought, her imagination going into overdrive.

'I can't help thinking this was meant to be,' she said quietly.

'Oh?' he asked, turning to her in surprise. 'What do you mean?'

'Well, I've been reading about cottage schools, and the farm would really lend itself to being one. We could have one central school and convert the barns and outbuildings to make houses and workshops, engage house parents . . .'

'Woa, girl, you have got the bit between your teeth,' he cried. 'I thought we were going to sleep on it?'

'I know, and we will. But let's face, we need to review our current practices and ensure we move with the times. We cannot remain in the past, Harry Higgins.'

'Indeed we cannot, Sarah Sullivan,' he said, gathering up the reins and heading for home.

Pern, your continued support is greatly appreciated.

Teresa Chris and everyone at Penguin, your guidance and expertise is invaluable

All my friends at BWC who encourage me to keep writing.

He just wanted a decent book to read ...

Not too much to ask, is it? It was in 1935 when Allen Lane, Managing Director of Bodley Head Publishers, stood on a platform at Exeter railway station looking for something good to read on his journey back to London. His choice was limited to popular magazines and poor-quality paperbacks – the same choice faced every day by the vast majority of readers, few of whom could afford hardbacks. Lane's disappointment and subsequent anger at the range of books generally available led him to found a company – and change the world.

'We believed in the existence in this country of a vast reading public for intelligent books at a low price, and staked everything on it'
Sir Allen Lane, 1902–1970, founder of Penguin Books

The quality paperback had arrived – and not just in bookshops. Lane was adamant that his Penguins should appear in chain stores and tobacconists, and should cost no more than a packet of cigarettes.

Reading habits (and cigarette prices) have changed since 1935, but Penguin still believes in publishing the best books for everybody to enjoy. We still believe that good design costs no more than bad design, and we still believe that quality books published passionately and responsibly make the world a better place.

So wherever you see the little bird – whether it's on a piece of prize-winning literary fiction or a celebrity autobiography, political tour de force or historical masterpiece, a serial-killer thriller, reference book, world classic or a piece of pure escapism – you can bet that it represents the very best that the genre has to offer.

Whatever you like to read – trust Penguin.